Outstanding Praise for the Novels of D. L. Bogdan

THE SUMERTON WOMEN

"With smooth prose that goes down like warm honeyed milk, D. L. Bogdan tells the story of Cecily and Mirabella Sumerton and their family saga of loss, jealousy and betrayal. Set in a time of religious upheaval and political chaos as King Henry VIII destroys the monasteries and plunges his country into war, *The Sumerton Women* is a story of love and redemption, beautifully told."
—Christy English, author of *To Be Queen*

"Delightful. D. L. Bogdan is a gifted storyteller. I gazed spellbound as an aristocratic young lady matured before my eyes and the characters surrounding her suffered through the psychological consequences of their moral failings, all set against the backdrop of the English Reformation."
—Mitchell James Kaplan, author of *By Fire, by Water*

"Bogdan's characters are complex and the story is riveting. Bogdan brilliantly portrays the transformation and conflict of Tudor England while mixed with the struggles of a broken family."
—Kayla Posney, *Pittsburgh Historical Fiction Examiner*

RIVALS IN THE TUDOR COURT

"Careful research and a gift for realistic and sympathetic portrayals give Bogdan's novel a sense of time and place."
—*RT Book Reviews*

"A fast-paced, quick and entertaining read."
—*Historical Novel Reviews*

SECRETS OF THE TUD~~OR COURT~~

"There is no doubt that Tudor fan~~s~~ novel starring Henry and his wives."
—*RT Book Reviews*

Books by D. L. Bogdan

SECRETS OF THE TUDOR COURT

RIVALS IN THE TUDOR COURT

THE SUMERTON WOMEN

Published by Kensington Publishing Corporation

The
SUMERTON
WOMEN

D. L. BOGDAN

KENSINGTON BOOKS
www.kensingtonbooks.com

KENSINGTON BOOKS are published by

Kensington Publishing Corp.
119 West 40th Street
New York, NY 10018

All Kensington titles, imprints, and distributed lines are available at special quantity discounts for bulk purchases for sales promotion, premiums, fund-raising, educational, or institutional use.

Special book excerpts or customized printings can also be created to fit specific needs. For details, write or phone the office of the Kensington Special Sales Manager: Kensington Publishing Corp., 119 West 40th Street, New York, NY 10018. Attn. Special Sales Department. Phone: 1-800-221-2647.

Kensington and the K logo Reg. U.S. Pat. & TM Off.

ISBN-13: 978-0-7582-7137-2
ISBN-10: 0-7582-7137-9

First Kensington Trade Paperback Printing: May 2012
10 9 8 7 6 5 4 3 2 1

Printed in the United States of America

In memory of two incredible women:
my grandmothers, Lily Bogdan and Helen Baer

Acknowledgments

I'd like to thank my agent, Elizabeth Pomada; I am so fortunate to have found not only a wonderful agent in her but also a dear friend. I could not have gotten through this process without my editor, John Scognamiglio, and his wonderful team at Kensington Publishing, especially Paula Reedy and Vida Engstrand. You have all been so encouraging and helpful; my appreciation for your hard work is deeper than I can ever express. To the authors, bloggers, and readers who have helped support my work and lift my spirits along the way, you are all indispensable to this process and I am so blessed to have you in my life—you know who you are! And I would not be able to have any confidence in anything I send out without my mother, Cindy Bogdan, who is always the first to screen my work scene by scene. Last but not least, my deep and heartfelt thanks to the love of my life, my husband, my best friend, and promoter extraordinaire—my Kim. All that you do and all that you are is appreciated more than you could ever know. You make my dreams come true.

The mind is its own place, and in itself
can make a heav'n of hell, a hell of heav'n.

—John Milton, *Paradise Lost*

❧ 1 ❧

Lincolnshire, England
Summer, 1527

She hid in her mother's wardrobe. The Sickness would not find her there. Shoulders scrunched, limbs hugged close to her body, eight-year-old Cecily Burkhart huddled against the silks, taffetas, and damasks of the baroness's elegant gowns. She fingered the materials, thinking of her beautiful mother, murdered by the dreaded sweat. She heard the servants' dresses as they rushed in and out of Lady Ashley's chambers. They rustled, stiff with starch, crude gowns of homespun and wool. They did not flow the way her mother's did when she walked across the floor.

But she was not walking across the floor. The footfalls that click-clacked against the rush-strewn chambers now belonged to the physician, the servants, and, finally, the priest as he administered the last rites.

Cecily's mother was dead.

Cecily buried her head against the fur hem of her mother's gown and offered silent sobs. Her mother was the last of them, her father, Lord Edward Burkhart, passing the week before. He had joined Cecily's four brothers, who met the angels when they were but infants. Now she was alone.

Someone called her name. She hugged herself and began to rock back and forth. She did not want to answer. She did not want to think of anything but her mother's gowns. She smiled to herself, remembering Mother gliding across the floor, hand on Cecily's father's arm, in the very gown her tears wetted now. How gentle she was and how merry was Cecily's father in her mother's company.

"Lady Cecily, do come out, lamb!" begged one of the servants, Mistress Fitzgerald. "You must come out of Lady Ashley's wardrobe now; we must know if you are ill!"

"Supposing she passed on and we're not being aware of it?" another of the servants added, her voice wrought with anxiety.

Silence.

"Lady Cecily!"

Cecily drew in a breath. She must not evade them any longer; it was cruel to cause them distress. "I am here," she said in soft tones.

Footfalls bounded toward the wardrobe. "Lady Cecily, child, are you ill? Do you feel hot, child, achy?" Mistress Fitzgerald's voice was taut.

"I am . . . well," Cecily assured her. She was not well. Her parents were dead, her family was wiped out, she did not know what was to become of her. But she was alive and there was no other response she could think of.

Mistress Fitzgerald threw open the doors to the wardrobe. Cecily squinted against the painful light and retreated farther back within its reaches. Meaty, chapped hands parted the gowns, revealing Mistress Fitzgerald's broad face and teary brown eyes.

"Lady Cecily," she said in gentle tones.

"What have they done with my mother?" Cecily asked, sniffling.

Mistress Fitzgerald expelled a heavy sigh. "Lady Ashley has been promptly put to rest, to help contain the spread of the Sickness." She narrowed her eyes and shook her head. "Blast the king for bringing God's wrath upon us and all for lust of that Boleyn Whore, witch and heretic that she is! And blast your parents for supporting him! That's why God took them, you know. They supported the Boleyns and their despicable lot."

Cecily covered her ears against this gloomy interpretation of God's will, averting her head from the round-faced maid.

"I'm sorry, my lady," Mistress Fitzgerald said. "It's just me being mad with grief is all. This sweating sickness came into our country with the Tudors . . . and sometimes I'm afraid it won't leave till the last Tudor is—" At this she cast her eyes to and fro, then crossed herself. It was treason to predict the death of any monarch and Mistress Fitzgerald had enough problems.

Cecily uncovered her ears and stared the maid in the face. "Then I am Baroness Burkhart now," she said as she realized the fact for the first time. "I am the lady of this house . . . of everything. . . ."

"Yes," said Mistress Fitzgerald. "Though this is hardly the time to gloat about it."

Cecily scowled. "I mean to say, madam, that I am the mistress of this house," she explained.

Mistress Fitzgerald bowed her head. "Of course, my lady. What can I do for you?"

"Close these wardrobe doors and leave me alone!" Cecily ordered.

Mistress Fitzgerald screwed up her face in confusion, shrugged her shoulders, and closed the doors.

In the darkness of the wardrobe, Cecily inhaled the traces of perfume on her mother's gowns. She wrapped herself up in them and pretended they were the beloved arms of the woman she would never see again.

Father Alec Cahill saw no valid reason for having to fetch the Earl of Sumerton's new ward. Now that the threat of the dread sweating sickness was on the decline he couldn't understand why the Pierces could not get the girl themselves. It was the least they could do for her, a child all alone in the world with no one to care for her. As for the Pierces, while a stag lived in Sumerton Forest they were not to be disturbed. Not when there was hunting and entertainments to be had.

Yet Father Alec liked the Pierces. They were warm and merry, and since being engaged as tutor to their children he could not say he didn't enjoy being a member of their household. The children were intelligent and eager to learn, the employers were generous and freethinking enough to allow him to teach in the progressive manner he felt would someday benefit the children in what was becoming a fast-changing world.

If there was any fault to be found with the Pierces it was that they were upper gentry and, as with most upper gentry, an inherent selfishness accompanied their station. It would not occur to them to fetch the Baroness Burkhart themselves, not because they were cold and unfeeling but because the thought would never cross their minds. He supposed it didn't matter. He would endeavor to make the child feel as comfortable as possible until her delivery to the Pierces, where he was confident they would do the same.

Father Alec drifted in and out of a listless sleep as the coach lurched and bounced along the rutted road. When not sleeping, he prayed for the girl's smooth transition, and it was as he was praying, eyes closed, mouthing the words, that the coach rambled up to Burkhart Manor. He opened his eyes to a sprawling green vista. The manor house was set on a hill surrounded by lush gardens and an imposing stone wall. Vines climbed the walls of the house toward the heavens and Father Alec inhaled the sweet smell of fresh rain and green things.

He was shown into the house, where he was instructed to wait in the great hall for the girl. It was a stunning hall, outfitted with imported Turkish carpets, intricate tapestries, and stained-glass windows bearing the Burkhart coat of arms. He shook his head, awed as always by such opulence. It, along with all of the treasures within, belonged to a single little girl now. Quite heady.

"I'm afraid she won't come down, Father," a stout servant informed him with a huffing sigh. "She's been devastated since her loss, sequestering herself in her mother's wardrobe. She takes her meals in there and everything—only leaving to use the chamber pot!" With this the round face flushed deep crimson. "If I may be begging your pardon, Father."

Father Alec smiled and waved a hand in dismissal. "Perhaps you should take me to the girl."

"I apologize, Father," the servant continued as she led him up the stairs to the chamber that used to belong to Baroness Ashley

Burkhart. "Lady Cecily has always had a bit of a stubborn streak in her and now aggrieved as she is—"

"I am not worried, mistress," assured the young priest with a slight chuckle.

The servant entered the chambers first. "Lady Cecily, there's a priest here waiting to see you, a servant of God! You'll not want to be angering a servant of God!"

"We're all servants of God, so I expect *he* should not want to anger *me*, either!" a little voice shot back.

Father Alec's lips twitched, but he refrained from breaking into a smile.

The servant balled her thick hand into a fist and pounded on the heavy oaken doors of the wardrobe. "Now we've indulged you long enough! You come out of there!"

At this Father Alec rushed forward, laying his hands upon the doughy shoulders of the servant. "Please, mistress, perhaps you should allow me. If you wouldn't mind stepping out?"

Scowling, the servant scuffled out of the room, slamming the chamber door so that the little girl within the wardrobe was certain her displeasure was heard.

Father Alec laid a slim-fingered hand on the door. "Lady Cecily, my name is Father Alec Cahill. Perhaps you wouldn't mind coming out and speaking with me awhile? If you do not like what I have to say you can go back in if it pleases you."

"No!"

Father Alec leaned his forehead on the door. He found himself wishing with more fervency that the Pierces had come to collect the girl.

"Then perhaps you will allow me to come in there and talk to you," he suggested in gentle tones.

Silence.

"All right, you may come in," she conceded.

"Thank you, my lady," said Father Alec as he opened the door and crawled inside the cramped, stuffy wardrobe. He folded his knees up under his cassock and thanked God he didn't have gout. "This is a rather nice spot, my lady, if I may say so."

"Thank you," the child replied, her voice thick with reluctance.

"I'm told you've made it a second home," he said. "Small for gentry folk, but I suppose it has all the amenities."

"Yes," she agreed. "My . . . my . . . lady's gowns are here so I stay here to be closer to her. To her smell." Her voice caught in her throat. "It makes her seem alive."

"My child, you will never heal from this. I know." Father Alec heaved a sigh, squeezing his eyes against memories of his own. He continued. "But God will give you the strength to go on and each day your burden will be easier to bear. You must honor their memory by living. There is so much of the world to see, so much that you need to do. You are the last of your family and it is up to you to be brave and carry on for them, to grow up, to marry and have children. You cannot do any of that if you hide yourself away in this little wardrobe."

"But if I come out it all becomes true. One day will go by and then another and another. And all without them," she said miserably. "In here it isn't quite real; in here I can pretend they're just away. They were always away so that is easy," she added with a sniffle. "I can still smell my mother's pomander, you know. I wait for her in here. Any minute, I keep thinking, she will throw open the doors and find me hiding, just like she used to when she was alive. She would laugh and put her hand to her heart as though I gave her an awful fright—but all along she knew I was there."

Father Alec was silent a long moment. "It sounds like a beautiful memory, Lady Cecily. I imagine your mother must have been a kind, loving woman. It would break her heart to see you hiding away. She cannot come find you now. So she sent God to. And God and your mother both long to see you come out and take your place in the world."

The child was silent.

In the hopes she was giving credence to his words, Father Alec went on. "I'm certain the wardrobe with all of your mother's lovely gowns can be brought to your new chambers at Sumerton," he told her. "And someday when you are big enough, the gowns can be updated and fitted for you. Your mother would love to know you would use them again, I imagine."

Cecily paused a long moment, then quietly, in tremulous tones, she asked, "What is Sumerton like?"

"It's a lovely place, much like your home," Father Alec told her. "It is surrounded by a lush forest teeming with life and there is a lake the Pierces keep their barge on. There are stables filled with beautiful horses and mews with regal hawks. And Lord Sumerton loves hounds. The king himself has called them among the finest in England."

"The earl—I am his ward now?" Cecily asked.

Father Alec nodded, then, realizing it was too dark for her to see, said, "Yes."

"Is he kind?"

"He is," Father Alec told her in truth. He had never known Lord Hal to be unkind. The man always smiled, always had a gentle word for his children, never raised a hand to anyone. "He is kind and quite young, in truth." He smiled in fondness. "He and Lady Grace, the countess, are both vibrant with youth and vigor. It is . . . well, it is a *fun* place, my lady—very alive. And me, I am tutor to their children, which means I will be educating you as well."

"Tell me of the children," Cecily prompted.

Father Alec's legs were getting sore and stiff within the confines of the wardrobe, but he continued. He would win this child. Rather win her than have to drag her kicking and screaming to Sumerton. He rubbed the backs of his knees as he talked.

"One, young Aubrey—they call him Brey—is just your age, and Mirabella is thirteen. They are loving children and eager to make your acquaintance," he said. "Why, the whole household has been in a thrall of preparations since news of your wardship. They will be so disappointed if I cannot convince you to join me." He paused. "Won't you join me, Lady Cecily?"

She was silent again. "Yes," she acquiesced at last. She pushed open the doors, squinting as blinding white light flooded the wardrobe.

Father Alec scrambled to his feet, then extended his hand toward the girl.

She accepted it, emerging from the depths of the wardrobe to reveal a stunning beauty with rippling waves of rose-gold hair and startling teal blue eyes set in a tiny face with skin the color of alabaster. Father Alec's breath caught in his throat. *An example,* he thought to himself. *I am looking at an example of God's art, for this child is nothing if not a masterpiece.*

He squeezed the little hand in his. She turned her strange eyes to him, eyes that were a mingling of so many emotions—fear, grief, anxiety, longing. Longing to trust, to be happy. To live.

Together priest and child proceeded out of Burkhart Manor, where waited the coach that would carry them toward Sumerton and Cecily's new life.

Cecily was well accustomed to opulence, but never had she seen such beauty as that possessed by Castle Sumerton. Father Alec had explained the history of the castle to her as they rode. Built in the fourteenth century and a favorite summer estate of Lancastrians and Yorkists alike, the palatial fortress was awarded to the Pierces, along with the title of earl, when their family assisted Henry VII in his victory over Richard III at the Battle of Bosworth. Since then not only had a little town of the same name emerged nearby to support its needs, but it had been visited by ambassadors and kings and prelates, scholars, princes, and pundits. An advocate of education, Lord Sumerton entertained Europe's most celebrated minds, men such as Thomas More and Desiderius Erasmus. The Pierces adored giving grand entertainments and feasts, Father Alec told her, and there was seldom a week that passed without guests.

It sounded very grand to Cecily. Yet even as her heart raced with anticipation she feared the transition. She feared liking her new home, liking her keepers. What if she grew too fond of them and forgot her own family? Even now, so soon after her parents' deaths, their faces were obscured in her mind's eye, forms that resembled the people she had cherished but were not quite right. Like paintings, their features were soft, a little lacking in definition. Guilt surged through her as she thought of it and she found herself focusing on the miniatures she had brought with her, staring for long hours at the little faces. But what were miniatures but paintings?

They were not her parents; in fact, these miniatures were very poor reproductions indeed.

But as she approached Castle Sumerton thoughts of her parents were replaced by fearful curiosity. The large keep with its climbing turrets captured her breath. She could not imagine playing hide-and-seek here. She took in the vast expanse of lush green forest that surrounded the fortress; it made it seem sort of isolated as opposed to the open, sprawling green fields that had made up the Burkhart lands. Somehow this comforted rather than intimidated her.

Taking Father Alec's hand, she allowed him to lead her into the great hall, which was being set for a feast. Servants bustled everywhere. The hall was being swept and sweetened, trestles set up, plates laid, and orders shouted. Cecily looked toward the cathedral ceiling, one side of which was outfitted with three large windows allowing the light to stream in and dance across the floor. She stood in one of the rays, watching the flecks of dust float and sparkle in the sunlight. She smiled.

"Ah! She has arrived!" a jovial voice cried, rousing Cecily from her reflections. She turned to face a well-built man in his early thirties sporting a close-cut beard, wavy brown hair that curled about his neck, and twinkling blue eyes. His countenance was kind. Cecily was immediately disarmed.

She curtsied. "Lord Sumerton."

Lord Sumerton dipped into a bow. "My dearest little lady," he said. "We mourn the loss of your parents; Baron Burkhart and I were educated together with the Wyatts of Kent." His eyes softened with fondness over a memory, perhaps of the carefree days of youth. He returned his gentle blue gaze to Cecily. "Please know that we will take good care of you and hope you will be very happy with us here at Sumerton." He took her hands in his, offering a bright smile. "I should like to present my family." He indicated a slim, fair woman beside him whose blond hair was pulled back beneath her gable hood. Her sleepy brown eyes were bleary and unfocused. "This is Lady Grace, my wife."

Another curtsy.

"And these are my children. Aubrey and Mirabella." Lord Sumerton gestured toward the children. Lord Aubrey offered a quick bow. He was fair haired and wiry, his smile slow and sweet. His cheeks flushed when he looked at Cecily. She smiled and curtsied in return.

Lady Mirabella was slender and tall, her black hair cascading down her back in soft waves. The green eyes peering out of her olive-skinned face were keen as they scrutinized Cecily. She shivered as she offered a curtsy.

"You will share the nursery with them, Lady Cecily, until you are older," Lord Sumerton told her. "Matilda is our nurse." He nodded to a short, buxom young woman with bouncing red ringlets who tossed her a reassuring smile. "And of course you know our tutor and chaplain, Father Cahill."

Cecily offered a fond smile to the priest whom she had placed all her trust in since this peculiar journey began. It comforted her to know he was a fixture in the household; perhaps it would make her adjustment easier to bear.

"Children, take her to the nursery and get acquainted," ordered Lady Grace in soft tones. "We will send for you at supper."

"Yes, my lady," they chorused. Cecily threw one pleading glance at Father Alec, as though begging him to stop them, to stop her life from moving forward, to suspend the moment of bittersweet uncertainty and anticipation a bit longer before Reality began.

Father Alec only smiled.

Cecily averted her head, allowing herself to be shown out of the hall and up a flight of narrow stairs to the nursery. It was a room far lovelier than her nursery. The tapestries depicted cherubs surrounding the Blessed Virgin, all enveloped in a light so welcoming Cecily longed to be embraced by it. The beds were dressed in sumptuous white lace with cornflower blue velvet curtains to match those that were drawn across the bay window. The floors were covered in soft bearskin rugs to warm their feet and a cheery fire crackled in the hearth.

"What do you like to do?" asked Aubrey as the three took to sitting upon his bed.

Cecily pondered. She liked to be with her mother and father, but they were no more. Aubrey and Mirabella would not want to hear about all that as it were. "I like to dance," she said at last. "And read. I like to sing and play the lute, too—my . . . my lady played all the time." She would not cry. They would think her a baby if she cried. She must still her quivering lip.

"Do you like snakes?" asked Aubrey. "I have one," he said, his tone growing conspiratorial as he reached under the bed to withdraw a little wooden box. Upon opening, it revealed a slim grass snake.

"Brey!" Mirabella cried. "Get that slimy thing out of here!"

"Do you want to pet him?" Brey persisted, thrusting the snake toward Cecily.

Cecily smiled, touched. "I am not afraid of snakes," she said as she reached out, stroking the creature's skin. He was not slimy at all.

"Eve wasn't afraid of them either and look what happened to her," Mirabella snapped.

Cecily bowed her head, ashamed. She had never likened herself to the woman who steered the entire world into sin.

"She wants to be a nun," Brey informed Cecily sotto voce.

At this Mirabella lit up. "The abbey is within walking distance," she told her. "I love to go there and help them with their chores; it is usually forbidden to outsiders, but they allow me to visit. Perhaps you would like to accompany me sometime?"

"Very much," Cecily told her. She had never seen an abbey before.

Her willingness to acquiesce seemed to please Mirabella, and Cecily's taut limbs relaxed as relief coursed through her.

At once memories of Burkhart Manor swirled before her mind's eye. Riding her pony through the fields with her groom, hiding outside the solar to hear her mother sing . . . Cecily squeezed her eyes shut. This was her home now. There would be new memories.

She must concentrate on making them.

It was an energetic young household, abundant with vibrancy. The Pierces surrounded themselves with people their age; few who entered were over forty and all who visited could count on being made merry. Because it was Cecily's natural inclination to be happy their enthusiasm afflicted her like contagion. She fancied God could not have sent better guardians, and as the weeks separating her from her parents' deaths turned into months her former life at Burkhart Manor became more dream than reality. Her parents were the undefined faces in miniatures, and while there were nights she awoke crying for her mother, she found that it was increasingly difficult to recall her mother's voice, her touch, her face.

It startled her; it riddled her with guilt. But then there was a feast to prepare for and lessons to be had, embroidery to do, ponies to ride, and Cecily was consumed with the task of daily living. And, perhaps since Cecily had known such a great deal about death, the mission of living was all the more precious to her.

She loved her lessons with Father Alec. The patient priest tutored the children on all manner of subjects, from Latin to history, from astronomy to arithmetic, and Cecily was a quick wit. She enjoyed the company of the other children. Brey stirred a lot in his seat and his blue eyes were often more engaged by the window rather than his books, but Cecily imagined he wouldn't need much book learning anyway, since he was the heir and would not be a gift to the Church.

Mirabella had little use for book learning as well, though her intelligence was never in doubt. No, her heart lay with the spiritual. She plagued Father Alec with questions about the Church, about the Holy Orders, her eyes sparkling with longing, her smile as wistful as a lover separated from her heart's desire.

"Mother says she just likes all the decorations," Brey would insist to Father Alec when Mirabella demonstrated her desire to take vows herself one day. "The golden rosaries and pretty statues."

"You hush up!" Mirabella cried.

Father Alec laughed. "If Lady Mirabella is called to join the Church, I am certain it would be for reasons more pure," he told the boy, resting fond eyes on Mirabella.

Mirabella rose from the bench in the library where their lessons were held and strolled toward the window, resting her long-fingered hand on the glass. "I would join because it is so peaceful there," she said. "There is nothing to do but talk to God. . . ."

"*All* the time?" Brey asked, his tone incredulous. "I would run out of things to say," he confessed.

"Don't you want to get married and have babies?" Cecily asked her.

Mirabella shrugged. "Anyone can do that; only special people are called to do God's work. Besides, He needs everyone he can get for the fight against the New Learning."

At this Father Alec arched an inquisitive brow. "What do you mean, dear child?" he asked her slowly.

Mirabella fixed him with an earnest gaze. "Well, to keep the Church strong. The book of Mark tells us a house divided cannot stand, isn't that right? God needs soldiers to combat evil people like Martin Luther and William Tyndale. That's what the abbess says."

Father Alec lowered his eyes, his face paling. "Yet we must re-member that everyone, no matter how . . . misguided you believe their faith to be, deserves to be treated with compassion. Remem-ber, Lady Mirabella, God is our only judge. You—know that, don't you, my child?"

Mirabella offered a fervent nod.

Father Alec drew in a breath, running a hand through the chest-nut waves that grazed his shoulders. "Well, I think that is enough for today. It is beautiful outside—perhaps you should all take some exercise."

As the children filed out of the room Cecily lingered. She was not like Mirabella; she did not want to talk to God all the time and could not imagine life cloistered away from the world. Yet religion concerned her. She remembered Mistress Fitzgerald's claim that Henry VIII had invoked the wrath of God for loving the heretical Anne Boleyn. She recalled bits of conversations at Burkhart Manor, her parents discussing something called the New Learn-ing. They spoke of it in hushed voices, sustained with excitement. They did not speak of it with malice, as though it were a plague to fight. They spoke of it with hope lighting their eyes.

But to Mirabella the New Learning encompassed all that was

evil. It was an enemy with which to do battle and God was mustering His soldiers.

"Father," Cecily asked after the other children had left, "is the New Learning evil?"

"There are those of authority who think so," Father Alec replied in gentle tones as he knelt before her. He studied the child's face, a face wrought with sincerity and kindness. A face that he enjoyed greeting, a face that could be tear streaked from tragedy but instead chose to meet each day with sparkling eyes and a bright smile.

"But what is it?" Cecily persisted.

Father Alec searched for a simplified explanation. "It means different things to different people, but the central theme is the belief that the Church should be reformed. That the wealth in the monasteries and churches should be dispersed among the people, that sin should not be expiated by paying indulgences—that is, paying the clergy for forgiveness—that church officials in power should not give offices to family members even if they are undeserving . . . There are many things, complicated things—"

"But they all make sense!" Cecily cried with a smile. "Why would people think that is evil when they just want to make things fair?"

"That, too, is complicated, little one," he told her, touched by her innocent summation of the situation. "Many people do not like their authority questioned, even if the suggestions seem reasonable. People fear change and those benefiting from the way things are now will no doubt fight to keep them that way." He sighed. "It is dangerous even discussing the New Learning, Lady Cecily, and you would do well not to speak of it to anyone but me. People, like Martin Luther, have been excommunicated for their beliefs and began what some would call renegade sects of their own. They are the lucky ones; others have even been put to death."

He watched the teal eyes grow round; the alabaster face paled to match the falling snow. "What do you believe, Father?"

Father Alec paused. He reached out to tuck a stray rose-gold lock behind her ear. "I will tell you. I believe in God the Father Almighty, maker of Heaven and earth. . . ."

Cecily smiled.

"Come now, my little theologian, let us to the outdoors!" he cried, sweeping her up in his arms. "I believe there is a pony waiting for its mistress."

Cecily snuggled against his chest, all thoughts of the Church forgotten as she anticipated riding on the snow-covered trails of Sumerton Forest with Father Alec and the children.

Father Alec had not forgotten, however. For the rest of the day his thoughts were dominated by Cecily's questions. He prayed that none would accuse him of leading her in a direction most would consider to border on heretical. On the heels of these thoughts was the knowledge of his own beliefs, beliefs harbored within the deepest recesses of his heart.

He thought of Tyndale's English Bible, hidden in a chest in his chambers along with other forbidden texts.

He trembled.

He must be careful.

❧ 2 ❧

It was Christmastide when Mirabella took Cecily to see her cherished convent, Sumerton Abbey. Together, dressed in thick
otter fur–lined cloaks, they trudged through the snow-covered
trails through Sumerton Forest to the Benedictine convent that
bordered the eastern edge of the Pierces' vast estate. Beneath a
canopy of sparkling tree branches they walked and chattered, their
voices tinkling like the icicles that chimed in the crisp breeze.
Mirabella patted at the heavy pouch of ducats on occasion. The
large donation her father sent with each visit was safe, snug in the
pocket of her gown.

Preparations for Christmas were being made when they arrived.
Pine boughs were being strung about the chapter house and all
throughout women's voices were raised in song, their harmonies
swirling, filling up the breadth and height of the little chapel,
which was lined with stained-glass windows and outfitted with
statues of female saints.

Mirabella took Cecily by the hand, leading her throughout the
cloister, introducing her to the sisters, who offered warm, cheerful
welcomes. All the sisters loved Mirabella and it was with them she
felt most at home. Unlike her own mother, who was caught up in
running Castle Sumerton along with planning the endless enter-

tainments for her illustrious friends, these gentle women always had time for her. They listened to her. They soothed her.

The two girls approached the altar to light candles and pray before they would join in the decorating. Mirabella cast an adoring face toward a portrait of the Blessed Virgin, drawing from her serene countenance a sense of inner calm she could find nowhere else.

"Here one lives for God and for charity," she explained to Cecily. "At home everyone is frantic and hurried—'Quick, we must prepare! So-and-so is coming! Quick, we must set table! Quick! We must impress Lord Who's-Its! Dress in your smartest gown— you must look your best!' " She turned, gesturing toward the nuns in their humble habits. "But here everyone casts away vanity. Here there is no one to impress. Here all one has to do is pray, sing, help others, and think. To be at peace, perfect peace." She drew in a deep breath, expelling it slowly. "I can *breathe* here. I never think about breathing at home. But here I can cherish it—I can appreciate it. And it fills me up completely."

"Do you expect that is what being in love is like?" Cecily asked her, finding Mirabella's sentiments terribly romantic.

"Yes," a young olive-skinned sister answered before Mirabella had the opportunity. "It is being in love. In love with the Lord. That is why we wear wedding rings and circlets." She held up her slim-fingered left hand to display the humble gold band.

"Sister Julia!" Mirabella cried, her face alight with joy as the nun, who seemed far too beautiful for convent life to Cecily, opened her arms. Mirabella ran into them, snuggling against her breast as Sister Julia stroked the thick, raven locks tumbling down her back. "You have brought a friend," she observed, smiling at Cecily.

"This is our ward, Baroness Cecily Burkhart," Mirabella introduced. "Cecily, Sister Julia."

Both curtsied. Cecily stared at the woman in awe. She looked peculiar in her habit, as though dressed for a masque. A courtly gown would suit her far more. A vision of her twirling about a ballroom in a fleet, graceful dance seemed far more appropriate than the idea of her on her knees before a prie-dieu all day.

Yet Mirabella and the nun were enraptured by their surroundings, as though they could not imagine being anywhere else. Both faces were made radiant; both were indeed in love with God.

There was something else about their faces, something unsettling. But Cecily could not identify it and as quickly as it was noted it was forgotten.

The girls returned home just as the dusky hues of twilight began to subdue the snow from bright white to a subtle violet. As they scampered into the great hall they encountered Lady Grace, who rested one slim white hand on her hip while the other clenched a cup of wine. She fixed Mirabella with a dark stare.

"Where were you?" she demanded. "You were to be home hours ago."

"The abbey, my lady," Mirabella answered, bowing her head.

"You know you shouldn't be going without escort, and especially with little Cecily," she said. "Anything could happen to you in that forest—there could be bandits waiting to do all manner of things to you," she chided.

"Yes, my lady," was Mirabella's automatic response.

Lady Grace shook her head, sipping her wine. "You are a fanatic," she spat, her words slurring. "And while men cherish piety in their wives, such extreme devotion will repulse a future husband. No doubt your father will have to bribe your prospects with a higher dowry as it is, that your high-mindedness might be made more tolerable."

"I will not take a husband," Mirabella told her mother. "As well you know. If a man will find me as offensive as you have always claimed then you should be relieved that I fancy embracing the Church. My dowry would be put to far better use with them than by fattening some lord's coffers."

Cecily began to tremble. She did not fear Lady Grace; most often she was quite gentle with her. Yet there was something in Lady Grace that was distressing. Something dark and to be avoided.

Lady Grace gritted her teeth, her cheeks flushing. "A dowry will be paid, but I will be goddamned if a cent of it goes to that abbey or any other!"

"Ladies!" cried Lord Sumerton, who insisted everyone call him Hal, as he made long strides into the hall. He wrapped an arm about Lady Grace's shoulders, squeezing her tight. "Now, now, my love, we do not wish to frighten little Cecily, do we?" he asked under his breath. Then to Mirabella, "Did you deliver the donation, sweetheart?" His eyes lit with tenderness as he regarded her, but the gentle smile on his handsome face did not reflect in them. At once Cecily believed she had never seen such sad eyes.

Mirabella nodded. "They were most pleased, my lord," she told him.

"You mean to say that the girls were alone in the forest with *money?*" Lady Grace cried. "God's wounds, my lord, do you ever think?"

Lord Hal drew in a wavering breath. "I apologize, my lady. I shall make certain the girls are accompanied on all future excursions." He cast his gaze upon Cecily, brightening. "And how do you find the abbey, sweeting? Fancy it as much as Mirabella does?"

"It is a beautiful place," she answered. "But I do not think I shall ever become a nun," she added.

"It is not for everyone," Lord Hal agreed with a chuckle. "But it is a divine calling and not to be disrespected." This comment was directed toward Lady Grace, who narrowed her eyes and sipped her wine.

Lord Hal wrapped one arm about Mirabella's shoulder, then stooped down, lifting Cecily with the other. Cecily relished his generous displays of affection. He was a kind man, never failing to demonstrate his love for his children. His attentions softened the pang of longing for her own father, who often had been distant and preoccupied.

"Come now, sweetings, let's remove to the solar and warm you both up. We shall send for some honeyed milk and bread and cheese," he told them. "Twelfth Night is coming soon and I need to know what my best girls will be expecting!"

As they quit the great hall Cecily peered over his shoulder where Lady Grace stood, head bowed over her cup of wine.

"We have to set to making a match for Mirabella," Grace told her husband in their bedchamber late that night. "She'll be fourteen soon. It cannot be avoided any longer."

"Of course it can," Hal returned as he removed his clothing and knelt before his prie-dieu. Grace's gaze traveled up and down the well-muscled torso, taking in the sight of skin made raw by the hair shirt he wore underneath his fine doublets. She shuddered.

"A betrothal, Hal," she amended in gentle tones. Tears pooled in her eyes. She rolled onto her side, back to him. "Just a betrothal." She would focus on that. Far better than the scars decorating what would have been an otherwise perfect specimen. "Brey's future is secured," she went on. "The little baroness will make a fine wife; add all her lands and ten thousand ducats a year into the bargain and you have one of the best catches in England. Which leaves us with Mirabella. An alliance must be made. We do not have to send her away for a long while. She could remain till she is seventeen, eighteen if she likes."

Hal crossed himself, then joined her in bed. "A worthy thought," he said. "Meantime, you will indulge me with peace under my roof." He rolled her toward him by the shoulder, appealing to her with his eyes. "Please."

Grace pursed her lips, scowling. She reached up, tentatively fingering one of the angry red sores. "When will you stop?"

Hal looked past her at the bedside table where rested a decanter of wine. "When will you?"

Grace flopped onto her back, staring up at the blue velvet canopy.

We will remain thus trapped, she reflected. *Each in our own twisted vices.*

The thought did not prevent her from leaning over and seizing the decanter, however.

She drank straight from it.

She did not need a cup when no one was watching.

*   *   *

Twelfth Night was ushered in with a feast that many celebrated nobles attended. The children were all allowed to sit at table, though Mirabella excused herself early so that she might devote the night of Epiphany to prayer.

Cecily absorbed the event with delight, however. She had never been to such a gala. Though her parents had socialized with their peers, Cecily was restricted to the nursery. Now she was allowed to be in the thick of things, to drink in the colors and flavors of the evening. It surpassed the bustling excitement of market day in the nearby town of Sumerton and far exceeded a fair—Cecily never cared for the disorganized chaos of fairs. This was splendid—a perfectly choreographed feast. The table was laden with mincemeat pies, mutton, haunches of venison, a fat stuffed goose, brawn, eels, cheeses, bread, puddings, and tarts. The guests attendant were attired in their finest silks, velvets, furs, brocades, and jewels. It was a display of sensory pleasure and Cecily savored every moment.

She and Brey, as the only children present, were the center of everything. She was dressed in a silver damask gown with a kirtle of white lace. Brey was dressed to match in a fine silver damask doublet with white hose. Both children's slippers bore silver buckles encrusted with pearls and they were displayed for the adult guests to pet and admire. Together Brey and Cecily showed the spectators the latest steps they had learned while Lord and Lady Sumerton sat at the high table, their smiles wide with pride.

After a fleet dance that left Cecily and Brey collapsing in each other's arms breathless and giggling, Lord Hal rose. "What a delight to watch these children at their revels! And what a delight it shall be to watch them grow in the sacred union we have chosen for them." He paused, casting fond eyes at the children who stood stock still before the assemblage. "Tonight we would like to announce the betrothal of my son, Lord Aubrey Pierce, to Baroness Cecily Burkhart." He raised his cup. "To the future!"

"The future!" echoed the guests.

None was more surprised than Cecily herself.

She stared at her intended with wide eyes, cocking her head, trying to imagine his features sculpted and angled with five, ten years of age added to his seven years. She could not.

Brey offered a shy smile. "I guess this means we can hunt snakes together for the rest of our lives!" he cried then, as though finding a great deal of refuge in the thought.

Cecily's shoulders relaxed as she imagined traipsing through the vast forest of Sumerton alongside of cheerful, gentle Brey. "And we can pick berries, too," she added.

"And go hunting and hawking," he said. "That will be fun." He cast a sidelong glance at his parents. Lord Hal was leaning in to offer Grace a peck on the cheek. "What else do you think we have to do?" Brey asked.

Cecily grimaced. "Certainly not that," she said. "At least not till we've grown proper."

"Yes," he agreed, sighing in relief. "Meantime, we shall look for snakes."

"Yes," said Cecily. "I should like that."

At once the children were swarmed by well-wishers eager to congratulate them. They were hugged and pinched and kissed. Brey grimaced and wiped the kisses away. Both were soothed from the onslaught by sweetmeats.

"What a commodity!" Cecily overheard one of the lords exclaiming to Lord Hal. "God's body, man, I expect this child is one of the wealthiest heiresses in the kingdom. A fine suit—I rather wish I had snatched her up for one of my sons!"

"Thank you, Lord Norfolk," answered Lord Hal. "We are most pleased with the arrangement."

Cecily's heart pounded. A commodity. An arrangement. When did a person become a commodity? She had never thought of herself that way. A commodity was a bolt of fabric, a fine jewel perhaps, but her? At once the heat of the room and stench of the different pomanders stifled Cecily. She suppressed the urge to gag as she removed herself from the assemblage. She needed a moment to think about her new estate.

She cooled herself in the hall. She longed to remove her sleeves and run about bare armed but dared not. She did not want to be unladylike. She rolled them up instead. No one was watching, after all. She sank to the floor and leaned against the cool stone wall, closing her eyes, blinking back tears. She could not stave off the dark thoughts.

She was betrothed. She wondered what her parents thought of the match. She supposed it was inevitable that she should, as the Pierces' ward, marry their heir. It was custom. It was one of the main reasons why people took on wards.

It was good business. She was a good commodity.

"Lady Cecily."

Cecily started at the husky male voice, looking up to find Father Alec standing before her.

"Are you well, little one?" he asked.

Cecily nodded, brushing the tears aside with the back of her hand. "Do you expect the Pierces like me?" she asked.

"I expect the Pierces love you," answered Father Alec. He paused a moment, then sat beside her. "Why do you ask?"

"I expect they like me a great deal more for the money and the lands," she said, scowling at her slippers. "And the title, of course."

The priest drew in a breath. "Well, Lady Cecily, I will not lie to you. I am certain your assets made you quite attractive as they thought of securing Brey's future. But even had your parents lived it is likely you would have been made a ward to someone and allied to their son in marriage." He sighed. "Someday you will have children, Lady Cecily, and you will want to secure for them the best future possible as well. There are obvious benefits of your wealth that please the Pierces no doubt, but look what else they're gaining! They will have a beautiful, bright, and sensitive daughter-in-law." He reached out, seizing her chin between thumb and forefinger. "For all you may be bringing to them, you, Lady Cecily, your soul, your self, are irreplaceably priceless and they know that."

Cecily brightened at the thought.

"This, Lady Cecily, is an opportunity," Father Alec continued. "You are very young and it may be hard to see now, but you have the chance to shape Brey's whole life, to mold him"—he offered a brief chuckle—"to train him, if you will, into your ideal husband. You have more influence than you know. What's more, Lady Cecily, is that you are not going to marry a stranger. You are going to grow up as *friends*. Few realize how special and rare that is to find in a marriage." He smiled. "Do you like the Pierces, Lady Cecily?"

Cecily offered a fervent nod. They were the only people she could call family now and they were easy to like. Easy to love.

"Do you like Brey?" he asked.

She nodded again. Indeed, Brey was as sweet a boy as one could find.

"Then I think you have a better start than most," he told her, taking her hand in his. He rose. "Come now! You'll be missed!"

Cecily rose and followed him back to the celebration.

She would dismiss her uncharitable thoughts and be what Father Alec said: irreplaceably priceless.

Lent sobered Sumerton, and though there was still a modest amount of entertaining, it was nothing compared to the rest of the year's revels. Mirabella enjoyed Lent; in its deprivation of physical pleasures she found solace. Quietude. She spent hours in prayer and meditation, enveloping herself in the rare peace her home afforded during this fleeting time of year.

When not absorbed in her devotions, Mirabella passed the gray winter days in embroidering, riding, and lessons. One favorite pastime for all of the children became listening to Father Alec's tales of his travels through Europe.

"After Cambridge I wanted to see a bit of the world," he told them one afternoon. "So I traveled abroad. I was given a letter of introduction to study under the great Erasmus; it was he who recommended me to your parents." He nodded toward Mirabella and Brey.

"What else did you do?" asked Brey, his tone fringed with impatience.

Father Alec offered a conspiratorial smile. "I camped with Gypsies, I preached to bandits and vagabonds—I was held at knifepoint on more than a few occasions." He chuckled. "I met greatness in humility and humility in greatness."

"Wasn't your family terribly worried?" Cecily asked him.

Father Alec's face softened. His hazel eyes grew distant. "My family was gone by then, victims of the sweat." He offered a sad smile.

Mirabella reached out, laying a hand over his. "It was God's will," she said, her green eyes grave with conviction.

Father Alec withdrew his hand. "Yes . . . thank you, Lady Mirabella."

Mirabella offered her sweetest smile, her heart clenching.

"Then we are orphaned together," commented Cecily, raising saddened eyes to the priest, eyes made wistful with the pain of loss.

Father Alec's eyes revealed fondness as he cast them upon the child. "That we are."

"Yet I suppose no Christian is really orphaned. God is always our father," Cecily added then, her face brightening with hope. "And He sends us people to look after us and help us, even though our parents were called to Him. Like the Pierces and you for me. That way we need never feel all alone."

Father Alec's eyes softened with unshed tears. "No . . . we are never all alone."

Mirabella's gaze darkened. She had spent hours discussing matters of faith with Father Alec and with unending patience he had indulged her, all while praising her intellect. Yet Cecily's oversimplified generalization, along with the mutual loss of their parents to the dreaded sweat, connected her to the priest in a way Mirabella's devoutness and keen mind never could.

She should not resent her for it. It was unchristian, uncharitable. She was above such things. Yet her gut wrenched and ached with unwelcome jealousy. Cecily was endearing; she was sweet without pretense. Her light permeated the darkest reaches of any room and any heart. Mirabella could not emit these qualities, not because she was not in possession of them but because she preferred her solitude. Her light was secret, sacred, preserved for God and a handful of others, one of them being Father Alec. To see his eyes light with admiration for another seized her with a sense of envy new to her.

She blinked several times. She must not think this way. Cecily was to be a sister to her and to resent a sister was tantamount to resenting Brey or her mother and father.

Besides, Cecily was just a little girl and everyone was sweet to little girls. Mirabella had no reason to fret.

Grace needed another distraction. *Curse Lent and its damnable deprivation!* It was all observed with falsehood, as was most everything Catholic. It was a religion of pretense and ritual, meant to satisfy the illiterate multitudes grasping for visuals. Those with any intellect at all did not appreciate with awe the carefully calculated "miracles" the priests concocted to keep their parishioners in thrall. Grace was never impressed. As it was, whenever she attended mass she could not stop calculating the cost of the exquisite chalices, statues, and other artwork gracing the chapel. And the extravagance of the bishops and priests she had encountered had filled her with unholy envy of its own account.

Grace had heard of Tyndale and Luther, and though she agreed with their various suggestions for reform, she was not a woman impassioned by conviction. Her beliefs were not fervent enough to pursue the New Learning any more than cling to the so-called True Faith. She valued her life, after all. Grace could admit with a dark chuckle that one of the only reasons she resented the wealth of the Church was because she wished to appropriate it.

Thus the matter of the New Learning was only reflected upon during Lent as she wondered what these reformers would do with the season. She couldn't imagine it being made any worse; however, given the reformers' views on simplicity it likely would not be any better.

So it was that Grace needed another diversion; the melancholy was lurking again in the shadows of her mind and brooding over religious and philosophical doctrine would not assuage it. Matters of religion became too heady for Grace and were best left to Father Alec to puzzle out with moony-eyed Mirabella. Meantime, Grace would plan an entertainment for May Day to usher in the spring.

The girls would need gowns. Grace lay back in her bed, steepling her fingers beneath her chin in thought as she envisaged little Cecily and Brey in another matching ensemble. The two were a perfect pair! What a boon the little baroness was! Not only did she bring in a worthy dowry, but she was the presence of beauty and poise. And Brey loved her; they were together all the time, playing as children do. Grace could not refrain from emitting a naughty giggle as she imagined the games they would turn to when adolescence struck. No doubt theirs was fated to be a love match; Grace could see it.

With this to lighten her heart, Grace summoned Mirabella and Cecily. She would invite them to participate in the planning process. Both girls needed to learn; after all, they would be running their own grand households someday and it would give them something to do during the interminable weeks of Lent.

The girls entered her bedchamber, rosy cheeked and breathless from their revels outdoors. Grace offered a bright smile.

"Is it a nice day?" she asked them.

"Lovely!" Mirabella cried. "You should come out, my lady, and take in the air. 'Twould be good for you."

Grace reached for her cup of wine and took a long draught, then set it beside her, dabbing her lips with her handkerchief. "Yes, perhaps . . ." she said offhandedly as she patted the bed. The girls sat, Mirabella at her feet and Cecily at her side. "Now. I've summoned you both to help me plan a grand occasion."

"Another one?" Mirabella groaned.

"Yes, Mirabella, another one," Grace said, weary of the girl's aversion to all things pleasant. "A sort of Beltane celebration to bring in the spring."

"Beltane! But that's a pagan festival!" Mirabella cried, scandalized.

"Oh, bother, Mirabella, I didn't say we would be dancing naked round the bonfire, did I?" Grace returned, thoroughly irritated. "It's just that I thought this would give us an opportunity to . . . well, to be together," she added with a wistful smile. "I thought to order some fabrics and we could design the wardrobe—"

"During Lent?" Mirabella interposed, wrinkling her nose in disapproval.

"Oh, my lady, we can plan our own dresses?" Cecily cried, her little face flushing with delight. "Can mine be blue?"

"Blue would be splendid, Cecily—it will bring out your lovely eyes," Grace conceded, endeared to the good-natured child. "Blue silk trimmed with lace, perhaps?" She reached out to stroke the child's cheek.

"I think it's wonderful!" Cecily turned toward Mirabella. "We shall have a good time, Mirabella, with your lady mother. You'll see! You would look stunning in red—red organza or velvet!" She returned her gaze to Grace. "Don't you think so?"

Grace nodded; truly Mirabella was an exquisite child, far more beautiful than she knew. A red dress would accentuate all of her assets and if she ever decided it pleased God to smile . . .

"I think this display is despicable!" Mirabella huffed, rising from the bed. "My lady, it is Lent, the time of repentance and restraint. To plan such an occasion now, especially one that rings of Beltane, is an affront to God."

"Oh, my self-righteous girl . . ." Grace shook her head. "Who needs Father Alec with you around to keep us in check?"

Mirabella turned on her heel and quit the room, leaving Cecily to sit stunned, lip quivering, beside Grace, who wrapped her arm about her shoulders and drew her to her breast.

"There, now, no worries, Cecily," she soothed. "If I told Mirabella the sky was blue she would say it was brown just to disagree. We shall never see eye to eye, I'm afraid." She stroked the child's silky hair, taking comfort in it. "You would still like to help?"

"Yes, my lady," Cecily said, offering a timid half smile.

Grace relaxed against her pillows. She retrieved her cup from the bedside table. "Empty," she murmured, scowling. "Cecily, be a lamb, won't you, and fetch your mistress another cup of wine?"

"Yes, my lady," Cecily answered as she crawled out of bed to do Grace's bidding.

Grace watched the child's competent little hands fill her cup with the soothing, crimson liquid. How good it was to have such an acquiescent child about!

"I should like it very much if you spent more time with me,"

Grace told her on impulse as Cecily handed her the cup. "It pleases me to be in your company."

Cecily smiled, offering another engaging flush of the cheeks. "Thank you, my lady."

Grace drank her wine. As it surged through her, warming her trembling limbs and calming her racing heart, she smiled. She would get through another Lent.

She had a ball to prepare for.

Hal Pierce spent Lent playing dice with a few other less observant members of the local gentry. He didn't mind the deprivation, the penance. He considered his life one endless Lent as it were, so the season had little effect on him. And a little dice was harmless enough. He never lost too much; he was careful with his assets. He would not deprive Brey of his rightful inheritance. It was fun, that was all, just a bit of fun. And he needed fun.

Hal was not a drinking man, he was not a whoring man, and that was more than could be said for most men. Thus he took some measure of pride in himself for being able to go through life with such uncanny restraint. A bit of dice and a hand of cards were his rewards.

He had married Grace at the age of eighteen. His heart contracted at the thought. She was the beautiful daughter of a wool baron from York and had brought with her a generous dowry. They got on as well as could be expected, though like most marriages, it did not begin as a love match. Since their wedding day they had been tested with rigorous consistency. His parents were ailing, both passing within the first two years of his marriage, leaving the running of the household and management of the vast lands that surrounded it to the young couple. Yet they endured and with endurance came love. They embraced their mutual passion for fun and good company. They shared a love of hunting, hawking, and dancing. Grace became the perfect social ornament. If he focused on those elements he could forget the rest, the lonely nights when their home was not teeming with guests, nights spent in separate bedchambers, nights of solitude and reflection on events that could never be changed.

That was when Grace slept with a decanter at her bedside. And that was when Hal played dice.

Because Hal was the only child of the previous Earl of Sumerton it was his hope to fill the house with children of his own. That there were only two and a succession of miscarriages could not be helped. It was the will of God, he supposed, and he cherished his blessings. Brey was a wonderful child, sweet and bonny. And Mirabella . . . well, he was certain Mirabella would come into her own when softened by marriage and children. It was his hope that she would abandon her fantasy of becoming a nun. Though he would never deter her, it was not the life he had dreamed of for her.

Dreams . . . Nothing had gone as expected. In that his life was a constant illustration.

He sat now, thinking of this life as he shook the dice in clammy hands, surrounded by other men who wondered after their own lives, all of them convening to stave off their own terrible loneliness for one night. They would listen to the rattle of the dice, the melody of their chuckling, the bawdy jokes.

And they would pretend to be happy.

Thus Hal would get through.

Father Alec was witnessing a change in the Pierce household. Though it had been lively with a superficial sort of energy, he could not say his patrons were happy people. Yet when Lady Cecily came . . . He was under no illusions. The little baroness worked no miracles. The Pierces were still imbued with their own respective vices. Yet she infused in them a tranquility that he had not seen before. Her innocence, her trusting nature, her resilient cheer endeared her to all she encountered. Brey had a playmate, a companion, an outlet for his restlessness. Mirabella had an affable girl-child to treat as a sister and pupil, someone with whom she could tout her knowledge, someone she could nurture and lead toward her perception of Right. Lady Grace adored the girl and spent entire afternoons absorbing her serenity; she was a buffer to the antagonism experienced with her own daughter. And Lord Hal was fond of her as well; she was his hope for the future. It was from her womb that would descend all future Pierces.

She was of no exceptional talent; she was the type who mastered all she attempted with competence. If she possessed any gift worthy of note it was in her ability to manage people. Though she was playful, she displayed no signs of being a coquette; she would not manipulate her way through life as would a woman of the court. No, it was her sweetness that won hearts. Her sweetness, her sincerity, her acquiescence, her comforting presence.

Cecily was that rarest of things. A soul of complete integrity.

Father Alec drank her in as well. She was as a daughter to him. Perhaps it was because the other children had living parents that inclined Father Alec to believe they needed him less. Perhaps it was that Cecily shared his acute awareness of loss. Or perhaps it was that she was so uncomplicated. So genuine. Whatever it was, Father Alec found that with her he could be as close to a true father as he would ever get.

Of course it was not productive to think like that.

Father Alec did not regret the choice he had made. What other alternative was there at the time? The priesthood made sense. He was the second son of a Welsh country squire. As such, his fate lay with the Church. He did not resent this. He needed an education and the only ones of his class with access to an education of any true merit were priests. Chastity seemed a small enough sacrifice for the enrichment of his mind and soul.

He found other ways to relate to his fellow man and being a tutor was one of them. It gave him the opportunity to experience a little of what he had chosen to forgo. He lived with the Pierces; through them he witnessed the pitfalls and triumphs of a family. He could not deny that he was still on the outside, a bystander living vicariously through others. The emptiness of it all enshrouded him and more often than not he felt like a fraud, a man dressed as a priest for a masque.

Then Cecily came and with her a new sense of fulfillment, a new sense of connection.

He cursed himself. He should not feel that need. He should be resigned to his lot, the lot that he chose. Yet what harm was there in pretending? Was he not called Father for a reason? He chose to be as loving as a father to God's people, to guide them, to nurture them. Surely God could not fault him for that.

So he pretended. Cecily called him Father and he reveled in the temporary fantasy that he was a family man, that he had a daughter.

That she called him Father not because he was a priest.

❧ 3 ❧

Winter shed its abundant white cloak in favor of the dewy
green gown of spring. Easter had come and gone, relieving
everyone at Sumerton of their Lenten deprivations. Now was a
time to celebrate the Resurrection, to savor the hope life brought
as it renewed itself in all its forms, the flowers pushing their bonny
heads through the moist, fertile earth, the trees budding and
blooming, the lambs and fawns struggling on their wobbly legs,
the pups opening their eyes to the warmth of the sun for the first
time.

The world was waking up.

Cecily was, too. She had grown to love the Pierces in the year
she had spent with them, and though she longed for her parents,
she realized she longed for them, less because of who they were
than what they were. They were her parents. It was her duty to
love them. She did not know them as people at all. They had
never interacted with her the way the Pierces did. To be fair, Cecily had been too young to interact with and was left to the nurse
for the most part. Most of her memories were of Mistress Fitzgerald rather than her mother, who was trailing after Cecily's father,
who was trailing after the court. Cecily could not blame them for
that; that was their noble responsibility.

She prayed for her parents' souls. The pain and guilt began to subside. She cherished their miniatures, keeping them on her bed-side table that she might always be close enough to consult their likenesses should nostalgia call. As time passed, it called less and less.

Meantime the Pierces served as her distractions. They were a strange group; she loved them. She feared them. Their pain was tangible to one as sensitive as Cecily. She knew it, she felt it, even as she could not identify it. It shone out of Lord Hal's wistful blue eyes, it rang like a mourning bell in Lady Grace's soft voice, and was illustrated in Brey's bewildered expression. In Mirabella it was disguised by an iron will and uncompromising conviction that Cecily did not bother to resist. It was far easier to acquiesce where she was concerned, and Cecily found Mirabella's rare smiles worth yielding to. Besides, Mirabella was at odds with Lady Grace enough as it was; she did not need Cecily to add to the melee. If Cecily disagreed with her on matters of principle and anything in between she kept it to herself.

Finally there was Father Alec, who wore a mantle of melancholy of his own. He masked it with a kind smile, but it was there, deafening in its tortured silence. Cecily could not hope to reach it, to nurse it as was her inclination with anyone suffering.

She longed to heal them all. They had come together, all broken things, it seemed. She did not know why; perhaps she did not need to know. What mattered was that she was there and, in whatever way she could, she would try to bring joy to these people who were to be her life.

She did not yet possess the ability to comfort with words. So she comforted with actions, leaving bouquets of fresh spring flowers for Lady Grace and Mirabella, treasures from the outdoors to Brey, anything she could catch—frogs, mice, moles. For the men, Lord Hal and Father Alec, she left messages of hope in the small things—feathers, vibrant blue-green grass, shiny rocks, birds' eggs. Anything that caught her eye.

She never told them; she was never one to tout herself. She knew she had given, after all, and sought no glory. She just left them. And hoped it cheered them as much as finding them cheered her.

Father Alec caught her one day. She had sneaked into his chambers and was leaving an interesting birds' nest on his pillow. It was woven with such perfection, such delicate intricacy, that it rivaled the richest tapestry.

He cleared his throat upon entrance. "Lady Cecily, you know these are my private apartments."

Cecily started, stiffening as she turned to face him. "I'm sorry, Father. It's just that . . . well . . . I—"

"Did you look through my things?" he asked her.

Cecily shook her head. "No, sir. Of course not."

His shoulders eased and he offered a smile. "I did not mean to frighten you. It's just that I do not own much. What I do have, I treasure."

"I understand," Cecily said, and she did. She did not have much either. In truth she had more land and money and possessions than she could fathom, but they were inaccessible. What she had that she actually valued was very little and she would not want anyone tampering with it either.

"What were you doing in here then?" he asked her, his smile widening.

Cecily retrieved the birds' nest, flushing as she handed it to him. "I saw it . . . I thought . . ." She could not speak. She did not want him to know.

"So it was you," he breathed in his husky voice that Cecily had come to grow fond of. He sat upon his bed as he examined the nest. "I've been wondering for weeks now . . . all these little gifts. I have enjoyed each and every one," he told her. "But why?"

Cecily bowed her head, embarrassed to be caught in the Act. She shifted from foot to foot, then slowly raised her eyes to the priest. "Because, Father, there is so much in this world to love."

Father Alec slid from the bed to his knees, taking Cecily in his arms. "Darling girl," he murmured against her hair. "Darling, darling girl, if there is any living proof of that it is in you. . . ."

Cecily wrapped her arms about his neck. No one hugged like he did. He engulfed her in his strong arms as would a great bear, holding her to his chest. She listened to his heartbeat. Strong, steady, and sure. A heartbeat she could count on.

There was no one in her world like Father Alec. With him she shared an inexplicable understanding that went beyond words. He always treated her with respect; he took her seriously. He answered all of her questions, even when Mirabella teased that they were childish and stupid. He was patient. He seemed to enjoy her company. He spent many an hour regaling her with tales of woodland creatures that talked, knights who rescued pretty ladies, or stories of the mischief he got into when he was a child.

He was the only person who seemed to completely belong to her. She did not know why. Yet somehow she knew it was reciprocated. That somehow, perhaps more than any little gifts she could offer him, it was her self that brought him the most peace.

What an uncanny privilege, she reflected as she looked into the kind hazel eyes, to know that she could be a comfort just by existing.

She did not leave him gifts after that day.

He did not need them.

"I cannot believe Mother and her May Day revels!" Mirabella fumed as the girls were dressed for the celebration Lady Grace had been planning since Lent. "I heard she is having bonfires after all! And she's going to let the peasants dance around the poles just like pagans! There are going to be all kinds of wicked masques where the ladies will be half-naked!"

"Really?" Cecily asked, her breathless tone betraying her eagerness to participate in the pagan frolic. "Oh, Mirabella, but you must try to have a good time! You look so beautiful!"

Mirabella turned, gazing at herself in the shining silver glass. The red organza gown that her mother had made was indeed splendid, if one put great store in material things (which Mirabella did not). Its red velvet stomacher was embroidered with cloth of gold and seed pearls; the resplendent sleeves were in the French fashion that the witch Anne Boleyn was making popular, with cloth of gold undersleeves and kirtle to match. Mirabella's black hair was brushed to a glossy sheen and flowed down her back in rippling waves under a red velvet French hood, embroidered with the same cloth of gold and seed pearls to match the stomacher. In all, a stunning ensemble.

She was beautiful.

She had not realized it before.

She put a slender hand to her face, taking in a slow breath. "Please send for Father Alec," she ordered.

"But we're expected to go down soon," Cecily returned.

"I said send for him!" she cried as the child retreated. Mirabella was agitated with the little girl. As sweet as she was, Mirabella lost patience with her even, affable attitude. She was so accepting, so content. Why could Mirabella not be content? Why could she not accept the life her parents would no doubt choose for her? It was exhausting, this constant fighting.

Yet it was a compulsion. It was as natural to her as breathing, as eating. She needed to fight. She would serve her Lord. She would not get caught up in these trappings. She would escape. And once free, she would learn contentment, acceptance. She would have what Cecily had.

"Lady Mirabella."

Mirabella turned to find Father Alec standing in the doorway of the nursery. He filled it up with his presence. Her heart clenched. She did not understand the feelings that stirred in her belly whenever she was in his presence. Perhaps it was his youth; at twenty-eight, Father Alec possessed an allure that was undeniably attractive. His well-muscled build seemed inconsistent with his calling; Mirabella could imagine him in a suit of armor or the finery of a courtier—imagine how hose would hug his legs . . . oh, what was she thinking? Mirabella squeezed her eyes shut, reopening them to find Father Alec bedecked in the humble robes of a priest. She lowered her head, feeling as though it were a sin just to look at him, as though somehow he would know she had involuntarily imagined him without his robes or a suit of armor or courtier's finery for that matter.

"Father, I need to confess," she said.

"You just confessed this morning, my child," Father Alec told her in his ever-patient tone. "What could have possibly transpired within the last three hours?"

"I have been vain," she said miserably. "I looked in the glass and saw . . . I saw that I was . . . well, I thought I—"

"That you were beautiful?" Father Alec asked, his lips twisting into a gentle grin.

Hot tears stung Mirabella's eyes.

"Lady Mirabella," Father Alec cooed as he held out his hands. Mirabella took them, trembling at the heat of his palms. "It is not vain to acknowledge your beauty. By recognizing it, you can demonstrate your gratitude to God for bestowing it upon you. I hardly think you will become as Narcissus, my dear."

"But nuns do not need to be beautiful," Mirabella said.

"Why? Don't they deserve beauty as much as anyone else?" Father Alec asked with a slight chuckle. "God made everyone beautiful, for His pleasure. It is not vain to appreciate it. Are flowers vain? Is a sunset vain?" He shook his head. "No, Lady Mirabella. They just *are*. Do you remember how God referred to Himself as *I am*? It is the same with the beauty He created. Beauty *is*. Do you see? Be, my girl. Just be. And find contentment in it."

Contentment. That word. It seemed so elusive here. Why was it she could only glimpse it at the abbey?

"It is hard to *be* at this celebration," Mirabella said. "It just is not who I am, Father."

"I know that," Father Alec said. "But you will find that in life there will be many occasions that are not tailored for you. We have to adapt to our circumstances; in adapting, but not yielding ourselves over completely, we can retain our true selves and endure the rest. Can you do that?"

Mirabella considered. Then nodded. "Yes," she said as she realized how simple he made things sound, how easy it could be. She did not have to like what was going on around her; she only had to be. She could exist in this world and be happy without conforming to it so long as she remained true to herself, to her Lord. "Yes," she said, brightening. "I believe I can."

Father Alec proffered his arm. "Good, then. Now. Let's go down and forget this nonsense about confessing. Save me a real sin."

Mirabella laughed before she could help herself and allowed

herself to be escorted on the arm of Father Alec to the entertainment.

She murmured a little prayer thanking God for him.

No one understood her like he did.

The May Day revels were held out of doors in the garden under an elaborate tent strung with lanterns. Lilies and roses were entwined about all the supports and a wooden floor had been constructed special so that none of the dancers' slippers would be spoiled by the grass. A table laden with the finest foods was set up; trays of pheasant, prawns, cheeses, breads, stuffed capons, and comfits assailed the guests with their aromas and any number of people could be seen nibbling throughout the evening.

Ladies in golden masks danced in gauzy white gowns trimmed with green to the assembly of musicians who entertained the guests, who were all dressed in their spring best. The dancers' costumes were indeed quite revealing, baring their creamy shoulders and arms, which were encircled in gold bracelets.

Grace was pleased with the children this evening. Little Cecily was dressed to match Brey in the blue ensemble Grace had designed with her. Grace watched with fondness as the little baroness rubbed the cool satin sleeve against her cheek. She and Brey made the perfect pair. Grace's heart contracted with wistful delight. Even Mirabella seemed happier than usual. She could not imagine what inspired the child to cooperate. Whatever it was, may it only continue!

Head tingling with the warmth of good wine, Grace threw herself into dancing till the soles of her feet throbbed and ached. When it came time for the ladies to unmask, Grace revealed herself to be one of the bare-armed dancers! Lord Hal's eyes widened in mock astonishment as he toasted his wife.

"You are full of surprises," he told her, drawing her close.

"I have to keep up," Grace answered before she could stop herself.

Hal's eyes lit with sadness. He averted his head. "You've outdone yourself."

Grace squeezed his hand. "Thank you, Hal," she said in gentle tones. "Isn't Brey charming? Look at him dancing with little Cecily and the others. They are splendid together. She's such a dear child."

"Indeed," Hal returned, his face soft as he regarded the children. "And Mirabella. Your choice of gown was exquisite. I have never seen such a stunning creature."

Grace stiffened. "No, I suppose not," she said blandly.

From across the tent she eyed her decanter of wine. She began to pull away.

"Grace, please, I didn't mean—" Hal attempted to seize her hand, but Grace jerked away from him like a horse gone skittish. "Grace. Don't."

"What?" she asked him. "Have I not the right to enjoy my own revels?" She sauntered toward the table, lifted the decanter, and held it to her lips. At once a collective thrill of murmuring was heard among the gathering.

Grace had forgotten to use a cup.

It did not matter to her. Face flushed in a mingling of rage and embarrassment, she tilted it back and drank. And drank. Her throat burned, her gut ached.

Still she drank. She would drink till it went away.

But it would come back, in spite of everything; it always came back.

Cecily watched the night unfold in frightened fascination. It had all been so magical at first—the golden hue of the lanterns playing off the masked ladies, the gauzy costumes that clung to their forms so rounded and splendid, capturing the very essence of spring and fertility, all those things that were woman.

The food had been delicious. Cecily and Brey had stuffed themselves, then hid under the table afterwards to play with the pile of caterpillars they had collected throughout the evening and feed them crumbs. The children were hoping to build a house for them to keep in the nursery that they might watch the caterpillars' transformation.

Even Mirabella was having a good time. She danced, favoring

the guests with her rare smile that was a transformation as stunning as that of the caterpillars, which Cecily and Brey anticipated with such eagerness. Her solemn, earnest face was made radiant with that smile, her eyes shone like emeralds, infecting Cecily with the need to laugh. She was thrilled to see her so happy.

Then something went terribly wrong.

The ladies unmasked, revealing Lady Grace to be the lead dancer. This in itself was a thrilling display and Cecily clapped at the sight. The countess was beautiful, as intoxicating as a faery with her white-blond hair falling around her shoulders in ringlets made limp from the dew of evening.

When she took to Lord Hal's side, the night that had begun as a fantasy faded into a horrific charade. Words were exchanged; Lady Grace pulled away. She strode toward the high table, seized a decanter of wine, and drank straight from it.

This was not unusual to Cecily. She had seen Lady Grace do it many times. But she knew it was not something Lady Grace would ever do in public. It was forbidden. It was unseemly.

Cecily and Brey had been searching out more caterpillars and heard the murmurs of the guests—unkind, snide remarks muttered with cackles of laughter.

People liked to see such things, Cecily realized with a heavy heart. She could not imagine such a display bringing pleasure to anyone. Yet they laughed.

"Why feign surprise?" one gentleman could be heard saying as Cecily and Brey returned to their spot beneath the table. "We know the woman cherishes her wine above all else."

Brey's lip began to quiver.

Cecily's cheeks flushed in anger. *How dare they criticize the hostess while they stand at her table and make pigs of themselves! They probably drink out of wine decanters all the time!*

"Don't worry, Brey," she told her companion, handing him the caterpillars that had been squirming in the lap of her dress. "We'll show them."

Cecily poked her foot out from under the table as the man who had uttered the rude comment walked by, tripping him clean on his nose, withdrawing her foot before he could be the wiser.

Blue eyes twinkling, Brey covered his mouth with his hand, and the two shared a conspiratorial giggle.

But it provided little relief. Lady Grace's breach of etiquette was only the beginning.

From beneath the table Cecily witnessed Lady Grace as she began to twirl about the floor, decanter in hand. While other guests were acceptably tipsy as well, Cecily knew with heart-pounding certainty the countess's antics were to be remembered. She had bypassed acceptable long ago. She was in a realm no one could reach. No one tried. They either derived amusement from it or were too shocked to move.

Lady Grace twirled about. "Prepare to be stunned, Hal!" She was laughing as her wine spilled down the front of her white chiffon gown, staining it crimson, as though she were bleeding from the heart.

She was wounded, Cecily knew. She longed to reach out but remained frozen, transfixed. From somewhere she heard Brey crying. She could not comfort him. She could only watch, helpless, hopeless.

Lady Grace threw the decanter across the floor, then began to tear at her gown. "Stunning, Hal?" she cried as she shed the gown, revealing her white body shining with sweat. She stood there, naked, trembling, beautiful, and terrible.

No one said a word. No one moved. Everything was happening as though underwater, slow, held back by forces too great to resist.

Lady Grace stared at the guests, shocked sober. She collapsed to the ground, drawing her knees to her chest, covering her breasts, and burying her head in them. Her white shoulders heaved with sobs.

The silence hurt Cecily's ears.

"For the love of God!" a man cried. The husky voice was instantly recognized as Father Alec's as he rushed forward, seizing a cloak from another stunned gentleman's shoulders and wrapping it about Lady Grace. He knelt beside her, murmuring softly. "Come now, my child. Let us remove to the house. Come now. You are all right. You are all right." He all but lifted her to her feet, then turned to the guests. "You've taken in your fill," he said, his voice laced with disgust. "Those of you staying with the Pierces this evening may retire. As for the rest, you best return to your homes. The lady of the house is unwell."

As Father Alec guided Lady Grace indoors, the world began to move again. Cecily was prompted into action. She reached out, taking Brey in her arms. "There, there, Brey," she murmured against the golden hair. "She is just unwell. The heat . . ."

"Her gown did not have sleeves!" he cried. "She could not have been hot!"

"But she was dancing so much," Cecily told him. "You know how hot one gets dancing. There, there, don't cry. She is just tired. She will rest and feel much better tomorrow."

"They will laugh at her forever," Brey returned, his eyes narrowing.

Cecily bowed her head. They would. She could not say otherwise. Brey was not stupid.

"Well, then they're just dense if that's all they have to laugh about," she said. "I can think of things much funnier than that. Can't you?"

Brey furrowed his brow in thought. "I suppose so." He leaned into her arms again. "Oh, Cecily, why is everyone so sad?"

Cecily swallowed the burning lump in her throat.

She did not know.

Hal did not know who to seek out first. More than Grace, Father Alec had made fools of everyone with his show of chivalry, not that Hal wasn't grateful for it. God knew he was too rooted in terror to be useful.

As Grace was ushered indoors the crowd began to disperse, shaking their heads and murmuring. Grace had wanted to give them an unforgettable celebration, he thought bitterly. He and Grace would be lucky to be received anywhere after this. He could not imagine how to undo the damage done this night.

He stood a long while, apologizing to the guests as they departed. How he hated that! The pity that lit their eyes as they regarded him, the amusement that was barely hidden in others. *May they all fall on the ends of their swords!*

His eyes searched the crowd for his children. Cecily and Brey were nowhere to be seen. He could only pray that they had missed the spectacle. As his eyes scanned the mass, he saw a shock of red organza.

Mirabella.

Oh, God. Mirabella.

She was running. He did not know if he could follow her. He could not imagine how to comfort her, how to assuage the terrible anger and shame the girl would no doubt be feeling.

He let her go.

He turned away.

All that was left of the evening was a table full of half-eaten delicacies, a shattered wine decanter, and a stained white gown.

Mirabella ran to the stables, fetching her palfrey. She was too beside herself to ride sidesaddle so rode astride. She could not imagine presenting herself as more offensive than her mother, so it mattered not.

She rode into the night, down the well-beaten trail to the only place that ever gave her any hope and comfort at all. Her convent. She would join them this night. She would leave her worldly life behind. They would hear her story. They could not refuse her. And her father would dare not deny her; he owed her this. He would send a large dowry. The sisters would be so happy!

Mirabella entered the cloister sobbing and breathless. The coos and hushes of the sisters filled her ears as Sister Julia was sent for.

"Mirabella!" the nun cried upon seeing her. "Darling, what is it?"

How could she tell her? It was too scathing, too shocking, for ears so pure. Yet she did. Somewhere God gave her the strength to tell Sister Julia. The story poured forth in all its ugliness. Sister Julia listened in rapt attention, green eyes tearing as she clutched Mirabella's hand.

When Mirabella finished, she hung her head, covering her eyes with a slender hand. She could not abide looking Sister Julia in the face after such a horrific confession.

Sister Julia wrapped her arms about her, drawing her near. She never found such comfort in anyone. Sister Julia's embrace was soothing, warm, filled with such tangible love that Mirabella absorbed it, as thirsty for it as the soil was for healing, nurturing rain.

"Oh, Mirabella . . ." Sister Julia began. "I do not know what to say, how to comfort you. Lady Sumerton . . ." She pulled away, cupping Mirabella's face between her slim hands. The face peeking forth from its hood was the most beautiful Mirabella had ever seen and the smile, even in sadness, was the most radiant. Sister Julia sighed. "Mirabella, you must not be angry with Lady Sumerton. She"—she lowered her eyes—"she has suffered much. She is a great lady, far greater than anyone could possibly know. I understand how difficult it has been between you. You must forgive her, however, as God requires. But more than that, you must love her. She is in such need of it."

"I never want to see her again," Mirabella said, her tone icy with involuntary hatred. "Oh, God, forgive me, I never want to go back to that house. I can almost taste the fires of Hell when I'm there—they are all steeped in the superficial, all taught to relish things frivolous and meaningless. No one pursues matters of the soul . . . well, save for Father Alec, of course." She averted her head, her heart pounding as she mentioned his name. "Please do not make me go back. Let me enter this holy place tonight as a postulant. My father will send a dowry. I will make him; he won't refuse me after tonight, I know it. Please."

Sister Julia sighed. "Do you not think that you can pursue matters of the soul there as much as here? Instead of passing judgment against your family, you can lead them by example with cheer instead of scorn." She gathered her in her arms once more and began to sway. "Mirabella, you must go back. They need you now more than ever. Lady Sumerton needs you and Ha—your lord father . . . he needs you, too. So very much. And what of the little ones? Surely they could benefit from your example."

"I do not want to leave you, Sister," Mirabella murmured against her coarse habit, which was more comforting than the smoothest satin. "You are my only happiness."

Sister Julia's shoulders heaved a moment as she pulled away. She bit her lip, her eyes luminous with tears. "Oh, Mirabella . . .

you must go." At Mirabella's stricken expression she continued hurriedly. "But you can come back. When you are ready, when you are here for the right reasons and not running away from unpleasantness. Meantime you must grow in your faith and endure the tests we all are bound by God to endure. Do you not think I was tested?" She shook her head, her eyes registering a bewilderment Mirabella could not decipher. "I was tested, Mirabella, oh, how much! But I prevailed. And you will, too."

Mirabella bowed her head, sobbing brokenly.

"Do not think I don't want you beside me," Sister Julia told her in gentle tones. "It would please me more than you could know. But it is not time. Not yet. Please understand that. You must go back, darling." She smoothed Mirabella's hair, then offered her a linen handkerchief to dry her eyes. "You must go back."

Mirabella collected herself, drawing in a breath.

It was a test, Sister Julia had said. Just a test.

She must prevail as Sister Julia had prevailed. She would show God she was worthy of His calling.

She rose and ordered her cloak. And went back.

This time she rode sidesaddle.

Grace opened her eyes. They had put coins on them, she was sure of it. Why else would they be so heavy? She opened them, though, and found them unencumbered. Her head was pounding. She looked down, drawing herself into focus. She was in her bed, wearing a nightdress. Father Alec sat beside her.

"My lady?" he asked, his endearingly husky voice just above a whisper. "Are you . . . well?"

Grace's lip quivered. Tears began to pave hot trails down her cheeks. "What's happening to me?" she whispered.

Father Alec shook his head. His smile was kind. "Why don't you tell me?" he asked her. There was no sarcasm in his tone, no judgment. It was the epitome of gentleness.

Grace regarded him for a long moment. Could she trust him?

"Lady Sumerton," Father Alec persisted. "I want to help you. There is no one here but you, me, and God. And He won't say a word, I promise." He winked.

Grace offered a half smile that reverted to a quivering frown as fresh tears welled in her throat. She regarded the young priest. He was so handsome; what a shame he was wasted on the Church!

But these thoughts were irrelevant to his purpose in her chambers. He was perhaps at this moment the only friend she had in the world after tonight.

"My lady?" Father Alec prompted again.

Grace began to sob.

And told him.

Lord Hal's explanation to the little children was about the same as Cecily's had been to Brey, therefore Cecily knew he was lying. But it didn't matter. Brey was not crying anymore and that was the important thing. What's more, they were assured that they could build their caterpillar house, so instead of focusing on the horror of the evening, Cecily distracted Brey with its design.

They constructed a pavilion in the nursery, pulling together tables and chairs and throwing the bedclothes over them so that a great tent with several different little "chambers" had been erected. In it they drew out the caterpillar's house while two dozen of the little creatures squirmed and wiggled about in someone's goblet they had taken from the table. To ensure the caterpillars would not escape, Cecily covered the goblet with a plate from the same unfortunate guest, who likely had to scope out new dining ware.

In their pavilion they drew and giggled and eventually fell asleep cuddled on one of the bearskin rugs. Brey held Cecily in his arms that night.

"I'm so glad I'm marrying you," he told her as they drifted off.

"Me too," said Cecily, and she meant it.

Despite anything else that would transpire, she didn't doubt that they would have a good life.

Hal entered Grace's chambers after Father Alec had departed. Hopefully the priest has shamed her into sense, Hal thought, anger flushing his cheeks as he pushed the door open with trembling hand.

Grace lay in her bed, blond hair about her shoulders in a wavy cloud. Angelic, Hal thought. How contrary to her display! He shook his head in wonderment as he beheld her.

He stood for a long while, one hand on his hip, the other roving through his hair over and over in an involuntary gesture of nervousness.

At last Grace sat up. Her tear-streaked face was stricken. "Oh, Hal . . ."

"Don't." Hal held up a silencing hand. "Please." He sighed. "Oh, for love of everything holy, Grace, why? Whatever you feel for me, why? We are ruined now. We will not recover from this. And what's worse is that Brey's chances may be ruined as well." He shook his head. "Do you know at all what you have done?"

Grace's eyes made their appeal. "I do, Hal, I do," she whispered. "I cannot say what came over me. It was like a devil . . . I just knew I couldn't bear it anymore. I couldn't bear any of it and I wanted it to go away. I remember the feeling of tearing at my clothes—in that moment there was a strange freedom." She regarded Hal, her eyes lit with the peculiar pleasure of the memory.

Hal shook his head again in disgust. "You enjoyed it, didn't you?"

"Yes. For one moment I enjoyed it," she said. "I was unfettered. I was free of all of it, all the pain and the constraints. And then I saw all the faces. . . ." Her voice broke. "And I knew I could never be free, not of the pain, not of anything. I knew then what I had done, how shameful it was. I did not plan to do such a disgraceful thing, God knows I would never have planned it. And I know what it has done to us." She paused. "We—we have to protect Brey. Perhaps when he and Cecily marry they can be sent away to court—"

"Do you think the king would receive him after he learns of the goings-on in our household?" Hal retorted with a bitter, joyless laugh.

"As if his goings-on are any more dignified!" Grace railed. "You know he plans to marry the Boleyn woman. There's even a special court being convened to set aside the queen! He's hardly one to—"

"It doesn't matter!" Hal cried. "He is the king and the biggest hypocrite in the land! Convenient for him to be one and the same. If he finds our son unworthy based on the scandal you created—"

"The scandal *I* created!" Grace seethed. "Who is the hypocrite now, Harold?"

Hal bowed his head. He hated this, confrontation, arguing. The pain was strangling them both. He drew in a slow breath.

"We must go on, Grace," he told her. "Somehow. We will keep to ourselves. We've no choice now. And after a while, perhaps it will fade away. . . ."

He turned from her. He did not want to lie to her face.

Such things never faded away.

❧ 4 ❧

Summer passed, fading into autumn. Time did nothing to alleviate the pain permeating every pore of the Pierce household. It seemed to ooze forth from the very castle itself, chokingly pungent as the pus of a plague sore.

A year passed. Then another and another.

Father Alec marveled at how one night, one incident, no matter how outrageous, could impact so much. What had been a vivacious, energetic household was sluggish, strained. The halls no longer teemed with the erudite and noble guests who once had flocked to the Pierces' door. It had once been an honor to receive an invite to the Pierce table; indeed, it was something of a competition and those who had been fortunate to stay on at Sumerton always returned to their respective homes boasting of the privilege, thus elevating their own status by association.

Now the extra apartments, which had always been kept ready and waiting for occupants, were empty. The great hall was vacant. The voices of the children echoed in rooms too big, rooms meant to be warmed by the bodies of friends. But had the Pierces any true friends they would have remained. It was a sad illustration of human nature to Father Alec, a lesson of hypocrisy and judgment at its apex. Bile rose in his throat whenever he thought of it.

Lord Hal was slowly welcomed back into the arms of a society moved to pity and he found other locales in which to gamble.

Except now he was losing. More and more, a piece of art could be seen missing, an expensive vase, a portrait, plate that had once belonged to Lord Hal's grandmother. Gone in a night. Jewels began to disappear as well and soon Lord Hal's fingers were bare.

Lady Grace remained cloistered in her apartments. She never went out of doors again after that night. She no longer took her meals with the family. She escaped her shame, or wallowed in it, alone in a world she created for herself, a hard world softened by decanters of wine no one refused her till she remained in her bed, quivering, drooling, and incapacitated.

Though Father Alec visited her, attempting to bring what comfort he could, she stayed her course with a steely determination that would have been admirable had it been directed into a more honorable pursuit.

"We all make our choices, Father," she had told him. Father Alec stared at her in bewildered consternation. She took in little nourishment, save bread and broth, and was reduced to a white, sore-covered, skeletal wraith. "This is my life. This is what I want."

It churned Father Alec's gut with both frustration and agony to see her willingly render herself mad. He shook his head. "You cannot mean that, my lady. You are destroying yourself and the body God lovingly fashioned for you." He retrieved a hand glass and held it before her. She averted her head as though she had just looked into the depths of Hell. Father Alec seized her chin and with gentle force faced her toward the glass again. She closed her eyes.

"Open your eyes, my lady," he urged her. "Open your eyes!"

Grace submitted, slowly opening her glazed eyes, struggling to hold her image in focus.

"Look what you have done to yourself," he told her, sitting beside her. "Lady Sumerton, you have children in your care and a husband. You must reconcile yourself with past transgressions that you might recover and be of some good to them!"

Grace offered a bitter, hoarse laugh. "No, no," she said in offhanded tones. She rolled on her side. "Your counsel is appreciated, Father. But I no longer require it."

He was dismissed.

And so he left, shoulders slumped, weighed down by the anguish of the household. Thus Father Alec took to distracting the children. They must be protected from the stranglehold of despair, and since no one else had stepped in, he considered it his sacred duty.

Mirabella was found in the chapel or praying before her priedieu. Her interactions with the rest of the family were limited and she saw Lady Grace as little as possible. But Mirabella still confided in Father Alec and he listened, trying his best to soothe her anger with urgings that she forgive and find peace in God. The ritual of her prayer and incantations became as much her escape as wine was Grace's. Father Alec did not know if this was a good thing. He had always fancied that the true calling to God should be taken up with a peaceful heart, not one filled with the acute desire to avoid reality. But then he could not judge Mirabella. His reasons for entering the priesthood had been no better.

The glimpses of hope and indeed the only place from which a measure of sanity prevailed came from Cecily and Brey, whose light seemed so misplaced in this dark place. Yet there it was, white, shining, emitted like rays of sunshine bursting through the clouds in their giggles and plots and shrill, happy voices. Bosom companions, Cecily and Brey collected animals and insects together, making the nursery a veritable menagerie. No one stopped them, and if anyone dared, Father Alec would have had their head. The children would be allowed their happiness and Father Alec thanked God they found it in each other. Cecily emanated joy; it came natural to her. She was by no means simpleminded. Her wise eyes could be seen making their observations and Father Alec wondered what went on behind them. What conclusions had she drawn about this place so tinged by tragedy? She did not reveal them. Instead she smiled her sweet smile, she laughed her infectious, lilting laugh, and pressed on, always inventing new ways to spread cheer.

Father Alec continued to pray for her and Brey, hoping nothing would invade the world Cecily so lovingly created.

For his part, he kept them busy. They took many of their lessons out of doors during the warm months. He utilized anything he could think of to tie in his lessons with the wonders of nature. Instead of studying astronomy in the stuffy library, they spread blankets out in the garden and looked up at the dazzling array of sparkling stars littering the night sky. The children snuggled against him as they pointed out each of the constellations and discussed navigation, astrology, and the myths from which the constellations derived their names.

Father Alec loved to discuss military history and reenacted battles with toy soldiers. This became a favorite sport of Brey's and together they spent many hours fashioning their soldiers and kings out of wood, painting them, and reliving the battles of old just as Father Alec described them.

The children learned of flora and faunae by taking long walks through the forest. Father Alec taught them about herbs and mushrooms with medicinal properties, in which Cecily took great interest.

With them the knot in his heart eased. They were the hope of this broken household. With love and guidance, they could still prevail to be productive, successful individuals.

What's more, and what was most important to Father Alec, they could be happy.

"The king has broken from Rome!" Lord Hal cried one evening as he burst into the solar where Father Alec had been engaging Mirabella in a game of chess while Brey and Cecily drew purposefully unflattering pictures of the servants.

Mirabella rose. "No!"

Lord Hal nodded, his handsome face ruddy from riding. "King Henry has been named Supreme Head of the Church of England by Parliament. It is because of the Boleyn woman, of course. It is almost certain he will marry her."

"But the Pope—" Father Alec began, rendered breathless at the prospect. He was more than interested in the whole affair. The king's will intrigued him. He seemed so intoxicated by this Anne Boleyn that he would rearrange the world for her. Father Alec could not imagine the power she must have over him. He wondered after her beauty. She must be in possession of something extraordinary for the king to be so taken with her. Father Alec had heard she held the New Learning in high esteem and for this he admired her. He wondered what influence that had on His Majesty's startling decision.

Lord Hal shook his head. "Is no more, not for England, anyway."

Father Alec could not imagine it. But others had broken away, though not on such large scale. It was interesting. "This could create a great deal of strife. Catholics loyal to His Holiness will never abide it." He wondered if he could abide it. He was alarmed at how unperturbed he was by the news. But what did he know of the Pope? Was he not as corrupt as every other church official jealously guarding his ill-gotten gains? Yet was he not God's representative on earth? Wasn't the king? What an opportunity this could be! Imagine the possibilities of reform he could be bringing! Imagine the new age of thought he could be ushering in, an age where simplicity replaced extravagance, an age where priests could not be bought, an age of humility and true devotion to God, not under the grandeur and illusion the Church provided. It did not have to be Lutheran per se but something different, something tailored for English people and English needs. . . . Oh, bless this King Henry!

Father Alec tried to rein in his enthusiasm as he speculated, focusing on the reactions of the room.

"Oh, Father," Mirabella interposed, addressing Lord Hal. "What is going to happen to poor Queen Catherine?"

"No one is sure yet, lamb," Lord Hal told her. "I suppose all we can do is wait it out."

"Oh, that Boleyn woman!" Mirabella cried, narrowing her eyes. "I have heard the names they have called her—all fitting, it seems! For her to corrupt His Majesty this way . . . she is an abomination!"

"Whatever she is or isn't, Mirabella, we are the king's subjects, you must remember," said Lord Hal. "And we are beholden to him. He is not one to tolerate differences in opinion."

"So we accept it? The displacement of an anointed queen and a split with the *Holy Father?*" Mirabella asked, eyes wide, incredulous.

Her father nodded. "Yes, Mirabella. Whatever the king's pleasure. If we want to keep our place, if we want to keep our heads, we keep silent."

"But you cannot think this is right!" she cried, appalled.

Lord Hal shook his head again, running a hand through his dark hair. "I am not one to judge what is right, Mirabella."

"Your father is wise," Father Alec said. "None of us can know God's will. There could be a message in this for us, a sign that things are meant to change—"

"But to break with His Holiness, Father Alec?" she cried, scandalized. "Let alone the notion of divorce!"

Father Alec pursed his lips. "You know that as a priest I do not support divorce in most cases. However, the king is far from most cases. He needs a legitimate male heir to succeed him and unfortunately the queen has not been able to provide that. In matters of state, my child, sometimes exceptions have to be made. I do not condone it, but to a degree I can understand its need for the stability of the realm. And as your father said, it is not for us to judge." He paused. "Regarding the situation with the Holy Father . . ." He drew in a breath. "I must pray on that."

"Oh, Father . . ." Mirabella's eyes were lit with disillusionment as she regarded him, causing his heart to lurch in unexpected regret.

But he could not change his opinion. Ever since his tour of Europe, observing the change and the excitement the New Learning was bringing, he knew he could support the king's split with the Pope. Likewise, he understood the king's Great Matter. And he felt he understood humanity. He was no fool. He knew it was not all about the succession. But he could not explain matters of lust to a young girl and disillusion her even more. Best cloak it in a (semi) noble cause.

"Pray for them, Lady Mirabella," Father Alec urged her. "Pray for all involved. And you must be confident that whatever happens, even if it is beyond your understanding, even if you do not agree with it, is the will of God."

Helped along by men, he added silently.

But it consoled Mirabella to the desired degree and she quit the room to indulge in her favorite pastime.

Father Alec excused himself to do likewise.

Unlike Mirabella, he did not pray for the preservation of the Church in England.

He prayed for continued change.

Cecily affected genuine cheer in Brey's gentle presence. With him there were no complications. The rest of the household had sunken into general decline, save Father Alec, who scrambled to uphold a façade of normalcy in the hopes of preserving some semblance of happiness. Cecily did the same. She steered Brey away from unhappy introspection with games and smiles. They rode, they composed little songs and plays together, they lay awake in the nursery, talking and conspiring about the next day's adventures till the sun began to filter through the bay window. Together they visited Lady Grace in her apartments, always an experience Cecily approached with a measure of dread and hope—dread that she must see the poor woman in such estate, hope that it had somehow improved. It never did. Though Brey was brave when he saw his mother, he cried in Cecily's arms afterwards. Cecily always let him. She would never tell him not to cry. If Lady Grace were her mother, she'd have cried, too.

Lord Hal attempted to cheer them by taking them hawking and hunting. Cecily proved an archer unmatched in her abilities, earning admiration and praise by all. With Lord Hal the children also indulged in games of dice and cards. Brey challenged him to games of chess that the boy always won, while Cecily had the luck of beating Lord Hal at cards. Lord Hal, who made the effort to be in good cheer around the children, smiled and laughed. "Two little cheaters I've got!" he would exclaim at the close of each game he lost. He'd shake his finger at them. "I don't know how, but wait till I have you figured out! Then we'll see who emerges the victor!"

Cecily and Brey exchanged a triumphant glance. They would never let Lord Hal win if they could help it.

It went along like this, a little routine of emotional preservation and survival that the children had fallen into until the beginning of their early teens. And then one ordinary day, for a perfectly ordinary reason, everything changed.

Cecily woke up with her courses.

She knew what had happened. For weeks her tummy had been cramping, her back aching, and the two tiny swells that served as breasts hurt so much she could not even cross her arms. For a while she just lay there, contemplating her new status.

She was something resembling a woman. It was an overwhelming thought. She did not feel altogether grown-up. She had imagined that when a woman began her menses she received some kind of epiphany, as though with the ability to bear children came the innate knowledge of how to be everything woman. She was disappointed. There were no divine awakenings; she was, in fact, quite uninspired, hungry, and irritable.

Mirabella had been removed from the nursery years before for just this reason. This meant she, too, would be given her own chamber. Her nursery days were over. No more conspiring with Brey until the wee hours of the morning, no more behaving as the carefree child. Everything was going to change. She closed her eyes, squeezing back hot tears.

At last she called for Nurse Matilda, who cleaned her up and gave her instructions on how to care for her new plight.

"What's happening?" Brey inquired upon hearing the commotion. "What's going on? What's wrong with Cecily?"

"Nothing!" Cecily and Matilda shouted at once.

The startled lad pouted and went back to bed.

Cecily, now cleansed and uncomfortable, quit the nursery.

She needed to be alone. She needed to think about womanhood.

"You will have to wear the proper corset now," Mirabella told her after Cecily imparted the unhappy news of her ascendance to Venus. They were in Mirabella's chamber, which was as unlike the nursery as a pup to a mule. There was a prie-dieu, of course, and several portraits of the Blessed Virgin, one of her holding baby Jesus to her breast, all surrounded in a halo of golden light, another of her alone with a sparkling rose. Cecily's eyes were treated to an ensemble of saints and statues the like of which belonged at the chapel. She could not imagine why Mirabella needed the convent with all this about her.

Cecily's thoughts were drawn from the décor to her own estate. A corset. Her shoulders slumped. She had not been looking forward to that. "I won't be able to breathe. How will I play with Brey wearing a corset?"

Mirabella laughed, but it was full of affection. "Poor girl, you can't *play* with Brey anymore, not like you used to. No rough-and-tumble, no children's pastimes. You are to be reared as a lady now and if my mother chooses to remain too incapacitated to guide you then I shall have to."

Cecily's throat went dry. Her timid smile reflected a mingling of gratitude and dread. "I thank you," she said in small tones.

Mirabella rose and in a flurry of black skirts went to her wardrobe. "Now! Let me see what I have. You're such a willowy girl . . . but I think I have some things you can get by on until we have you measured."

Mirabella smiled at the girl, pleased that she had come to her. She was happy to have someone to take under her wing. Now that Cecily was unable to be coddled as a child she would have a proper ally. Mirabella rifled through her wardrobe until she arrived at some corsets she had grown out of and had failed to give to the poor. God must have meant for her to save them for Cecily.

"Here," she said. "We should put it on you."

"Now?" Cecily asked, eyes wide. "Today? But I am not going anywhere today."

"It doesn't matter if you're going anywhere," Mirabella explained patiently. "You must always be a lady, modest and goodly as God intends."

Cecily grimaced as she allowed Mirabella to dress her. The stiff shafts of wood that would confine and shape her body could be felt through the linen and they dug into her hips. Her breathing was restricted and her cheeks flushed as she struggled to modulate it.

"You're thinking about it too much," Mirabella said, resting her hands on Cecily's shoulders. "Just breathe. You will grow accustomed to it. If you think about it, though, you will swoon."

Cecily closed her eyes. Specks of light danced against the backs of her eyelids, or wherever her eyes went when she closed them. In, out, in, out. "It's too tight," she told Mirabella.

"It certainly is not. You will get used to it," said Mirabella. "Just as we all have to."

Cecily took a step with caution. Everything was different, from sitting to walking—she could not imagine what it would be like to ride a horse. She wanted to slouch, but the corset held her upright. She regarded Mirabella, who seemed perfectly adapted to wearing this torture device. At eighteen, Mirabella filled out her gown with a figure Cecily had caught the male servants gawking at. What could be glimpsed of the breasts peeking out over the top of her neckline revealed a fullness Cecily envied; the Gypsy-toned skin was soft and flawless. Her black hair, though pinned up in an unflattering chignon under a stiff black gable hood, was shining and splendid when she let it fall down her shoulders. In addition to her figure, Mirabella's face bore a full sensual mouth, small, straight nose, and intense green eyes that shone with determination. She could have any man she wanted and still she chose God, Cecily thought wistfully.

"I know what you are thinking. Stop looking at me," Mirabella demanded.

"What are you about?" Cecily countered.

Mirabella bowed her head. "You are thinking, 'What a waste, Mirabella going into the Church when she is so beautiful.' "

Cecily gaped at her. She hadn't wanted to be so transparent.

"I hear the servants laughing at me, the piggish things the men say," Mirabella told her. "You are just like them. You do not understand. I will be the bride of Christ, someone who will not paw at me and gape at me like some starved animal. Someone who will respect and cherish me for what is inside, for what is eternal, not for the beauty that will pass."

"But Jesus . . . well, he is not exactly here, Mirabella," Cecily dared observe. "He can never be to you what an earthly man can be."

Mirabella clenched the material of her gown in frustration. "Oh, earthly men—such worthy creatures! Haven't you witnessed enough marital bliss for you to see what it's really about? Look to my parents. Look at my mother, shutting herself away that she might drink herself to death. Look at my blustering fool of a father, eking out what little pleasure he can find in his cards and dice while losing his fortune." She shook her head. "And there are others even worse off. I will not be in their numbers, made the wife of someone who will be ungrateful for the children I give him, someone who will use mistresses and whores while I keep his house. Look what joy marriage brought poor Queen Catherine of Aragon. Now she is banished and made Princess Dowager, pushed aside so King Henry can elevate a common whore." Mirabella sighed and shook her head. "I will not be put last for anyone and you can bet with a man that is just what you will be. Maybe that is a life for some." Mirabella shook her head emphatically. "But not for me."

"Of course not," said Cecily. For the first time she began to understand Mirabella's choice.

"Of course you will never have to worry about any of that," Mirabella said in gentler tones. "You're marrying Brey."

Cecily smiled. "Yes . . . Brey." She bowed her head, then. "It will have to be different with Brey now, won't it?"

Mirabella nodded gravely. "Yes, yes, it will."

Cecily suppressed a sob. She did not want it to be different.

Brey did not understand Cecily's withdrawal. She did not chase him in the woods anymore. They did not tumble down hills or hide in haystacks and she always rode sidesaddle, never astride as she used to. And she sat so despicably straight! Mirabella must be behind all of this; Cecily has been spending an inordinate amount of time with her of late. And now she didn't even sleep in the nursery anymore! Nurse Matilda told him she was a lady now and ladies must keep their own chambers. What did she know? He had heard Cecily fart before—she was a champion, for love of God! Who could hear that and call her a lady?

"I just don't understand it, Father," he told Father Alec when the two were riding alone one February day. Cecily was indoors doing some stupid thing that no doubt "ladies" occupied themselves with, so Brey took this opportunity to pour out his troubles to the caring tutor. "And it is not just that she won't play most of our old games; she's moody, too. She snaps at me and gets quite huffy like Mirabella. She never used to be like that!"

Father Alec laughed. "Cecily is at a crossroads, Brey; you must be patient with her." He turned toward Brey as they slowed their mounts. They were riding in the snow-covered fields today, which glistened against the noonday sun, bright and blinding. The air was crisp but pleasant enough to enjoy.

"What kind of crossroads?" he persisted, annoyed. If he were at a similar sort of crossroads he'd be scolded no doubt.

Father Alec shifted in the saddle a moment, then cleared his throat. He shifted again. "Well . . . er . . . I'm surprised your father hasn't made you aware of this, Brey, but there comes a time in a girl's life when—"

"Oh, no!" Brey smacked his forehead with a chapped hand. "You don't mean she's—that she's . . . oh, repulsive!"

"So you have heard about it." Father Alec chuckled. "If it is repulsive to you imagine how it must be for them."

"I don't want to," Brey said with a grimace. "I don't know why I didn't think of it. I suppose I could not really imagine something like that happening to Cecily." He turned to Father Alec, his face perfectly straight. "When do you suppose she's going to have the baby?"

Father Alec sat stunned.

This was going to be a long ride.

"He did it!" cried Lord Hal as he rushed in from a day of visiting friends, no doubt his pockets much lighter than before. "The king has wed Anne Boleyn in secret!"

Father Alec and the children had been dining in the solar when he burst in, flushed from wine and excitement.

"What's more, she's with child!" Lord Hal cried. "They think it happened when she went to France with him to meet King Francois."

"Then it is over?" asked Cecily. "All the trials to undo his marriage to Queen Catherine, everything? Lady Anne is queen now?"

"She will never be queen." Mirabella glowered.

"She will be and you best respect it," warned Lord Hal.

Cecily smiled. "My parents knew the Boleyns. They would be pleased at her ascension," she said, her tone reminiscent as an image of her parents swirled before her mind's eye. She could not quite latch on to it. Their forms evaded her, their faces no more than smudged paintings on miniatures. She smiled away the thought as she anticipated the reign of the young, witty Anne Boleyn.

"Support who the king supports is what I always say," said Lord Hal.

Mirabella shook her head as she quit the room.

Cecily surveyed the faces in the room, one a bright-eyed, golden-haired boy, the other a handsome courtier, the other a humble tutor, all of them so dear to her. As she looked at them she thought of another, the forgotten one, lying alone in her chambers.

And went to her.

"Lady Grace, I thought you would like to know the news," she told her, ignoring the stench of the room as she sat at Lady Grace's bedside. As discreetly as possible she averted her eyes so she did not have to look at the withered, yellow figure that lay under the covers.

"News?" asked the raspy voice.

"The king has married the Lady Pembroke—Anne Boleyn—in secret!" she cried, forcing cheer into her voice. "Isn't it exciting?"

"I should be scandalized," said Lady Grace with a weak smile.

"Mirabella is scandalized enough for everyone," Cecily told her with a slight giggle. "But Lord Hal doesn't seem to mind. Neither does Father Alec."

"Father Alec has taken all of this quite in stride, hasn't he?" Lady Grace inquired. "The break with Rome. Now this. It is interesting."

"Interesting, how, my lady?" asked Cecily, who could not see anything unusual in it. Father Alec's nature always seemed so affable and accepting of whatever fate doled out that it did not seem peculiar to her.

"A man of the Church accepting the will of a mortal king . . . and such a peculiar will it is." Lady Grace smiled. "He is a reformer."

Cecily's heart pounded. She knew the Church of England only differed from the Church of Rome in one way. It deferred to the king rather than the Pope. The Pope was referred to as the Bishop of Rome. Otherwise England was a Catholic kingdom; masses commenced as they had before the split. Anything else was considered heresy. Henry VIII, once called Defender of the Faith by the Pope, was a son of the Catholic Church. That matters of doctrine should cause this separation was said to have devastated him. Cecily began to shudder. England was not a safe place for reformers. The Church, under the king's direction, was reformed enough. Those who opposed it fled or were executed.

"But, Lady Grace, it could be dangerous—"

Lady Grace nodded. "Which is why I won't say a word. Who do I talk to besides? And why would I betray him whom I hold so dear?" She reached for her decanter, taking a gulp. Her chin was slick with liquid. Cecily retrieved her handkerchief and wiped it away, ashamed to be doing so, not for her own sake but for Lady Grace, that she had been reduced to this, that Lord Hal let her, and that there was nothing anyone could or would do about it.

"Maybe all these changes in the kingdom are a sign for all of us," Cecily ventured with a nervous laugh. "Maybe . . . maybe we all need to change a bit. I know I have. Getting used to all these new undergarments—this corset!" She placed a slender hand to her belly and tried to laugh. "I swooned three times the first day I wore it!"

Lady Grace's eyes closed.

At once Cecily was seized by an overpowering bravado she did not express save in the presence of Brey. She could not fight the words that came forth next. "Lady Grace, you must come out of your apartments now." Her girlish voice was taut with urgency. She did not understand what emboldened her. Perhaps she was inspired by Anne Boleyn, a woman who got just what she wanted no matter if the world had to be set on its back for her to get it. Maybe it was being in the presence of the steely Mirabella. She did not know. All she knew was that if she did not intervene somehow, Lady Grace would die. She could not let her die.

Lady Grace's eyes fluttered open. A lazy smile. "What on earth are you going on about, girl?"

Cecily took her hand. "You've punished yourself enough for your sins. You *must* come out now. You still do not have to leave your home, but at least come out of here. See Mirabella, what a beauty she has become. I know she does not visit you often—perhaps she is afraid." Cecily drew in a breath, saddened that she must say it aloud. "It is frightening seeing you. Brey cries afterwards. Every single time."

Lady Grace averted her eyes.

"Lord Hal is lost without you," Cecily went on, hoping she was reaching her somewhere. "He probably does not know what to say or how to say it, but it shows in everything he does, in everything he does not say. It is not for me to know how it is between you and if you cannot come out for him alone I understand. Thus you must come out for us. I need you, too, Lady Grace. I am so overwhelmed with all of these changes. Soon I imagine we will want to begin planning my wedding to Brey. I know it will not happen for at least three or four years yet, but we should start planning my gown and I know you want to be a part of that—"

"Enough, Cecily," Lady Grace interposed. "God knows you have good intentions. But I am tired and you must go."

Cecily rose, looking down upon the wraithlike creature with a mingling pity and frustration as she turned away and fled.

Grace was stunned. Little Cecily could bite! But such a gentle little bite. The child did mean well. Grace struggled to sit up in bed, drawing her bony knees to her chest as she thought.

Hal came to see her. For a time they had been as a husband and wife, but as her health deteriorated their relations did, too. He attempted to coax her out of her self-imposed prison with promises and fair words. When that failed, gentleness evolved into threats and curses. Then he stopped seeing her altogether. She did not blame him. If she could avoid seeing herself she would.

But the children came. Cecily and Brey every day, and Mirabella now and again, though they had little to say to each other. Mirabella usually prayed with her. Father Alec did the same, though he tried to offer counsel as well. But she did not know what to say to him anymore. She had already said too much.

Yet Cecily said what none of them would.

I need you.

She had forgotten what it felt like, what it meant to be needed. She had forgotten that she once valued it.

I need you.

Grace sank back against her pillows. She ached all over. She had lost her beauty. She had lost her self. She would not emerge the woman she had been when she entered these apartments four years ago.

But she must come out. They needed her.

Why did it take a child's simple words to make her understand? It mattered not. What mattered was that she would emerge, that she would live.

Because they needed her.

❧ 5 ❧

Thomas Cranmer, the newly appointed Archbishop of Canterbury, announced that the marriage between Henry VIII and Catherine of Aragon was invalid in May of 1533. By now, the king's intended's belly swelled with what was hoped to be the Prince of Wales.

Anne Boleyn was Queen Consort of England. Her coronation was set for the first of June. The Earl of Sumerton and his family were invited to attend.

"We will go, won't we, Lord Hal?" Cecily asked, her cheeks flushed with excitement. She found all gossip surrounding the new queen cruel and irrelevant. She wanted to attend the coronation, to see the beautiful woman who had brought a king and his kingdom to their knees.

Lord Hal sat before the fire in the solar, idly shuffling and reshuffling a deck of cards. "I am uncertain. . . . London will be overflowing to stinking."

"But you have a home on the Strand," Cecily persisted. "And I've never even seen it, not in all the years I've lived here. Couldn't you open it up?"

"Oh, Father, but it would be grand!" Brey cried. "To see the court!"

"And the gowns!" Cecily added. "And all the pretty jewels. Oh, Lord Hal, you must take us!"

"Please!" Brey smiled, falling to his knee. He was growing tall. Angles and lean muscle had replaced puppy fat from hours of training with the sword while wearing a heavy suit of armor. The promise of becoming an intuitive young man shone out of a boy's eyes.

"We will go."

All heads turned toward the low voice.

From the doorway stood Lady Grace, dressed in a rose velvet gown. Her limp blond hair was pinned back in a chignon beneath a fashionable French hood. She was thin, her neck had aged considerably for one so young, and her skin was tinged with a yellow hue.

But she was there.

Lord Hal arose slowly, his eyes wide as though he was beholding a ghost. She may as well be for all he had seen of her these past years. A momentary onset of guilt surged through him as he regarded her. How much of this was on his head? He held out his hand.

"Grace . . . my God . . ." Tears clutched his throat.

"Mother!" Brey cried, running toward her, throwing his arms about her tiny waist. She was caught off balance and the boy all but held her up in his strong embrace.

Tears streamed down her cheeks as her eyes met those of Cecily, who offered an encouraging smile. Father Alec, who had been playing chess with Cecily, rose and offered an elegant bow.

Mirabella stood by the fire, her face somber.

Lady Grace held out a hand to her.

Mirabella remained where she was. "Do you expect me to congratulate you on doing something you should have done years ago?" Her tone was laced with bitterness.

"Mirabella!" Brey cried.

Lady Grace's arm fell to her side. "No, it is all right. Mirabella is . . . correct."

Mirabella bowed her head. "Still, it is good to see you about, my lady," she told her in grudging tones.

"Thank you," Lady Grace said.

Father Alec addressed the matter at hand. "Are you certain you would want to make such a long trip, Lady Grace? It might be quite taxing."

"I want to go," said Lady Grace. "And the children deserve to go. We have all been shut up here long enough. And," she added in thoughtful tones, "if I do not leave here now I never will. Those who were in attendance that night will scoff. Let them scoff. They will whisper. Let them whisper. I will go."

"Oh, Lady Grace!" Cecily cried as she joined Brey in embracing her again. "We will all take care of you!"

"I am happily outnumbered," said Lord Hal as he cast fond eyes upon his wife. "I suppose we best get packing."

With this the children and priest left the room to sort through their belongings and prepare for the most exciting event in the kingdom.

Grace was about to do likewise when Hal caught her hands.

"Grace . . . you have no idea how proud of you I am," he told her, his voice wavering with tears. "I admit that I had given up on you. I am sorry."

"You were right to give up," said Grace. "I did."

"Is this our new start?" he asked her, his eyes lit with hope.

Grace nodded. "Yes, Hal. This is our new start."

Hal drew her toward him, then pulled back. She was so fragile; he could feel every bone.

"Come now, you won't break me," Grace teased in sad tones.

He drew her near once more, holding her for a long time.

Cecily had never been to London before. The manor on the Strand overlooked the sparkling Thames and Cecily could watch the river traffic, a procession of barges making their way to the Tower of London, ships, and little rowboats containing delightful characters. The elegant manor stood as an understatement compared to the palaces that lined the famous street. Nonetheless, it was beautiful with its collection of Italian art of which Lord Hal was so fond. Sumerton Place had its own courtyard bearing lush gardens and a large fountain with porpoises on it that had been a gift from the Duke of Norfolk, a reward to Lord Hal's father for fighting beside him at Flodden Field, where was slain James IV, King of Scots. Cecily marveled that they did not visit the manor more often; she could not imagine returning to the isolation of the countryside when they could be so close to the happenings of court.

There was not a more exciting place in the world, Cecily decided as they prepared to ride in the procession that would traverse Queen Anne from Cheapside to Westminster Hall. Merchants peddling souvenirs to commemorate the special event, ladies and gentleman of the nobility, urchins waiting to pick pockets, clerics and prelates, soldiers and shining knights, horses trimmed in the colors of their noble owners, cats and rats scampering about, eager to feast on any delicacy dropped in their midst.

The streets, indeed the whole place, teemed with activity, with *life*.

"Overflowing to stinking," Lord Hal muttered as he surveyed the throng for the grand procession, but he was smiling.

They had brought an entourage of their own for the ride, bedecked in the Pierce colors of yellow and white. Cecily's horse and attendants wore her colors as Baroness Burkhart of brown and orange. In her russet gown with its brown kirtle threaded with cloth of gold and matching hood, Cecily felt every inch the grand lady. Mirabella, though disapproving of the whole enterprise, was dressed in her yellow and white gown and earned many an appreciative glance. She turned her nose up at each and every one while Cecily waved, thrilled to be favored with such open admiration.

At Cheapside Cecily took the opportunity to scrutinize her new queen. She had never seen the old one, who was rumored to be quite beautiful in her time but after years of strife and suffering became overweight and dowdy. This queen was the antithesis of such descriptions. Bedecked in cloth of gold and wrapped in yards of soft ermine, the queen allowed her raven black hair to trail down her back in sleek waves brushed to a glossy sheen. On her dainty head was a bejeweled circlet and on her alabaster face a triumphant grin. Something about her features reminded Cecily of a mischievous and very satisfied cat. From the comfort of her litter, also swathed in cloth of gold, Queen Anne waved and blessed her new subjects, who seemed none too receptive.

Cecily's heart sank. It seemed a shame to think that after years of waiting to become queen she should not be received with more enthusiasm. She was what the king wanted, after all, and it was the duty of his people to accept her. Though a few doffed their caps, most stood silent, their faces a mingling of bewilderment and disgust.

At one point Cecily heard the queen's fool shout, "You all must have scurvy heads, since you so fear removing your caps!"

Cecily cried, "God save the queen!" with extra enthusiasm, encouraging Brey to do likewise.

Mirabella rode her horse, silent, head bowed.

Cecily ignored her show of disrespect, turning to take in all around her. Tapestries were hung everywhere and the queen's badge bearing her falcon symbol was in every corner the eye could fall upon. Hans Holbein, the renowned court painter, had designed a beautiful arch where a tableau was being performed. Apollo and the four Muses played instruments and sang, each a remarkable display of talent. Cecily clapped her hands, enthralled by the sight.

All throughout the procession they were treated to similar displays of choirs and pageants. Cecily's heart raced and her head tingled as she marveled that they were included in such an event.

"Look!" cried Brey as he pointed to one of the conduits. "Wine!"

Cecily's eyes widened in awe. "Is there nothing King Henry cannot do?" she cried in delight.

"Nothing," Father Alec murmured, taking in the sights about him with the same interest. But his eyes were not wide with awe. There was something else in them, something Cecily could not quite decipher.

It was very akin to fear.

* * *

The next day they witnessed Queen Anne's coronation at Westminster Abbey. Cecily was able to get a closer look at the woman King Henry so desired. She was small, save for the curving belly she displayed with pride, with tapering limbs and delicate hands.

"Where's the sixth finger?" Brey whispered.

Cecily searched for the rumored deformity, but to her dismay, the queen's hands were hidden beneath her resplendent sleeves. She shrugged and placed a finger to her lips, urging Brey to hold his peace.

Under a cloth of gold canopy the queen walked with measured steps. Her train was carried by her cousin the delicate Mary Howard. It was said the queen's aunt, the Duchess of Norfolk, so disapproved of the new queen that she refused to attend. Cecily's heart churned in sympathy. It must be difficult being Anne Boleyn.

Queen Anne took her place in St. Edward's Chair and allowed the Archbishop of Canterbury to crown her. The choir burst out in a Te Deum and Cecily's heart thrilled with delight at the sound.

She turned toward Father Alec, whose wide hazel eyes were lit with tears as he regarded the scene.

But he was not regarding the queen.

His eyes had fallen upon another, one whose face bespoke eternal gentleness.

Thomas Cranmer, Archbishop of Canterbury.

After the coronation they attended a celebratory feast at Westminster Hall. It was a strange affair, uncomfortable for Lord Hal and Lady Grace, the latter of whom was avoided by all and who with trembling hands tried to sip sparingly from the cup of wine before her, though her eyes lit with undisguised desire for it.

Mirabella, claiming fatigue, had been allowed to be escorted to the manor by her guard. It was just as well.

"Now she can't spoil it for us," Brey told Cecily, who could not help but giggle, though she chastised herself for being uncharitable.

Course after course was served and Cecily ate her fill, taking in the splendor of the court that ushered in the new reign of Anna Regina. The Duke of Suffolk, the king's brother-in-law and steward for the evening, still was handsome at forty-eight as he made sure everything was to the queen's pleasure. The queen's cousin Henry Howard, Earl of Surrey, also attended. Three years Cecily's senior, Surrey, though married, stole several admiring glances her way throughout the evening. He was a handsome lad with his aquiline nose and penetrating dark eyes. Cecily offered him a bright smile. She did not know how to flirt but, as she watched the lords and ladies about her, thought this just the place to learn.

The next day jousts were held at York Place. Cecily and Brey clapped and hooted in the stands as they watched the champions tilt each other. The gleam of the armor, the sweet smell of upturned grass, the clank of the lances against shields thrilled them, and their voices rose in a chorus of gleeful anticipation as they speculated on who would prove victorious.

Brey reached out to still her clapping hand at one point, leaning over to whisper, "And someday when I am here, besting all the champions with my lance, will I be carrying your token?"

Cecily scrunched up her shoulders and giggled. She squeezed his hand. "No one else, Brey," she told him, and on impulse leaned in to kiss his cheek. Brey had turned his head, however, and their lips brushed against each other's for the briefest of moments.

Cecily pulled back, flushing deep rose with embarrassment. She bowed her head.

Brey had averted his head and was making a show of cheering on the jousters.

Cecily pressed a hand to her tummy, which, for some reason, would not stop quivering deep within.

"Well, I cannot wait to get back," Mirabella said, allowing the maid to undress her as she readied for bed that evening. "Such extravagance and waste. Can you imagine if the king invested what he spent on the coronation into charity for the poor? The coronation banquet alone could have fed hundreds for months!" She shook her head. "Sheer waste."

Cecily was shamed. It was a waste. Guilt surged through her as she tried to stop reliving what, to her, had been the happiest, most exciting event of her life. Was she a creature of vanity? Did she not care for the world and her fellow man as much as Mirabella? Tears stung her eyes.

"Would that we all could be treated to such a testament of someone's undying love," was all she could think of to say.

Mirabella grunted in response. "The king's love is famously fickle," she said. "Oh, Cecily, but you aren't thinking of the king, are you? You are thinking of Brey. I saw what happened at the joust."

Cecily flushed. "I suppose you have been rehearsing my scolding."

Mirabella's eyes widened. "On the contrary, I was pleased. Do you know how rare it is for one's love and one's betrothed to be the same person?"

Cecily regarded Mirabella, awed that she showed some capacity for understanding. "You mean . . . you aren't angry with us?"

"Of course not," Mirabella said. "I am relieved and happy. I wish nothing but happiness for you and my brother."

Cecily threw her arms about Mirabella, who returned the embrace.

It seemed London brought about all sorts of unexpected joys.

The next day was to be devoted to hunting with the court, but Brey woke up nauseated, plagued with a terrible stomachache and remained abed.

"All this rich food," Lord Hal told him in jovial tones. "We eat good but never this good!" He ruffled the boy's hair. "Are you certain you wouldn't like us to stay?"

Brey shook his head. His brow glistened with sweat. "For what? To watch me sleep? Go ahead. Cecily should be among her own; this has been such a treat for her. And it's good for us, too, for our name." He grimaced in pain and gestured for his father to leave.

"Where's Father Alec? Perhaps he can sit beside you," Lord Hal suggested.

"He's been at Westminster Abbey, probably bribing someone to allow him audience with Archbishop Cranmer." Brey laughed. "He's mad with admiration for the man."

Lord Hal chuckled. "I suppose he needed a little time to himself, too. Ah, well, then, if there isn't anything you need—"

"Go on, Father. Really. I'll be fine with Mirabella," Brey assured him, waving him away with a hand.

Lord Hal leaned in and kissed his golden hair. "We'll tell you all about it tonight."

Brey smiled to his father's retreating back and, once certain he was gone, drew his knees to his chest in agony. Deep in his gut, on the right side almost near his leg, something clenched and twisted him into knots of pain. It was excruciating. He could not imagine what he could have eaten to cause such severe indigestion.

Mirabella attended him with soothing words and cool compresses, but nothing helped. Soon he was retching into the chamber pot.

"I should fetch a physician," Mirabella said.

"So they can tell me I ate too many artichokes?" Brey countered, with a weak chuckle. He clutched his right side, which rebelled against any attempt at laughter.

"It's more than that, Brey." Mirabella's brows furrowed in concern. "Something is wrong."

"Nothing some small ale won't cure," he said. "Be a lamb and get me a cup, won't you?"

Mirabella backed away, her face lit with fear as she regarded her brother's writhing form.

Nonetheless, she went to do his bidding.

When she returned, she sat at his bedside. "Here, Brey. Small ale."

No movement. The tension in Mirabella's shoulders eased. Perhaps he had found some relief in sleep. She reached out to stroke his face.

Something did not feel right.

"Brey?"

She shook his shoulder. Stillness.

"Brey!"

In a terror, she leaned in. No breath. She placed her fingers against his neck. The throb of life had ceased.

Brey was dead.

Lord Hal, Lady Grace, and Cecily returned from a happy day of hunting in the company of a young, merry court. Though they were not joined by the king and queen today, the day was just as dazzling and Cecily found herself taken in by the glamorous ladies and handsome lords in attendance. How she wished Brey could have been there! What fun they would have had together sharing their observations!

They returned to Sumerton Place to find Father Alec waiting. His handsome face was drawn, his hazel eyes lit with unshed tears.

"Father!" Cecily cried, immediately concerned.

"What is it, Father?" Lady Grace asked, taking his hand. "Are you well?"

Father Alec shook his head. He took her hands in his. "My lady . . . dearest Lady Grace . . . Lord Hal . . ." His eyes scanned the anxious faces. He squeezed the thin hands in his. "You must be very strong for what I am about to tell you. Rely on the Lord to give you the strength."

"Out with it, Father!" Lord Hal demanded.

Father Alec squeezed his eyes shut. "It is Brey . . . he has been called to the Lord."

Silence. Then, from Cecily, "No! No! You are wrong! Why would you say such a wicked thing? You are wrong!"

"Lady Cecily—"

He could not give her his attention, for at that moment Lady Grace slumped to the floor, unconscious. Lord Hal took to her side, gathering her in his arms, sobbing. "Oh, God, no! Not Brey! Not Brey!"

"What happened? He just had a stomachache!" cried Cecily, approaching Father Alec to seize his wrist. Her teal eyes shone bright with tearful accusations.

Father Alec shook his head. "I do not know, my lady."

"Didn't Mirabella call for a physician?" Lord Hal cried.

"She did, but it was too late," Father Alec told him. "It—it was God's will," he added helplessly, knowing this was the least comforting of any answer he could supply and cursing himself for supplying it anyway.

"Oh, Grace." Lord Hal turned his eyes to his wife, who lay limp in his arms, her breathing shallow, her eyes moving restlessly beneath closed lids. "What are we going to do?"

Cecily rested her fingers on her lips, her eyes searching the space above Lord Hal's head for answers.

"Take Lady Grace to her apartments, my lord," Father Alec said in gentle tones. "Once she is settled, see to Brey. We shall return home directly that he might receive a proper interment. I shall send a messenger with all the instructions."

Obedient as a child, Lord Hal rose to do as he was bid, Lady Grace in his arms.

Cecily continued to stare at the vacant spot at the foot of the stairwell.

"Lady Cecily," Father Alec began. "Oh, my lady, I am so sorry."

Tears spilled onto Cecily's cheeks, rolling and tumbling over one another, racing toward sorrow. "Brey . . . how could it be? He was here this morning." Her voice was soft, puzzled. She furrowed her brows in confusion. "I do not understand. We were laughing together yesterday. The joust—" She clenched her eyes shut. "Oh, God, the joust . . ."

"My child!" Father Alec cried, unable to bear her pain any longer. He rushed forward, taking her in his arms and holding her tight. She sobbed against his chest. He stroked her silky rose-gold hair. "God will grant us the courage to persevere. He always does. We are made strong through Him—you must believe it."

"I know you speak true," Cecily murmured against his robes. "But these words bring me no comfort. Just now, there is naught to do but mourn."

Father Alec could think of no response. She was right, of course. There was naught to do but let mourning run its natural, healing course. But would they ever heal from this? He squeezed his eyes shut against an onset of tears. He did not want to think of the future without happy, golden Brey.

He held little Cecily close, drawing what comfort he could from her and hoping she could do the same.

Mirabella had kept vigil by her brother's bedside. After the physician came and left she had bathed Brey herself, preparing him for his long rest until the Lord came to claim his sweet soul on Judgment Day. When Father Alec returned from the abbey he had tearfully anointed him and together they had sat, hand in hand, praying for gentle Brey.

Now that Father Alec was with the rest of the family and she was alone, she felt a peculiar comfort wash over her. Brey was gone and yet more than ever she felt his presence, gentle and encouraging. His death was a sign to her, the sign she had needed but did not want, not in this form, that it was far past time for her to pursue her destiny.

After Brey's interment she would enter the convent and no one would stop her.

Until then she would try to be what comfort she could to her family and poor little Cecily, who would no doubt be lost without her bosom companion.

But now, just now, she wanted to be alone. She wanted to be with her brother.

She took his hand, holding it in hers, casting her eyes at the face, so serene in his eternal sleep. Such potential, now gone, all gone. She could not think of it.

It was God's will. She must tell herself that.

She believed it, truly.

The family broke fast the next day in silence. None were attired in black as they had not brought mourning clothes with them. It seemed a mockery to go on donning the colors of life when one of the liveliest things in their world was no more.

Father Alec, struggling to remain collected, shifted his eyes from one member of the family to another in growing concern. Lady Grace drank cup after cup of wine undeterred. Lord Hal stared at his plate, picking at his bread with fumbling fingers. Mirabella did not eat but sat, staring at the table before her without seeing it. Cecily, her eyes swollen and red from sobbing the night through, her lips puffy and nose chapped, held her piece of cheese without eating it.

"There is nothing left now," Lady Grace said, breaking the suffocating silence with her low voice as she stared into her empty cup.

"More wine?" a servant asked.

Lady Grace scowled, waving the servant away. She shook her head, pushing her cup away from her. It fell on its side with a clatter, causing Cecily to start and Mirabella to avert her head.

"Nothing!" Lady Grace screamed.

"My lady—" Father Alec began.

"No!" Cecily clenched her fists, rising. "You still have your daughter. You cannot forget her!"

Lady Grace fixed Mirabella with a hard glare. Then, to everyone's horror, she began to laugh. She rose. "I have no daughter." She smiled. "As I said. I have nothing."

"Grace!" Lord Hal seized her wrist. Lady Grace withdrew it.

Mirabella stared at Lady Grace, her mouth agape, her eyes filled with tears. "You cannot mean it, my lady. For all that has been, I am always your daughter. Please . . . take comfort in me."

Lady Grace shook her head, her disconcerting laughter low in her throat. "You are not mine. You have never been mine. You belong to your father, that much is so. But I am not your mother."

"Stop!" Lord Hal commanded.

But it was too late. The words were out.

Lady Grace tipped back her head and laughed. The grating, joyless sound pierced Father Alec's ears. "Ask your father about her. Who was she, Hal? Ah, yes. Julia was her name. The daughter of his father's treasurer. The jewel of his family, his gift to the Church. *Sister* Julia. So holy. So pure. So irresistible to the lusts of a hot-blooded nobleman."

"For God's sake, Grace!" Lord Hal screamed.

Mirabella quit the table, Lord Hal chasing after her.

Cecily sat, stunned and trembling.

Lady Grace's face went slack. She held out her cup. Wordlessly, a servant filled it.

Father Alec shifted in his seat, uncomfortable with the scene. At last he sighed. "Perhaps, since you found it appropriate to favor the young ones with this knowledge now, you would like to explain further to Lady Cecily," he said at last.

Lady Grace regarded the startled girl before her, her heart clenching in agony. What had she done? All that she was capable of doing, it seemed. Wreaking havoc, destroying lives. But she did nothing that had not been done to her! Was she not destroyed, irreversibly destroyed, years ago? Since then she had slowly degenerated into despair.

And now she was required to explain.

"You were never to know," Hal told Mirabella, who lay face-down on her bed, sobbing, her shoulders quaking as he sat beside her to rub her back. "It had been agreed to long ago, to save us all. To save you. And your mother."

"Which one?" Mirabella seethed as she sat up, wiping her eyes with the backs of her hands, the gaze she fixed upon her father accusatory.

Hal bowed his head, his heart sinking. "Both, I suppose." He drew in a shuddering breath. "Julia was the daughter of my father's treasurer, it is true. She was set to enter the convent; it was her calling, like you. I was newly married to Grace then, a woman I had not set eyes on till my wedding day. Julia Grayson had been a childhood companion and it so happened that she grew into a beautiful woman—"

"This talk is vile," Mirabella spat, her voice thick with horror.

"Yes, Mirabella, it is vile. It is shameful and all that is bad. But you must know," said Hal. "I cannot undo what has been done. Now that you know the truth some sense of it must be made."

Mirabella was silent.

Hal continued. "I was drunk when it happened. Had been out with the lads. My memory of the actual night is so hazy . . . suddenly all I knew is that I was with her. It was one time only."

"You . . . violated her?" Mirabella's voice was low as the realization settled upon her. She shook her head. "Only one time? As if it would make a difference if it were one time or a hundred for what you stole from her! One time. That is all it took? *One time?*" She clicked her tongue in incredulous disgust.

Hal nodded, his face wrought with shame. "My father told me from my earliest childhood days till manhood to rise above my peers, to hold myself to a higher standard: God's standard. He said that women were creatures of God to be protected and cherished, never misused as many men are wont to do, and that few sins were as selfish and wicked as adultery. I failed my father; I fell short of everything he taught me. I failed God. And in that failing my guilt has plagued me; no self-imposed torture is enough to expiate it. I have repented for that 'one time' ever since. I have begged God for a forgiveness I am not worthy of, but, Mirabella, you must know how sorry I am for taking that woman's innocence. I have worn a hair shirt since that day. I—"

"It does not matter," Mirabella said, shaking her head. "You took what was not yours, a gift that was saved for God alone, and you broke your marriage vows to do it."

Hal bowed his head, tears trailing slow, even paths down his cheeks. "Yes. I deserve all of your hatred."

"You have it," Mirabella said, her tears dry, her voice hard. "Tell me what happened to my mother."

"She was with child," Hal said. "She kept it to herself a long while. She still planned to enter the convent after the child was born. It was kept quiet. A dowry was arranged that no abbess could refuse and I would raise the child—you—acknowledged. It was only right and fair. I would not let my child be raised by anyone else. I had brought you into this world and would be responsible."

"And Mother?" Mirabella inquired. "Or should I say 'Lady Grace'?"

"I went along with the plan," Lady Grace told Cecily, who sat silent, riveted by the haunting tale. "What else could I do? I was not about to be disgraced by a bastard, legitimized or not. Better the child be seen as mine. I had heard of other women humiliated by their husbands who allowed their bastards by servant wenches run of the house. I would not be one of them. So the servants were dismissed and our house was run with a skeleton staff. I had taken on peculiar fancies during my 'condition' and could not abide any number of people about. I padded my gowns and received guests. But I never allowed servants to attend me—it was odd, of course, and earned its share of gossip. But it was a small sacrifice compared to what life would be if the truth came out.

"As for Mistress Julia, she was housed in a cottage with a well-paid midwife, who delivered 'my' daughter, bringing her to me under the cover of night. Thank God she hadn't been born a boy or Hal would have gone so far as to make her his heir, no doubt," she added as tears gathered like storm clouds in her eyes. "But I had Brey. *I* had the heir. And now he is gone. Gone." She raised her eyes to Cecily. "Now you see why I have nothing."

Cecily shook her head. "But you do not. You chose to live as Mirabella's mother; it did not have to be. She could have been raised by a nurse and still be acknowledged as Lord Hal's. The gossip would have faded; your dignity could have been spared in your character, in how you handled the crisis. Instead you lived a lie, allowing the hatred to cripple you until you caused more agony for yourself than need be. Because of that you have become a source of gossip anyway. Mirabella is not to blame for that. She is not to blame for any of it; you cannot punish her for her father's sins."

"You do not understand!" Lady Grace cried, slamming her fist on the table. "I wanted to love her! I tried to love her! But from the moment she was born all I could see was that woman. She served as a constant reminder of my husband's indiscretion, taking after her mother in every way, from her looks to her fervent devotion to God. She has mocked my good intentions at every turn! She has been nothing but an affront to me!"

Cecily bowed her head. Too much pain. She was drowning in it. She covered her ears with her hands and allowed her head to sink onto the table.

She could not bear to hear more.

Father Alec drew in a breath. His voice was soft. "If your mission today was to make everyone feel as aggrieved as you, my lady, you have been successful," he said at last.

Grace pushed back her chair, letting it fall to the floor behind her with an angry thud as she fled the table.

* * *

"Do you believe I am sorry, Mirabella?" Hal asked his daughter in urgent tones as he seized her by the shoulders. She withdrew with a jerk. Hal's hands fell limp and useless to his lap. God, she was afraid of him. He did not want her to be afraid of him. "Ever since that terrible night I have tried to make it up to you by giving you the best life I could think of, with the best of everything—gowns, tutors, anything. I have tried to make it up to Lady Grace, to the convent, to everyone I sinned against. I'd make a pilgrimage to Jerusalem if I thought it would expiate my sins. I would do anything. Oh, Mirabella, please forgive me."

"I am bound by God to forgive you," Mirabella said in hollow tones. "But you cannot think that anything will ever be the same between us."

Hal buried his head in his hand. "No . . . I could never expect that." He reached up to stroke her face. Mirabella pulled away. "Can you understand the depth of my remorse?"

"It is not important for me to believe how sorry you are," said Mirabella. "But for God. He alone can read the sincerity of your heart. I pray for your sake you are as repentant as you appear."

Hal nodded. He sniffled. "I do love you, Mirabella. It matters not how you came to be but that you are mine. I have never viewed you as anything but a gift from God."

Mirabella nodded to acknowledge the statement. When Hal could see she would say no more he rose. With one last look at her, he made his retreat.

Mirabella flopped back on her bed, staring at the canopy until it became obscured by a veil of tears.

☙ 6 ❧

Day yielded to night. Cecily crept into Mirabella's apartments and the two girls held each other, sobbing themselves to sleep. Father Alec sat up with Hal in his apartments while Hal begged for absolution. Father Alec, who knew the man was sincere if nothing else, gave it. He had known the story since Lady Grace's infamous display at her last entertainment so many years ago. He could not say he was shocked. Such things happened with more frequency than one supposed.

"The damndest thing, Father, is that I do love Grace," he said. "Yet I failed. I failed her. I failed everyone. God knows how I've tried to make it up to her. . . ."

"It seems to me you are both to blame," Father Alec observed. "You have been at odds, her with her drink, you with your guilt . . . it has separated you far more than Mirabella or the initial betrayal ever could. And now with Brey's passing . . . it will take a long time to heal from this. But if you want to, if you both have the desire, you can. All of you. I would very much like to help you."

"I accept the offer, Father," Hal told him. "God knows how much we need it."

Father Alec reached out, taking his friend's hand. "Jeremiah chapter twenty-nine, verse eleven, tells us: 'For I know the plans I have made for you, plans to prosper you and not to harm you, plans for hope and a future.' "

Hal bowed his head over their joined hands and sobbed.

Grace could not sleep. Memories swirled in her mind, relentless, comforting, painful. She recalled when she first learned she was with child. She had two miscarriages before Brey and when she felt him stir within her she knew he would live. With each stretch and kick, she reveled in her estate. She would be a mother, a real mother to a child who was hers. Hers and Hal's and no one else's. A child born in the light and the truth, not surrounded by darkness and lies. He was born, golden and beautiful, happy and serene. All his life Brey was happy, growing from a happy baby to a happy boy. His laugh was like no other; it was like the tinkling of icicles on the pines. It was heartfelt with sincere joy.

He was to marry Cecily. Together they would bring her grandchildren and a legacy that she was partially responsible for. Now he was gone. Cecily would marry someone else; she would no longer be a part of them. Mirabella would go; she would join her precious convent. Even if she did not, she would leave. Grace's actions had chased her away. There would be no redeeming their already-fractured relationship. And Hal . . . How could Hal ever forgive this? This was to be Their Secret.

Grace had lost everything.

She climbed out of bed, throwing her wrap about her shoulders.

Carefully, noiselessly, Grace slipped out of doors.

"I have nothing," she said to the great manor that loomed in the darkness.

"We cannot leave without her!" Hal cried the next morning as the family prepared for the long, unhappy journey home for Brey's interment. "Where in hell would she have gone to? Has anyone seen her?"

Cecily and Mirabella shook their heads. They clung to each other, both fragile and frightened, battered by the whirlwind of events that had left its brutal mark on the last few days.

At once Hal's steward rushed in from out of doors, leading in a young, startled boatman.

"What's this?" Hal demanded.

"News, my lord," said the steward with an apologetic bow.

"M-milord," the boatman stammered. "I was in front of your house when it happened. . . . I had trouble bringing up my oar. Something seemed to be grabbing at it. I jerked it up and . . . that's when I saw it. I thought it was riverweeds tangling it up, but it was not. It was a lady's wrap." He choked back a sob.

"No . . ." Hal whispered to the servant, who offered a reluctant nod.

Cecily's shoulders began to convulse with silent sobs. Mirabella held her close, her body rigid as she absorbed this new onslaught of tragedy.

The two men led Hal to the scene. In the bottom of the boat was a bloodied wrap and a tangle of blond hair. Gingerly, Hal fingered the sopping wrap. His hand trembled when he encountered the hair entwined about the boatman's oar.

"Is it hers, my lord—the wrap?" the man asked in anxious tones.

Hal offered a slow nod, his blue eyes stormy with bewilderment.

"She must have been caught on a branch before the current carried her off," hazarded the boatman.

Hal clutched the wrap to his chest. He began to shiver uncontrollably as he sobbed. "Oh, Grace . . . oh, Grace . . ." At once he regarded the stunned assemblage, his face lit with an epiphany. "She may have survived," he ventured at last. "We will alert the proper authorities. Any females of Grace's description pulled from the Thames shall be examined."

"Of course, my lord," Hal's steward answered in gentle tones.

Hal would be appeased. There would be a thorough search. But all knew no one survived the Thames. Brey was gone. Grace was gone. And all in three days. The amount of time it took for the Lord to die and rise from the dead.

How would Hal ever survive this? Could *he* ever rise above it?

* * *

After two weeks of Hal dashing off to examine the bloated corpses pulled from the Thames on a daily basis, Father Alec accompanied him to his apartments. He laid a hand on Hal's shoulder.

Father Alec's lips quivered. He did not want to say it. "Hal, we must return to Sumerton. Brey needs to be interred properly. It does not mean we have to stop searching for my lady, but we must at least begin to face the prospect—"

Hal jerked his shoulder from his friend's grip, drawing a hand up over his eyes as though by doing so he could blot the latest tragedies from his vision. "I know! By God, I know!" He removed his hand, fixing Father Alec with an angry stare. "And after? After I have faced that I drove my wife to her death? After I have returned her son to his final resting place? Then what?"

Father Alec bit his lip. Once again, he took Hal's shoulders beneath his firm grasp. "Then, my dear friend, you keep living. As we all must. There still remain those in your care who depend on you."

The priest had to summon all of his willpower to meet the naked pain lighting Hal's eyes. He held the blue gaze, allowing his own eyes to fill with tears. He reached up, cupping his friend's cheek in his hand. There were no words for such grief.

Hal nodded, then bowed his head. "Then it is time to return?"

Father Alec nodded. "Yes. It is time."

A requiem mass was celebrated for Grace, and Hal made arrangements for a tomb bearing her effigy to be erected in her honor beside Brey's. Brey's interment immediately followed. Father Alec officiated at Lord Hal's request, though he felt inadequate for the role. He had not presided over any kind of ceremony in several years and he felt too close to the family to offer any real comfort. He stood over Brey's casket as stupefied as everyone else. His exterior was calm and collected; his voice rang out with false confidence as he recited the requiem mass, and to those in attendance he was the model priest, strong and self-contained. In truth he was wrought with discomfort. He stared at the helpless, bewildered faces of those who remained, each lost in their own separate spheres of misery, and could not imagine how they would survive. One loss was enough, but two, and in such quick succession, were staggering, more than most minds could wrangle with.

Hal kept to himself once the mourners made their departure. There was no one to comfort him; he had no immediate family. His friends were tactfully turned away. Grace's family, who abounded in Yorkshire, refused to attend. She had disgraced them and they would not forgive her even in death. Father Alec wished to visit each and every one of them, that he might box all of their ears.

Mirabella allowed him to visit her in her apartments, where she knelt before her prie-dieu, murmuring fervent prayers he hoped would bring her some kind of peace. If her anxiety-ridden face was any indication, however, they had not.

He laid a hand on her shoulder. "Mistress."

Mirabella turned her face toward him and he could not help but be struck by her dark beauty, beauty she would never acknowledge as an asset. It saddened him.

"I will not pretend to imagine what you are going through," he told her. "But if I can be of any help . . ."

Mirabella rose, throwing herself into his arms. He held her a long moment before pulling away and guiding her to her small breakfast table, where they sat. She took his hand, squeezing tightly.

"So many feelings, Father," she told him, her voice thick with agony. "All conflicting, all pulling me in different directions. Do I stay to comfort my father, even as I can hardly abide his presence now that I know the truth? Or do I leave at last, take my vows, even as I fear entering the cloister knowing that *she* is there, knowing what she is to me?"

Father Alec shook his head. "I do not know," he said, his voice huskier than usual, made thick with unshed tears. "I will tell you this. Despite everything, your father is not a bad man. He is a good man who did a bad thing, a terrible thing. But you must forgive him, you must see that he has tried to amend himself to the best of his abilities, and that is all God can ask of any of us. You have lost the only mother you have ever known, and though your relationship was strained I know that you grieve for her, for what you never had with her if nothing else. You grieve for your brother, the innocent whose life was taken from him before his time, and it is his loss to which there is no easy comfort. But if you examine your circumstances as compared to your father's and Lady Cecily's I would say that you make out better than either of them."

Mirabella screwed up her face in confusion.

"Your father has no one. No wife, no heir. Lady Cecily finds herself in a similar position now; not only are her parents gone but her betrothed as well. And while you share in their loss, you still have a mother and a father. And from what you told me of Sister Julia, she loves you very much," Father Alec said, his heart pounding as he dared make the suggestion. "I do not think you would lose by lovingly confronting her with the truth. You must realize that she is not a contributor to what you may perceive as a betrayal any more than your father was. Like him, she was trying to protect you. You have to see that. Now you have the opportunity to know her as a mother in an environment both of you cherish. Perhaps now more than ever is the time for you to take the step you have been longing to take for the better part of your life. What drew you toward this calling may be the same force that drew you toward her, something in the blood."

Mirabella bowed her head. "There is no doubt of my calling," she told him. "But to see her again knowing what I know. How has she abided looking at me all these years, knowing how I came to be? I must have been such a painful reminder to her, just as I was to my moth—to Lady Grace." Her voice broke. "That is all I have ever meant to anyone. Pain. Heartache." She heaved a deep sigh. "How could I put her through that every day?"

Father Alec's heart clenched with compassion as he reached out, stroking her tearstained cheek. She leaned into his hand.

"Yet she saw you before you knew of your connection," Father Alec told her. "Did she seem pained then?"

Mirabella's face softened in thought. She shook her head. "No. She seemed . . . happy." She regarded him in awe, as though shocked at the possibility.

"Because, no matter what, you are her daughter and she loves you," Father Alec told her. "Go to her, Mirabella. Take comfort in one another."

Mirabella rose, Father Alec rising in turn.

"Oh, Father, you have been so good to me, to our family," Mirabella told him, wrapping her arms about his waist again and burying her head in his chest.

"You have all been as family to me," he said. "The only family I have known for many years. You all have brought me as much comfort as I hope to have brought you."

Mirabella drew back, her arms still about him. She reached up, stroking his cheek. "You have. So much." She swallowed several times, overcome with emotion. "Oh, Father . . ."

To Father Alec's utter astonishment she leaned up and pressed her lips to his. They were full, moist, and not unpleasant, but his body went rigid. Mirabella may be a beauty, but never at any moment had he been attracted to her. He had never suffered a lapse in chastity before, though he had been visited by temptation many a time. Despite this, he tried not to lose sight of the fact that he was a priest and, unless there were drastic reforms made, he was constrained to celibacy.

He pulled away. "My girl . . ." He cleared his throat. "If I have in some way led you to believe—"

Mirabella had backed away from him, covering her mouth as though her lips had been set aflame. "Forgive me, Father! I do not know what possessed me! Oh, Father, I am out of my head! Please forgive me!" She fell to her knees. "Please, grant me absolution. I had no right. . . . I am no better than the Boleyn creature. Oh, Father!"

Father Alec knelt beside her. "Lady Mirabella, collect yourself," he said gently. "Your emotions are running high right now given your remarkable circumstances. It is both expected and acceptable for you to be a little out of sorts. You are forgiven. But," he added, bowing his head as his cheeks flushed in embarrassment, "you must realize that this cannot happen again. I am a priest."

"Of course, Father," Mirabella said. "I also wish to take vows.

As I said, I do not know what . . . I just . . . I suppose I just wanted to feel the nearness of someone, the comfort. . . . Is that strange?"

"Not at all," Father Alec said. "We are human beings. And God said it is not good for man to be alone. We need each other. Now and then there is a special nearness that a man and woman cherish. But for those of us called to serve God alone, we sacrifice that nearness for a different kind of fellowship and take comfort in something a little more abstract. It is a hard life and not one to be entered into lightly. That being said, we still cannot deny our humanity. Now and then we need to be embraced, to feel a sense of closeness to another human being just as anyone else. There is nothing wrong in it, Mistress Mirabella, as long as it is done in chastity."

Mirabella nodded, averting her head. "Yes, Father."

Father Alec rose. The room had suddenly become stifling and he longed to leave it. "Bless you, my child. I pray peace will find you."

Mirabella said nothing.

Once certain he had retreated she drew her knees to her chest and sobbed. How could she have betrayed herself like that? Was there not enough to grieve over?

No matter how he would try to pretend, it would be different now.

She had lost him as well.

Cecily had watched Brey's casket be slipped into its dark crypt and shuddered. The image would not flee, stalking her even in dreams. It swirled relentless before her mind's eye; the grating sound of the casket scraping against the stone of the tomb was chilling, causing goose pimples to rise on her flesh.

Brey was gone. Lady Grace was gone.

She almost expected the latter. For years she had prepared herself for it as she watched Lady Grace's health decline. But for her to die like this . . . it was a tragedy she could not grapple with.

And if she could not grapple with that she could not begin to make sense of Brey's death. One moment there, the next gone. Something inexplicable, a stupid stomachache. And gone. She would never hear his infectious laugh. They would never again ride together through the lush forest of Sumerton, never hawk together. She could never tease him about his poor aim with the bow. He would no longer be there to conspire with, to dance with, to play games with, to talk to, to accompany her to entertainments in their silly matching ensembles.

He was her best friend.

And soon he would have been her husband.

They had kissed at the joust. Her first kiss. A little kiss it was but a kiss nonetheless, the first of what she had imagined would be many more. But Brey took his kisses with him.

They would never marry now. She would never be the mother of his children.

Brey, her Brey, was gone.

Cecily lay in her apartments sobbing until she could sob no more. And when the tears stopped, remarkably they would start again. She would remember something Brey had said, a jest, a story, a song he sang in his off-key voice. And the tears rolled down her cheeks in a hot torrent.

The house was empty without him. She, Mirabella, and Lord Hal lived in separate worlds. No one interacted. No one commingled. They ate separately. They prayed separately. The joy had been sapped from the house, and Cecily, who had once been so adept at spreading joy, could not summon forth the strength to bring it back.

Father Alec attempted to comfort her but at last gave up.

"There is nothing I can say or do," he told her at last. "Simple answers will not suffice, not for one as astute as you. I hate being helpless. I hate watching all of you suffer like this. All I want is to be here if you need me."

"Many thanks," Cecily whispered. "Just stay beside me," she told him. "You don't have to say anything. Just be here."

So Father Alec stayed beside her. Sometimes she fell into a dreamless slumber. When she awoke he was still there.

At least he did not fail her. At least he would always be there.

*   *   *

Not only had Hal lost his wife and treasured son but all hopes of a dynasty. He was the last of the Pierce line. The future had rested on Brey's slim shoulders, it shone out of his bright blue eyes.

Hal wondered how it was his grief had not killed him. Grace . . . how he had hurt her over the years. But he could not abandon his daughter, not for anyone. He had to do right by her. And in doing right he had done so much wrong. . . . Grace's happiness was sacrificed, his family was compromised, and all for a night of uncontrolled lust.

He had never stopped punishing himself for a night he could not remember. Ever since he learned of his shame he wore the hair shirt, save for those few weeks before his ill-fated trip to London when he and Grace had embarked on their "new start."

New start.

Hal's throat constricted with tears. Imagine how many tears a body could hold!

He had killed her the same as if he had thrown her into the river himself. A slow, agonizing death soaked in water and wine.

Grace was no more.

And Brey . . . his triumph, his beautiful boy. His blessing, his redemption . . .

But he did not deserve blessings or redemption. God knew that. So He took Brey from him. He took him away. And he was not enough, so He returned for Grace.

Now Hal was alone.

He could not face Mirabella's angry stare or Cecily's bewildered one. He did not speak to Father Alec much. There was nothing to say.

He remained in his room. He shuffled his cards. He rattled his dice.

He cried.

Until at last one day Mirabella came to him.

They embraced. Hal held her fast, thrilled at the contact with another human being, thrilled that it was his daughter. Surely this was some sign that forgiveness was possible. . . .

"I cannot promise things will ever be the same for us," she told him. "But I thought to seek your blessing. I would like to take my vows now. It was my hope you could arrange the dowry."

"Of course," said Hal, his heart sinking. Of course she would want that. It was all she had ever wanted. Now, despite or because of the knowledge that her mother resided at the cloister, she was more determined than ever to get there. "I will make the arrangements directly."

Mirabella offered a low curtsy. He detected a trace of mockery in it.

"Thank you, Father," she told him.

He inclined his head as she left him.

Alone.

ॐ 7 ॐ

"**Y**ou are leaving now?" Cecily cried, furrowing her brows in consternation as she regarded Mirabella. "Now, when everyone needs you so?"

"How could I stay?" Mirabella returned. "The arrangements have been made. Father is offering a generous dowry and I will be entering as a postulant. At last. You know this is all I dreamed of, that it is my calling. Can you ask me to deny what God ordained?"

Cecily wiped her tears away with her sleeves as she sank onto Mirabella's bed. She shook her head. "No, I cannot. I know that. And I would never try to stop you. I know how long you have waited for this. But, oh, Mirabella, what's to become of me? I am so alone!"

Mirabella's lip quivered as she sat beside Cecily. She gathered Cecily in her arms, cupping the back of her head. "Oh, darling, I am so sorry. Would that I could stay. But I cannot. I just cannot. If I stay I will be poisoned with bitterness. I must leave before that happens, while there is something in me to salvage. I feel it creeping in every day. This house, this terrible place . . . I cannot abide it, the sins of the past are too great. They choke me. You can understand that, Cecily, can't you?"

Cecily offered a miserable nod. "I suppose I am being selfish. But I am so alone," she repeated brokenly. "There is no one in the world for me, no one but Father Alec, perhaps. And I am not fool enough to believe he will remain here forever. Oh, Mirabella, what will become of me? Where will I go? Before my future seemed so assured. I was to marry Brey . . . my Brey. . . ." Her shoulders quaked with sobs. "I am thrust into this world of uncertainties. Perhaps I will be married off to one of the men you told me of, someone who will take mistresses or hit me. Someone who will always put me last. I am so afraid, Mirabella!"

"Oh, darling!" Mirabella cried, rocking with urgency. "You mustn't be afraid. For whatever Father's past sins, I know he will choose you a fine husband."

"No one like Brey," Cecily said with fervency. "There will never be another like my Brey."

The girls clung to each other, sobbing for what was lost and what was yet to be.

Both were filled with gut-wrenching helplessness.

Despite Mirabella's momentary guilt over leaving Cecily behind, she was at peace the moment she entered the convent, no longer as a visitor but as a postulant. Her hair was cut. The long black locks that had been such a stunning feature were abandoned and what remained was tucked beneath a coif. She was unadorned, free of the stares of wicked lusting men, free of her own startling desire for a man she could never have. Free to *be*.

Her days were devoted to prayer and chores. For the most part silence was observed. She learned she had been an exception to the long-preserved rule that few visitors enter the convent.

She was there two months before she approached Sister Julia. Mirabella had skillfully avoided her, stealing glances at her whenever she could but never allowing herself to speak to her. Sister Julia offered confused glances of her own but never approached her, respecting what seemed to be an obvious wish to be let alone.

But one night when Sister Julia was grinding grain in the courtyard Mirabella approached her. They were alone, a rare enough occasion, as the convent teemed with silent females, greatly restricting one's freedom to speak. It was Mirabella's natural inclination to be silent. But she would have years for that.

Now was a time for words.

She only said, "I know."

Sister Julia ceased grinding. The mortar fell to the ground. She did not raise her head. At last she sighed. "I thought you might." At last she regarded her, her eyes filled with tears.

How could Mirabella not have seen it? She was looking into a mirror, a mirror that had aged her seventeen years. On impulse she reached out, touching her mother's face. She knelt before her.

"You do not have to explain a thing," she assured her. "I know what he did, how he stole your gift to God. How I wish you could have been spared the pain—"

"You must not say any more," said Sister Julia, averting her head, clasping Mirabella's hand. "You do not understand."

"But I do!" Mirabella insisted. "Oh, how did you ever find it in your heart to forgive him?"

Sister Julia shook her head emphatically. "But, Mirabella, he needs no forgiving! The only one who he betrayed besides God was Lady Grace! For what he took I gave to him!"

"Wh-what?" Mirabella sank to the ground, her knees unable to support her. "B-but he said . . . he said—"

"My father convinced him of that, to be sure," Sister Julia said. "Poor Hal was so intoxicated that night it was a wonder he could remember his own name. It was the only way I could . . . I could—"

"You mean you *seduced* him?" Mirabella cried in a hoarse whisper, withdrawing her hand. "Was this before or after your decision to become the bride of Christ?"

Sister Julia shook her head. "It is never that simple. I knew I could never be a wife to him, not only because of our difference in rank but because I was inclined to the Church. But I could not take the veil until I had one night, *one* night of humanity. I could not think of a better person to share that with than Hal; we were on friendly terms as it were, having grown up together, though I cannot say either of us harbored any romantic feelings toward the other." She shook her head in awe. "I never imagined that night would lead us to this. Yet despite it all I thank God it did."

"You have no idea the misery you caused," Mirabella breathed, awed and nauseated by the revelation. "Lady Grace's life was ruined; all the while I resented her not knowing I was the cause of her pain. Now she is dead. Did you know that? By her own hand, though to save face the family claimed it was an accidental drowning." Mirabella's brows ached from furrowing them in frustration. "Do you not realize the impact your night of—of careless lust had on my entire family? My father has punished himself ever since! And you thank God for it!"

"Do you think that is what I was thanking God for? Do you believe that I meant for such tragedy to unfold?" Sister Julia cried. "I was seventeen, Mirabella. I was passionate, I was impulsive. But I was devout, despite the image of me you may have now. I did feel a calling. But to know for certain which world I was to give myself over to I had to experience what it meant to be a woman." She lowered her eyes in shame. "My quest for certainty destroyed more lives than I could have ever in my darkest fantasies imagined. And living this life has been as much penance as calling now." She regarded her with tearstained cheeks. "Mirabella, is there enough compassion in your heart to understand any of what I have been telling you? Have you never felt these emotions? Can you honestly tell me that in your almost twenty years of life you have never longed for the love of a man?"

An image of Father Alec swirled before her mind's eye. She blinked it away, bowing her head. "I—I have loved. But I cannot . . . I cannot have him," she said softly, her heart pounding in shock that she should reveal this vulnerability to Sister Julia knowing all she knew of her now. She raised her head, resolute. "And even if I could I would not. I accept the sacrifice I must make without having to dabble in the forbidden."

Sister Julia gazed at her, her expression filled with tenderness and something Mirabella could not discern. Pity? Fear? Both? "Then I commend you, Mirabella. Some are clearly stronger than others. I gave in to my weakness and I have paid the price along with many others ever since. You will never be able to fathom the depth of my regret."

"I am weary of people's regrets," Mirabella sighed. "It does no good now. It is too late for it."

Sister Julia covered her eyes with her hand, expelling a heavy sigh. "I did not expect your entrance into my life," she whispered through tears, "and God knows I was not called to be a mother. But I do love you, Mirabella. And you must know how Hal tried to do right by you. Blame us for everything else that happened; I take full responsibility. But know this: You were not conceived in an act of evil. And when I thank God, I thank God for you. Nothing else. Just you."

Mirabella buried her face in her hands. "Oh, poor, dear Father," she murmured as she sobbed. "How could he not have known?"

Sister Julia shook her head. "Perhaps he did know, in the beginning. But I imagine between his father and mine, he was convinced . . . oh, if only I had . . . but I was kept away from him. I have not seen him since that night. I vowed never to see him again; it is a vow I will adhere to. You must get a message to him."

Mirabella's heart was pounding. Tears clouded her vision. It was all too much to absorb. "There is so much heartache. . . ." She shook her head, sniffling and wiping her eyes. She rose.

Sister Julia caught her hand. "Can you forgive me?" she asked her.

"As God requires," said Mirabella, defeated by her virtue as she made her retreat, closing her ears and heart to the sobbing woman behind her.

She had come searching for clarity and peace. Instead she was tossed into another turbulent ocean of confusion and unrest. It seemed the running theme of her life.

She entered the chapel, falling to her knees before the crucifix and crossing herself. The familiar image eased the knot in her chest. She inhaled, expelling the breath slowly. She inhaled again, closing her eyes, opening them to find the image still before her, her one anchor in this relentless storm.

Mirabella did not speak to Sister Julia after the night, adhering to the general silence observed by the sisters. They communicated through signs, whispering when necessary. She marveled at the change. It seemed when she visited as a child it had been different, the sisters warmer and more free in their ability to communicate. Mirabella's infatuation with their lifestyle had shrouded actuality in illusion. In truth it was to one sister that she had spoken in all her years of visiting, besides the obligatory exchanges with the abbess, and that was Sister Julia.

But nothing was the same now. Being housed in the same cloister was not designed to bring them closer together as women; it was instead a place where women could in relative safety be excluded from the outside world, a place devoted to discipline, reflection, prayer, and the personal, individual pursuit of closeness with God.

In order to achieve the closeness they once shared, one of them would have to leave. This was not a world for friendship, not even between a mother and her wounded daughter.

And so they went on. Mirabella's disillusionment traded itself for the clarity she longed for. Sister Julia was not viewed as a mother but as an equal. They were not friends, they were not enemies. They just were. Somehow, it was enough.

Mirabella gave little thought to her remaining family. Removed from Castle Sumerton as she was, the grief for her brother and Lady Grace began to subside to a dull ache, where once it had been an all-consuming throb. She welcomed a new feeling: hollowness, emptiness. Nothing touched her inside the cloister. It softened worldly pain and disappointments. Life outside began to fade away, hidden behind a misty veil, illusion of another kind, and she would not let herself pass through.

Even had she wanted passage, the rules of the cloister would prevent her. Because of the strictness enforced to uphold and preserve the morality of its inhabitants, Mirabella's contact with the outside world was limited. But she was able to write her family. Thus far she only had sent one message, a carefully worded letter to her father that told him all he needed to know.

> *Dearest Father,*
> *I have it on authority that the gift you believed you*
> *stole was given to you. I pray this knowledge brings you*
> *peace.*
> *Your loving daughter,*
> *Mirabella*

Hal reread the letter again and again. The crumpled parchment was damp with his tears. He could not believe it. All of these years . . . how could he not remember? That spirit-drenched night was so long ago, so hazy, that to this hour he had little recollection of it, save for the sensations. And though he had convinced himself of the crime committed, never in his years of self-examination had the memory of those sensations resembled anything cruel or violent. Yet, he had thought, it must have been so. His father had told him thus. Her father had told him. He was too far gone in the spirits to rely on his own judgment.

But it was his judgment, that flicker of reason stirring in his gut insisting his innocence, that was indeed correct.

He was not a rapist. He mouthed the words over and over, letting the knowledge settle over him. Relief surged through him like a cleansing river. He had felt some measure of it, even before this revelation, when Mirabella learned the truth of her parentage at last. The knot in his gut had eased somewhat as he realized the charade could stop.

And now this, a sudden gift of mercy from God to assuage the pain of his great losses. To know that he was not All Bad. But the comfort this brought him was transient. His heart still throbbed with pain. It was still too late. Too late for his poor Grace. He could never tell her, the woman who despite it all he had still sinned against, that the sin had at least not been one of brutality. Would it have made any difference had she known, or would her resentment toward Mirabella's existence still have fueled her every action since the day the child was brought into his home?

There was no use speculating. Grace was gone. He could never pray her back.

He could only pray that she was with Brey, eternally young and free from her great pain, that somehow she knew the truth.

And that, somehow, it made a difference.

Castle Sumerton was empty, large, and looming. Echoes of laughter rang in the halls, childish and innocent, only to fade away, sucked into the stone walls, claimed by the faery folk, who gathered in the happy noises of the children to fill their own mysterious world.

Cecily was alone. She haunted the halls, a little ghost. Everything was so big. The exciting passageways and secret places she had explored with Brey were dark, filled with shadows and goblins and terrible things waiting to carry her away.

Brey . . . her dearest friend. Brey, her betrothed.

What would she do without him? What would become of her? No one knew.

Mirabella was gone. She was where she belonged, shedding her former life as a butterfly sheds its chrysalis. Cecily never heard from her. She supposed it was easier for Mirabella that way; contact with Cecily would serve as a constant reminder of the pain she had left behind. Cecily hoped she had found the peace that eluded her in the outside world. There at least she had her mother. As strange as the circumstance was, it must prove some comfort.

As for Cecily, she had Lord Hal and Father Alec. They slipped into the predictable monotony of routine, which proved a strange sort of comfort. Monotony did not betray or abandon, monotony did not die. It persisted, dull and mundane. Safe.

Father Alec diverted her with their lessons and she pretended enthusiasm, going through the motions in a weak imitation of what had existed before. Father Alec remained a font of understanding; when she needed to talk, they talked. When she needed his strong silence, he was silent. As she grew she began to realize that he did not have all the answers to life's mysteries.

"What I know about life can fill a thimble," he had told her with a rueful smile. "I am as capable of being bewildered as you are." His eyes clouded. "And we have had our share of bewilderment," he added in soft tones. "Some things we will never be able to make sense of. But we must never stop trying because it is that trying which keeps us growing and learning. And the more you learn, the more you hunger for it, the more you *need* to know." He winked. "Your thimble might begin to overflow and yet still, still, it is never enough. With every bit of knowledge acquired, there is still something we have yet to learn. It is endlessly humbling."

Rather than being disillusioned by his confession, she found it brought them closer together. The blinding light of her ideal began to fade, leaving in its place a man trying to understand his world just as she was. Knowing that she was not alone in this very human struggle brought her comfort, far more so than if she had maintained the impression that he was a creature of the divine, above mortal failings. And so it was that for the first time she felt on equal terms with someone else. There was no pretense, no displays of superiority. Just two people searching for peace.

Lord Hal offered another sort of peace, peace through mindless activities. He played games with her in the evenings, chess and dice, sometimes cards. They sat by the fire. Some nights he asked her to play her lute and sing for him; her clear voice would ring through the silence of the room and he would close his eyes, tipping back his head, his lips quivering. Now and then she noted a stray tear rolling down his tanned cheek.

Other nights they would sit in silence while she embroidered. He would stare into the fire, into the past, or regard her nimble fingers with gentle eyes. Perhaps he thought of the daughter-in-law he had lost in her and the son who was gone forever. She did not know. She did know he found a measure of peace in her company and she was happy to provide it.

For whatever passed before, he deserved that.

Hal had to give some thought to Cecily's future. It was not seemly for her to remain under his care anymore, a young girl with none but himself and a male tutor for company. The practical side of him cursed the thought of losing her wardship. But what could he do with her? He had no son now. . . .

His throat constricted with a painful lump.

He had no son now.

No heir. No immediate family to pass down what remained of his wealth and lands. No one to inherit his title. He imagined after he passed Sumerton would revert to the Crown, to King Henry.

Unless . . .

*   *   *

"She is far too young," Father Alec insisted when the two men were alone in Hal's apartments one summer evening. "Even if she were of a more suitable age you have not even been widowed the summer! And with the shady circumstances surrounding my lady's drowning . . ."

"What are you implying?" Hal demanded, his tone sharp.

"My lord, I should hope you would know better than to think I would imply anything," Father Alec returned, matching Hal tone for tone. He sighed. "It is others I worry about. At the very least, you must understand that such a move would appear disrespectful to your lady wife's memory. Was she not disrespected enough in life?"

"But I told you—"

"It does not matter," Father Alec cut him short as he rose from the chair to pace before the fire. "Innocent or not, Lady Grace was still sinned against and deserves the respect of at least a full year of mourning. Let Lady Cecily grow up a bit."

"Then she cannot reside here any longer, you must know that," Hal said, his heart sinking. "If I send her away, she will no doubt be betrothed to another to benefit the house—"

"That is all she has ever meant to you, hasn't she?" Father Alec cried, whirling upon Hal, his face contorted in a display of rage so contrary to his usually calm countenance that Hal was shocked into momentary silence. "You wish to amass her lands and wealth for yourself!"

When Hal found his voice it was sharp. "Father! Don't be naïve! You know how fond of the girl I am, that she would be cherished and well cared for. But you must also know that from a practical standpoint, the Baroness Burkhart is an asset to any house granted her wardship. You know that was why we took her in, that is why she was to marry Brey. That is life, Father. The fact that we came to love her as we did was an unexpected, and much appreciated, gift."

"Then if you love her so, wait," Father Alec advised him. "Wait till the girl is sixteen at least."

"And who will care for her in the meantime, Father?" he asked.

"I have no living relatives. And no one else will take her in if they cannot benefit from her themselves." He ran a hand through his chestnut brown hair in frustration. "And in truth, Father, I cannot bear the thought of sending her to strangers. D'you honestly wish to see her uprooted from all she has known after she has been through so much already? God knows who she could end up with. I may be far from perfection, Father, but I would never be cruel to her. I would never raise my hand to her and God knows the marriage will not be consummated till she is of a proper age! . . ." His voice softened. "And I would never stray from her—believe me that is not a mistake to be made more than once. With me she would at least have some of the life she had planned on before . . . before . . ."

"You are not Brey," Father Alec said in low tones.

"I *know* that," he said. "But neither am I a lecher. I am young and vital, still in my thirties, for love of God! I need heirs, Father, or all that my family stood for ends with me. My fortune will revert to the Crown and that is the reality. My God, man, you behave as if it has not been done before! Why, I can name dozens—"

"They do not matter." Father Alec's voice was soft with disillusionment. "I had hoped *you* were above such things." His shoulders slumped. He sighed. "But you know better. You are noble. I am but a humble tutor. Be advised, however, that I will not stay on. The lady of the house will be far too preoccupied in acquainting herself with her new station to carry on with the lessons of childhood."

"I had hoped you would remain as our personal chaplain," Hal said, his tone thick with sadness. "As our friend. Lady Cecily loves you so."

Father Alec shook his head. "That is not possible," he told him. "I am sorry, my lord. For your friend I am, but this . . ." He searched Hal's face. "Yet you will stay your course, won't you?"

"There is no other way, Father," Hal said. "I am sorry you cannot see that."

"I am not leaving because I cannot see it," Father Alec said. "I am leaving because I can."

With this he turned on his heel and quit the apartments, leaving Hal alone to contemplate this new decision, one of the biggest and most startling he had ever made, that of taking on a second wife.

Never in his wildest imaginings had he thought life would necessitate such actions.

And never in his wildest imaginings had he thought the bride in question would be his ward, the Baroness Cecily Burkhart, the child selected for his son.

❧ 8 ❧

Hal had taken her to practice archery the day he broached the subject. Dressed in a smart gray velvet gown, her rose-gold hair flowing down her shoulders, she was the picture of a lady, drawing back her bowstring and hitting her marks with ease. Hal's shoulders slumped. However ladylike she appeared, she was very much a child. Her face was tender even in concentration; the sweep of her jaw, the curve of her neck, the soft glow of her skin indicated that beneath the blossoming figure was an innocent.

If he could convince her that it made sense. If he could convince her that he cared as much for her welfare as his own . . .

He began with as much gentleness as possible. "Cecily—my lady—"

She started at this, not accustomed to him addressing her as such, and she offered a timid smile.

"There is something you must know," he said. "Before I say anything else I want you to know about—about what happened with Sister Julia."

"You do not need to tell me," she said in her soft voice. "I was informed."

"But you must know," he began awkwardly, "you must know that . . . that I did not—that I did not . . . violate her."

Cecily averted her head, her cheeks flushing.

Hal flushed as well. "I had believed that for many years but was recently assured by her that—that it was not the case," he told her. "I know this makes me no more honorable, that I still sinned against the Lady Grace, and for that I am eternally remorseful. But if it elevates your opinion of me in any way—"

"My opinion of you has never been affected," Cecily told him. "I always knew you were a good man, Lord Hal. Even the best of men do terrible things and I know you have endeavored to lead a righteous life since then."

"Still," he said, bowing his head and shifting his weight, uncomfortable with the conversation. "I thought it important that you know."

"I am honored you told me," Cecily said, reaching out to squeeze his forearm.

He fixed his eyes on her little hand, the slender, tapering fingers, the immaculate, well-sculpted nails. He covered it with his own.

"Lady Cecily, we have been grieving, you and I, for so much," he went on. His heart raced. He could hear it pounding in his ears. His throat was painfully dry. "For Lady Grace and for our dear Brey. And I know what I am about to say will hardly seem fitting now, but . . . Regarding your future, Lady Cecily." He cleared his throat and swallowed hard. "H-have you given it any thought?"

Cecily's face paled. Her hand trembled in his. "I did not want to. I have been afraid of this moment, but I knew it would come. I knew you could no longer care for me given the circumstances. You have found another place for me." She squared her shoulders, squeezing her eyes shut a long moment before reopening them. They shone luminous with unshed tears. "Where will I be going, my lord?"

Hal bowed his head. "It is my hope that you will remain here with me, if that is to your pleasure."

"Oh, yes!" Cecily cried, blossoms of hope coloring her cheeks rose. "But who will attend me? Who will be my chaperone?"

Hal drew in a deep breath, expelling it slowly. "If you are agreeable to my . . . suggestion one will not be needed." He regarded her carefully. As yet she showed no sign of comprehension. "Lady

Cecily, as both of our situations have changed drastically we are both in a position to help one another." Another long-suffering sigh. "I need heirs. You need someone to care for you, someone familiar, someone you know will never hurt you, and I swear to you that if my past has taught me nothing else it has taught me that—"

"Lord Hal?"

Hal nodded as realization settled upon her countenance. "I know I am a good deal older than you are and that till this point you regarded me as a father. But if you can find it in your heart to see me as something else . . . I would make you happy. And you would be here in familiar surroundings instead of being sent off to a new family whom you may not take to, betrothed to a man who might not treat you with the kindness you know I will."

"Lord Hal . . ." Cecily's hand slipped from his arm. Her bow slid out of her hand, leaving her arms to dangle at her sides.

"You may not believe after everything you witnessed between Lady Grace and me that I am capable of making someone happy, but I know if you give me the opportunity I—"

Cecily shook her head. "No, it is not that. I am certain you are capable of it. It is just that . . . it is so unexpected. Brey . . ." She sighed, sinking to the ground. Hal sat beside her, wrapping an arm about her shoulders. "What would Brey make of it?" she whispered.

Hal shook his head. "It is my hope he would bless the union . . . after mocking it, of course."

The smallest smile played across her button mouth. "He would do that," she agreed. "It is just that it is not what I thought would be happening to me now," she sighed.

"I know," he said, his voice soft. "Nothing has gone as expected."

She shook her head.

"If you cannot do it, my lady, if it is too much to ask"—he drew in a breath, stifling a peculiar urge to cry—"I will understand. I will try to secure for you the best match possible with another family."

"I could not bear the thought of leaving here," she said. She turned toward him. "Or you. For however unexpected this may

be, perhaps it is as Father Alec said, that this is the will of God, beyond our understanding but for our own good nonetheless."

Hal smiled, touched at the simple thought, grateful Cecily did
not know how against the match Father Alec was. He was certain
the priest believed this as much against the will of God as was possible.

"I will be a good husband to you, my lady," he said.

"And I will be a good wife," she assured him. At once her face
hardened with a rare sternness. "But there will be conditions."

Hal was taken aback. "Name them, my dear."

"I will oversee the management of the finances," she told him.
"With the help of a treasurer of my choosing. I have noted since
my arrival there has been no treasurer and learned that the ap-
pointment has been vacant since Mirabella's birth. Now, of course,
I know why. But there is no excuse for it to have remained unfilled
for so long."

Hal's eyes widened in surprise. He never imagined Cecily
would have paid such close attention to the running of the household. But then Cecily had been close to Grace. No doubt she had
proved an able instructor, even in her weakest moments. In any
event, this was an asset he had not counted on and he smiled inwardly.

"Of course," he told her. "Is there anything else?"

"I will allot you a small amount for gambling, as I know that
pleases you," she said, her tone all business, the tone of a woman.
"But you will not fritter away my fortune or that of your future
children."

"You are very wise," Hal said with a chuckle. "And I will not
take to the sport so often."

Cecily shrugged. "You may do as you like, but I will have you
know that while I am very young, Lord Hal, I am no fool. I came to
understand my value many years ago, when I first became betrothed to Brey. I will not pretend to believe your motivations have
changed. Our fortunes will be joined just as you have always
wished. But I will not let you squander it away. In turn I will give
you heirs and your name will be passed down through the ages."

Hal shook his head, impressed. "Be my governor, my lady. I give you all authority over my person!"

He felt Cecily relax against his side. He drew her to him, holding her close. She giggled, a girl once more.

"I promise you, Cecily, I will be good to you," he said with fervency. He cradled her head against his chest, stroking the silky rose-gold tresses. "I promise you."

Cecily nuzzled against his chest. "I have no doubt," she told him.

Hal closed his eyes, allowing his tears to fall, murmuring a prayer of thanks to God that she was receptive to the news. He only hoped he could make her as happy as she would no doubt make him.

Cecily found Father Alec in his apartments. As the door was slightly ajar, she offered a polite knock before allowing herself entrance. Her heart caught in her chest.

He was packing.

"Are you going on holiday?" she asked him.

He regarded her, his hazel eyes lit with a sadness she knew somehow had nothing to do with their losses.

"Where are you going, Father?" Her voice rose in panic.

He averted his head, attending to his trunk once more. "London. I have secured a position in the Archbishop of Canterbury's household. It is a wonderful opportunity, more than I could have ever hoped for."

Cecily's heart pounded against her ribs in a painful, erratic rhythm. Her cheeks tingled. "Oh, Father, no! Why?"

"It is time," he said, his husky voice low.

Cecily knelt beside him before the trunk, reaching out to still his hands. He avoided her eyes.

"But, Father, I need you now more than ever," she told him. "I came to tell you that I . . . I am to marry Lord Hal." Her voice was taut with urgency.

"So he stayed the course," he muttered.

"Pardon?"

He waved the thought away. "Pardon me, my lady." He turned

toward her at last, offering a strained smile. "May I offer my congratulations?"

Cecily nodded, tears pooling in the base of her throat. "Oh, Father, it is all too much to take in. So much has happened to us and now this. I know marrying Lord Hal is the right thing to do, and I do bear him affection. Yet still I am so afraid." She lowered her eyes. "But not nearly as afraid as I would be had I been sent away. Mirabella told me of the men in this world—"

"Not all of which are the monsters and devils she painted them as, Lady Cecily," he told her. "You may have been wed to someone of your own age—"

"Or not," Cecily finished for him. "I could have been wed to someone even older than my lord. I could have wed someone cruel . . . and I would have been all alone in a foreign place. This is my world, Father. I belong here. It may not have all come to pass as I had once hoped, but . . ."

"I have underestimated your wisdom," he told her, his voice wavering with admiration. "And your strength."

"I am not strong," she confessed. "I tremble with fear. I am to be a wife now and perhaps a mother soon. I admit I am not ready for it. But I must be. That is why I urge you to remain here with us." Her eyes made their appeal. "Please. We are your family, after all. Do you really think you can help the archbishop more than you can help us? We need you."

Father Alec laid a heavy hand on her shoulder. "Have faith that God will guide you. And have faith in yourself, Lady Cecily, just as I have always had faith in you," he told her. "I am sorry, my lady. Please know my leaving has no bearing on you personally. It is just that I have outlived my usefulness. With you taking on the duties of a countess, you will have no need of a tutor. I cannot be expected to wile away my hours living off your charity. I need to be stimulated again, to find out who I am and what I am about. I feel a call to London. I feel that something is waiting for me there, something that I must be a part of, and that somehow the archbishop is tied to all of that."

Cecily bowed her head. She understood. How could she not? "Then it would be selfish of me to ask you to remain where you would be unhappy," she said in soft tones. She raised her head to meet his tortured hazel gaze. "There is only one thing I request of you, Father."

"Ask and I shall try to accommodate," he told her.

"I want you to officiate the ceremony," she told him. "You have been a part of our lives from the beginning. It was you who brought me here, you who comforted me through all of my trials. What passed before is gone, but something new is about to begin. Be the one to bless the beginning of this journey."

Father Alec swallowed several times, bowing his head. He took her hands in his. They were small, smooth like lilies, the hands of a child-woman.

"Yes, my lady," he told her. "I will."

Father Alec did not understand his reaction to Hal's decision. His unspecified sense of objection was gut wrenching, frustrating him to no end. Certainly he understood the practical necessity of the match—to a degree he even approved of it. It reassured him to know that Cecily would not be sent to a stranger's house where there was no guarantee of her safety and happiness. At least with Hal that much could be counted upon.

Yet the reaction remained, the tightness in his throat, the desire to throw things and shout at the injustice of it all. It was Cecily's age. That must be it. If she were not so young then perhaps he could be more supportive . . . yet what was atypical about her age? It was not unusual for noblewomen to be wed much younger than commoners. Countless cases proved politics and wealth were put before any sensitivity to extreme youth.

Father Alec shook his head, cursing himself. He had grown too close to this family. London would be a welcome change. Things were happening there, exciting things. Changes were being implemented that he would be a part of. And working alongside the archbishop would be a thrill. In London he would be far too preoccupied to be troubled by the complexities of the Pierces.

But before he left there was this last thing, this last request. He was to marry Lord Hal and Lady Cecily, he, whose heart screamed out against some unknown force, was to go against his every sensibility and join them in holy matrimony. He would do it, of course. It was the least he could do for Cecily. And Hal was his friend. He must never lose sight of that, disagree with him though he might.

It was a small wedding with a handful of the local gentry in attendance. Cecily was dressed in a pale yellow gown of silk and a white kirtle embroidered with seed pearls. About her throat was a collar of amber, matching the circlet on her head. Her hair hung loose, flowing down her back in a cascade of rose-gold waves. The candlelight of the chapel was no competition; as she walked down the aisle she emanated a glow from within, softening her features like a painting. A living light . . .

She was escorted by Hal's friend Sir Edward Camden, a grizzled knight who had fought with Hal's father at Flodden and resided at a nearby estate with his brood of sixteen children by three different wives, two of whom had died in childbirth. His latest was a young bride as well, three years Cecily's senior, who had already given him two children. Father Alec gazed at the girl, at the dark circles smudged beneath her eyes, the pallid skin and drawn countenance; she exuded exhaustion. He wondered if he was staring into Cecily's future and shuddered.

He shifted his gaze to Hal, who, he must say, looked splendid in his yellow brocade doublet and hose, which hugged his legs in fine form. He was a handsome man, a youthful man, and when happy radiated a contagious passion for life. Father Alec swallowed an unexpected lump in his throat. This man deserved happiness after his great tragedies. There was no doubt Cecily would provide it.

The couple knelt before the altar. Father Alec raised a hand in blessing, commencing with the ceremony.

When Cecily saw her groom at the altar her heart lurched. Had God's plan been different, a few years from now that very man would have been escorting her down the aisle rather than this crusty old knight, leading her to his son, Brey.

But this was not to be. Hal stood at the altar, not Brey, and now she was beside him. They knelt before Father Alec and Cecily was grateful; her knees were trembling so violently she was certain they would buckle at any moment.

Cecily drew in a breath and slipped her trembling hand into Hal's steady one. He offered her reassuring glances throughout the ceremony, accompanied with cheery smiles. Her own smile was timid. She had never been timid around Hal before; she had always been comfortable to be who she was. Now everything was different. Would he expect her to be someone else now? To be grand and composed and regal?

She had never fretted about such things with Brey. There had existed no pretenses between them, no discomfort, no awkwardness. With him she never questioned herself, never second-guessed.

Brey . . .

She saw him in Hal, in his gentle smile, his twinkling blue eyes, his endearing sweetness. No doubt Brey would have grown into the image of his father.

Brey . . .

Never had she dreamed she would be spending her wedding day with anyone other than him. But here she was, hand in hand with her bridegroom, the father of her former betrothed. He squeezed her hand, spreading an unexpected tingle of warmth throughout her entire body. She fixed her eyes upon him, tilting her head in thought. Hal's tender gaze was filled with nothing but gentle respect. At once she was overwhelmed with reassurance.

He would never expect her to be anyone other than herself, she realized with sudden certainty. She would not have to pretend around him any more than she would have around his son. Now more than ever she saw that Brey had been but an extension of Hal, a boy who was the essence of everything that made his father such a wonderful man.

She squeezed his hand in turn. There was hope.

The rings were exchanged. She slid the gold band up Hal's slim finger. Father Alec's voice swirled around them, husky and low, familiar, another source of reassurance as he blessed their union.

They arose, hands joined. Hal leaned in, brushing his lips against hers in a chaste, gentle kiss.

Cecily faced the guests in attendance for the first time as the Countess of Sumerton, Baroness Burkhart, and Mrs. Harold Pierce.

The wedding banquet was course after course of delicacies— stuffed capons, brawn, puddings, tarts, sugared comfits, breads, and cheeses, all of which Cecily could not enjoy under the scrutiny of the guests. She was no longer a child free to devour everything in sight but a young woman who must exert self-control at every turn. So she picked and nibbled, vowing to make up for it later.

When the trestles were taken down, the floor was open for dancing. Musicians had been hired and the wine flowed freely. Ruddy-cheeked guests clapped their hands and stamped their feet, alternating between hearty country dances and the elegant steps of the court. Hal and Cecily twirled about the floor until the soles of her feet ached. All eyes were upon her, boring into her until the back of her neck prickled with self-consciousness. She heard the whispers.

"Not even a full year of mourning . . ." some said, while another piped in with, "But look at her . . . with her under his roof what choice did he have?" "But she was betrothed to his very own son!" still another cried, scandalized. "Just because the son is no more doesn't mean the father shouldn't still benefit!" a man laughed. "And how he will benefit!" Soft chuckles followed. They were as subtle as possible, gathered in their corners, but wine never improved anyone's ability for discretion and the whispers were stagy and harsh, grating on Cecily's ears.

She pretended to ignore them, taking hold of Hal's hand and tipping back her head, emitting titters of girlish laughter so as to appear the carefree, happy bride.

"They're mad with jealousy," Hal told her. "And I've created scandal once more."

"A happy kind of scandal," Cecily assured him with a smile. "We can be proud to enliven their boring lives!"

Hal laughed, holding her close. He was happy, his voice alternating between soft and low and a crescendo of zeal that tickled her. Like Cecily, Hal's natural inclination toward gaiety abated the deepest melancholy. Tonight he radiated with it and Cecily was thrilled to be the source.

As they returned to the high table, Father Alec joined them. The smile fixed upon his face was incongruent with his somber expression.

"I wanted to offer my congratulations before my departure," he said in soft tones.

"What, you can't be leaving," Cecily breathed in horror. "Not now! What are you thinking?"

Hal's plea was communicated through his expressive blue eyes.

"I am expected sooner than I thought," Father Alec told them, not quite meeting their eyes. His smile was distracted, apologetic.

Cecily's heart sank. "But you cannot leave tonight! It could be dangerous! There could be highwaymen and bandits and all sorts of—"

"Lady Cecily is right, Father, you cannot—"

"Please." Father Alec locked eyes with Hal. His soft tone resounded with underlying intensity. "I must."

Hal bowed his head. He drew in a wavering breath. "Then if you must . . ."

Father Alec turned to Cecily. "My lady, what a pleasure it has been serving you all these years." He bowed over her hand, offering upon it a soft kiss.

On impulse Cecily flung her arms about the priest. "Oh, Father, would that you could remain with us a little longer!" she sobbed, wetting his neck with her tears. "We shall miss you so!"

He rubbed her back a moment before withdrawing. "I am sorry to have to make such a hasty retreat, but my duties lie elsewhere now." His face softened. "Know I shall always remember you and keep you in my prayers."

"You will write to us, won't you?" she asked, her voice small.

Father Alec nodded. Why was he so cool, so offhanded? This had been his home for years and he was behaving as if it and those who resided there had never meant a thing to him!

"Come, Father, let me walk you out," said Hal. Both men bowed toward Cecily, leaving her to stand bewildered, uncertain, and angered by what just came to pass.

"Father, I am saddened that you chose this moment to leave us," Hal said when they were in the crisp coolness of the court-yard. "Lady Cecily did not deserve such disappointment on her wedding day."

"I apologize," Father Alec said in wooden tones.

The men had made it to the stables, where waited Father Alec's horse and cart.

"Are you so very angry with me, Father?" Hal asked. "Even knowing I do not plan to consummate it?"

Father Alec heaved a sigh. "No. I am not angry. I commend your integrity, in fact. And any man of property with the same cir-cumstances and opportunity would do the same," he told him. "I do understand that. Truly."

Hal searched for insincerity, for anger. He found none. He reached out, gripping the priest's forearms in a sign of affection. "If you understand then why not stay? Be our chaplain?"

Father Alec's expression contorted with pain. "Your offer is gen-erous. But I cannot. I find my soul is in a state of . . . unrest, my lord. I need this change."

"But to leave us tonight?" Hal persisted. "Why not at least wait till the morning?"

"I must go now," he said. "I cannot jeopardize my new position by being late."

Hal shook his head, puzzled. Father Alec had always been such an understated man, a font of calm. He was steady, nonchalant, and whenever Hal thought of him brought to mind were his easy smile, his offhanded tone, his self-deprecating humor. For years he had been so much more to his family than mere tutor. He was con-fessor, compassionate counselor, wise adviser, and treasured friend.

The man standing before him now was a stranger—uneasy, skit-tish. He was a man in agony.

"Father, in all the years I have known you, you have been nothing but a friend to me," Hal told him in gentle tones. "If there is something I can ever do to help you, I would hope you would trust me enough to let me."

"I appreciate that," Father Alec said, bowing his head. "All I ask of you is to let me go. I—I must go."

Hal released his forearms. Tears clenched his throat. "You will visit us, I hope?" he asked.

Father Alec offered his best imitation of a smile. "Of course." Tears trapped in moonlight glistened off his cheeks, shimmering like opals. He laid a hand on Hal's shoulder. "Thank you for your hospitality these years past and for your kind recommendation; I shall never forget it. You are a good man, Lord Hal. I know that."

"Godspeed, Father," Hal said softly.

Father Alec climbed up on the cart, flicked the reins, and was consumed by the blackness of night.

He did not look back.

Father Alec wondered what Hal would have made of his lying to him, for there was no reason he could not have stayed the night through. He was not late. Indeed, he was not expected in London for another two weeks. The inn he had chosen to stay at was a mere ten miles from Castle Sumerton.

Father Alec left on impulse. He simply had to get away. He could not be there tonight; he could not bear the thought of Hal taking the love of that sweet innocent.

And, for love of God, he could not understand why.

And so he rode through the night, listening to the hooves pounding against the road, matching the beating of his racing heart. As each mile was put between him and Sumerton, leaving the suffocating complexities of its world behind him, the painful knot in his gut eased. He had no desire to analyze his feelings.

He was getting out.

❧ 9 ❧

The hour that Cecily had been anticipating with the most fear had arrived. Exhausted revelers had departed or taken to their beds and she was led to her apartments, where she would await her bridegroom. She was dressed in a white silk nightdress trimmed with yellow ribbons. Nurse Matilda, who was elevated to the station of lady's maid, brushed her hair to a golden sheen.

"You mustn't fret, my lady," she murmured sweetly as she smoothed her hair with her hands. "The pain passes very quickly."

Cecily trembled. "Pain?" she squeaked. Her voice was caught in her throat, mingling with a sob as she was tucked into bed. Matilda sat beside her, stroking her cheek.

"It is a pain we all bear, and not nearly so bad as childbirth," she told her in tender tones, offering a chuckle. "You will not even remember it come morning."

Cecily doubted this but accepted the well-meaning words with a smile.

When Lord Hal arrived dressed in naught but his shift Cecily drew the covers over her shoulders with an involuntary shiver.

Matilda bowed, offering Cecily a conspiratorial wink as she made her exit.

Hal sighed, stretching. "And now what I've been waiting for!" he cried as he fairly jumped into the bed.

Cecily's heart lurched. This was not a side of Lord Hal she had been expecting.

He leaned over, brushing his lips against her cheek. "I am exhausted! Good night, my dear," he told her as he settled against the pillows, drawing the covers to his neck.

"You mean . . . you mean you're not . . . ?" Cecily hoped the relief in her voice would not offend him.

Hal chuckled. "What manner of scoundrel do you take me for?" he asked her. "I am only sleeping in here to satisfy the guests. I even brought in a wineskin filled with pig's blood for the sheets!" He laughed at his cleverness, then reached over to stroke her cheek. His teeth shone bright white in the moonlight and Cecily found herself smiling in turn.

"Lord Hal . . ." Cecily said, touched. She slid closer to him, snuggling against his warm chest, finding solace in his steady heartbeat. "Thank you."

"Not a minute before you're ready, sweeting," he whispered, wrapping his arms around her and kissing the top of her head. "Not a minute before . . ."

Cecily nuzzled her head in the crook of his shoulder.

How easy he is to love, she thought.

Mirabella analyzed the latest news from home while tending the gardens one afternoon with Sister Julia. Her hands trembled with rage as they worked the earth. Her father . . . her father and Cecily. A thirty-nine-year-old man and a fourteen-year-old girl! This made him no better than King Henry when he had taken after Anne Boleyn's sister, Mary! She had never thought to liken her father to the king. Had he no shame, no decency? Let alone he was supposed to be in mourning for his wife and son—Cecily's former betrothed! The affair filled her with disgust.

"What did you expect him to do?" Sister Julia asked in gentle tones. Mirabella had chosen to confide in her; she found she could not shut her out. What's more, she did not want to; the relationship they were developing was akin to the friendship they had known before and Sister Julia proved Mirabella's only confidante besides the confessor. "Did you think someone of your father's standing would let his legacy die with him? Mirabella, you are nothing if not perceptive."

"But Cecily!" she whispered, ever observant of their muted world.

"She was his ward, under his protection," Sister Julia said. "Would any man in his right mind send her away with what she had to offer? Mirabella, you must think in reality."

"It is disrespectful on both parts," Mirabella pouted. "She was to marry Brey! And now look, a stepmother five years my junior—"

"You are no longer of her world," Sister Julia interposed. "Thus her world should not concern you, save to keep her in your prayers. Keep in mind how limited her choices were. Would you rather she had been warded to strangers? You know as well as I what could have befallen her. Yes, she was to marry Brey, but he was called to God. You can thank that same God that she has your father—and that your father has her. They have a common bond in their familiarity. And Cecily is good and sweet, you know that. She is young and strong and will give him heirs."

Mirabella grimaced. "It is a disgrace. My father grows foolhardy in his dotage," she muttered.

"Oh, my dear girl, your father is hardly in his 'dotage'! Why do you insist on turning your back on peace?" Sister Julia asked as she rose, balancing her basket of vegetables on her hip. She shook her head at the stubborn postulant.

Mirabella raised her face to the nun who was her mother. "I turn my back on peace?" she asked in low tones. "I, who reach out for it, only to grasp at nothing?" She shook her head. "No. Peace betrayed me. It has evaded me since the day you brought me into this world."

With that she rose, quitting the garden. It was time for Vespers. She had best go through the motions of being at peace with God.

Hal and Cecily fell into the same routine they had known before their nuptials, with one exception. Father Alec was gone. Every corner seemed to reflect his vacancy and Cecily's heart clenched with grief whenever she thought of her tutor. She found herself missing the oddest things, things she hadn't even realized she cherished—the distinct huskiness of his voice, his offhanded manner, his gentle eyes, his lazy smile, the faintest trace of an accent betraying his Welsh heritage. Strange little things, the way the veins stood out in his hand when he wrote, the way his brows knitted together when he lectured, the low timbre of his voice when he discussed something he was passionate about. She missed him. She missed him, but he was gone. He wanted to go; indeed, he had seemed desperate, a fact that she would never understand. Yet there was nothing she could do but savor the memories of a childhood he had enriched, knowing beyond any doubt her transition into the Pierce household would not have been made with as much ease had he not been there to guide her.

And so she kept the priest in her prayers, along with Mirabella and all those who went before, while she tried to concentrate on her present estate.

Hal was the center of her world now. Cecily was married but not quite a wife. She still found herself regarding Hal as a kind of father. The affection he bore her was only altered by the fact that they were completely alone. The love once spent on Brey and Mirabella was now lavished upon her. In his loneliness he reached out to her; she curled in his lap before the fire at night for long hours as he spoke of his day, of the antics of his tenants, of a particularly good hunt, or an amusing anecdote he had heard about the court. They still played games together, still went hunting and riding. The golden bands about their fingers uniting them as man and wife seemed not to affect their relationship in the slightest.

Though they did take on a treasurer to manage the finances, Hal was still allotted a modest amount for gambling and paid calls to his friends to indulge in the sport, leaving Cecily alone with no one but the servants. It was at these times that the suffocating loneliness closed in around her. She was assaulted by thoughts of the past. What would she and Brey be doing now? What would Lady Grace be doing? Was there any chance she could have stayed well? They were useless thoughts, these, and only served to knot her gut with anxiety. Nonetheless, she was stalked by relentless reflections, for with her only distraction away, there was naught to do but think and pace and think some more until Hal at last came home.

One night he did not come home at all. He arrived the next day in the midafternoon, blustery and ruddy cheeked from riding against the autumn wind.

Cecily, gripped with anxiety, had been pacing the great hall for hours. When he burst in all smiles her relief was replaced by unexpected anger. She resisted the urge to throw her arms about him, stamping her foot instead.

"Lord Hal!" she cried. Her lip quivered.

"Darling!" he cried, making long strides toward her to grip her upper arms. He planted a kiss on her forehead. "What is it, dearest?"

"What is it?" Cecily retorted, pulling away and folding her arms across her budding breasts. "Oh, my lord, how could you stay out all night without sending word? I was worried unto death! No doubt you were treating yourself to a marvelous time while I paced and waited imagining all manner of ill fortune befalling you! Not to mention the company you could be keeping . . . How do I know you're not with—with—" Tears clouded her vision as a strange sensation caught her off guard. Jealousy. It shocked her beyond measure. The feeling seared through her breast like an arrow's tip as her mind's eye conjured up a buxom blonde sitting on Hal's lap, stroking his cheek, running her fingers through his hair. And yet was this an unreasonable fear? Hal was a handsome still-young man, in good form, and in possession of great charm. When a woman, a grown woman with breasts and hips and woman's charms, learned he was married to a girl with the décolletage of an eight-year-old boy . . . Cecily squeezed her eyes against the unwelcome imagery.

Hal drew her close, rubbing her back and making little shushing noises of consolation. "I had no idea," he said, his voice soft with surprise. "I am unaccustomed to people wondering after my whereabouts. I will never be so thoughtless again." He kissed the top of her head. "And as for the company I keep, don't fret. All old curmudgeons." He pulled away, cupping her cheek in his hand.

The fondness in his twinkling blue eyes sent a wave of reassurance warm as wine through Cecily as she leaned into his hand.

"And their wives? How do they occupy themselves?" she asked him, sniffling. "The same way I do? Pacing and waiting?"

"I am a witless idiot," he said, lifting her in his arms. She wrapped hers about his neck as he carried her into the solar. He lowered them onto the settle. "I suppose I never considered how lonely it must be for you here now that . . ." He let the thought hang between them.

Cecily, knowing there was no need to expound on it, pressed her cheek against his. "I am sorry, my lord, for being cross," she said in small tones, still shaken by the sense of protectiveness that overtook her at the thought of Hal in danger, even if that danger meant falling prey to another woman's charms. "All I could think of as I waited out the night was, 'What if something happens to my lord? How will I live without him whom I have come to love so well?' "

Hal drew in a wavering breath, clutching her to him as he kissed her cheek.

"I am to pay Sir Edward Camden a visit tomorrow," he told her in husky tones as he swayed from side to side. Cecily recalled Sir Edward as the gentleman who had escorted her down the aisle at her wedding. "How would you like to accompany me? You and his wife, the Lady Alice, are of an age; perhaps you would enjoy her company?"

"Oh, yes!" Cecily cried, snuggling even closer against him. "Do take me with you!"

"Wherever I go, sweetheart," he said, holding her tight.

As he held the slight creature in his arms, relishing her scent, her softness, her sweetness, his heart constricted with a love he had never imagined possible, at least not for him. He had never loved the woman who became Sister Julia. Theirs was a connection based on sheer lust. Now that Hal knew the truth of it he considered it divine irony that devout Mirabella was born of such a union.

The love he bore Lady Grace was based on companionship, forged in mutual strife and pain. That pain tainted everything, every touch, every smile, every act, at last devouring every tangible sensation. At the end of the day, there was nothing left to give. Empty apologies had been made. The words floated around them, useless. The love that had waned and waxed over the years had in the end, the very end, proved itself unsalvageable.

Now Cecily, this gift, this miracle, remained to heal his shattered heart, his broken soul. Cecily, more than he could have dared dream of. Cecily . . . He would not repeat his mistakes. He would make her happy, despite their age difference, despite everything, he would make her happy.

And if God was as merciful as He was proving thus far, perhaps He would see fit that she love him as he so completely and inexplicably loved her. . . .

Cecily was so struck by the reaction her loneliness for Hal had inspired that she did not want to sleep alone that night. Since their wedding guests had departed they had taken to sleeping in separate chambers, and though Cecily was still not ready to consummate the marriage, she thought it would do no harm to at least sleep beside her husband. And so she followed him to bed that night.

"This place is too large. Our apartments are on opposite wings," she told him. "It is silly. And it does become so cold. . . ."

"If I did not know you I would call you a vixen," Hal told her with a throaty chuckle. "I do not know, Cecily." He drew in a breath. "To be honest, it is far easier for me to be honorable if we are in separate chambers."

"Oh," Cecily said, bowing her head. "I suppose I did not think of it like that."

"Do not think I am turning you away . . ." he reassured her. "But I am afraid I will lose control." He bowed his head. "And I do not want to frighten you."

Cecily smiled. "You could never frighten me, my lord." She strode toward him, reaching up to stroke his beard. "We are joined together under God, Lord Hal. Our bed is sacred and I am not afraid of what may take place in it. We will sleep beside one another. Whatever happens is meant to be."

"Dearest girl," Hal murmured, drawing her into his arms for a tight embrace.

Cecily crawled into his bed, drawing the covers to her neck as she watched him remove his doublet, revealing beneath it, to her utmost horror, a hair shirt. "My lord!" she cried.

"Oh, this," he said with a careless shrug. "I suppose you have never seen me unclothed before. . . . I— It is my penance."

"For what, my lord?" Cecily asked him, crawling out of bed to approach him. "For sins you have more than paid for?"

Hal shifted from one bare foot to the other, averting his head, as though caught committing some grievous sin instead of trying to repent for one.

Cecily drew in a breath. *How much sadness this man has known!* she thought as her eyes found themselves resting on the sandglass Hal kept on his bedside table. Brightening, she retrieved it, tipping it back and forth, watching the grains of sand slide from one end to the other.

"Do you know what this represents?" she asked him in soft tones.

"Time," he answered, matching her tone with his own.

"This kept time in the past," she told him. "Each grain of sand represents every old sin, every old hurt." Cecily headed toward the bay window, unlatched it, and pressed it open. For a moment she held the sandglass by her fingertips. "God forgives, my lord," she reminded him. "Our sins to Him are as these grains of sand." She let go. The sandglass plunged to the earth, shattering. "Cast to the winds. Forgotten."

She approached Hal, removing his hair shirt. "We will have a new sandglass, one that keeps time for our *now*." She smiled. "No more hair shirts. No more punishments. Now is a time to begin again. First with a bath to cleanse your wounds," she added with a smile. "And then a healing ointment. It is time to heal, my lord. Time to renew and start again."

Tears glistened off Hal's cheeks as he regarded her. "Cecily . . ." he breathed in awe. He opened his arms. Cecily ran into them, holding him close.

Hal turned down the bed and Cecily crawled in once more. He slid in beside her, wrapping his arms about her to hold her close.

"I meant what I said, though," he told her. "About waiting. I never want to hurt you, Cecily."

"I know," she said, squeezing him about the middle. "I know."

And after a warm bath was ordered for Hal that the cleansing of his self-inflicted wounds might start, they passed another chaste night.

To his surprise, Hal found that his love for Cecily made this easy to do.

Cecily awoke to the ringing of bells. "I haven't heard the like since Queen Anne's coronation!" she cried, running across the rush-strewn floor to the window, flinging it open to a burst of warm air. Below, the gardener was clipping at the ivy that crawled up the side of the castle like a great searching hand. "What news, sir?" she cried.

"That'd be the birth announcement, milady!" he shouted back with a smile of his own.

"Oh!" she cried, pressing her hands to her cheeks in excitement. "Have you heard? Is it a prince?"

The old man shook his head. "A wee princess," he said. "Poor little mite."

Cecily's heart lurched as she thought of the new queen, who had held the hopes of a kingdom in her womb. Now she would be considered a disappointment, and after all the grief she went through in her elevation to queenhood. Oh, the poor lady . . . Cecily found her hand straying to her flat belly, wondering how disappointed Hal would be in her should she bring him females.

Of course there was no need to fret about that at the rate they were going. Hal was so respectful of her sensibilities that Cecily ruefully believed she would not become a mother till she was forty and toothless.

Cecily pushed the thought from her mind as she waved to the gardener. "Well, God keep her!" she cried, shutting the window. Hal had risen and dressed.

"A girl," he breathed. "Poor Harry."

"Poor Harry!" Cecily cried. "The poor queen! She must be mad with fear." She paused to call for Matilda. "Everything is different in Henry's England," she said. "He put one queen aside for providing naught but a female. Nothing will prevent him from doing the same with her."

Hal waved the thought away with a laugh. "He wouldn't want to go through all that trouble again. That was a six-year ordeal! No. Our Queen Anne is young and has proved herself fertile. So the first one's a girl; it will make the birth of their prince all the sweeter."

Cecily recalled the confident woman riding in her litter all covered in gems. "I suppose if anyone can hold a king she can," she said.

"Only because his eyes have not beheld you," he said with such profound sincerity Cecily was touched.

"Who would want to be a queen when they could be your wife?" she asked him, and found that it was not mere cleverness that motivated the retort.

She meant it.

Sir Edward Camden was visibly shocked when Hal called upon him with Cecily on his arm. The rheumy eyes lit with pleasant surprise, however, abating the knot of awkwardness in Cecily's gut as they were shown into his solar.

"Well, isn't this wonderful!" said the old man as he limped to his chair. He flagged down his steward. "Albert, send for my wife," he ordered, returning his attention to Cecily. He drank her in with his eyes; it was not a comforting assessment. Cecily shifted in her seat. "So pretty," he murmured, stroking his beard.

Cecily bowed her head. "Thank you, sir," she replied, entwining her hand in Hal's, who offered a squeeze of reassurance.

"I had thought on your wedding day that your beauty was exaggerated by the stunning attire. . . . I see now I was wrong," Sir Edward said, wagging his bushy gray brows at her. "And still so young; imagine when your beauty has reached its peak! Hal, you're a lucky man!"

"You honor me with your fair words, sir," Cecily said, stifling her annoyance and feeling an immediate sympathy for his wife, who was making her entrance.

The men in the room rose, offering bows, while Cecily inclined her head with a timid smile at the pale-faced girl who seemed to drown in her pink taffeta gown. Sir Edward wrapped his arm about her waist, then, to Cecily's utter shock, squeezed her rump. The girl averted her flushing face with a grimace.

"Here she is!" He laughed. "This is my Lady Alice." He jerked his head at Cecily. "You remember Lady Cecily, Hal's young bride."

Cecily rose. "I am afraid we were prevented from getting better acquainted due to all the wedding festivities." The smile she offered was warm. "I am glad for the opportunity to know you better."

Alice extended her hand. Cecily took it, noting a sense of desperation in the squeeze offered.

"Shall we leave the men to their conversation?" Alice asked, Cecily's hand still in hers. "I should love to show you the tapestry I have been embroidering."

Cecily nodded.

"Behave yourselves, ladies!" Sir Edward called after them as they quit the room.

As the girls navigated their way through the manor they encountered a passel of children, boys and girls of ages varying from four to what looked like Cecily's own, running about like a band of wild Scots. While some screamed and squabbled, leaping and turning about in somersaults, the older lads paused to gawk at their stepmother and her guest, causing goose pimples to rise on Cecily's flesh as she averted her head to find two of them engaged in a mock sword fight on the table of the great hall!

"Oh, these?" Alice quipped when noting Cecily's overwhelmed expression. "Yes, the house is positively crawling with them—and there used to be more." She grimaced. "Thank God two have married and two have become monks—not that there is a pious bone in the body of any Camden," she went on as they walked. "Nine were born of his first wife," she explained. "The last five are from the second. I suppose the reason for their deaths warrants no explanation," she added with a smirk. Then to the boys: "Can't you pretend civility for one blooming day, at least in front of the company?"

The boys paused a moment, looked at her, then shrugged and returned to their amusements.

"A pox on you all, then!" she murmured.

Alice did not relinquish Cecily's hand till they reached her apartments. There she collapsed against the wall, giggling. "Oh, thank God you're here!" she cried, trading her weariness for animation. "I shall go mad without some gentle society!"

"I see why!" Cecily cried before she could help herself.

Alice, a plain-faced, auburn-haired girl with keen brown eyes and a boyish figure, exuded cheer and good humor despite circumstances that Cecily regarded as intolerable. Her heart constricted with a mingling of empathy and admiration for the girl as she watched her swagger to the large embroidery frame across which was stretched plain white fabric.

"My tapestry," she said, with an elaborate hand gesture. "As you can see, it's nearly done."

Cecily laughed. There was not a single stitch on it.

"I call it 'Clouds,' " Alice went on.

Cecily laughed harder, till her gut began to ache. Alice added her own laughter; it was a robust sound that bordered on hysteria. When the girls wiped the tears from their eyes, Cecily noted that Alice's expression had converted from one of merriment to tragedy.

"You married an older man, too," she said in soft tones. "Does he treat you well?"

Cecily's throat constricted in guilt as she thought of gentle Hal. She almost did not want to admit her good fortune, lest she make the poor girl regard her lot as even more pitiable.

"He is a good man," she said.

"He is not rough with you?" Alice asked, lowering her eyes.

Cecily's heart sank. Now she understood more than ever why Mirabella took the veil. Sir Edward was the type of man Mirabella had referred to when she shared her fears. At once Cecily hated him and all men like him.

"It must be wonderful," Alice said in wistful tones. "Edward is an ass and his sons, the older ones, they're just as bad. My only relief comes when they go carousing in Lincoln." She shrugged, then offered a rueful smile.

"Oh, my lady!" Cecily cried, taking her hand once more. "I am so sorry."

Alice shook her head, drawing in a wavering breath. She wiped her eyes, then brightened. "Do you want to see *my* children?"

"Very much," Cecily answered.

Alice led her to the nursery. A two-year-old girl just out of swaddling bands toddled toward them, stretching her arms toward her mother. Alice lifted her up, squeezing her tight as they made their way to a cradle in which was snuggled another infant girl of about eight months. She scrutinized the visitors with earnest brown eyes.

"My daughters," Alice said. "Ellen and Margery."

Cecily's heart lurched with an unexpected longing as she reached down to caress the silky cheek of the baby. "They're beautiful."

"They're girls," Alice said, her tone soft with fear. "And I pray I can ward them off to the convent as soon as they are able." She lowered her head, kissing the blond hair of the baby in her arms. "It is not good to be a girl in this house."

Cecily did not know how to address the statement, or if it even should be, so remained silent a moment while Alice set little Ellen on her unsteady feet once more.

"Is it very painful having babies?" she decided to ask.

Alice laughed. "I'm still here," she told her. "And I had Ellen when I was about your age. It isn't pleasant, but we're all proof that it can be done."

Cecily offered her own uncertain laugh.

"It is harder afterwards," Alice said, her tone contemplative as she regarded the cradle. "They are so foreign, you know? The nurse takes them and there is naught to do but have more." She offered that rueful smile again, a smile that Cecily was certain was her feeble attempt at masking immense pain. "They grow on you, though," she added with her infectious chuckle.

Alice blew a kiss to Ellen, who returned it with a little giggle as they quit the nursery and alighted to her apartments. Alice sent for some bread and cheese and they took to playing a game of chess. Alice proved herself quite the strategist and bested Cecily at each turn.

After three games Sir Edward's voice rang through the hall. "Ladies! Supper!"

Alice grimaced toward the sound, then turned to Cecily.

"I hope you come again," she said, her eyes lit with anticipation.

"I shall," said Cecily. She cast her eyes toward the tapestry frame. "We will work on your tapestry together."

"I will like that."

Cecily stood. She could not wait to go home, to throw herself in Hal's arms and tell him that no bride was more blessed than she.

The longer Father Alec Cahill served as a secretary in Archbishop Thomas Cranmer's bustling household, the more he was able to distance himself from his former life at Sumerton. Even had he the inclination to reflect upon the past, he would have little time for it. Almost every waking hour was devoted to assisting the archbishop in the management of his personal affairs, and as Father Alec learned more about Cranmer he found his admiration for the man evolving into genuine affection. The man was never anything but amiable, despite an enormous amount of pressure, but the archbishop carried himself with a poise, graciousness, and remarkable gentleness that Father Alec respected. It was, to his delight, a regard that was mutual, for Cranmer had nothing but kind words to bestow upon him, praising his sincerity, wit, and easy manner.

"We are two nobodies who were elevated by great Somebodies!" Cranmer would tease, his squinty brown eyes narrowing even more as his lips curled up into a gentle smile. "You by your fortunate encounter with Erasmus and the Earl of Sumerton and me by our loving Sovereign! To think it was all because I made the suggestion for him to interview men of learning when he was pursuing his annulment from Princess Dowager Catherine. 'I had the right sow by the ear,' he had said," he added with a chuckle.

It was an overwhelming circumstance for both, who emerged from relative obscurity to hold positions other men envied. What was most remarkable, however, was the genuine affection both held for their employers. Cranmer loved King Henry and Father Alec loved Cranmer. Subtle, gentle, and kind, the Archbishop of Canterbury stood for many of the reforms that Father Alec held dear. If Cranmer could keep that certain sow by the ear his reforms had a chance of being brought to fruition.

Working closely with Cranmer gave Father Alec the opportunity to observe his "loving Sovereign," who fairly radiated with the light of his own power. Despite the king's magnetism, Father Alec found himself far more drawn to his scintillating wife Queen Anne, a fascinating woman of sharp wit and humor. Bent on keeping the court spiritual, the queen gave all of her ladies prayer books to hang from their girdles at all times and encouraged acts of charity to the poor. She was a glib creature, unafraid to speak her mind, and often challenged the king to daring duels of wits regarding matters of religion and affairs of state. It was clear she was in favor of reform, and for this Father Alec admired her.

For all his admiration, however, he feared for the dark-haired girl whose edgy nature and intensity was too reminiscent of Mirabella Pierce. Such traits may not favor her. Already the king's affection was waning; she had brought forth a girl, a burden and liability. Anne would have to prove herself, and quick, if she wanted to keep her place at his side.

And King Henry would be a difficult man to be beside, Father Alec noted as he recalled the moody, charismatic man with a laugh as robust as his appetites. Father Alec could hardly disguise his disillusionment, for it became obvious to him that the king's split with the Pope had nothing to do with reform or doctrine and everything to do with getting his own way. Father Alec kept his peace around the king, wary of the man who daily demonstrated a range of startling emotional extremes. At the slightest provocation, his boisterous, merry nature that was so much larger than life could convert into a temper tantrum with disastrous consequences for the offender. Despite this, Cranmer's deep affection for the king was real.

"There is a thread of the divine in him," Cranmer had told Father Alec with conviction when they returned from Westminster one evening. "Our king is ordained by God to rule and I am ordained by God to serve. As servant to the king I must try to guide him, mentor him . . . protect him. Above all, however, I must obey him." Cranmer turned searching brown eyes to the priest. They flickered with fear. "We all must."

The advice was sobering, alluding to the power King Henry had, power given by none other than God. His ways, God's and Henry's, were not always easy to decipher and yet they must be accepted. For God's will and Henry VIII's were one and the same.

Father Alec tried to believe this.

❧ 10 ❧

Cecily was determined to fulfill at least part of her wifely oblig-
ations to Hal and decided if there was one thing she could do
for him it would be to reestablish his place in society. Before the
scandal of Lady Grace's last entertainment, Hal had been included
in the uppermost realm of the elite and his was considered envi-
able company to keep. Now he lived in obscurity, retaining friend-
ships with a select few. Cecily knew well he feared never being
able to emerge from the shadow of his late wife's indignity, but
now he had a new wife. And this wife would make herself the most
charming, sought-after hostess in the land. If at first they would
not come for Hal, they would come for Cecily, out of curiosity if
nothing else.

She enlisted the help of her new friend, Lady Alice Camden,
hoping to rescue the girl from her wretched household as often as
possible, as she organized her first grand entertainment. Drawing
on her many lessons in the running of a household from Lady
Grace, Cecily planned an exquisite menu and set to hiring the
finest musicians in northern England for the guests to dance to.
The castle was sweetened, all the rooms cleaned and aired, made
ready to be filled with people, with friends.

She did not only plan to enchant the nobility, those many con-
nections that had been made with Sumerton since before her time;

she wanted the respect of Sumerton's tenants as well. Cecily rejuvenated another tradition Hal had let fade away since the fall of
Lady Grace, that of holding feasts on saint's days, inviting all of
their tenants to partake. Cecily's heart swelled at the joy of the
peasants, whom she introduced herself to, trying to learn as much
as she could about each of them and their families. She planned to
call on them and attend to their needs in the manner of a true lady.

In the span of a few months' time, Cecily had made tremendous
progress, demonstrating all the organizational skills of one called
to run a noble house. As she planned her debut, Cecily invited the
nobility, local gentry, bishops, artists, and thinkers to dine at
Sumerton. She and Alice referred to these evenings as "audition
suppers," where Cecily would establish her reputation as the
charming, hospitable, and fashionable Lady Sumerton. She entertained her guests by playing her lute, at which she had become
quite accomplished through the years of hoping to impress Mirabella and Brey. She also sang ballads that brought tears to men's
eyes.

With the ladies she shared her flawless embroidery and discussed household management, flattering them with her display of
eagerness to learn from their wisdom. Though she kept herself educated on the latest news from court, including both politics and
gossip, she could never be accused of offering opinions containing
the faintest scent of scandal. Cecily remained witty, vibrant, and
smiling alongside a husband whose own exuberance grew with
each passing day.

Her reward was the compliments he received on her behalf.

"Lord Hal," one gentleman had told him at the end of an
evening as he clasped his hand, his gaze never leaving Cecily's
face, "you have yourself a true lady."

Cecily glowed under the praise.

To her great satisfaction, the invitations requesting Lord and
Lady Sumerton's presence began to pour in and they did not
refuse a single one. When the time came for their great entertainment, the castle was overflowing with guests to the point where
some had taken to sleeping in the stables.

She spent the evening dancing in a satin gown the color of yellow topaz. No cruel whispers reached her ear this evening. Forgotten was the fact that she and Hal had married before the period of mourning had elapsed and the image of Lady Grace as a figure of scandal had faded; gossipmongers were too caught up in the charms of Lord Sumerton's new bride to obsess over the antics of the old. Cecily was grateful to be the distraction. She did not want Lady Grace's name to be sullied any longer. If the only way for that to happen was in her being relegated to obscurity then so be it; Cecily was certain Lady Grace, with her wry wit, would understand. As Cecily reflected on this she wondered what Brey would make of her strategy to restore his father. Yet in his restoration was not Brey's memory being honored as well? Cecily bowed her head, offering a quick prayer to him, hoping he knew that her every action was motivated by love. The squeeze she received from Hal's hand in her own sent a wave of reassurance through her and she lifted her face to him. The tenderness shining forth from his sparkling blue eyes told her everything she needed to know. Her heart swelled.

"How can I ever thank you for everything you have done, for the life you have returned to this empty place?" Hal asked.

"If I have made you happy in any way, Hal, it is in an effort to thank you." She cupped his face between her hands. "Because I am so grateful to you for being the man that you are."

"I wouldn't be anything without you," Hal said, his voice catching as he held her close.

Cecily closed her eyes, nuzzling against his chest.

I have done a good thing, she thought with an air of triumph.

The Sumertons' triumphant entertainment brought a close to a season of socializing as Lent made its stoic approach. Cecily found herself thinking of Mirabella and sent her a letter once a week, updating Mirabella on all the news, but the responses she received were rare, brief, and impersonal.

Hal heard from Mirabella even less.

"Perhaps it is the marriage that has upset her," Hal said softly one night as they sat before the fire, burning low in its hearth. "You are so young, after all. . . ." He rose to fetch the stoker.

Cecily bowed her head. She admitted to being troubled by that thought as well, but Mirabella's absence from their daily lives made it easier for her to accept the probability that she was disappointed.

"I suppose we have to acknowledge the fact that we just are not a part of her world any longer," Hal went on in decisive tones. "I only wish we could visit now and again. . . ."

"Strange to think how easy it was for us to visit the convent when we were younger," Cecily mused as she stared into the embers, swallowing a rising lump in her throat. "But that was due to Sister Julia."

"It was due to my generosity," Hal corrected. "A generosity that continues. It is unfortunate, Cecily, but even the holiest institutions can be bought."

"Then why not see her?" Cecily asked him. Her stomach lurched with a peculiar dread as she imagined him beholding Sister Julia again. "We could go together," she added.

Hal smiled, leaning on the stoker a moment and massaging his forehead with his fingertips before speaking. "I would much rather she came here."

The knot in Cecily's stomach eased. She sighed, fearing she was betraying her relief. "Perhaps something can be arranged," she said hopefully.

"Perhaps," Hal said as he approached her, taking her hands in his.

"Hal . . ." Cecily bit her lip. She cursed herself for her need to know. "If you saw Sister Julia again . . ."

Hal met her eyes with a steady, unyielding gaze. "I would say, 'Sister Julia, I would like to present to you my wife, Cecily, Lady Sumerton.' "

Cecily dissolved into tears of gratitude and embarrassment as she wrapped her arms about his neck. He embraced her with one arm, then began to shrug his shoulder several times.

"I . . . can't . . . raise . . ."

Cecily pulled away. "Hal, what is it?"

His eyes were panic stricken. "M'arm," he said through the right side of his mouth. "Cec—"

"Hal!"

Hal slipped from her arms to the floor.

"Apoplexy," Dr. George Hurst said after examining Hal. They stood at the foot of his bed, and though Cecily listened to the physician's words, her gaze did not leave Hal's sleeping face.

Don't take him, was her urgent plea to God as she regarded Hal, rendered useless by a force no one understood. *Please don't take him, too!*

"It can cripple a man for life; it can kill him," Dr. Hurst went on. "No one knows how and no one knows why."

Cecily's heart pounded as she sat beside Hal, reaching out to clasp his limp hand. "So you do not know if he will ever recover?"

The old man shook his head. "Regrettably, no. I do know that the longer my lord remains asleep the less likely it will be that he recovers. I am afraid it is in God's hands now. I shall pray for you both, my lady."

Cecily offered a brief nod of thanks as the kindly physician quit the room. She was alone. She collapsed to her knees beside the bed, never loosening her grip on Hal's hand.

"Please, God," she prayed in fervent tones. "Please do not take him. He is a good man, a young man without heirs to succeed him. And he is my everything. Please . . ." She sank her head onto the mattress, sobbing and repeating her prayer till her throat was raw.

At last she fell into a dreamless slumber, snuggling against her unconscious husband. She would not let him go.

She had enough will to sustain them both.

"My lady, you cannot mean to take this on yourself!" Matilda, the maid, cried as Cecily undressed Hal and ventured to change his linens for the first time. "Such work is beneath you—such work is beneath *me!*"

Cecily whirled upon the servant, raising her hand, then lowering it in shock. She had never thought to slap anyone before.

"I am his *wife*, Tillie!" Cecily told her. "Did I not take a vow that required my presence in sickness and in health? Who then is better suited to care for him?"

Matilda bowed her head. "But he may never recover—"

"That is the last time you will say that unless you wish to be dismissed," Cecily said. "Lord Sumerton will recover and anyone who cares for him will speak nothing but words of encouragement. Why, look, already the color has returned to his cheeks!"

Cecily searched his pallid face. "Well, they are a little rosier," she insisted as she drew the covers back. She bit her quivering lip. She had never seen Hal unclothed before and never imagined it would be under these circumstances that she would behold him for the first time. Ashamed that he must suffer such an indignity, she averted her head as much as was possible while she completed the task of cleansing and changing him.

A hand rested on her shoulder and Cecily tilted her face toward Matilda.

"God bless you, my lady," Matilda told her, her voice wavering with tears.

Cecily reached up, squeezing her faithful servant's hand. "I'm sorry I lost my temper, Tillie," she told her.

Matilda shook her head in wonder as Cecily sat by Hal's side once more and commenced to chatter with him about nonsensical things, things that seemed far removed from where they were just now.

Hal did not awaken for three days and when at last he did open his right eye, bringing the face of his precious Cecily into focus, he found his body would not obey him. His left arm and leg were all but numb. His mind told them to move, but they would not. He groaned in frustration, finding that the left side of his mouth was not inclined to be useful either.

"Hal!" Cecily cried, flinging her arms about his chest and kissing his cheek. Tears streamed down her alabaster cheeks. "Oh, Hal, you've come back to me. I knew that you would."

He attempted to smile.

"Can you move at all?" she asked him.

"Yes," Hal said as he shook his throbbing head. He scowled. He didn't know why he said yes when he meant no.

Cecily smiled. "Well, we have time to work on that later. First you must eat. I have broth all prepared for you and bread and some cheese." She fluffed the pillows behind him and, with a strength he had no idea she possessed, pulled him into an elevated position. "Here now, take this." She clasped his right hand, placing a cup of wine in it. "Drink."

Hal's hand trembled as he raised the cup to his lips. Half of it poured down the side of his face. He thrust the cup into Cecily's hands in despair. He longed to rail against the fates but didn't trust what would come out of his mouth so remained silent.

"It will take some time, Hal," Cecily said. "You only just woke up." She held the cup to his lips, dabbing away at each stray rivulet of wine. After he had taken in his fill she fed him some warm fish broth, then soaked bread in it, breaking off tiny pieces and placing them in his mouth. She did the same with the cheese.

Tears rose in Hal's throat as he regarded her. "What life for now you?" he asked, frustrated that the words should come out so out of order and again unable to make sense of it. They were right in his head.

"What do you mean?" Cecily returned, the translation not at all lost on her. "I am your wife, Hal. My life is dedicated to taking care of you as you take care of me." She straightened. "Come now! Take some more broth. We must get your strength up."

Hal sipped the broth, allowing his tears to trail down his cheeks, tears of shame and gratitude, love and fear.

He could not imagine what life would be like for either of them if he remained in this estate.

Cecily refused to allow Hal the luxury of pitying himself. After a week she began making him feed himself with his able right hand, and though she still helped with his basic maintenance, she would not let him get out of doing something he was capable of himself.

"If you do not do for yourself, you die," Cecily told him with conviction. She was certain most illnesses could be beaten with sheer determination and, though there was no lack of it in her, she could not do it alone. Hal would have to assist in his recovery process.

When it was discovered that Hal could wiggle his toes and fingers on his left side Cecily was more convinced than ever that he would return to her a whole man. She began to make him hold a ball in his left hand and try to grip it. He protested at first, using any excuse to avoid it, but Cecily persisted with unwavering cheer coupled with steely resolve. Soon Hal was clenching and unclenching the ball, gaining strength in a hand he never thought he would use again.

By late spring Hal was sitting up and able to extend his left leg. Though it trembled violently, Cecily made him exercise it by repeatedly lifting it, bending it at the knee, and stretching it. The same strategy was implemented with his arm.

By the time the justice of the peace came calling, Hal was able to sign the king's Oath of Succession seated at his high table in the great hall, dignified as any able-bodied lord. It was an effort for him; he did not want to lose face in front of the JP by receiving him abed in his apartments. Upon the JP's departure, however, Hal returned to his chambers, all but carried by his faithful steward, George Hunter.

When Hal was settled and comfortable, Matilda burst into their apartments, dropping into an apologetic curtsy, then rising with a bright smile.

"My lord, my lady!" she cried. "A visitor!"

Hal closed his eyes, leaning against his pillows. "What they want now? I signed the damned oath—Anne Boleyn is queen undisputed and her children rightful heirs—" He could not continue. The words would come out jumbled; he could feel it. It seemed his speech was taking the longest to recover, and he wondered if he would ever be able to communicate with the ease he had so taken for granted before.

Matilda shook her head, twitching her lips, unable to suppress her smile as she stepped aside, allowing a slim figure donning a nun's habit entrance.

Hal's jaw went slack. "M . . . ira . . . bella," he said slowly.

Mirabella, whose beauty was so incongruent with her sober attire, offered a slow smile. "Hello, Father."

"How manage you get here?" he asked her, trying not to grit his teeth in frustration as he struggled with the words.

Mirabella's green eyes lit with pity. Her lips quivered as she ran to her father, wrapping her arms about his shoulders and holding him close. "Cecily arranged it. She—made a very generous donation. I am accompanied by the abbess herself." She buried her head in his cheek. "Oh, bless you, Father! Thank God He has seen fit to spare you!"

"Thank Cecily," Hal told her, grateful at least that this simple sentence could escape his lips unspoiled.

Mirabella righted herself, inclining her head toward Cecily. Her eyes reflected genuine gratitude. "Thank you, Cecily, for being what my father needs."

Cecily ran toward the girl, this figure that represented so much of her childhood, and embraced her. "I am so glad to see you, Mirabella! How I have missed you!"

They clasped each other a moment, then returned to sit beside Hal. He took in his fill of Mirabella, managing to hold a conversation with her by speaking as little as possible. She intuited his need to remain silent and told him of the convent and her dangerous opinion on the Oath of Succession.

"Sir Thomas More, the king's former chancellor—he hasn't taken the oath, you know," she said in low tones.

"Oh, the dear man," Cecily said, her heart thudding with fear. "If he doesn't sign the oath, he will be accused of treason! He'll be imprisoned or perhaps even die!"

Mirabella's gaze was level. "Then he will be a martyr." Her voice was rich with admiration. "More never wanted a break with Rome, as forward-thinking as he may be. His dispute with the king is based on conscience. He cannot acknowledge the king's whore's children as the rightful heirs."

"Mirabella!" Cecily cried. "The justice of the peace has only just left us. Please desist in this talk. You have come to see your father, after all."

Hal, who had remained quiet throughout this conversation, gazed at Mirabella thoughtfully. There was a glint of fear in his blue eyes as he beheld her. Was he afraid of her or for her? Cecily wondered. Perhaps, like her, it was a mingling of both.

Mirabella seemed content to close the subject and returned to more neutral topics. They spoke of their landholdings, the forest, and the price of wool, all trivial things. Safe things. At last Mirabella took Hal's and Cecily's hands in hers and led them in prayer for his recovery.

When Hal was happily exhausted from the company, Mirabella and Cecily removed to the solar.

"Are you happy there, Mirabella?" Cecily asked her when they were settled. "Is it all you ever hoped for?"

Mirabella nodded. "It is," she said with confidence.

But as she regarded her father's bride the conviction in her heart did not match her tone. There was something about Cecily, a tangible love she emanated that Mirabella found herself at this moment envying. What would it be like to love like that?

She dismissed the thought. Surely everyone in the monastic community had moments like these, enhanced by exposure to the outside world. Mirabella's hands trembled. She longed to return to the safety of the cloister, where disturbing images like these could not taunt her.

With abruptness she rose. "I am afraid I must leave."

"So soon? But I thought we would have time together as well . . ." Cecily protested, tears lighting her vibrant teal eyes.

Mirabella averted her head in guilt. She had planned on a lengthy visit but knew the longer she stayed the more she would question herself. She did not want to question herself.

She had always been so certain.

And so she took Cecily's hands. "It was a blessing to be permitted such a visit as it is, you know that. I will write more often, however. I promise." She leaned in, kissing Cecily's cheek, closing her ears to the soft tears Cecily shed as she departed.

Her father was recovering, Cecily was a good wife. That was all she needed to know.

Now she could go back. She must go back.

* * *

"So you ran away," Sister Julia observed after Mirabella confided the details of the visit to her the next day in the courtyard of the cloister.

Mirabella wanted to protest but found the words sticking in her throat. Sister Julia called life as she saw it and had never been wrong about Mirabella. For this candor Mirabella respected her.

Sister Julia took Mirabella's hand in hers as they promenaded. "Mirabella, why are you so afraid to love?"

Mirabella averted her head, blinking away an onset of unexpected tears. "I . . . have loved," she said as an image of Father Alec conjured itself before her mind's eye. "But those I love are constrained not to love me."

"But I love you, Mirabella," she said. "And so do your father and Cecily." Sister Julia paused. "But that is not the type of love you fear, is it?"

"I am called to love only God," Mirabella told Sister Julia.

"I know you believe that—"

"I am!" Mirabella insisted, frustrated that her vulnerability lay thus exposed. "You are proof that even the most dedicated servant of God has moments of doubt," she added.

"Yes," Sister Julia agreed. "My moment of doubt gave me you. But it also gave me the courage to pursue what I truly did love most and that was the Lord. Mirabella, my course of action did irreparable damage to some," she added in soft tones as she lowered her eyes. "You do not have to go to that extreme to figure out what it is you want most. But you do need to resolve this battle you are fighting with yourself."

"When I am here I am as close to being at peace as I have ever been," Mirabella told her. "So here I will remain."

"But is it to seek an intimate relationship with God or is it to escape from emotions you cannot seem to grapple with in what some would refer to as 'real life'?" Sister Julia challenged her.

Mirabella shook her head. "I . . ."

"You do not owe me an answer," Sister Julia said. "You owe yourself. Please reflect, Mirabella. Do not live a lie. This is a difficult life; I would hope you would not remain because you were afraid of losing face should you change your mind."

They continued their walk in silence, Sister Julia's words echoing in Mirabella's mind again and again.

But still, not even to her own self could she admit the possibility that she had chosen the wrong path.

That would change everything.

Hal had regained almost full use of his limbs. The traces of his sudden and baffling illness remained in his speech and in the slight droop of his mouth that caused him a great deal of embarrassment.

"I think it's charming," Cecily told him one night as she reached out to run a finger along his lips.

Hal kissed the finger. "A crooked mouth, charming?" he returned with a slight chuckle. He sighed as he organized his next words in his mind. He spoke slowly. "These past months have taken you toll on," he told her. "Few enough would ever have . . . done what you did. Do not think it goes unappreciated. I would still be abed were not for you."

"Nonsense," Cecily said, though both knew it was true.

She snuggled against his chest, savoring the closeness she so feared would be stolen from her. Hal's summation had been correct; the past few months had taken a toll on her. She spent the days seeing to Hal's every need and the nights in an exhausted state of anxiety, listening to Hal's every breath, judging his every movement, beside herself with fear that he would relapse.

He did not. He grew stronger. With her beside him, pushing him relentlessly, he thrived. Each day was easier than the day preceding and Cecily was filled with hope. When Dr. Hurst came to visit he marveled at Hal's improvement.

"Lady Sumerton is a born healer!" he would exclaim with a chuckle.

Born healer or not, Cecily had managed to will Hal through. And now there was nothing more that she wanted than to be a wife to him in every sense of the word. Her glimpse of Hal's mortality shook her to the core and she vowed not to let him leave this world without the heirs she had promised him.

What's more, she longed for that closeness. For the past few months saw her transform from girl to woman. Her willowy figure had blossomed; curves replaced the flat landscape of childhood. The face that stared out of the glass was no longer a child's and the mind behind the eyes longed for things she had never experienced.

Now, feeling Hal's kiss upon her finger caused her lower abdomen to clench in a not altogether unpleasant sensation. She trembled. She had dreamed of this moment for months now, and though she still regarded it with some measure of fear, she did not doubt what she wanted to happen next.

Cecily stroked his cheek. "I love you, Hal," she told him with all the sincerity in her heart, leaning in to press a gentle kiss upon his mouth.

"Oh, Cecily . . ." Hal breathed, rolling to his side to take her in his arms. "I love you. So much." He held her close.

"I am thinking there is one more exercise we need to indulge in, to make certain you are . . . quite recovered," Cecily suggested, flushing.

Hal laughed. "Cecily, you minx!" His eyes lit with concern as he stroked her cheek. "You are sure?" he asked, offering his crooked smile.

Cecily nodded. "I have never been more certain. Let me be your wife, Hal."

Hal leaned in, kissing her in a way he never had before. Cecily moved her mouth along with his, her body thrilling with a rush of sensations foreign to her.

That night she became Hal's true wife at last.

This new dimension to Hal and Cecily's relationship found them in a state of befuddled rapture. They could not get enough of each other. For Cecily, this was a time of exploration and she absorbed each new sensation as if she were a student taking in a particularly stimulating lecture. For Hal, Cecily was his joy and to be allowed to demonstrate his love for her in the manner of a true husband made the struggles of his life easier to bear. Cecily made everything easier to bear.

In August, when they had been married a year, Cecily's womb quickened with Hal's child.

She did not know why she was so surprised. She knew that missed menses meant a child was growing within her, but to feel it stir, to feel its presence, gave the condition a renewed certainty. It was real. The creature inside her was a person, who would have a name and a personality. The creature was a child and it was hers.

She could not fathom something belonging to her in such a way. Though the Pierces had served as her family since the deaths of her parents, nothing could match this new feeling, the knowledge that she was the founder of a family, that she was to be a mother.

Hal doted on her endlessly. "I will try to care for you as you cared for me," he said, measuring his words with care, as his speech still gave him difficulty.

His actions more than compensated for what he could not artic-ulate. He showered her with gifts, beautiful collars of jewels and strings of pearls, bolts of fabric for baby garments, and any dish she craved. He waited on her himself and ordered the retiling of the nursery with tiles imported from Flanders.

"You know," he told her, "if a girl, no matter."

Cecily stifled a sob of gratitude when he told her this one warm autumn evening as the two sat in the gardens. Because of her tiny figure, Cecily had already begun to show, and Hal was rubbing the curve of her expanding belly with tear-filled eyes.

"As long as I have you," he went on. "That is all."

He met her gaze. It was mingled with tenderness and fear.

Cecily clasped his hand.

"You won't lose me," she assured him, though she began to fear the prospect of childbirth more and more with each passing day. "You will never lose me."

Life proceeded in the manner they had grown accustomed to. They still entertained, and if it was not quite as lavish due to Ce-cily's condition, they still enjoyed a steady stream of guests and circulated throughout Lincolnshire and York paying calls. As Cecily's condition progressed she had to keep adding panels to her gowns, but she retained her slender limbs and tiny face. Hal watched her with adoring eyes. After his illness each day was a precious gift to them, to be savored and appreciated with renewed vigor. The new life growing within Cecily was treasured all the more and seemed to contain all of their hopes for a happy future and a healed past.

When it came time for Cecily to enter confinement, where she would lie abed in her darkened bedchamber for the last month of her pregnancy, Lady Alice visited her as often as possible. No more could Cecily pay calls or entertain or take in exercise. She despised it and her restlessness sent her into fits of anxious tossing and turning. She was never comfortable. The baby sat low in her belly and she felt as though it would drop out of her at any moment. At times the little one offered lusty kicks square in the bladder, causing the immediate need to void. She found no position adequate for rest and often slept propped up against pillows. She alternated between hot and cold or both at once and found the condition of pregnancy far more glorified than in reality. She did not glow at all, as ladies with child were purported to do. She was sweaty and irritable and wanted to have this baby yesterday.

"This is the worst part," Alice told her as she sat embroidering at the foot of her bed. "Thanks to Margaret Beaufort."

Margaret Beaufort had been the king's grandmother and it was she who set out the strict practices for noblewomen in childbed. Cecily did not understand why the birth of a noble should differ from that of a peasant, who often delivered their babies in the fields at harvesttime and seemed to do well enough. But gentlewomen were to be regarded as fragile, dainty roses to be preserved in the darkness of an airless chamber lest a breeze scatter their petals to the winds.

Cecily, who was accustomed to activity, did not relish this new estate and prayed for an early delivery. Though Hal did his best to entertain her, she was lonely and frightened. Her hours alone in her chamber gave her too much time to ponder her condition and it was now more than ever that she longed for the presence of her mother so long departed from this world.

She also thought of Lady Grace and a pang of longing stirred in her breast for her. She would have made a merry conversationalist . . . but of course, were Lady Grace alive to converse with, Cecily would not be in confinement with Hal's child at all. No, Hal and Lady Grace would have been looking forward to the grandchildren Cecily would provide with Brey.

Cecily squeezed her eyes shut against the weight of heavy tears.

"Cecily?" Alice leaned forward, concerned. "Are you all right?"

Cecily nodded, swallowing hard. "I was just thinking," she confided. "Of all the changes. Had life gone as expected I would be carrying Brey's child, not his father's. And yet, as much as I miss him and Lady Grace, I have never been so astonished to realize how much I truly love Hal. . . ." She trailed off, as always mystified by her love for her husband. "At first I thought it was out of gratitude. Hal brought me into his home and heart and has shown me nothing but kindness and respect. But then, when we were alone, I spent more time with him and came to appreciate the tenderness of his soul, the strange sort of innocence . . ." She laughed as she recalled his twinkling eyes and contagious enthusiasm. "And I knew then that I loved him for who he was, not simply because he was my protector. Now, despite the terrible tragedy of our losses, I know that God has His reasons, that Hal and I are meant to be." She drew in a breath, comforted by the thought.

"When I thought I was going to lose him I knew I would fight anyone and anything who tried to come between us, even the force of death itself. Death has taken so much from us. . . . But it yielded its grip over Hal and returned him to me. And now I am to give him a child." It was at this point that she was overcome with a fear she hadn't known since Hal was first struck with his illness. She cast wild eyes to Alice. "After everything we have survived I should feel triumphant. But I am more afraid than I have ever been. What if I die, leaving Hal all alone with a little one? Or what if the baby dies? How will poor Hal endure it after all of his heartbreaks . . . and if we both . . . ?"

Cecily began to cry, gasping and hiccoughing like a child, as Alice rushed forward to sit beside her, taking her hand.

"Even now you only think of Hal," Alice observed in awe. "I

cannot even fathom such love . . ." she said, her voice thick with sadness.

Cecily at once regretted her confession and cast her eyes to their joined hands. Alice squeezed hers in reassurance. "You are stronger than a seasoned knight," Alice told her in her uncompromising tone. "You will get through this, Cecily." She smoothed Cecily's hair off her face. "And when you do, you are going to know a happiness few ever experience. How many of us belong to families who truly love each other?"

Her voice rang with the faintest trace of agony, causing Cecily to shift the focus from her own concerns to Alice's loveless existence. She stroked her friend's hand. She felt selfish.

"Thank you, Alice," Cecily said in gentle tones. "I am very fortunate. Even more so to have a friend like you."

Alice took Cecily in her arms and held her tight. "Well then!" she exclaimed, drawing back and wiping tears from her cheeks. "D'you expect you'll have time to call on me in a few months when I enter my confinement?"

"Alice!" Cecily cried, tears of joy replacing those of trepidation as she beheld her friend. "Oh, how wonderful—you know I shall be beside you! And our children shall be companions!"

Alice offered a sad little smile. "It will be wonderful, won't it?"

As she regarded her friend, Cecily found herself once more overwhelmed with gratitude.

Hers was not a bad lot.

Father Alec Cahill was growing used to the fast-paced routine of Lambeth Palace and had become so comfortable with the archbishop that there were few subjects the two did not discuss. Cranmer had an easy manner about him as well, a quality he shared, and the two were as content in a lengthy conversation as they were in silence. Father Alec intuited many of Cranmer's needs and was excellent at being at the right place at the right time.

Except once.

Father Alec had been composing a series of devotions and prayers that he tentatively titled *Meditations for the Common Man*. The work was endorsed by Cranmer in private, but he advised Father Alec to use caution. Despite pure intentions, the book could be considered heretical. And no one wanted to burn. Despite fears for how the piece would be interpreted, Father Alec was proud of it and often sought out Cranmer for advice, which he was always generous about dispensing.

The men had developed an informality between them and it was not unknown for Father Alec to enter Cranmer's apartments unannounced. He was always received and it reassured him to know there was a place for him to go and a friend to talk to any time he needed. Tonight he needed counsel; Father Alec was frustrated about his loss of inspiration for his book and decided to seek out his friend.

But Cranmer was not alone. A woman was with him. This was not remarkable; there were noblewomen who sought audience with him. But at this time of night and without chaperone . . . and the fact that she was clasped tightly in his arms . . .

Father Alec's gut lurched with disgust, and before either could react he rushed from the suite.

Once in the privacy of his own quarters he found himself battling tears.

He is just like old Cardinal Wolsey, he thought, clenching his fists in rage as he paced back and forth before his bed. Once one of the king's dearest companions and advisers, the cardinal had indulged in all manner of depravity, living the life of a king, taking mistresses, fathering bastards, all while taking great pains to remain in the king's favor, that he might attain more power for himself. In the end, Wolsey earned the king's wrath by failing to procure his annulment from Catherine of Aragon and died alone and in disgrace on his way to his own execution. He was an unforgettable example of what lust for worldly gains did to a prelate, the antithesis of what Father Alec wanted to be.

To think that Cranmer could be of his like . . . No. It could not be true. He could not wrap his mind around it. Cranmer, gentle Cranmer, who seemed so devout and in touch with God's desires. No, not Cranmer. Surely his eyes had betrayed him. After all, who did not need a chaste embrace now and again?

But alone and at night?

Father Alec gritted his teeth, his face aching from the intensity of his scowl. He was a fool; priests often had mistresses—*housekeepers* and *servants* were the polite terms for it, but they were mistresses nonetheless. The rank of the priest offered no exception; a man was a man and lust was lust.

Father Alec cursed himself for expecting more from Cranmer. He cursed himself for his naïve idealism, his hero worship. . . . It was all fantasy.

He did not know how much time had passed, minutes, perhaps hours. He did know that when the knock sounded at the door he would face Cranmer. And, out of obedience, he would not be able to question him.

He opened it, kneeling before the archbishop to kiss his ring, then rising and allowing him entrance.

Cranmer sat at the breakfast table, cocking his head, regarding Father Alec with a gentle countenance capable of inspiring a shameless liar to confess of his deepest sins.

"I know you have questions, my son," he began in his soft voice. "And I understand why you may feel angry and betrayed. Know that what I am about to tell you I reveal because you are one of the few men that I actually trust." His gaze did not leave Father Alec's face. "The woman you saw with me is my wife."

Father Alec's gut twisted in a knot. Wife? He was uncertain of whether or not this was worse than keeping a mistress. Both were forbidden to a priest. . . . He could not begin to grapple with it.

Reading his confusion, Cranmer went on. "My son, I was always inclined to marry, to have a family. I did so before I became a priest, but alas, my first wife died in childbirth along with the baby. So I returned to my calling. I lived up to my vows and for a time succeeded at forgoing the love of a woman." He sighed. "Until I became ambassador to Charles V and was in Germany. There I met Andreas Osiander, the theologian. I fell in love, Father, with his niece and I knew then that I must marry her." Until this point Father Alec believed he knew Cranmer's every expression, but this was one he had not seen before. Cranmer's face reflected the enraptured tenderness of an infatuated youth mingled with the happy bewilderment of a man who is realizing for the first time that his soul mate is the same woman he has been married to for the past thirty years. The expression was fleeting, however, converting to his usual melancholy gentleness as he went on. "I also knew then that it could not be wrong to serve God and love a woman at the same time, for God made man and woman to be companions and helpmates. I knew it from my innermost being, from every facet of my soul. Rather, this tie to the Lord and the world He put me in set me closer in touch with the struggles of men."

"But it is so dangerous, Your Grace," was all Father Alec could think of to say. He did not even know how to begin to explore the level of danger it put the archbishop in, with the king, with God. . . . His head hurt. He put a hand to it, rubbing his temple as he tried to wrangle with this knowledge.

"Yes, it is dangerous," Cranmer said. "Which is why I am sending her back to Europe, that she might be safe." Only now did he lower his eyes, though not in shame. Father Alec perceived nothing in the movement but sadness. "We pay for what we want most, Father. Despite that, if what we love is in the realm of the Lord, it is always worth the pain."

Father Alec swallowed the lump rising in his throat. It would not go down. He slipped from the chair to his knees before the archbishop, taking his hand in his. "I am so sorry for what this is costing you . . . and more for what it could cost you. Please, for love of God, man, be careful."

"I was right to trust you, Father," Cranmer said. "We are of like mind, perhaps more so than you know. I was careless tonight. It will not be repeated. This is the last time I shall see her."

He rose, his face set with pained determination. "I do not know if I shall ever see her again . . ." he added wistfully, as if to himself.

Father Alec let tears of compassion slide down his cheeks. At once it did not seem so sordid; Cranmer's agony was in no way comparable to that of a scoundrel like Cardinal Wolsey.

And who was he to say that a priest should not be allowed to marry? He did not set down the doctrine, after all. Imagine all the terrible crimes that could be avoided if they were allowed . . . Father Alec's chest constricted in anxiety. This was dangerous thinking.

This was reformer thinking.

But there was no going back, not after tonight.

This was the night that solidified Father Alec's support of, if not the New Learning, *a* new faith, for good.

❧ 11 ❧

Dorothy Mopps, the midwife attending Cecily, was not at all what Cecily had imagined. She had pictured a gnarly old witch, truth be told, and was reassured by the presence of the young, sturdy woman who seemed to intuit her every need. She was in her midthirties and had boasted of bringing the latest generation of Sumerton into the world. She had attended Alice and would do so again when her time came. Cecily thought this must be a very interesting profession, meeting all the ladies and handling the babies. Had she not been born noble she would have considered pursuing it.

Her musings on midwifery were cut short by the piercing pain in her back. Her waters had broken in the middle of the night and, though it did not hurt, she had screamed frantically for Hal, who immediately sent for Dorothy and her assistants. Alice arrived in the morning and was prepared to sit with Cecily till the baby came.

All of the women reassured her with their own experiences in childbearing. The pain was normal, they told her, she was not going to die, they made sure to reiterate, and that everything would be forgotten when she was holding her new little lamb in her arms.

Cecily doubted that. How could one forget a pain like this? It was excruciating. Her belly was taut with cramps; it seemed as though a dagger was fixed in her lower back, stabbing her but not enough to kill. She panted and cried out with each contraction while Alice swabbed her burning forehead with a cool, wet cloth.

Periodically Dorothy checked Cecily's woman's parts to see if she was getting any closer to delivery and each time her broad face revealed disappointment.

"It is taking too long," she said. "She should be ready by now."

"Don't scare her, for God's sake," Alice snapped at her, but she was unable to mask the fear in her own eyes.

The last strains of evening faded into night. The apartments were dark, save for the candles, which cast eerie shadows about that Cecily had never pondered before. Was one of them the shadow of Death? She was growing weak and fanciful, she decided, and must concentrate on the birth.

"Isn't there anything we can do to speed things up?" Alice asked.

Dorothy shook her head, expelling a sigh.

Cecily moaned, yielding to another terrible pain. The night dragged on; there was nothing to measure the time but the light that filtered through the curtains. She knew not how long she labored. Her limbs trembled violently. She did not have the energy to scream anymore, so she whimpered now and again. She could not think of anything, not the baby, not the gentle voices swirling around her. All she could think of was the pain and that she wanted to rid herself of the creature causing it.

The light was gone. Cecily wondered if she was dying, then realized with a sense of wryness that it was night again. Her hair was matted to her head in sweat; she was slick with it despite Alice's efforts in trying to cool her.

"Cecily." The voice did not belong to the women but to Hal. Cecily offered a feeble smile. A warm hand stroked her brow. "My love . . . you are so strong," he told her. "Stay strong, my dearest, just a little longer."

Cecily knew the words were well intended but could not imagine how to implement them. She was too weak to say his name.

Hal was called away and Alice took his place beside her. Cecily closed her eyes and ears. There was nothing but pain; it reverberated throughout her whole body, as resonant as a church bell. She hummed and tingled with it.

Snatches of conversation permeated the fog.

"It is very risky," Dorothy was saying in her brusque tenor. "But I believe she has less of a chance dying of that than she does if we leave her like this, my lord. She is going on forty hours. . . ."

She could not hear Hal's response.

"A Caesarian section," Dorothy said.

"Mother Mary preserve us," Alice murmured.

Cecily heard no more. Fleetingly, she wondered if the word *Caesarian* was derived from the old Roman emperor Julius Caesar in some way, but it did not really matter. She did not know what it was or why it applied to her, only that it might get this thing out and that was enough.

Cecily's head lolled to one side.

She wondered vaguely if she was going to die.

There was no pain like it in the world, the searing pain of being cut down her middle, this despite a cautious dose of dwale. Cecily was certain her insides would fall out when she felt the scalpel delve into her tender flesh, into her womb. By God's grace they did not and it was not long before a squalling infant was heard somewhere in the distance. Cecily could not hear much; the pain eclipsed everything else. Her belly burned and throbbed as Dorothy's needle restored her to wholeness.

"She is not safe yet," Dorothy told Alice and Hal. "There was a great deal of blood loss and she could get an infection. Her recovery will be long if she does live. But you have a fine, healthy heir out of it and women are easy enough to replace."

Did she say "heir"?

Cecily tried to open her eyes but could not. She managed a throaty whimper but could not communicate her desire to see the child.

"You ignorant fool. This woman is irreplaceable," Hal snapped. "And you'll take care to hold your tongue, madam, if you would like to keep your position lest I drive you out of Sumerton and brand you as a witch!"

Cecily would have smiled if she could. Dear Hal, her faithful rescuer. She wondered if Dorothy knew he was far too gentle to hurt a fly, let alone a woman, and that it was his fear speaking through him.

"Cecily, look," Hal said, his voice wavering with emotion. "Look at our fine son!"

Cecily managed to open her eyes a slit. In Hal's arms was a tiny bundle with golden hair and fair skin. Hal held the baby closer, that she might see his little face.

Hal pulled the blanket aside and Cecily gasped.

"Brey . . ." she whispered.

Then he was gone and she was engulfed in darkness.

Those first days of Cecily's recovery were critical, Dorothy warned the terrified household. If Cecily developed a fever or inordinate swelling and pus, she would likely die. She drifted in and out of consciousness while Hal kept vigil at her bedside, never releasing her hand. He spoke to her in soothing tones, telling her of the baby.

"He shall be named Harold," he said. "Harold Aubrey. But we'll call him Harry. How shall that be?" Hal still spoke at a deliberated pace, measuring his words and phrases that he might get them out coherently. Speaking was still very difficult for him. But his ability to communicate was the last thing on his mind now as he beheld the frail creature on the bed. His heart surged with admiration for her. She had already demonstrated great strength in the past by nursing him through his illness. Now she had lasted through over forty hours of labor to be hacked into as if she were meat to be butchered. The thought of it caused Hal to shudder with fear. He had remained while the terrible procedure had been performed; nothing could keep him out, least of all propriety. He had seen the blood spurt forth from the gaping wound and at seeing it could hardly appreciate what else entered forth, his beautiful son Harry. The only thought dominating Hal's mind was that Cecily would die; he would lose the only person he had loved with his whole self and he could not bear it.

Cecily sanctioned Hal's suggestion for the name with a tiny smile before drifting off to sleep once more.

Now and again her eyes would flutter or she would grimace in pain or expel a heavy breath. Hal took these as signs of life, and though he regretted her discomfort, he was reassured by the fact that Cecily had made it through the worst. A week had passed and there were no signs of fever or infection. She would live.

Hal felt it was safe enough to resume some of his duties and leave Cecily's side now and again, but he took care to spend as much time with her as he could, bringing the baby with him to cheer her, though, to his regret, she showed little interest in Harry thus far. But she was still very ill and he expected it would take time so tried not to worry.

What worried him most was Cecily's countenance. Once so hopeful and filled with gentle cheer, her expression was now melancholy, distracted. He feared she was slipping into despair and did not know how to revive her. It was not like his illness, which was physical and seemed to respond well to exercise. Her troubles lay somewhere in the soul, somewhere he could not reach. It frightened him.

She never complained, even when she winced in pain, and sometimes he wondered if it would be better if she did, if it would serve as some kind of release. But he knew it was not in her nature. And so all he could do was pray for her recovery both mentally and physically while remaining by her side to offer all the cheer and support he could.

Cecily meantime was attended by Matilda, who rubbed salve made from marigolds, beeswax, and honey given to her by Dorothy on her angry red scar to encourage healing, and she remained abed. The baby was nursed by a sturdy and loving young woman called Bertie Stokes and Cecily was just as content to leave him to her care. She would have no energy for it. As it were, Cecily did not enjoy one pain-free moment; her breasts had filled and she endured the agonizing process of drying up while her belly still cramped. The wound with its massive stitches frightened her when she saw it in between dressings and she found herself filled with self-loathing for her inability to recover. Now she had a better sense of the frustration Hal had felt when recuperating from his illness.

Cecily received visits from the local noblewomen, Alice among them. Even some of the tenants' wives called with bread and cheese and blankets sewn by their own loving hands. Cecily was grateful for the solicitousness of those around her, but nonetheless the feeling of gloom remained. She was possessed by dark fancies and had nightmares while she was awake about someone killing the baby. The image that terrorized her most was that often that someone was herself. She did not understand it. She had never entertained such notions before, even in her angriest moments, and that the object of her dark fantasy should be her own innocent baby terrified her. She was shaken with fear. Surely these thoughts come straight from the vilest depths of Hell, she thought, and she prayed for forgiveness, hoping God would rescue her from these fiendish visions.

She longed for Mirabella, remarkably. She did not want to confess her imaginings to a priest, who would probably say she was taken by a devil, and thought that the novitiate nun might prove a little more understanding.

In the end, however, she told no one and tried to suffer through them. She found the less she saw of the baby the less the disturbing images taunted her. Instead she was left with the hollowness of sadness undefined and all consuming. She had every reason to rejoice; she had lived through her ordeal, delivered a healthy son, and, though she did not feel like it, was recovering with remarkable speed according to the midwife.

But she could not rejoice. She found, much to her dismay, that she could not do much of anything.

She was as immobilized as Hal had ever been.

It was overwhelming.

One afternoon while Cecily nibbled on some savory goat milk cheese, Hal burst into her apartments, wearing a bright smile and carrying a sack.

He sat on the bed. "I've been thinking," he said. "Do you remember what you told me?" He shook his head. "Of course not, you tell me so many things!" he added with a laugh.

Cecily could not help but smile in his presence. "What did I tell you, Hal?" she asked, her curiosity piqued.

"When you convinced me to stop wearing the hair shirt," he said, casting his eyes downward as though the memory of the shirt and the reasons he had employed it still brought him great pain. "You took the sandglass and threw it out the window, saying it represented the past and we were to start anew." At this point Hal reached into the sack and retrieved a new sandglass, this one elaborately carved out of beautiful mahogany with roses and ivy twining about the supports. The glass was large enough to time one hour.

"A new sandglass," he said. "To represent our new life." He gave it to Cecily. It was heavy in her hands. "We have both endured a great deal of pain. But every day is a new start, Cecily, a chance to heal from old wounds. Every time we need to start again, whether we have had an argument or have suffered a tragedy, we will turn this glass about to remind each other that we can begin again. You see?"

Cecily's eyes brimmed with tears. Her heart constricted with love as she ran her hand over the wood. Her fingers ran across something, a defect perhaps, and when she looked down she found two dates carved into it. One was their wedding date and the other the birth date of their son.

"Oh, Hal . . ." she murmured, allowing her tears to fall.

"Every time we need to turn it about—when we're not actually using it to keep time, that is—" he added with a little chuckle, "we will carve the date of our new beginning in it. Even if it marks the end of something sad."

"It is a beautiful notion," Cecily said. She sat up with great effort, swallowing the urge to cry out as a searing pain flashed down her belly, and wrapped her arms about Hal's neck, kissing him firmly on the mouth.

She would banish the bad thoughts and start living again. She had a baby to care for and a large household to run.

She turned the glass about, watching the grains of sand drizzle to the empty base.

It was time to begin again.

Cecily was moving about slowly. She was still in a tremendous amount of pain and could not stand straight, but she managed to attend to the needs of her household, finding that the distractions kept her startling melancholia at bay. She began to receive visitors on a regular basis and soon the house was a hive of activity.

Harry was four months old when she felt safe enough to interact with him; even so, she felt a disconcerting distance. Harry was attached to his nurse, Bertie, and cried for her when she left the room. His eyes searched her out frantically if she was not in his immediate line of vision. Cecily swallowed tears whenever this happened. It was natural for children to be more attached to their nurses than their parents, she knew, but it did little to comfort her. She resolved to spend as much time with him as possible, tending to as many of his needs as she could, that the two might develop a closer bond. She cuddled and played with him and soon his face lit with delight upon seeing her, causing her heart to constrict with relief.

"He knows who my lady is," Bertie told her, her voice warm with reassurance.

Cecily hated the fact that she needed this kind of encouragement, but she had done it to herself, hadn't she, wallowing in that strange sadness she had fallen into after his birth? Now she had regrouped and was determined to be the best mother possible.

It was not without a trace of bittersweet sadness that Cecily observed Harry resembling Brey more and more with each passing day with his blond curls and inquisitive blue eyes. Cecily was not the only one haunted by it; now and then she caught Hal gazing at the child, his eyes soft with wistfulness. There was no doubt that he was recalling his first son.

Cecily found it a little disturbing that she was the mother of Brey's brother. She did not know why this should make any difference, but she was disconcerted nonetheless. She could not stop thinking of her, Brey's, and Hal's blood flowing through the same veins—they had all become one in the body of this remarkable creature.

Yet, strange as it was, it was that thought that consoled Cecily. In little Harry life was renewed. He was their hope, their new beginning, and whenever she looked upon the sandglass Hal had given her she ran her fingers along the carving of Harry's birth date.

Someday she would tell him of his sweet brother and how she had loved him so. But that would not be for a very long time.

If Harry resembled Brey in temperament as much as he did in looks, he would be a lad in whom to take much pride.

"We live in dangerous times," Archbishop Thomas Cranmer was telling Father Alec when they were alone in Cranmer's apartments at Lambeth Palace.

Father Alec found the words to be a gross understatement, but then who could articulate best the horrors of the past three years? Words could never encompass the tragedies they had witnessed. Thomas More, the former lord chancellor who would not sign the king's Oath of Succession, was dead, beheaded on Tower Green, as Bishop Fisher had been. Princess Catherine of Aragon had died in January 1536 and was buried the same day Anne Boleyn was delivered of her stillborn prince.

Within months, Queen Anne, that pretty, spirited girl, was accused of treasonous acts that included incest with her own brother, adultery, and witchcraft. She was beheaded along with her brother while the other men who had "criminal knowledge" of her were hanged and eviscerated. But when Father Alec looked into those hard, proud black eyes the day she knelt before the French swordsman, he knew in his soul she was not guilty. The only reason she was condemned to die was because she failed just as her predecessor had failed. She could not produce a son for the king. Now there was a new queen, the pious Jane Seymour, who was meek and dainty and would not push for reform as clever Anne had done. Henry VIII would not be manipulated by a woman again.

"All we can do is cautiously move forward," Cranmer was telling

Father Alec. "We must push our reforms through as subtly as possible. And everything, absolutely everything, must be credited to His Majesty."

The thought of the king, whom Cranmer still loved with a devotion Father Alec would never understand, made him want to retch. Henry VIII had grown fat over the years and his paranoia increased with his belt size. No one was safe around him; he raised men up and cast them down on a whim. The Howards, Anne Boleyn's ambitious family and once the shining stars of the kingdom, were all but in hiding, yielding to the rise of the favored family of the moment: the Seymours. Father Alec wondered how long it would be before they committed some concocted offense against His Majesty and tumbled from grace. One had only to look at the king the wrong way to do so.

As long as Father Alec was beside Cranmer he felt safe. Cranmer was one of the king's most beloved companions, and as Father Alec lacked political aspirations for himself, he immediately set men at ease. His only aim was to serve his archbishop, who was a living manifestation of his every ideal.

The unspoken bone of contention between the men was that the archbishop's only aim was to serve his king.

And the king frightened Father Alec to death.

"I believe in him, you see," Cranmer said, as though reading his thoughts. It was a disturbing habit the archbishop indulged in often, and sometimes Father Alec entertained, albeit briefly, the notion that the man did possess some otherworldly quality about him. "I believe in the strain of the Almighty that runs through his veins and it is that strain which will ultimately compel him to do good—if he is guided correctly, delicately, and with love."

"You truly do love him," Father Alec observed, trying to contain his awe.

"He is my king . . . and he is greatly troubled. He needs . . ." He searched for the words. "He needs our help." He sighed. "If you could only have seen him when I first met him. He was so vibrant, so inspired. His depth and breadth of knowledge is still incomparable. He loves to learn; he tries so hard to understand and make sense of the world around him. He is driven by a conscience we sometimes do not understand, but when you look into his eyes you cannot doubt its existence." The passion in Cranmer's tone touched Father Alec. "He longs to be a good king. In his eyes to be a good king means ensuring the succession with a male heir. He will feel as though he has failed if he does not." Cranmer's eyes were lit with the intensity of his convictions.

"And what of Queen Jane?" Father Alec was compelled to interpose. "If she cannot bring forth an heir . . ." He cocked a speculative brow. There was no need to say more.

Cranmer squeezed his eyes shut a moment, as though warding off a terrifying vision of Hell itself. He drew in a breath. At last he said, "I am constrained to help His Majesty, to pray for his soul. It is difficult to see now in the light of recent events, but we must have faith in the fact that King Henry is, in his soul, a good man."

It was a convoluted analysis, justifying the king's horrific actions through the biased eyes of one who loved him, but Father Alec would not dispute him.

In his heart, of course, he thought no such thing.

Henry VIII was a madman and Father Alec knew without a shred of doubt that the indirect murder of Queen Catherine followed by the slaughter of Queen Anne signified a new chapter in their lives.

It was the beginning of Henry VIII's reign of terror.

"He is mad," Mirabella seethed to the abbess, Anna Shelby, when the older woman tearfully explained the fate of Sumerton Abbey in chapter that evening.

Anna Shelby fixed Mirabella with a steely stare. Though chapter was the time to air out grievances, she seldom tolerated outbursts, no matter how justified they may be.

"Sister Mirabella! You will be silent!" she admonished in harsh tones.

Mirabella rose, the slender hand that rested on the table curling into a fist. "Forgive me, I mean not to disobey, but I cannot be silent. I cannot accept this. You have just told us that our beloved convent, along with almost every other monastic house in England, is to be closed and plundered for the sake of filling King Henry's treasury! How can you expect any other response?"

"I understand your resentment, Sister Mirabella, but what would you have us do?" returned Anna Shelby, her eyes brimming with tears. "We are but humble women; we cannot fight His Majesty's will."

"No, of course we cannot fight him," Mirabella said. "But we can resist. Perhaps the king will have mercy—"

"My dear lady, when have you witnessed an act of mercy from this king?" returned the abbess.

Mirabella was trembling with anger. "Then what are we to do? Accept our pensions, retire to the country, useless, while our world crumbles about us? How can we accept that?"

The room burst into nervous chatter until the abbess raised her gnarled hands, gesturing for them to be silent. "Sister Mirabella, change is an inevitability of life. Perhaps this is God's will—"

"It is *not* God's will!" Mirabella cried, feeling a tug at her wrist, knowing it was a warning from Sister Julia to hold her peace and ignoring it. "This is a test for us to uphold the will of God, opposing sinners who mean to work against it!" she cried with passion. "It cannot be God's will that His devoted servants be cast into this cruel world like grains of sand—"

"Perhaps it is," the abbess interposed, her voice soft. "Perhaps, Sisters, we have been isolated for too long. Perhaps God wishes us to be out in the world, that we may perform His work—"

"I cannot accept that," Mirabella said with a shake of her head. "There are those called to the monastic world and those called to live outside. To take away our place of calling is tantamount to taking away our very lives." As she spoke she noted Sister Julia searching her face. She flushed, feeling the need to defend herself against something she did not understand.

"You are wrong," Anna Shelby said. "The king may take away our home, our property, our books, and our treasures." She looked beyond the gathering of anxious females, fixing pale blue eyes on a plane so distant it could only be viewed from within. "But those are all things, my child. Just things. He cannot take away that which belongs to God—our souls. And that is where our calling lies. Whether cloistered or out in the world, if your soul belongs to God, nothing, not even the injustices of this life, can touch you."

Mirabella shook her head again, squeezing back hot tears. How could the abbess betray them so easily? How could she yield to that bastard devil-king, Henry VIII?

Mirabella righted herself, standing straight and tall, her shoulders square as she addressed the chapter house. "Sisters, does no one have the courage to fight, to preserve our way of life? Can we remain passive and allow this tyrant to separate us from our Mother Church? The devil reigns in this land, cloaking himself in the New Learning, and our king has been seduced by it. I tell you, the Archbishop of Canterbury and that crony of His Majesty's the vile weasel Thomas Cromwell—you remember him as that wicked man who slinked through here two years past to examine our fitness as a convent? Yes, that same Cromwell and Archbishop Cranmer are out to destroy the Church! Together they lead England farther away from our Lord and closer to the gates of Hell!"

The tables were silent. All of the nuns' eyes were riveted to Mirabella, who tingled and trembled with inspiration as she spoke.

"I call you to fight for our Lord, for His Church!" Mirabella cried, raising a fist and shaking it before the assemblage. "Stand beside me when the guards come! Do not accept pensions and a life denied your purpose! Remain with me and fight! And if we should die, we die martyrs!"

The women burst into applause and Mirabella flushed with peculiar delight. She would save the convent, and if not, her sacrifice would be remembered. Someday, when the world was set right, they would speak of the brave, selfless sisters of Sumerton Abbey and how they died defending the Lord's honor. . . .

"But, Sister," a young novitiate said in timid tones, "we have no arms."

"We need none," Mirabella told her. "We will not fight them as soldiers. We will stand our ground. We will simply refuse to leave. They will have to run us through to move us and who would dare harm a holy woman without fear for their souls?"

"Sister Mirabella!" the abbess cried. "To my knowledge you

have not been elected abbess of this institution, yet you fall into the role of command as though you are entitled to it."

Only now did Mirabella feel the first strains of genuine humility flow through her as she fell to her knees before her superior. "Forgive me," she said in soft tones. "Whip me if you desire, discipline me in the manner you see fit . . . but know that I cannot be moved from what I am being called to do."

"Is it God calling you, Sister?" Anna Shelby intoned as she seized Mirabella's chin, lifting it up to gaze into her eyes. "Or are you driven by something far worldlier? Beware, my child, the sin of pride. It is pride that will separate you from God with far more success than King Henry ever could."

Mirabella bowed her head, annoyed. How dare the abbess presume that her intentions were anything but pure?

"I beg of you, Sister, do not do this," Sister Julia cautioned Mirabella as the two quit the chapter house, where, to the surprise of everyone and the dismay of some, Mirabella did not receive punishment for her diatribe. "You have great sway over the women here—you could lead them all into danger. Do not persist. You must accept our fate and trust in God to care for us."

"It isn't always that simple, Sister," Mirabella told her with a sigh of annoyance. "God requires us to serve Him above and beyond what we sometimes feel capable of. I am fighting for His Church. I am not going to slink off into the country to lick my wounds while the monasteries are looted and my brothers and sisters in God are thrown to the wolves. Perhaps some can live with that on their souls, but I cannot."

"Mirabella." Sister Julia's voice was soft as she spoke her given name. "You are my child. . . . I beg you, for the first and last time, as your mother, not to do this. Come with me. We will retire to York. I have an uncle there. I am certain he will extend his generosity to me. We could be so happy. And we could establish some sort of monastic community of our own, perhaps not as formal as this. Perhaps it does not need to be like this. As long as our hearts are pure in their intent to serve and know the Lord, I do not think it matters where we reside."

Mirabella stopped walking and turned to Sister Julia, fixing her with eyes hard as mirrors. "If you think you can use our tie of blood to manipulate me, you are wrong, *Sister*."

Sister Julia flinched at this, then averted her head.

"As it is, I do not expect you to understand," Mirabella went on. "You are accustomed to running away from life; you ran from me, you ran from scandal, you ran from my father. Why would now be any different?"

Sister Julia straightened, raising her chin in defiance as she regarded her daughter. Her voice when she spoke was low, laced with venom. "If I have been running my whole life, then indeed so have you. Did you not run away from the scandal of Lady Grace, from Brey's death, from your feelings for the man you love and can never have? Don't lie to me, Mirabella, not to *me!*" At once her face softened. She reached out, cupping Mirabella's cheek in her hand. "Above all, don't lie to yourself. Examine your motives, my girl. Examine your soul."

Mirabella bit her lip until she flinched from the pain. At last she said, "You do as your conscience advises and I shall do the same."

Sister Julia cocked her head, her eyes filled with irony. "Well, then. If your introspection is sincere, I have nothing to fear. Do I?"

Cecily watched her son, Harry, romp through her garden in the company of his favorite companion, Alice's daughter Joanna. Together the two children toddled about, exploring their surroundings, pinching flowers off their stems, fingering the delicate petals in amazement as they took in the bright colors of summer.

The young mothers looked on through fond eyes. Nearby Alice's daughters Ellen and Margery played, shifting to other locales as soon as the babies caught up to them.

"The little ones always get left out," Alice laughed.

Cecily smiled as she rubbed the slight swell of her belly. Her womb had only just quickened with her and Hal's second child. She was as happy as she was terrified. She did not know if she could live through another birth if it proved as difficult as Harry's. It seemed, however, that as fearful as she was, Alice was far more anxious.

She observed her friend now, noting the pinched, pallid complexion, the puffiness beneath her eyes, the distant gaze.

"Alice, what is it?" she asked at last.

Alice pursed her lips. She bowed her head. "I have been thinking of the future, of my daughters. With the dissolution of the monasteries, I cannot imagine it possible that they ever be sent away now. I had hoped to send them soon, but now . . ."

Cecily's heart lurched at the thought. "Alice, but they're only babies!" She laughed in nervousness as she covered her friend's hand with hers. "You need not send them off so soon."

"I do. The sooner the better." Alice bit her lip, averting her head.

Cecily's heart pounded with some unnamed dread. "Why, Alice?"

"He . . . he just won't leave me alone. You know?" She rubbed her neck absently as she spoke. "Every day, every night, he is on me. I'm so exhausted. And the babies keep coming, all of them blasted girls." She began to tremble. "Had God granted me a different life and a different husband, I wouldn't have minded them. They would have been a comfort to me. . . ." She shook her head. "But not here, not now. Now they are as much a curse as they are accursed. Edward and his eldest sons . . . they descend upon us like vultures. No one is safe. They *are* just babies, Cecily!" She hugged herself, stiffening a moment, perhaps stifling a sob before continuing. "If it were just me it would not matter. I can stand it. I have stood it," she added in soft tones. "But Edward says it's our duty to satisfy the hot blood of the family males. Far better for him and the boys to get it from home than contract the pox by whoring." The meaning of the statement hung in the air like a dense, strangling fog. Burning bile rose in Cecily's throat. She swallowed hard. "You see, he has his heirs," Alice went on. "It makes no difference to him now who my children look like—if they resemble one of his sons more than him. . . ." She shrugged.

Cecily's stomach churned. "Oh, God, Alice . . ."

Alice buried her face in her hands, dissolving into sobs.

Cecily wrapped her arms about her, holding her close, her heart wrenching in terror as all of her suspicions about Alice's household were at last confirmed.

"Is there not something to be done?" Cecily breathed. "Perhaps my Lord Hal—"

"No!" Alice's tone was sharp, edged with tears. "Not a word to a soul, Cecily, do you hear me? I told you to relieve my burden, to seek your comfort, nothing more. There is nothing more can be done."

"But Lord Hal could help," Cecily urged. "He is a gentle, honorable man. If he knew what Edward was about he would see justice done."

"Justice for a woman?" Alice returned, her tears replaced by a cynical smirk. "Cecily, don't be naïve."

Cecily's shoulders slumped. "All right," she acquiesced. "I won't tell him." Whether it was right or wrong she did not want to ponder. She would do as Alice asked. She was her friend, was she not?

Alice visibly relaxed, her features softening, her shoulders easing. She sighed. "As it is, there will be no more children."

"How will you manage that?" Cecily asked. She couldn't fathom it, especially given the circumstances.

"There is a woman in the forest," Alice said. "She has ways, herbs and the like that can stop a child from starting—"

"A witch?" Cecily's cheeks burned at the thought. "But if Sir Edward ever found out—"

"He won't find out," Alice said in low, certain tones.

"But how can you be sure?"

"Cecily! He won't find out!" Alice said again. "Unless you tell. And you will not, will you?"

Cecily's heart sank. She felt queasy as she shook her head.

At once she was certain she trod on dangerous ground.

❧ 12 ❧

It was agonizing watching the nuns trickle forth from the convent into the world, leaving the safety of the cloister behind them perhaps forever. With tearful good-byes, the women left the only home they had known, some for the better part of their lives. Some were collected by family members, some ventured out alone. The abbess thought to stay till the last sister in Christ departed but in the end shook her head at Mirabella, her rheumy eyes glazed with tears.

"I will not stay for this," the abbess said. "My heart cannot take it." She made the sign of the cross before Mirabella. "Bless you, child. I pray you are directed in wisdom—and right."

And it was so that only three remained as servants to Lord Francis Morton, the gentleman who assumed temporary management of the abbey for the Crown, which would now be a sheep farm, like any other ordinary landholding. Nothing more.

When the guards came to dismantle their home of its treasures, Sister Julia, with great reluctance, Sister Agnes, the sub-prioress, and Mirabella awaited them. They made for a pathetic resistance, gathered in the chapel, pretending as they had pretended to for so many days now to be occupied with the mundane tasks of servitude to their new earthbound master.

"Three is not so bad a number," Mirabella quipped with forced cheer as her heart thudded in time with the hooves thundering up the road. "We do remarkably well with the Father, Son, and Holy Ghost," she added, feeling clever.

Sister Agnes began to wring her hands. "They are coming! Oh, blessed Christ, they are coming! Today is the day!" She began to cry. "I should have gone. Taken my pension and removed myself to safety. Now we will be seen as rebels. Poor old Lord Morton will have been betrayed, and him just doing what he's told," she rambled. "I should have followed the abbess's advice; didn't she tell me we were two old women, unfit for the battles of men? God's truth will reign in the end, with or without our interference. Now I will never know a day of peace."

"Take heart," Mirabella assured her in tones gentle but firm as she reached out to still her hands. "If God is for us, who can be against?"

The doors to the chapel burst open as the small regiment of guards entered.

"Good day, ladies. We mean you no harm. If you will simply step aside that we might carry out our orders, all will go smoothly," said the lieutenant, his tone not altogether threatening as he regarded the three women standing at the altar.

"I am afraid you will be disappointed," said Mirabella. "We are sisters in Christ and stay to remind you that you are in peril of your souls if you desecrate this holy place."

The man tossed a smirk at his comrades-in-arms before returning his attention to Mirabella, who fixed him with her uncompromising stare, all the while hoping he could not hear her heart pounding against her ribs. She entwined her hands in those of the two nuns at her sides.

"You expect to hold us off then from our duty ordained by the king?"

"Yes," said Mirabella. "For we are ordained by one even higher than the king: God."

The man laughed as he approached her. "Not anymore," he said. His breath was foul, his cheeks ruddy. He appeared to be in his middle thirties and was built with the shoulders of an ox. He reached out, laying a heavy hand on Mirabella's shoulder. She resisted the urge to tremble. "Lass, I respect your determination, but 'tisn't wise to meddle in the affairs of the world. Leave this place. 'Twould be better for you."

"We will not," Mirabella said, shrugging his hand off of her shoulder as she stepped closer to the altar, as if hoping to absorb some supernatural strength from it. "Nor will we allow you to defile the house of the Lord by robbing it of its holy treasures. You will go now! Go in the name of the Lord!"

"My lady," the man said, his voice low and menacing as he stepped even closer. "I am still here. I am a man, not a demon to be cast out, and I have not a saint's patience. Remove yourselves and no harm will come to you. Remain and you will be dealt with in the manner I see fit."

At this Sister Agnes began to wail.

The man turned to her, a dark smile twisting his lips. "You want to leave, don't you, my lady?" he asked, his tone an exaggeration of gentleness. "Go now. We'll not detain you. Go."

Sister Agnes tossed Mirabella and Sister Julia a fleeting glance of wild fear mingled with apology before hurrying out of the chapel, the heavy oaken doors slamming with the resounding crack of finality behind her. Mirabella's throat went dry.

"Men! These ladies prefer to watch us do our bidding! Let us commence as we have been commanded!" he ordered then.

At once, with the practiced efficiency of seasoned soldiers, the men took to loading up trunks and chests with all manner of décor. The carts were already heavy with loot: paintings, books from the library, tapestries, plate, altarpieces for the treasury. Mirabella swallowed an onset of tears. In weeks prior, all rents and lands owned by the abbey had been reverted to the Crown without incident. But this . . . this was tantamount to rape.

Sister Julia clasped Mirabella's hand. "We best leave while we have the chance," she whispered. "Before we are in real danger."

Mirabella shook her head. She swallowed hard. "Lord Morton will protect us."

"Lord Morton is with *them*, don't you see?" Sister Julia said in a frantic whisper. "He doesn't care what happens to us. If we are seen to be working against the king's will he'll just as soon help them be rid of us. Do not be a fool to expect his protection—"

"Then go if you are afraid!" Mirabella snapped. She did not want to hear arguments, logical or not. Nothing could be allowed to mar her victorious fantasy.

Sister Julia remained rooted in place, her breathing shallow.

When the lieutenant began to chisel away at a golden statue of the Holy Mother from its marble base, Mirabella could stand it no more. She hurled herself upon him.

"Blasphemer! How dare you? No!" she cried, pummeling him with her fists. Tears of fury streamed down her cheeks. Was nothing sacred? How could this man go about these evil deeds so carelessly?

"Look at this!" he cried, delighted with the spectacle. He wrapped his arms about her, pinning her to his body. "Gentlemen, perhaps we have been too hasty in our efforts to dismiss these lovely ladies," he muttered as he removed her hood, revealing her cropped dark curls. He stroked her jawline. Mirabella averted her head, bile rising in her throat as she at last began to realize the enormity of the danger she had placed herself in.

"Come now, lass, I told you I would be reasonable!" he teased as he backed her against the wall. He pressed himself against her groin; she attempted to wriggle away. "If you're a good girl, I'll even give the other lads a turn with you. . . . I've never had a woman of God before. I expect the experience to be . . . divine?"

He began to chuckle as he ran his hand under her gown, along her bare leg to her secret parts. Mirabella squeezed her legs together, yelping in pain as he inserted his fingers. This seemed to excite him further, for his breathing quickened as he forced her legs apart with his own and attempted to hike up her gown. Mirabella squeezed her eyes shut, emitting an involuntary sob.

In all her life she had never been as afraid as she was at that moment. She began to scream. It had all been for nothing. She had failed God and now He was punishing her.

"You will stop this!" a voice thunderous with authority cried. Sister Julia! Her mother . . . Yes, her mother would save her. . . .

Time seemed to stop. There was no sound, not that Mirabella could make out, and everyone's movements seemed too slow to be real, as though they were exaggerating them in a masque mocking movement itself. Maybe that's what this was: a horrible, evil masque. Yes, that had to be it. It couldn't be real. It couldn't have all gone this wrong. People couldn't be this wicked.

Mirabella turned panicked eyes to Sister Julia, who was charging toward the lieutenant with the very chisel he had been using on the statue. She raised it above her head. Mirabella drew in a sharp breath as she watched Sister Julia's green eyes widen. Slow, fluid as a dancer, the soldier turned from Mirabella toward her mother and manipulated the chisel from her hand by a twist of her delicate wrist while with his other hand he brought the hilt of his sword crashing against the side of her temple.

As slow as time seemed to be moving before, now it lurched forward with dizzying speed. Sister Julia was flung—or was she flinging herself?—into Mirabella's arms and the two collapsed to the floor.

"Sister!" Mirabella cried, cradling her mother's bloodied head. "Oh . . . please . . ."

In a movement almost spasmodic, Sister Julia seized Mirabella's face between her hands, fixing her with a hard, uncompromising gaze. "Forgive," she whispered, her voice audible only to Mirabella. "*Let go.*" With that, the eyes glazed over and the surge of life that gave Sister Julia the strength to utter this last command receded. Her hands slipped from her daughter's face, her head lolled to the side.

Mirabella cast helpless eyes at the lieutenant, whose sword was already in his scabbard as though that unpleasant episode had just been in a day's work. She swallowed an onset of bile, reverting her gaze to Sister Julia once more. In awe, she watched a pool of deep crimson surround her mother's head, some nightmarish perversion of a halo.

"You." The lieutenant's voice. Mirabella raised her eyes, dazed. He towered over her, the darkest shadow in her world. "Now I've had enough from high-minded bitches. Let me to my business."

There was naught but to obey. He had won, he and the king,

Cromwell and Cranmer. She had lost. How much she had lost! Mirabella clasped her mother to her breast. She lowered her head, forcing herself to look upon the face of the woman who had loved her completely, without condition, the woman for whom she had shown nothing but disrespect. Even in the end she had accused her of being a coward, of running away from life, from her. . . . Yet when Mirabella's life was in jeopardy Sister Julia did not hesitate once. She would have killed for her. This sister in Christ would have killed to spare her daughter's virtue. In that brave, selfless attempt she lost her life.

And Mirabella was to blame. Mirabella had killed her the same as if she had been wielding the sword.

Mirabella began to rock the body back and forth. In vain she felt for the pulse of life in Sister Julia's neck. Nothing. What had she done? Surely she could have found a better way. . . . She could have appealed to her father. He would have raised an army for her. . . . No. Not Hal Pierce. He was too passive, too obedient. He would never risk the king's displeasure.

Oh, Mother, forgive me . . . forgive me. . . .

"My lady . . ."

A warm hand stroked Mirabella's forehead. She grimaced, her eyelids fluttering as a strangled whimper stuck in her throat. Images came swirling back to her, merciless, terrible.

"Oh, my dear lady . . ." The soft male voice once more.

Mirabella's eyes opened at last, allowing her to draw into focus the face of the abbey's new steward, James Reaves, stooping over what she assumed to be her bedside, though how and when she arrived in a bed she never knew. She had the presence of mind to recognize the infirmary, however, and fresh tears stung her eyes at the thought of the many hours she had spent there nursing the sick. She squeezed her eyes shut against the memory.

"I didn't know," Master Reaves was telling her. "The soldiers . . . everything was happening so fast and I was detained. I found you in the chapel unconscious and Sister Julia . . . oh, the poor, dear lady . . ." He bowed his head, stray locks of blond hair sweeping across his forehead.

"Where is she now?" Mirabella demanded in tones sharper than she intended.

"She has been laid to rest, Sister Mirabella," Master Reaves assured her. Then softly, "Do you know . . . who did it, my lady?"

"It matters not," Mirabella replied in hoarse tones. "Justice will not find them in the England of Henry VIII." She rolled on her side, back to the young steward.

"Sister, you cannot mean to keep this quiet!" he cried, resting a hand on her shoulder. She jerked it away, drawing the covers to her neck. He withdrew his hand, backing away. "I am sorry . . . I meant no disrespect. It is just that I want to help you. Please."

Mirabella remained silent.

"Your family," he said. "They should be informed."

"I will go to them when I am ready and not before," Mirabella said in sharp tones, rolling over to face him. "Until then, we will not speak of it to anyone. Please."

Master Reaves shook his head. "But, dear mistress, why?"

"I am not your dear mistress," Mirabella hissed. "I am Sister Mirabella, do you hear?"

The bewildered steward nodded. "Yes, of course. But—but you do recall what has come to pass?"

"I do," Mirabella said. "That changes nothing." With this she laughed a shrill, joyless sound that caused the steward to shiver. "Do you honestly think I remained to be a mere servant to Lord Morton? No. I stayed to fight for my home, for my calling, for everything holy that King Henry and his—his *minions* are stripping the land of." Tears rolled down her cheeks in smooth, slick trails. "But I lost . . . I lost."

He shook his head, this time in sadness. "No, Sister. Any fight for God is won in Heaven, even if we still suffer here." He leaned closer to her, threading his fingers through hers. She was too exhausted to withdraw. "I will tell you," he whispered. "I am a convinced Catholic of the old tradition. I abhor the king's 'reforms' and so do a great many others. Even now an army is being raised against His Majesty. It is an army of which I am part. We challenge His Majesty's authority over the Church and more—so much more!—and we are to march on Lincoln." A storm of fervor gathered in his gray eyes. They were clenching each other's hands. Mirabella was sitting up, everything, all the pain, all the turmoil of the last days, swallowed up in the enthusiasm of a man she hadn't paid a scant of attention to before.

"How many amass?" she asked, afraid to hope.

"A good forty thousand brave souls," answered the steward.

"Forty thousand!" Mirabella cried. "That is a sizable force! Then perhaps something can be done. Perhaps it won't have been in vain. . . ." Her voice broke. She cast her eyes at their joined hands, then slowly disengaged. She could not bring herself to meet his eyes.

He nodded. "All of the vile crimes that have been committed in the name of the king and his perversion of the Church will be avenged."

"May God bless and keep you, Master Reaves," Mirabella whispered, sinking back onto the pillows.

The steward's tone was tender. "But what of you? Do you truly intend to remain here, after everything?"

Mirabella pursed her quivering lips. "I don't know," she confessed brokenly. "I don't know what is to become of me now. I have a family and a home and yet to return to them, to that world, is to return to a world where I am of no use—"

"No use! But you are of noble blood," Master Reaves observed. "You *do* have power. A voice at court! You could seek audience with Queen Jane. She is said to be of gentle nature and sympathetic to our cause. . . ."

Mirabella regarded him with wide eyes. "It is . . . our cause, isn't it?"

Master Reaves offered a slow nod. "More than ever, good Sister."

Almost against her will, a new purpose began to surge through Mirabella's veins.

As soon as Mirabella recovered herself enough to keep her composure, she set off to Sumerton. She sent no word, no message bespeaking her ordeal. Her father and Cecily were well aware of the abbey's closing and that she had chosen to remain with Sister Julia as a servant. Though they had pleaded with her in letters to return home rather than suffer such indignity, she had made it clear that her place was beside her mother.

Now Mirabella bore the painful responsibility of disclosing Sister Julia's death. She did not want to lie, but neither could she bear to tell the complete truth. If her father knew what really happened, that Mirabella was to blame . . . She could not abide it. He must not know. There had to be a way to hide the truth while not offending God. By the time she arrived at Castle Sumerton, Mirabella believed she had contrived a proper account, vague enough so as not to seem too deceitful, detailed enough to satisfy.

So it was with squared shoulders and a high head that she quit her coach and entered the home of her childhood. The castle was a hum of activity. Servants bustled here and there, the guests who always managed to find a warm welcome with the Pierces cavorted with one another at dice and cards, while a new sight, something Mirabella had not expected at all, made its presence known above all others. Children.

A small boy was leading a pack of little ones, waving about a wooden sword. "Enemies afoot!" he cried, charging toward Mirabella. "Who goes there?"

His demand, in an exaggerated brogue, disarmed Mirabella despite everything.

"I am Mistress Mirabella Pierce," she said in haughty tones of equal exaggeration. "And who, might I ask, are you?"

The child's face screwed up in confusion as he regarded her, his blue eyes bright and intent under their fringe of thick blond lashes. *Brey's eyes*, Mirabella thought, her heart constricting in a moment of anguish.

"Mirabella Pierce?" he returned, his shrill voice a thrill of enthusiasm. "Then you are my sister! I'm Harry!" He dropped the sword with a clatter and rushed toward her, throwing his arms about her waist.

Shocked at the show of unexpected affection, Mirabella wrapped her arms around the child, a lump swelling her throat. She bit her lip. So this was the little brother of whom she had been written. She had never once come to see him, nor did she allow Cecily to bring him to the abbey. Guilt coursed through her. It must have pained her father and Cecily a great deal to think she had wanted nothing to do with their much-anticipated heir.

"Where are you, you little imps?" A musical voice interrupted Mirabella's reverie.

She beheld the owner of the voice—a very radiant, very pregnant Cecily.

The two women stood before each other in a moment of shock. The emotion between them was tangible; even Harry's lip began to tremble under its power. At last, Mirabella offered a curtsy.

"Lady Cecily," she said in low, formal tones.

The tears that were welling in Cecily's eyes spilled over as she rushed toward Mirabella, seizing her hands in her own. "I have never been 'Lady Cecily' to you," she told her, gathering her in her arms.

Mirabella relished the embrace as she held the woman who had shared most of the important moments of her life. She held Cecily as close as the pregnant belly between them would allow.

Cecily pulled away first, reaching up to stroke Mirabella's cheek, now slick with tears of her own. "Oh, Mirabella, when we learned of the abbey's closing we knew not what to do. We followed your instructions, stayed away." She lowered her eyes a moment as though the thought of it still pained her. "It was all I could do to keep Hal from charging there and collecting you himself." She sighed. "But at last he agreed honoring your wishes was the best thing we could do for you." At this her expression converted to one of the child always eager to please. "Did we do the right thing?"

Mirabella could not bear to answer that question. Neither could she begin to examine the agony her father and Cecily had undergone on her behalf as they wondered what her future may hold now that the dream of a monastic life was extinguished.

Mirabella knew she must say something, however, so nodded. "I do not think anyone really knew what the 'right thing' was." With this she thought of James Reaves, the steward who was probably at Lincoln by now. They knew what the right thing was. She swallowed hard. "Anyway, it doesn't matter now. I've come home. To stay."

Cecily's teal eyes sparkled with a joy Mirabella could not fathom her presence inciting.

"Truly?" Cecily pulled Mirabella into her arms once more. "Oh, Mirabella! You have no idea how happy this will make Hal!"

At this Mirabella felt the sadness creeping in, invading the joy of the reunion. She had no right to feel happiness of any kind, not after all she had done. She extricated herself from Cecily, steeling herself against the sensations she had allowed to permeate the discipline she prided herself on, cursing what a few moments in the world outside the cloister had done to her.

"And Sister Julia?" Cecily asked, her tone softer. "Has she chosen to stay on?"

This was it. The beginning of the Lie. Mirabella squeezed her eyes shut a long moment.

"What is it?" Cecily asked, taking her arm. "Mirabella?"

Mirabella expelled a breath she did not know she was holding. "My mother has passed into the next world. An apoplexy. It was . . . fast. She knew little pain."

Cecily's hand flew to her milky breast. "Apoplexy . . . how frightening. Oh, Mirabella, I am so sorry. I'm certain your mother was grateful to have had you with her. She loved you so—"

Mirabella averted her head. "Forgive me, Cecily, but I cannot yet speak of it. I am still too fresh in my grief."

Cecily hesitated. Mirabella felt her eyes upon her, scrutinizing, searching. Did they detect her guilt?

"Of course," Cecily said at last. "Do know that when you are ready, I am always here for you."

Mirabella offered a curt nod of acknowledgment. She sighed in relief. The hardest part was behind her. It would be easier relaying the story to her father now that she had tested it on someone else.

"Where is Father?" she asked.

"Hunting," Cecily said, then looped her arm through hers as they made the familiar promenade to Mirabella's chambers. "You must be exhausted. How about I have your things sent up? I will arrange to have some food brought as well and you can take a long rest. By the time you awaken, he'll be here."

Her voice was so soothing, the suggestion so thoughtful, that tears stung Mirabella's eyes once more. She was unworthy of her friend's solicitude.

Nonetheless, she yielded to it. "That would be wonderful, Cecily. I should like that."

Cecily wrapped her arm about her waist. "We shall have a great deal to catch up on at supper tonight," she told her as they walked. "And now at last you have a chance to get to know Harry."

"That will mean a lot to me," Mirabella said automatically.

By the door of her chambers they paused. Cecily placed her hands on Mirabella's shoulders, fixing her with a gentle, significant gaze that caused Mirabella's heart to race.

"For all that is known and unknown, I am truly sorry."

She left it at that.

❧ 13 ❧

A wave of tenderness enveloped Cecily as she watched unchecked tears pour down Hal's tanned cheeks when he beheld Mirabella. Rested now, she had changed into a black mourning gown that suited her better than a nun's habit ever had.

"Home at last," Hal breathed, cupping the back of her head with one hand as he clasped her to him with the other. "Now the family is complete."

Cecily watched Mirabella's face contort with pain. All knew the family had not been complete since Brey's death. And now with the combined blows of her mother's passing and the abbey's closing, Mirabella must feel more incomplete than ever. Cecily's heart went out to her.

The family sat down to a private dinner in the solar while the guests were treated to the usual revelry in the great hall. They feasted off the boar Hal had killed that day, along with some warm bread, cheese, and figs Hal had imported just to satisfy Cecily's craving.

After Harry had been sent to bed with the nurse, Mirabella imparted the news of Sister Julia's passing to Hal. His face clouded with fear at the word *apoplexy*, then quickly converted to grief.

"Hers is a great loss to you, I know," he said in gentle tones as he laid a hand over hers. "She was a good woman." He bowed his head a long moment. "A very good woman."

Mirabella shifted in her seat, withdrawing her hand to pick at her food without eating anything. Cecily covertly watched, wondering if she would ever learn the truths behind her silences, if Mirabella would ever trust her enough to share them. Such moments could not be forced, however. She would never coax or pry. She could only wait.

"I am certain you are aware of the uprising, then," Hal said, diverting the subject from one source of grief to another.

But Mirabella perked at this. "Yes, I am. Any word?"

"It has been quelled, under threat of the Duke of Suffolk's army descending," he answered. "Thanks be to God."

"Thanks be to God!" Mirabella cried, appalled. "It is for God that the army was fighting! They fought for *me!* For all those like me, those who simply wished to dedicate their lives to God." Tears choked her. The words came out in short gasps.

"Mirabella, I know you think that. And perhaps they believed it as well," Hal told her. "But to fight against a king such as Henry, a king who will move the *whole world* to obtain his desires, is foolhardy. King Henry will crush those who oppose him with lethal precision. Please be careful, my love. You must not be seen to sympathize with rebels, no matter how you may feel in your heart."

"There are no rebels to sympathize with now," Mirabella said in tones thick with defeat. "So you need not worry."

"This rebellion is far from over," Hal informed her. "Now it's being called the 'Pilgrimage of Grace.' They are led by a lawyer, Robert Aske, and gather at York."

Cecily attempted to urge Hal into silence with scowls, eyes, and bared teeth, all hints he did not seem to pick up on. Cecily wanted to scream. Could Hal not see that this latest report incited in his daughter *hope,* not fear?

"My friend . . ." Mirabella breathed. "I wonder if . . . if he joins them."

"We must pray for a safe outcome, that no lives are lost," Cecily said, hoping to neutralize the conversation.

"Those who lose their lives for God are martyrs," Mirabella said in hard tones. "Saints."

Cecily bit her lip, exchanging a fearful glance with Hal, who at last understood the gravity of imparting such news.

It was clear to both of them. Mirabella had not changed at all.

As Mirabella eased herself back into life at Castle Sumerton, she found she was allowed all the solitude for prayer that she desired. She did not pray in the family chapel, where mass was held in the new fashion, but remained alone at her prie-dieu, where she was free to practice the True Faith.

When not maintaining a schedule that was as close to convent life as possible, she was drawn to the boy, to her little brother, Harry, who to her unexpected delight seemed to adore her. He could not comprehend the fact that she was indeed a half sister, not to mention the fact that she was *older* than his mother. While he was kept ignorant of the technicalities, Mirabella explained that she was born of another mother, many years ago, all the while trying to banish the last images of Sister Julia from her mind, her eyes glazed and sightless, her hair coated in blood. . . . No! Mirabella must not think of that. She would die if she did.

Instead she focused on Harry. She petted him, spoiled him with sweetmeats, read to him, told him Bible stories, and seemed never to tire of his childish prattle. Together they walked all the trails of her youth, places Father Alec had taken her, Brey, and Cecily as children. She told Harry of Brey, of his resemblance to him, of his mother as a little girl and how she had rejuvenated the castle. She told him of Father Alec, a tutor without rival. She even told him a little of Lady Grace, the gentle things, the good things.

"You have a way with him," Cecily observed one evening after Harry was tucked in bed. Her eyes were wistful as she rested her hand on her belly. With effort she lowered herself onto a sedan chair in the solar. "I am so glad. Sometimes . . ."

Mirabella eyed her with concern. "What is it, Cecily?"

Cecily averted her head. "I was very ill for the first few months of his life. Sometimes I feel as though because I missed those first few months, that something crucial may have been lost between us forever." She shook her head, squeezing her eyes shut a moment. "Oh, there is no shortage of love and I am certain he feels it. And yet . . . There are times I feel as though I cheated him."

"You were ill," Mirabella reasoned, strangely honored to be privy to Cecily's innermost thoughts. "You could not help what came to pass. You mustn't punish yourself for that, Cecily."

Cecily raised her head to Mirabella, reaching for her hand. Mirabella took it, marveling at its perfection. What man could resist such a dainty little hand?

Cecily went on. "I feel selfish for being so glad that you're home. Sometimes I think I could have borne things much better had you been with us then. That you would have understood what I was going through." She drew in a shuddering breath. "But you are here now and that is what matters. You'll see me through this next baby."

Mirabella shuddered at the prospect. She feared childbirth almost as much as she feared death. She could not imagine waiting in the airless, darkened chamber while Cecily labored with another one of her siblings. The thought of it caused her belly to churn with a mingling of disgust and anxiety.

She patted Cecily's hand to distract herself from the vision. "Of course, Cecily. Of course I'll be here."

Cecily regarded her with eyes so filled with trust it pained Mirabella doubly to lie.

"Father, I wonder if you could arrange for me to visit the court," Mirabella told Hal as the two went riding together one crisp December afternoon. "You have always been in favor with the Seymours." She offered a warm smile. "You are in favor with everyone," she added fondly. "But I should like to be presented to Queen Jane."

Hal's blue eyes widened at the suggestion. "I never fancied you a lady of the court, Mirabella, but if it is what you want I shall set to it directly." He searched her face a long moment. "You have endured so much. I know I cannot change the past. I cannot right the many wrongs. But I promise you, Mirabella, I will always try to help you any way I can." With this he nudged his horse closer to her palfrey and leaned in to kiss her cheek.

Mirabella reached up to finger the moist spot his lips had left behind. "I appreciate it, Father, truly."

But the sincerity of his declaration was lost on her.

She could only think of the queen, of Henry's court, and of her own private mission.

"Court? No!" Cecily cried upon learning of Mirabella's plans. "For how long?"

"Only a short while," Mirabella promised her. They were in Cecily's confinement chamber. Already the fear of another complicated birth had sent Cecily into a panic. Wild-eyed, she imagined every horror fate could hold and spent many an hour in restless anxiety.

"But you said you would be here to attend me in childbed." Cecily's voice was thick with disappointment as she regarded Mirabella. "Mirabella, I told you how awful it was last time. I thought . . . I thought . . ."

"You have the midwife and your friend Alice," Mirabella reasoned. "She knows more about childbed than I ever would want to—" *spitting out brats one after the other,* she added in her mind. "You cannot think I'd be any comfort to you. Besides, I must go. There are things happening in London that I *must* be a part of."

"Just like Father Alec," Cecily muttered, casting her eyes down at the coverlet.

"What do you mean?" Mirabella's tone was sharp.

"He left for the great happenings of Henry's London," Cecily explained. "Left on my wedding day," she added in tones soft with reminiscence. "I suppose I am just one girl. What's one small girl in comparison to all London has to offer?"

"Cecily, it's about the convent," Mirabella said, dismissing Cecily's remark. "About all the monasteries Cromwell is dissolving in King Henry's name. It's about the Pilgrimage of Grace. You cannot pretend to think that wouldn't matter to me, that I would just accept my lot without some kind of protest?"

Cecily shook her head, defeated under Mirabella's crushing, resentment-fueled determination.

"I had just hoped you would find some kind of happiness here," Cecily said. "That you could let go of the past, start again."

"You have no idea what you are saying." Mirabella rose from Cecily's bed and began to pace. "If you had only seen what I have seen, you would understand."

"Then tell me," Cecily urged, tears clutching her throat. "Make me understand."

Mirabella whirled toward Cecily, her face wrought with grief. Her lips parted to speak, but no words came forth. She clamped her mouth shut and looked down at her hands, which clenched and unclenched a rosary. All that could be heard for long moments was the sound of beads rubbing and clicking against one another. A shiver coursed through Cecily at the grating sound, causing her arms to be dappled with gooseflesh.

At last Mirabella raised her head. The beads were silenced. "Robert Aske, the leader of the Pilgrimage, has been invited to court for Christmas to establish some kind of peace. I should like the opportunity to meet him. And if I am presented to Queen Jane, I can tell her . . . everything. She can tell the king. Perhaps some difference can be made."

"Are you daft?" Cecily cried, unable to contain her anger another moment. "Do you really think anyone has any sway over this king, least of all his *wife?* One wrong word and he'll have her head!" Cecily sank against her pillows, closing her eyes against Mirabella's illogical ambitions.

"So I am supposed to stay here and do nothing, to cloister myself in my own little world where everything is lovely and safe and no one disagrees, where the biggest problem is what is on the menu for the evening?! Well, forgive me if I cannot be as accepting of tyranny as you and my father are!" Mirabella spat.

"So now we are the ones seeking escape?" Cecily observed, fixing Mirabella with a hard stare. " 'Cloistering ourselves'? I did not take you for a hypocrite, Mirabella." She expelled a heavy sigh, rubbing her belly. "We accept what is going on around us because we cannot change it. We will not try to change it. That does not mean we like it. But we have more than ourselves to think of. We have Harry. We will not jeopardize our children's future because we disagree with policy, no matter how unjust. How will it do to have Hal's or my head on a spike? So our children can keen, 'Why did they give their life?' Why, indeed? For some intangible point? To make a statement? The only statement it makes is foolishness and carelessness for your own family—your father and Harry and me, whose lives you could put in jeopardy. But you would not think of that." Cecily expelled a heavy sigh. "Sometimes the greatest heroes are those who survive these ordeals by keeping silent and waiting it out."

Mirabella's sigh betrayed her exasperation. "I see we will never agree on this. I *do* think some things are worth dying for. But I will not remain to debate this with you and upset you further in your condition. I am going to London and that is that. I am opening up Sumerton Place on the Strand."

"After everything that happened, you can still stay there?" Cecily regarded her, eyes wide with incredulity. It seemed nothing could penetrate Mirabella, not the fact that Sumerton Place was the locale of Brey's and Lady Grace's deaths, nor the fact that the elegant riverside home was also where Mirabella had learned of her parentage.

"It is only a house," Mirabella said. "It is immune to the events that transpired within."

"But you are not," Cecily said. "Are you?"

Mirabella scowled. "Of course not! But it makes sense to stay there. I am not going to dwell on what happened. It is a lovely house and I will make good use of it. I will refurbish it, perhaps. Make it my own. Father said I could do what I like with it."

"Well, then," said Cecily. "It seems you have everything figured out."

"Yes, I do," Mirabella said in cool, unaffected tones. She rose. "I best make ready." She leaned in, kissing Cecily's forehead. As she pulled away, Cecily reached up, cupping her cheek.

"There are some things worth dying for," Cecily said. "Family."

Mirabella bit her lip, blinking several times, then shook her head as if to shake away an unwanted thought before quitting the room.

Father Alec Cahill knew this would be no ordinary Christmas. The king had invited the notorious rebel leader Robert Aske to court. Just that month the Duke of Norfolk had successfully negotiated a truce in the king's name. It was such a slick transaction only Norfolk could pull it off, with his rumbling voice and silvery tongue. To the rebels he assured a pardon, promising that all of their demands would be met. He was a predator luring in his prey. A skilled manipulator, he would summon every wile at his disposal to quell the Pilgrimage of Grace with as much efficiency as possible to please His Majesty and obtain the favor he once enjoyed when his niece Anne Boleyn was at her apex.

The rebels were fools to believe any promise made by King Henry or Norfolk, Catholic as he may be.

Yet, pity the rebels' fate though he might, Father Alec knew the Pilgrimage had to be stopped. Reforms must be pushed through, a precarious ordeal as it were with Henry's attachment to the Catholic religion, sans Pope though it may be. The rebellion posed a real threat to the ambitions of the reformers. Archbishop Cranmer was as hated as he was loved. It was his Ten Articles, the list of sacraments to be celebrated by the Church of England, that was as much at the heart of the rebellion as the dissolution of the monasteries.

Father Alec did not want to see violence committed in the name of progress, even in matters of faith. He did not believe in holy war—the taking of a life could not be called godly, even if done in His name. It was his hope that wily King Henry and the hawk-nosed Norfolk could diffuse the Pilgrimage before more lives were lost.

That said, Father Alec could not say in honesty that he supported the dissolution of the monasteries himself. Though he had read Cromwell's reports of the corruption that took place behind cloistered walls, he knew the committed Lutheran Privy Seal to King Henry had trumped up the charges that he might further his own agenda. Father Alec had not the tolerance for Cromwell that his master did. A narrow-eyed, jowly man who reminded Father Alec of the result of a terrier-weasel union, Thomas Cromwell would not hesitate to take one life or a thousand if it meant achieving his goal—the Lutheranization of England. He had stood by and watched innocent lute player Mark Smeaton tortured into confessing his "affair" with the late Queen Anne with a delighted twinkle in his eye. No doubt he would stand hundreds more "confessions" if he were to prosper from it.

Father Alec knew no religious agenda was worth such blood-drenched intrigue. One could die for one's faith, but one could not kill for it.

These were the thoughts that whirled in Father Alec's mind as he strolled through the cold gallery at Windsor. He was wrapped in a cloak lined with soft otter fur to ward off the bitter winter chill and found himself clutching it around him, his fingers burrowing into the fur like worms desperate to shake the frost. He watched steam escape his lips as he expelled a heavy sigh, sniffling. He hoped he didn't run into anyone too illustrious. The cold always made him sniffle and it was most unbecoming facing a nobleman or -woman with drippage running down his face.

As he reached up to wipe away the crude reminder of his connection to humanity, his eyes beheld a woman dressed in black damask, tendrils of cropped curls spilling out from her gabled hood matching. Green eyes flashed from an olive-skinned face. Father Alec was rendered immobile.

Mirabella Pierce.

She was cocking her head at him now, her face drawn in concentration, immersed in the task of recognition. As he approached, her face softened into a hint of a smile. She extended her hands.

"Father Alec," she said, the smile growing wide as he took her hands in his. She shivered at his icy touch.

He withdrew them immediately. "Lady Mirabella, what a pleasure!" To his amazement, it truly was. Despite the many heartaches he had witnessed at Sumerton, there was still something about its residents that would always evoke in him a sense of home, of family.

"You're here." Her voice was soft. "Really here."

"*You're* here," he returned, his easy, husky voice bright with uncharacteristic enthusiasm. "You must tell me everything. Unfortunately, I haven't occasion to write to anyone, I've been kept so busy these past few years. And you, what are you doing here?" In his excitement the words came out all a-jumble. He emitted a soft laugh.

Mirabella laughed in turn. "Father is well. They had a baby, you know, a little boy, Harry, and Cecily is expecting another any moment."

Cecily, a mother? Father Alec's heart lurched, he supposed for the little girl who once was, his little pet, his little Cecily.

"They are happy, then," he said at last. "I am glad they are happy."

Mirabella nodded.

"And you?" His voice softened as he returned his gaze from his reverie to the woman before him, taking note for the first time of the fierce glint in her eyes, the expression lit with an intensity burning from within, the proud set of her jaw. For some unknown reason, he shuddered.

"No doubt you have heard of my abbey's closing," Mirabella said in tones not altogether accusatory.

Father Alec drew in a breath and nodded. Now he understood her presence at court. He braced himself for her next words, no doubt an onslaught against him and Cranmer and anyone she perceived to be in on the destruction of her dream.

But they were no such thing. Instead she said, "It was an honor and privilege to spend the time there that I did. I will remember it well."

After a moment's hesitation, Father Alec asked, "And Sister Julia? What became of her?"

"She passed on," she answered without breaking her unflinching gaze.

"My deepest condolences," Father Alec managed to say. Something seemed wrong with her response. It was too cold, too detached. Too hurried. And yet what could he expect? Mirabella knew who his master was. He could not expect her to divulge all of her secrets to him as she had in days gone by.

"Mistress, if it means anything at all," he began to venture, then stopped himself. He could not share his views about the dissolution, not even with Mirabella. As he had noted only moments before, they were no longer at Sumerton. She was a papist. He was a reformer. Her convent had just been closed and her mother was dead. He would be a fool to trust her. But he cursed himself for mistrusting her, along with the world that had made them this way.

Mirabella studied him, reading his expression. Sympathy, kindness, reluctance, wistfulness. All the expressions she had cherished in him and had somehow forgotten over the years. Her heart constricted at the sight of him, his wavy brown hair flecked with snow, his tanned face ruddy from the wind, his hazel eyes sparkling. And when he took her hands . . . It was the same reaction. It would always be the same reaction.

If fate were kind she could have remained a nun, cloistered away with her mother. If fate were kind she could have remained kept from this world of sin and vice. But fate was not kind. She was in the world now, in the world where he was. She had to learn to bear it if she was to survive.

Forcing these thoughts from her mind, Mirabella decided to rescue him from the awkward moment that had insinuated itself between them. "Robert Aske is here, I am told. It seems as though my prayers are being answered at last, that compromises are being reached."

His face, his honest face, changed once more, registering an expression Mirabella knew all too well. Pity. She averted her eyes.

"The king does not compromise, Mistress Mirabella," he told her in soft tones.

"You are a man of faith, Father Alec," she returned. "Do not tell me you have been jaded by this court, that you have become doubting."

To her surprise Father Alec released a small chuckle. "Just practical, mistress." He reached out, touching her nose in the fond gesture of a parent to a small child. "But I see you have lost none of that fiery spirit of yours. My prayer is that it serves you well."

A furious flush heated Mirabella's cheeks as she bowed her head, touched and flustered.

"Are you staying at court then?" he asked her.

"I am staying at our home on the Strand if you would like to visit," she said.

He regarded her strangely at this but said nothing except, "I will." And then he bowed. "I am afraid I must be off. Bless you, Mistress Mirabella. God keep you."

And then he was gone, leaving Mirabella breathless and fighting against the hope that she would see him again soon.

Mirabella did not have too much time to dwell on Father Alec or the strange stirring in her gut when a vision of him was summoned to mind. Today she was being presented to Queen Jane. Today she was going to make a difference.

Because of her father's connection to the Seymours, Mirabella was secured a private audience with Her Majesty. She had brought to Windsor with her one servant, a widow woman named Sarah Lucas who served as chaperone and lady's maid while she stayed at Sumerton Place. She was the perfect company for Mirabella, quiet and reserved. She asked no questions. She did what was expected of her, no less and no more.

Now she waited in the antechamber while Mirabella was shown into the queen's presence chamber. She could not appreciate the sumptuous chambers, the silks and brocades, the tapestries, the carpets. She could only focus on her good fortune of actually being invited into the queen's presence. It was a rarity to be granted audience without Her Majesty's ladies in attendance. Mirabella planned to make the most of it. Her heart raced as she dipped into her deepest curtsy before her sovereign, and as Mirabella raised her head she met one of the gentlest countenances she had ever seen. Though the tiny queen was no beauty, with her dusty blond hair, pasty complexion, and chin that suggested weakness, there was something in her delicate grace that reminded Mirabella of Cecily. Momentary guilt surged through her. She did not want to think of Cecily as she had last seen her, her eyes begging her not to leave in Cecily's time of need. If only Mirabella had told her why it was so imperative to make this journey, then perhaps she would have understood. . . .

"We are glad you have come to court, Mistress Pierce," Queen Jane said in soft tones as she gestured for Mirabella to rise.

Mirabella did so but kept her head lowered. There was something so pious about the woman it seemed disrespectful to gaze upon her.

"We remember your father fondly. He used to come to Wulfhall to hunt with our father and brothers," she went on. "Is the earl well?"

Mirabella nodded, eager to be finished with trivialities. "Yes, quite well," she answered in wavering tones. "Thank you for asking, Your Majesty."

Queen Jane's lips curved into a smile. "But you didn't request a private audience to discuss pleasantries. Please sit. Tell us how we can be of service."

The words, so sweet and sincere, caused Mirabella's throat to constrict with tears.

Mirabella sat in a stiff-backed chair nearest the queen. "I hardly know where to begin, Your Majesty." But she did begin. Through sobs the story tumbled out, word upon ugly word, and before long, with the exception of Sister Julia's relationship to Mirabella, the queen learned the tragic account of the sisters of Sumerton Abbey. "I can neither dream nor fathom any other life for myself outside the convent. I do not know what to do, where to go, where I belong. . . . I heard that you are kind." Mirabella's tone was soft, timid. "That you have begged the king to preserve the monasteries—"

Queen Jane averted her head. Her voice was very soft. "And did you also hear our husband's response to our pleas? That we should not speak of such things else we should meet the same fate as . . . as . . . ." She did not finish. Soft blue eyes fell upon Mirabella. Tears glistened against the queen's pale cheeks. "God bless you for thinking we had the power to intervene on your behalf. But we do not. . . . I do not. You have heard my motto, have you not? 'Bound to obey and serve'?" The queen offered a sad shake of the head. "My duties here are very specific. You must understand the repercussions for not meeting them. I cannot afford to direct my attentions elsewhere. It was naïve of me to try."

Mirabella regarded the queen, stunned at her dropping the royal *we*, at her condescending to share such personal thoughts with her.

Mirabella expelled a tremulous breath. "No," she said at last. "It was I who was naïve." Tears paved cool trails down her cheeks. Embarrassed, she daubed them away with her kerchief. "I am sorry for troubling you, Your Majesty."

"We are sorry we cannot be of help," Queen Jane said, returning to protocol once more. "Please do not be under the impression that we were not deeply moved by your story; we are touched that you would share it with us. If there was something we could do . . ." The queen trailed off, shaking her head once more. "We will keep you in our prayers, be assured."

Mirabella nodded, numbed at the revelation that raged through her, the thought that perhaps prayers were not good enough. In good faith she had told this woman all, this woman, supposedly the most powerful in the land. She did not want her prayers. She wanted action. But not even this exalted personage could be of help. She was just another lamb to Henry VIII's merciless lion.

"Meantime," Queen Jane was saying, "we extend our hospitality to you. Stay with the court for Christmas. There is someone we would like you to meet."

Mirabella could only curtsy and nod. "It will be an honor," she managed to say.

And with that the audience was over.

❧ 14 ❧

At the Christmas celebrations held in the sumptuous great hall of Windsor, Mirabella noted tapers rising from golden candlesticks, treasure no doubt stolen from one sacred place or another. She trod rich carpets that once warmed the floors of cathedrals, her head bowed to disguise the effort it took to choke back her disgust. When the floor beneath her feet became a blur of warm tears, a gentle voice beckoned her, so soft, in fact, that it took a moment for Mirabella to register it as being real and not a whisper of Divinity.

She raised her head to find Her Majesty, surrounded by her attendants. The little blond woman offered an ethereal smile. "Mistress, we are so pleased you have chosen to remain with us."

Mirabella offered a low curtsy, swallowing the painful lump of disappointment swelling her throat, disappointment in a humanity that never failed to prove its great capacity for failure, disappointment in all that had been lost, and the greatest disappointment, that she, as a member of this useless mass, had no ability to reclaim it. She was a voice struck dumb. A woman and a bastard, nothing more.

"Mistress Pierce, may I present His Majesty's daughter the Lady Mary?" The queen's gentle voice proved a respite from her introspection.

Mirabella raised her eyes to the slim, dark young woman beside the queen. Dressed in a modest gown, boldly wearing a rosary at her hip and a crucifix at her throat, she had the carriage of her rightful but long-denied title: princess.

A woman and a bastard, like her.

For the first time since her arrival, Mirabella found her lips curving into a smile of warm sincerity. She curtsied once more. "My lady."

"Her Majesty has told me a great many things about you, Mistress Mirabella," Lady Mary said in soft tones, but unlike Queen Jane, there was an underlying intensity fueling each word. "I should like to promenade with you."

"Yes," Mirabella said, hope surging through her veins, causing an unexpected giddiness.

Linking arms, the two women began to walk through the crowded hall, through the carefree revelers who were no doubt celebrating a richer Christmas than last year, their pockets fattened from robbing the Church. Mirabella trembled, enraged and disgusted by the display of blatant disrespect for all that was once held holy and sacred.

It seemed Lady Mary's thoughts followed a similar path. As soon as the two women found themselves a peaceful alcove in the hall, her dark eyes narrowed. "I know what they did to you, mistress. You and countless others. Our faith has been raped," she stated. Mirabella flinched, squeezing her eyes shut against the memory of the attempt to steal her own virtue that instead robbed her mother of her life. How small a price would it have been to sacrifice her chastity rather than Sister Julia? She swallowed bitter tears, concentrating on Lady Mary's words. "Raped and made sacrifice to avarice," Lady Mary went on. "His Majesty is promising to negotiate with Aske. There will be no negotiations. You know that. Perhaps even Aske knows that."

Mirabella was told as much. She did not want to acknowledge the truth in Lady Mary's words, but there it was, naked. Raw. Cruel. "Then . . ." She swallowed an onset of unexpected tears. "Then there is no hope?"

"Not while one reformer lives in our kingdom. Not while one

Cranmer or Cromwell lives to corrupt the conscience of His Majesty and lead him into darkness," answered the bastardized princess.

Mirabella bowed her head, recalling Father Alec and his devotion to Archbishop Thomas Cranmer. *For him to see so much to admire in a man must mean there is something there to . . . No. Father Alec is as corrupted as the other reformers like him.* At this Mirabella's throat contracted. Father Alec could not be corrupted. Misguided, perhaps, but never corrupted.

"But how can the reformers be driven out? How can the True Faith ever be restored if so many are enveloped in the Lie?" Mirabella asked again.

"Do you know my bloodline, Mistress Pierce? Do you know my grandmother was Isabella of Castile?" With this, Lady Mary drew herself up to her full height, standing as proud as the royal blood running through her veins gave her right to.

Mirabella offered a slow nod.

"She was a warrior-queen," said Lady Mary, her voice laden with conviction. "And she didn't have to drive the Infidels and Jews out of Spain."

Mirabella shuddered. No, the great Queen Isabella devised another way. The Inquisition. And looking upon her granddaughter, a woman of equal ferocity and drive, convinced Mirabella that the Lady Mary bore as much hatred, as much single-minded devotion to an ideal, so she would not hesitate to bring the Inquisition to England had she the opportunity.

Something about the insinuation caused Mirabella to shiver. She pulled her cloak tight about herself, knowing nothing could ward off the internal chill.

"Surely His Majesty would not bring the Inquisition here," Mirabella said.

"No, that is too much to hope for," Lady Mary answered, her tone low. "However, when God is merciful and restores me to my rightful claim . . ." As any treason-fearing subject would, she let the thought hang.

"My lady!" Mirabella cried, struck at the boldness of the insinuation. "But the line of succession, the . . . the—"

"The bastardy?" Lady Mary's tone was flat. "I am a Princess of the Blood, just as my mother was. No one can take that away from me. It is God's will that I be restored, for God knows the truth of my legitimacy. For my restoration, I will thank the Lord for seeing me through my struggles by someday guiding this kingdom to the one True Faith."

The courage of her grandmother and the conviction of her mother, Catherine of Aragon, made for a formidable woman, thought Mirabella. She should admire this woman, draw comfort from her unswerving determination. And yet why with each word spoken did a terrible fear surge through her?

"I want to assure you that your fight has not been in vain," said Lady Mary. "Such devoted servants to Christ and his cause deserve to be rewarded—and not by what *their* perverted philosophy of rewards is." She indicated the Christmas festivities, a display of drunkenness and overeating few could rival, and all off of gold plate plundered from holy houses.

"I thank you, my lady," said Mirabella, wondering if Lady Mary was deluded or brilliant, wondering how she thought she could manage to be reinstated as princess and have her rightful place in the succession.

Yet with or without the title, Lady Mary had powerful allies and was not without assets. She was the king's daughter, she was strong in mind, though weak in body. Despite that, she was determined and shared the same goal as Mirabella, the return of the True Faith to England.

Sometimes blood had to be shed for the glory of God, Mirabella reasoned. There was nothing to fear in the Lady Mary's plan for justice.

Then why couldn't she stop trembling?

"Come," Lady Mary said, cutting through Mirabella's reverie. She seized her hand. "Let me present you to Master Aske."

At this Mirabella brightened. Together the women rose, crossing the hall to where a band of men surrounded King Henry. Laughter swirled around the group, the loudest of which was emitted from His Majesty. The trembling returned. Mirabella had yet to be presented to the king.

"Ah! My daughter!" he cried upon seeing Lady Mary, though his beady blue eyes did not reflect the joy of his exclamation. "How are you enjoying the festivities?"

"I am pleased to have been invited to court, Sire," Lady Mary responded, her tone void of emotion. Mirabella could only imagine how it was for Lady Mary to face this man, this man who had cast aside her mother, removed Mary from the succession, and stripped her of her titles, leaving her to grow ill and bitter in a drafty northern castle. This was the man who, for love of a woman he would eventually kill, would remove himself from the Pope and thus God's grace.

"May I present Lady Pierce?" Lady Mary said as Mirabella dipped into a deep curtsy.

"Rise, child." The king's voice thundered with merriment. "Pierce? The Earl of Sumerton's daughter."

"Yes, Sire," Mirabella answered, keeping her head lowered. She could not bear to look him in the face.

"And how are you enjoying our court?" he asked, putting his hands at his hips, as though challenging her to utter her dislike for it.

Mirabella offered a frosty smile. "It is a fascinating place, Your Majesty."

"Indeed it is," he returned, his tone thoughtful as his eyes roved her body in a slow, methodical fashion. Mirabella took an involuntary step back.

"Your Majesty, we were hoping to be presented to Master Aske," Lady Mary said.

"Ah, my guest," said the king, his smile strained. "What a stir he creates." With this he turned to the throng of men gathered about him. "Robert, my boy! Come meet my daughter and her friend Mistress Pierce."

A strong man in his later years came forward, cutting a fine figure in his humble but presentable courtly garb. His jaw was set, his eyes a fierce blue, shining out of a clean-shaven face and crowned with thin graying blond hair. He emanated strength and determination. Mirabella's heart pounded as he offered a low bow. She curtsied in turn.

"Well, there you have it! Make merry as my guests!" the king cried, clapping his daughter on the shoulder. "Come, Mary, dance a pretty turn for me."

"Yes, Sire," Lady Mary answered in her dull tones as she set to the floor, leaving Mirabella alone to face Robert Aske.

He inclined his head once more. "I am pleased to know you, my lady."

Mirabella's lips quivered. "I—I so admire you, Master Aske," she blurted at once. Hot tears stung her eyes as he took her hand in his. "I am a true Catholic," she whispered. "And I support the Pilgrimage. I pray the king honors his negotiations."

"God bless you," he returned, his voice low and strong. "I have every reason to believe the king will be good on his word. Take heart and have hope, my lady. We may see a return of the old ways yet."

"I pray," Mirabella said with fervency. "The things that have happened . . . the horrors I have lived . . ." She swallowed hard. "I was a sister in Christ. My cloister was robbed of its treasures and one of my—one of my fellow sisters was killed."

Aske closed his eyes as though in pain, shaking his head. "My condolences. Know you are not alone, Sister. I have heard similar reports from across the kingdom. Let us pray that now that I have met with His Majesty these terrible days are behind us."

If she could have she would have crossed herself. Instead she contented herself with his words, praying that the king would go against form and honor the promises made.

Mirabella took Master Aske's hand, hoping the fervency of her dreams for their cause translated in the squeeze she offered. "I shall never forget meeting you."

"Nor I you," he replied, squeezing her hand in turn. "God be with you, Sister."

"And also with you," she replied.

With that he rejoined his comrades, leaving Mirabella to close her eyes a long moment. For the first time in months she felt peace. Perhaps the Lady Mary and her father were wrong; perhaps Robert Aske was just the man to negotiate with the king.

"My lady?"

Mirabella opened her eyes to the familiar male voice. She flushed, realizing that she had been standing there, her arms wrapped about herself in her moment of private triumph.

It was James Reaves, the steward from Sumerton Abbey.

"Master Reaves!" Mirabella cried. "I did not know you were here as well!"

"I have accompanied Master Aske," he explained. "Oh, my lady, how goes it with you?" His brows furrowed in concern.

"I am well," she answered. "Oh, but it is wonderful. Do you think he has succeeded?"

"Things look very hopeful," Reaves replied, his voice warm. "If any man can accomplish this great thing, it is Robert Aske. He is a wonderful orator and a man of unmatched honor. I believe the king recognizes that and admires it. One can't help but admire it. He is a most dynamic man."

"Indeed," agreed Mirabella. "I am so glad to see you safe. When I heard about the rebellion in Lincoln being quelled I was frightened for you."

Reaves bowed his head. "It has been a long, hard fight. But nothing is more worthy of fighting for than the return of the old ways. Soon all will be as it should be, my lady."

"All of my prayers are with you and Master Aske," she said.

"I thank you, my lady," he answered. For a moment he stood before her, chewing his lip. The gesture was so boyish Mirabella couldn't help but laugh. He was such an innocent creature, though he must be in his twenties. He bowed his head again. "My lady, when we return north, may I call on you at Sumerton? As—as your friend?"

Mirabella was touched. She could see no harm in that. Reaves was a sweet man and his intentions were as pure as the soul shining out of his stormy gray eyes. "Of course you may," she answered in warm tones.

He bowed low. "Until then, my lady."

"Until then," Mirabella replied.

On Christmas Day, the newest Pierce was delivered after a remarkably short labor. Cecily was haunted by images of her last delivery and had insisted on Hal's presence that she might seek reassurance from his eyes. Seven hours later, Dorothy Mopps, the midwife, had brought forth a wailing baby girl with brassy blond hair discernable despite being wet.

Now Cecily sat in awe. She had been denied the experience of joy during her first tumultuous birth and her heart lurched in guilt as she beheld her daughter. The feelings that stirred within her now eclipsed any tangible happiness she had ever known and it pained her that she did not know this with Harry.

The howling little creature was cleaned and placed in her arms.

"And what shall we call this passionate little orator?" Hal asked as he allowed the baby to suckle at his finger.

Cecily gazed at her daughter. "Kristina," she said. "Our little Christmas gift. Kristina Ashley Pierce, Ashley for my mother."

"Perfect," Hal said, admiring the pair. At last the baby found some contentment and closed her eyes.

Cecily stroked the child's silky cheek. "Hal . . . the fact that she's a girl—"

"Gives me another princess to spoil," Hal assured her in gentle tones, placing a kiss on her forehead.

Cecily smiled, the knots in her shoulders easing in relief. "Somehow I don't think this little lamb will give us a choice!"

> *Mirabella,*
> *We have heard of Master Aske's victory at court and congratulate you.*
> *Our Christmas was made spectacular by the delivery of your sister, Kristina Ashley. It seemed an easy birth and Cecily is making a speedy recovery. Harry has taken quite fondly to Kristina and seems most protective. I am praying you will return to Sumerton soon that you might meet her yourself. She is strong and lusty and makes her presence known; perhaps there is a little of you in her? Do come home to us soon.*
> *With love,*
> *Your father*

Mirabella received the dispatch at Sumerton Place in early January. She did not understand her emotions. Certainly she was happy for her father and Cecily, relieved that the labor anticipated with such dread had gone well. The fact that it had produced a girl did not trouble her; after all, with Harry secured as the Sumerton heir the need for a boy seemed less imminent. Then what was the bittersweet constricting of her heart?

She cursed herself. She had known this feeling before. Envy. Raw and primal envy. Now that her calling to God had been denied her, her life was a void of uncertainty. She was young with no prospects and no identity. As a novitiate nun, her life was defined, laid out before her, predictable, neat. Now she was unsettled, afraid. Would she marry, then? Would she ever know the happiness of a family? What's more, did she even want that? How could she so easily slip from one way of life to another? Did she owe it to God to remain chaste, alone in service to Him? Or was there another way to serve? Her chastity was bought at such a great price; would she mock her mother's sacrifice to give it in marriage?

Mirabella settled in the solar before a cheery fire incongruent with her mood and reread the dispatch. She wondered if her father's legitimate daughter would somehow usurp whatever rank she held in his heart, then chastised herself for the childishness of the thought.

"A visitor, mistress." The voice of her steward cut her fancies short as Mirabella waved them in.

"Mistress Mirabella."

God, it was him. Father Alec . . .

Mirabella's heart lurched. She rose from her seat, turning to find Father Alec behind her. He stood, cloak draped over his arm, his face somber.

She offered a timid smile. "How kind of you to call on me."

"How are you, mistress?"

"I am well," she answered. "I received a dispatch from Father today—they had a girl."

Father Alec lowered his eyes. His smile was fixed, grim. "Congratulations to them." He bowed his head. "Mistress . . . have you heard any news from court?"

"The court is too exhausting for me to keep up with." She sat, gesturing for Father Alec to take the wingback chair across from her. He sank into the seat, drawing in a breath.

"I thought to come, to tell you myself," he began. "It's about Master Aske. Another rebellion broke out in the North."

"Another rebellion? But the king—c-compromises were made at Christmas . . ." Mirabella stammered, her heart racing.

"Master Aske wanted to stop it," he explained. "But he couldn't." He sighed. "I'm afraid the instigators have been executed."

Mirabella's gut lurched. Her hand flew to her stomach, her face began to tingle and flush. "Executed? And Master Aske?"

Father Alec met her eyes, pointed. "I believe his days are numbered. The Pilgrimage of Grace is all but put down. It is no more."

Tears clenched Mirabella's throat and obscured her vision. "No! And the compromises? The promises?"

"I am certain you know what will become of those," Father Alec told her. "My dear, it is the king's will or no will." He reached out, taking her trembling hands in his. "I am so sorry."

Mirabella sank her head into her hands, shoulders quaking with sobs. "It can't be . . . then my cause . . . there is no hope. There is no hope for any of us. I will never know the life I knew before. Everything has been for nothing!"

"It is a stain on the reforms," Father Alec commented. "But perhaps this should be a sign to you to begin again, forge a new life for yourself. While I do not approve of some of the king's reforms, not all of the strides being made are negative."

Mirabella raised her head. "How can you say that to me? When everything I have done has been for God, for the True Faith? I am denied my calling; I am denied everything now. And everything I tried to accomplish, everything has been for naught! My poor mother—her death—"

Father Alec furrowed his brow in puzzlement. "Your mother's death?"

"Yes, my mother's death!" Mirabella seethed, rising. "When we

were defending our pathetic cause, my mother died trying to protect *me!* Another who sought to execute the king's 'reforms' killed
her with the hilt of his sword after she stopped him from . . .
from—" She dissolved into sobs. She hadn't meant to say it; she
had never meant to say it.

"My child." Father Alec rushed forward, gathering her in his
arms. "Oh, my poor, dear child."

She gave in to the embrace, burying her head in his chest, relishing the closeness as she sobbed.

"And your father and Cecily—they do not know—"

"Of course not!" she cried. "I wouldn't upset their nuptial bliss,
would I?"

Father Alec said nothing. He stroked her hair.

"My mother is dead and I am to blame. And now there is nothing left for me. I have nothing," she went on in small tones. "I am
nothing."

Father Alec drew back, gripping her by the shoulders, meeting
her intense emerald gaze with his. "That is where you're wrong.
You are not to credit yourself for your mother's death; she did what
any mother would do and you may be assured that she is rewarded
for it in Heaven." He cupped Mirabella's face between his hands.
"You have suffered a cruel blow—more than anyone should suffer.
But God has plans for you; He will not fail you. The world you
know is ending, but something new is being born in its place. You
have the opportunity to be a part of that, to be a part of creating a
new and more perfect faith—"

"How can we create a faith more perfect than that which God
Himself set down?" Mirabella returned, appalled at the suggestion.

Father Alec shook his head. "Men set down the doctrine; God
set down the ideal. It is to that ideal which we must strive."

Mirabella shook her head. "I've done all I can to defend the
faith that I hold as true. I can do no more; that is clear to me. I do
not want to do more. I want no part in these . . . 'reforms.' "

Father Alec sighed. "God will not leave you behind," he assured. "Yield to Him. His will may surprise you. Meantime, forge

ahead with a new life. You are an educated woman; you could be a governess, perhaps, or a lady-in-waiting. I could help secure you a position with a respectable family, if you like—"

"I could not bear that kind of degradation," Mirabella told him. "As far as being a governess, no one would appreciate what I have to teach." She bowed her head, defeated. "I suppose there's naught to do but return to Sumerton and be of what little help I can to Cecily and my father."

"It is a good start." Father Alec offered a small smile. "A place to reflect, to collect your thoughts."

"And you, Father?" Mirabella raised her eyes to him. "Can you really remain here? Can you truly abide the travesty our world has come to?"

Father Alec bowed his head. "I will remain where I am needed and pray that good comes of it."

"Then I suppose there's nothing left to say," Mirabella said. "Except, if I may ask, will you write to me at Sumerton, Father?"

Father Alec's face softened. "I will do that." He pulled away, bowing. "I must return."

"As must I, it seems," Mirabella noted, resting a hand on his shoulder. "Godspeed, Father."

Father Alec's smile was sardonic as he made his exit, leaving Mirabella to stand alone in a house that seemed far too big and a world that seemed hopelessly bigger.

❧ 15 ❧

At Sumerton Mirabella was pleased to be introduced to her new sister. While in London she had purchased several bolts of fabric to have garments made for her, and Cecily cooed over them with delight. Mirabella went through the motions of helping her plan the baby's new wardrobe, and as time placed itself between her and the life she had once known she found herself falling into a sort of routine. Mornings were spent with the children; the afternoons she passed sewing with Cecily. The evenings were hers, devoted to prayer and contemplation. When the weather was pleasant, Mirabella went riding with her father or called on his tenants, that she might see to their needs. In this she felt she was at least fulfilling her charitable obligation, and she took to mending clothes for them and caring for their sick, finding the much-needed solace of a purpose.

Of the rebellion, not a word was said, not even when Robert Aske was hung outside of York Castle in chains, a grisly illustration of what became of "traitors."

This and any other horrors remained unspoken. Her family spoke of the children, of impetuous little Harry and Kristina's latest antics, of Cecily's plans to increase the family further. Light-hearted things, things that did not require thought or emotion. Or the pain of remembrance.

Yet everything was forced. There was a palpable discomfort in Mirabella's exchanges with Cecily and her father. No one wanted an impassioned treatise on the state of religion in England; no one wanted to be uncomfortable. So Mirabella kept her thoughts to herself. She yielded to the monotony of the mundane, quelling her restlessness, quelling her grief, in fact, quelling everything that required feeling.

When the bells tolled the birth of the long-awaited Prince of Wales, little Edward, relief surged through Mirabella. Perhaps the birth of a living prince would soften King Henry; perhaps this gift from God would show him the error of his ways. . . . But God had other plans. He always mocked the world with His plans the moment one became complacent. Twelve days after Prince Edward's birth, the bells heralded the death of Queen Jane, perhaps the last Catholic queen England would ever know. There would be no softening the king now. Time, that invisible army more exacting and lethal than any human one, marched on, relentless. By 1540 the king procured for England a Lutheran bride, the German Anne of Cleves, a woman who was said to repulse His Majesty at first sight.

Sporadic letters from Father Alec delivered a grim scenario.

> *Lady Mirabella,*
> *Four months after his marriage the king has put Queen Anne aside in favor of a fifth bride, Catherine Howard, executing Lord Privy Seal Thomas Cromwell, the newly made Earl of Essex, as a wedding present to the Catholics. Cromwell was the foremost reformer at court. His arranging the king's marriage to the Lutheran Anne of Cleves proved his undoing.*
>
> *My heart goes out to our young Queen Catherine. At fifteen, it would be difficult to know one's own mind, and I doubt she is espoused to any doctrine. She is ruled through another, her uncle, the Duke of Norfolk. It is his desire to return England to the old ways. You may yet get your wish.*

Otherwise I am well. My service to Archbishop
Cranmer is most rewarding. I contributed to the
Bishop's Book, which helped outline the tenets of our
Church of England. In addition, the composition of the
Six Articles last year holds true to Catholic tradition as
well. . . .

Hope warmed Mirabella's veins like wine. Though she regretted the reluctant nature of Father Alec's missive, the fact that the
True Faith had powerful supporters encouraged her. She rejoiced
in the death of Cromwell, the man who had pursued the dissolution of the monasteries with the spite of a jilted lover. No, his was
no loss to be sure. This new Church of England was a perversion
of the True Faith, a cheap mirror of Catholicism sans the Holy Father. It could never be blessed by God; its followers were bound to
suffer, just as Cromwell suffered. They were not martyrs, they
were traitors of the highest degree—betrayers of God.

Yet this strange new faith was important to Father Alec and his
palpable disappointment over its possible demise saddened her.
His calling was as important to him as Mirabella's had been to her.
She could empathize with his plight. She was grateful he wrote
her; she wanted to share his thoughts, his ideas, disagree with
them though she might. Whatever his letters revealed, good or
bad, Mirabella treasured each word.

It was all of Father Alec she would ever be allowed to hold dear.

Winter, 1543

"We have a new steward," Alice Camden informed Cecily and
Mirabella one afternoon as they embroidered in the bower. "James
Reaves. He was the steward for Sumerton Abbey. He seems a gen-
tle and capable young man."

"James Reaves?" Mirabella raised her eyes from the garment
she had been sewing for little Kristina. "I know him. He was in the
Pilgrimage. . . ." Cecily noted a flush lighting her cheeks. "He is a
gentleman, a kind man."

Cecily smiled inwardly. Perhaps it would do Mirabella good to have a caller. "Does he have a family, this young Master Reaves?"

Mirabella shot Cecily a glance, pursing her lips.

"No, he's a bachelor," Alice answered, her lips curving into a knowing smile. "I can't imagine how he has remained one so long. He's a handsome enough fellow."

Cecily cocked a brow. "What does he look like?"

"Brownish hair—"

"Blond," Mirabella corrected. "A sort of dirty blond."

"Oh, pardon me." Alice giggled. "Blond. Hazel eyes?"

"Gray," Mirabella snapped. "His eyes are gray."

"Ah, yes, how could I forget? Gray eyes." Alice turned to Cecily. "A nicely made man as well. And such a pleasant disposition."

"You must allow him to accompany you to Sumerton one of these days, then," Cecily told her. "I'm sure he'd welcome a diversion from his duties now and again. And there are some lovely diversions here—"

"Cecily, really!" Mirabella cried, casting her embroidery aside as she rose. "I'll not have you playing matchmaker!"

"How could you insinuate that I would play matchmaker?" Cecily teased.

"Honestly, you are touchy, Mistress Mirabella," Alice added. "After all, give credit where it is due. *I* am playing matchmaker!"

The two women dissolved into laughter at Mirabella's discomfort as the girl shook her head and quit the room.

"We haven't offended her overmuch?" Alice asked, mirth still misting her eyes.

Cecily shook her head. "It is good natured. Mirabella knows we worry after her. She isn't happy. Sumerton bores her to tears. Oh, she is good with the children and loves them well. But in truth she doesn't know what to do with herself. These past years all she has lived for are Father Alec's letters, and they are few enough. She needs a diversion herself. And this young James may be just the thing. . . ." She sighed, swallowing a lump swelling in her throat. "Life hasn't turned out at all how Mirabella hoped. I know her first calling was to God. But it seems God wishes her to be a part of this world."

Alice's eyes grew distant. "It is a hard enough world to get along in," she commented. "It is no place for women." She bowed her head. "It is no place for my daughters and me," she added in a whisper.

"Alice?" Cecily abandoned her embroidery, reaching out to touch her friend's hand. Her heart lurched in sudden, inexplicable fear. "What are you about?"

Alice expelled a giddy laugh, waving the statement off. "Nothing. We are quite well. Really." She shrugged and made a show of going back to her embroidery. But her manner was distracted and she stitched at random. There was no pattern to her design.

"Alice." Cecily's voice was low. "Is it Sir Edward? His sons?" She leaned forward, stilling her friend's hands once more with her own. "Do you need help, Alice?"

Alice's smile was fixed. Her eyes were bleary. "I am getting all the help I need," she said. "No worries, Cecily. Truly."

"What kind of help? From whom?" Dread pooled in Cecily's gut. On instinct, her hand fled to the base of her throat.

Alice shook her head once more. "You are a fussy one, Cecily. I tell you, I am quite well. Better than ever, in fact. I was being silly. Really."

With that she returned to her embroidery, leaving Cecily to sit, disconcerted and afraid for her friend without quite knowing why.

Alice seemed well when she brought James Reaves with her to Sumerton one warm winter day. Mirabella found her heart pounding in a peculiar sense of anticipation as he made his way to her in the solar, where she had been attending little Kristina, who at six had grown into a curious and precocious little girl.

"My lady." James dipped into an awkward bow. "I do hope I am not disturbing you. Lady Camden and Lady Sumerton directed me in here. You—you once said I might call and when Lady Camden extended the invitation I thought to take the opportunity."

Mirabella smiled despite herself. His unease touched her. She extended her hand. "Of course, Master Reaves. How good it is to see you." At once a lump swelled her throat. "I was never able to convey to you my deep regret about Master Aske—the Pilgrimage . . . Oh, Master Reaves, I am so sorry."

James bowed his head, placing a light kiss on her outstretched hand. "It was brutal, my lady. Time seems never to dull that grief." He swallowed several times before raising his eyes to her. Unshed tears sparkled off the stormy gray orbs.

"I understand, Master Reaves," Mirabella told him, her voice wavering with sincerity.

James did not let go of her hand; it was enfolded in his and, strangely, did not feel uncomfortable. "It seems hope for our cause must lie in a different path," he said then.

Mirabella sighed. "I cannot imagine any hope for our cause," she confessed, withdrawing her hand.

"There's always hope," James corrected her. "As long as there is a prayer left on our lips, there is hope."

Mirabella smiled at this. There was something innocent about this Master Reaves, something untainted by tragedy and disappointment. Something endearing.

"Your optimism is refreshing, sir," she told him. "I am very glad you came."

James offered a crooked smile. "I am, too," he told her. "Perhaps I may call again?"

"I would like that," Mirabella admitted. Then, with more confidence, "I would like that very much."

James Reaves was as good as his word. He called upon Sumerton often, either with Alice Camden or alone, and Mirabella found that his visits rescued her from the monotony her existence had slipped into. Though James was not a man of high education, he possessed the kind of intelligence many seasoned scholars lacked, that of common sense. With him Mirabella could at last air her opinions on the rebellion, on the faith that she felt Henry VIII was trampling on more and more by the day, and on her lost life. He was a good listener; he rarely interjected his own opinions. He was gentle, quiet, and believed the solution to any problem could be found through prayer. And so together the two prayed on many subjects, and if solutions were not granted from the ritual the very act of praying together brought Mirabella a sense of comfort and fellowship that she had not known since Father Alec. . . .

Mirabella was not the only one to notice the changes James wrought in her.

"You must congratulate me," Cecily told Hal. Summer had arrived to the place that honored her with its name, balmy and ripe as an apple ready to fall. Cecily fanned herself idly and giggled at Hal's puzzled glance. She nodded toward the picture window of the solar, through which Mirabella could be seen greeting a breathless James in the gardens.

Hal chuckled. "I should have known you were behind this."

"I believe Master Reaves has been calling on Mirabella as much as four times a week for the past six months," Cecily went on. "Perhaps before long there will be wedding bells tolling at Sumerton." She offered a happy sigh. "He is a dear man, always bringing some token or another for the family. He carves toys for the children, and always has a book or some tasteful piece of jewelry for Mirabella, and even at times brings fresh game for the table. He's a marvel, Hal. Just what Mirabella needs."

"Indeed it seems so," Hal agreed. He sighed, stroking his beard with an idle hand. "Maybe with him she can find the peace she's always longed for at last."

Cecily smiled. "Let's hope so." She rose, placing a hand on her belly. "Then by the time this next baby is born, perhaps Mirabella will be thinking of giving you some grandchildren!"

Hal's eyes misted with tenderness. "Cecily . . . another baby? Truly?"

Cecily nodded.

"By God, I am a lucky man," Hal said as he rose to gather her in his arms.

Cecily nuzzled against his shoulder. The warmth of her own peace washed over her as a new confidence filled her. Life was good. At last, for everyone, life was good.

Someday she would curse herself for her naiveté; she knew too well that nothing lasted. Nothing stayed the same.

* * *

> *Dear Father Alec,*
> *There has been a tragedy at Sumerton. Cecily was*
> *recently delivered of a son, blessed little Charles, but the*
> *poor lamb was small and frail and was called to God*
> *not a month after his birth, leaving her in an*
> *inconsolable state of melancholy. Father is fated to*
> *handle grief with grace and keeps much to himself. But*
> *I worry after Cecily; for so long she has been all the*
> *strength and light of Sumerton. Now her flame flickers,*
> *fading; I know not how to stoke it.*
> *In times like these, we miss your guidance, your sense*
> *of calm confidence. How we need it now.*
> *Blessings,*
> *Mistress Mirabella Pierce*

"A sign, perhaps, Father?" Archbishop Cranmer asked after Father Alec finished reading the letter aloud in the archbishop's privy chamber at Lambeth.

Father Alec cocked a questioning brow. "Your Grace?"

Cranmer offered his gentle smile. "It is a dangerous time for men of faith. Indeed, it is a dangerous time for any who live in England. One of the saddest duties I ever undertook was that of the interrogation of young Queen Catherine Howard, the poor child. Though no innocent, her fate was . . . harsh."

Father Alec closed his eyes against the memory of the fair young girl as she laid her head upon the block, another victim of Henry VIII. A queen for only two years, she was condemned to death for the crime of loving one her own age. It seemed a brutal consolation that the only light to be shed on such a dark time was that with her died the ambitions of the Catholics at court. By 1543 a new Catherine sat on the throne of England: Catherine Parr, a bold supporter of the reformers' cause.

Once again, Cranmer indulged in the disconcerting habit of perceiving Father Alec's thoughts. "Though our new Queen Catherine is of our persuasion, her influence on His Majesty is shaky at

best. Bishop Gardiner will stoke the fires of Smithfield with reformers as long as there is breath in his body. If this queen can be
counted in those numbers, he would have her join them." He
trembled.

Father Alec shook his head. "It is a perilous time."

"For simply believing that the body of Christ is mere bread and
is not transubstantiated into flesh when celebrating Holy Communion, one can be put to death. Our cause is at a disadvantage. We
are all but at a standstill." He sighed, his heavy-lidded eyes softening with sadness. "And our King Henry is not well. The leg in-
jury he sustained at the joust in '36 is ulcerated. In his pain he
grows more agitated, quicker to provoke than ever before. He is
unpredictable. One day he may be in favor of reforms, the next we
could be put to death for them." He shook his head. "He has
changed. I fear for him," he added in hushed tones. "I fear for us
all." He bit his lower lip a moment before continuing. "I have long
since sent my wife out of England, as you know. I have hidden my
work, any work that could be considered . . . controversial. I pray
you do the same."

Father Alec nodded. "I have, Your Grace."

"Father, would you say you love Sumerton?" he asked then, his
tone suddenly light.

Father Alec's heart lurched in an unexpected moment of nostalgia. "Love Sumerton? . . . I suppose I do. My life has been a
drifter's life, you could say. Sumerton afforded me the only home I
ever truly knew, besides with Your Grace, of course."

"Do not flatter me, lad." The archbishop chuckled. "Though it
has pleased me to have you in my service. You are a man of rare insight. As such, I fear for you. I have read your work; I know your
thoughts and I will leave them unspoken, for it is too dangerous a
time to voice anything which might oppose His Majesty's at times
contradictory will. You could be compromised. You are a priest and
unfortunately more expendable than higher men who have already lost their lives to the stake." He rose and paced before his
fire. "I believe God has plans to utilize you in a time when England sheds the veil of ignorance at last. I believe you will help
shape our faith and bring in a new age. But for that, Father, you

must be kept safe." He offered a pointed gaze. "And this is not a safe place for you."

Father Alec's heart dropped in his chest. He shook his head. "You are sending me away, Your Grace?"

"For your own good, my friend," the archbishop reassured him. "And I believe Sumerton is just the place. It is tucked inconspicuously in the north country. There you may write, you may work, and not under the shadow of the axe," he added with a wry laugh. "They are a fruitful people, are the Pierces you served. Two living children now, is it? They will be in need of a tutor, I am sure. Oh, Father, take heart. We will keep correspondence. And you will return when it is safe—and it will be safe again someday, Father, I promise you."

Father Alec struggled to keep his mouth from standing agape. He knew it was the right thing, that he would not dare go against his mentor's authority. But to leave London, to leave his dreams behind, to leave the hub of all religious decision and reform for the country of Sumerton, where news traveled slow and life commenced in a sort of suspended reality so alternate to what he came to know and treasure in London . . . His stomach churned.

"My friend, I appreciate how difficult this is for you," Cranmer told him in gentle tones. "But you are too crucial to England's future to make a martyr of you. I will not have it. I pray you will understand and forgive me."

"There is nothing to forgive," Father Alec assured him. "And I am honored that you hold me in such high esteem, that you believe me to have some place in our land's future. But I admit it is almost unbearable leaving." He bowed his head. "I am avowed to obedience, however. And I suppose it is God's will. One can never get too comfortable." He shrugged, swallowing an onset of petulant tears.

"Consider it a sabbatical," Cranmer suggested. "A respite where you might compose your thoughts in relative safety. Not that you should get careless; I advise you conceal your work with the utmost caution. But it will be easier for you there. And you will prove a comfort to the family as well."

The family. Hal and Cecily and Mirabella. How had the years

changed them? Would they fall back into the easy friendship they once shared? Or would it be awkward returning to them? Yet he could not deny that it would be an honor educating a new generation of Pierces. It was perhaps a perfect cover.

"It is settled, then, Father," Cranmer stated, bringing Father Alec from his reverie. "You will return to Sumerton and wait this out. When the time is right, we will know what to do with you."

There was no argument to make. He would obey his dear friend and mentor and remove to the manor where so many memories were made. There he would live, he would dream, he would work.

And wait.

❧ 16 ❧

"Father Alec returning to Sumerton?" Mirabella cried as Hal made the announcement in the gardens. It was a warm autumn evening and the women savored their time in the outdoors before winter set in. Together with the companionable James Reaves they watched the children romp and play.

Cecily raised her head to Hal, a spark lighting the eyes that the loss of baby Charles had dulled.

"I just received his dispatch," Hal affirmed with a grin. "He has offered to resume his post as our tutor."

"Oh, Hal . . ." Cecily murmured, her heart stirring with the first real hope she had known since the baby's death. Everything had become such an effort for her; it was almost impossible to take any pleasure in day-to-day life. Her mind was tortured with thoughts of her little one, the warm weight of him in her arms, the feel of his downy soft hair against her cheek, his sweet, clean smell. How subtle, how quiet, was his passing. She had put him to bed one night, blissfully unaware of the fact that it was to be his eternal slumber. It seemed suffering had become her unwelcome companion. It haunted her, these thoughts, and wracked her soul with guilt; if she or the nurse had only checked on baby Charles more that night, perhaps they could have foreseen, maybe even prevented . . . Yes, it was a good thing that Father Alec was returning. Perhaps he could offer her counsel as he had in days gone by.

"We shall make ready his old apartments," she said, her tone decisive. "And celebrate his return with a feast!"

"Set the preparations in order, my darling," Hal told her as he leaned in to kiss the top of her head. "Give our friend a proper homecoming."

Cecily reached up, cupping Hal's cheek in her hand. This was a much-anticipated homecoming. Reuniting with one of the most integral figures in her childhood filled her with renewed purpose and would be a welcome distraction from her grief. Father Alec would prove a loving instructor to her children and the impartial friend the family needed to guide them through.

Mirabella anticipated the priest's appearance with a pounding heart. All the preparations had been made. Mirabella helped Cecily oversee the freshening of his apartments and even stocked a trunk with newly sewn shirts for his use. Two boars had been slaughtered and the kitchens were busy making ready a feast in his honor. Cecily had even assembled a group of tenants to serve as musicians for the occasion. Like Lady Grace before her, it seemed Cecily was a master of revels.

Even Mirabella found herself choosing her wardrobe with more care the day he was set to arrive. Red had always been her color in years gone by and she wore a sumptuous velvet dress of rich crimson with slashed sleeves to reveal fitted taffeta undersleeves of gold. Her dark hair she wore curling past her shoulders with a simple red and gold headdress.

"My God, Mistress Mirabella, you are the most beautiful thing I have ever seen," James Reaves told her upon seeing her that day in the gardens.

Mirabella smiled, proud of dear James. Never did he lose his faith; never did he seem to even question God's will. He was an example of acceptance and she strove to emulate him.

"My lady," he went on, taking her hand. "I did not know the proper time to say this, but . . . I have spoken to your father and—

and he gave his blessing. . . . Mistress Mirabella, it is my hope that I could plight my troth to you."

The color drained from Mirabella's cheeks. Marriage? To James? She could not trick herself into believing this would not happen someday. They had grown close. There seemed an easy chemistry between them. They shared similar beliefs and enjoyed each other's company. But marriage? As ever she was reminded of when the abbey's treasures were confiscated and her virtue almost compromised. As ever she was reminded it was her mother's self-less act that preserved her. James was one of the few to know of that tragedy. He tended her himself, after all. And yet the thought of being his wife . . . the thought of abandoning the last vestiges of her dreams to domesticity . . .

"My lady?" James furrowed his brows. He squeezed her hand.

"Mirabella! He's here!" the voice of young Harry was heard exclaiming as he burst through the gardens, trampling every flower and shrub that had the misfortune of finding itself in his path. At eight he was the image of Brey with his shock of curly blond hair and sparkling blue eyes that betrayed his enthusiasm for life. "Your friend, the priest you told me so much about! He's riding up now!"

"Oh, James!" Mirabella cried, rising and disengaging from him, grateful for the distraction. "He's here! He's really here!"

Ignoring the hurt lighting James's eyes, she hurried past him, following Harry to the courtyard.

This talk of marriage could wait.

Mirabella found her father and the children congregated in the courtyard. All were dressed for the celebration, Hal in a fine orange velvet doublet and hose. The children were attired in their best as well and little Kristina wore a russet gown to offset the waves of blond hair worn in plaits across her shoulders. The excitement was contagious, and though the little girl didn't know who they were expecting, she was caught up in it regardless. Hal rested his hands on her shoulders to contain her from bouncing about in restless anticipation.

James caught up to them as well, but Mirabella shifted her gaze from him to Father Alec, who had dismounted and was making long strides toward them, a smile broad across his face.

The children surrounded him first, Harry offering a bow and Kristina tugging at his sleeve. "I am Kristina! You have not met me yet, but I am far smarter than my brother and I know more, too!"

"Well, I am sure I will learn much from you," Father Alec said in indulgent tones as he took the child's hand.

"She's a liar, anyway," Harry told him. "I am the oldest, the strongest, and the smartest!"

Father Alec laughed. "Well, then perhaps you have no need of a tutor? Shall I return to London directly?"

"No!" both children cried at once. "We still need a tutor," Kristina added. "Harry has to learn how to be a gentleman, besides. It should take him a proper lifetime."

"Ah, then there's no danger of me going out of work," Father Alec commented with a smile as he approached the rest of the family.

He offered his hand to Hal, only to be taken into his arms in a great bear hug. "My dear friend!" Hal said. "I feared we would not see you again." He pulled away. "So much has happened." His eyes misted over. "But there's time for that kind of talk later. Now there's but to celebrate your homecoming and reacquaint you with Sumerton."

"My deepest sympathies for your loss, my lord," Father Alec said in soft tones. "And I thank you for allowing me to return."

Hal pursed his lips, as though warding off tears as he waved him off. "Of course, man, you'd be daft to think we'd refuse you!"

After introducing James, who remained quiet throughout, Mirabella lowered into a curtsy. "Father." Her voice was tremulous with reverence.

Father Alec smiled, taking her hands. "I am glad to see you, Mistress Mirabella. It seems Sumerton has had a healing effect on you after all."

Mirabella felt her cheeks burn. "Yes, in some ways," she told him. His hands enveloped hers, warm and steady. She did not want to let go.

At once Father Alec's eyes fixed on a point beyond her. His mouth parted. He stood stock still, as though frozen by a force greater than he. His hands went limp in hers. Mirabella turned. Cecily stood on the stone steps in the entrance of the castle mid-stride, caught in similar estate. She was dressed in a pale yellow gown that accentuated her delicacy, and her hair was in a loose twist, wound about a simple gold circlet. Rose-gold tendrils framed her face. She regarded Father Alec with the same wide-eyed expression with which he beheld her. Both seemed suspended in time.

Mirabella bit her lip. She understood well this exchange. This helpless exchange that conveyed far more than words ever could. Mirabella snatched her hands away from Father Alec. The movement seemed to jar him to his senses once more and he offered a small laugh.

"Lady Cecily," he said. "You look well."

Cecily's smile was forced. "I have done very well these past years. My lord and I have a wonderful family." With this she found Kristina and seized her hand as though desperate to illustrate this.

"I look forward to being a part of it." His tone was soft.

"We will make a merry time of it," Hal said as he slapped Father Alec on the back. "It will be as though you never left us."

As they made their way into the courtyard, Mirabella kept shifting her gaze from Father Alec to Cecily. Maybe she was being uncharitable. It had been years since the two saw each other and it was normal to register a certain surprise in seeing each other again.

And yet Mirabella's gut lurched with a strange foreboding.

She almost wished he had not returned.

Almost.

Father Alec wanted to deny what he felt upon seeing Cecily again, how his heart raced, how his face burned, and how enslaved he became under those strange teal eyes. As the evening commenced the two skillfully avoided each other. Father Alec made a show of acquainting himself with the children, giving them his undivided attention. He tried not to allow his gaze to wander toward the girl who had grown into such a beautiful and poised woman. He cursed himself. Could it be that this was what possessed Archbishop Cranmer to go against doctrine and marry? He longed for his friend now; no doubt he would offer sound advice without Father Alec ever having to ask.

It would pass, he decided. It must. Cecily was married to Hal and he was a priest. No stronger argument existed against further development of these foreign feelings than these two constraints. Yet was this a foreign feeling? Years ago when Father Alec objected to Hal marrying the girl, was it indeed because he found her too young or had there been something more? He did not want to explore it. He would surround himself with the children, he would do what he came to do and count down the days till his release.

Never had he thought he would liken Sumerton to a prison.

Cecily had no right to the stirrings in her heart. She was married; she was in love. Hal had been everything to her these years past. He had given her children, he had given her a life beyond what she dreamed possible. But the love she bore Hal and the strange sensation Father Alec evoked were two different things. It must be lust, she decided, her gut churning in guilt. The years had been kind to him, after all, the only testament to his age being the subtle streaks of silver through his chestnut hair and the lines that crinkled around his soft hazel eyes when he smiled. He was still in fine form; he emanated strength and confidence, and though Hal was a handsome man, there was just something about Father Alec. . . . Yet she could not say it was all looks with Father Alec. She had always cherished his manner. He was kind, straightforward, and gentle in his counsel. She admired him. Perhaps it was simply that. She had placed him on a sort of pedestal since childhood, and seeing him again renewed those feelings of awe. It was all foolishness regardless.

As Father Alec settled into life at Sumerton, Cecily invented every reason to evade him. The children adored him and he kept company with them even when he wasn't tutoring. He took them riding and exploring and stargazing, occupying them with the same pastimes he had entertained her, Mirabella, and Brey with as children. She was grateful for the easy rapport they established.

The counsel she had longed for she did not seek. His presence alone distracted her from her own tragedy, and though she would never be at peace with it, she could at least keep it in perspective. She never ceased praying for the soul of her little one, but beyond that, there was nothing else to be done.

If Cecily was avoiding the priest, so he was avoiding her, and she was grateful for that as well. And if Hal noted a difference in their exchanges, or lack thereof, he had the grace to leave it be.

Only Mirabella seemed to sense that something was amiss. She conveyed it in a pointed gaze that caused Cecily to avert her eyes and bow her head. She cursed the guilt Mirabella evoked. She had done nothing wrong and she wouldn't.

Mirabella's eyes told her otherwise. It was as though she was condemning and challenging her at once.

Whereas Cecily kept her distance, Mirabella sought out the company of Father Alec, and together they spent many a long hour discussing the True Faith, reforms, and the philosophy of the fledgling Church of England. No one stimulated her mind like Father Alec and she cherished their conversations. He was a good companion, a good friend, and she didn't mind that they disagreed on almost everything. The banter was good natured, and both left each debate with as much respect as they had when beginning it.

"And if your Cranmer gets his way, priests will no longer have to be celibate, will they?" Mirabella asked as the two took to riding through the forest one crisp spring day.

Father Alec slowed his horse. "This speculating on possible reforms is considered heretical, Mistress Mirabella. You must not fault me for being cautious when discussing them."

"Do you not trust me, Father?" Mirabella asked, her tone betraying her hurt.

"You are a former novitiate nun," Father Alec told her. "You were, as I remember, a supporter of the Pilgrimage of Grace and a practitioner of what you call the 'True Faith.' " He turned, raising a brow and smiling. "So, my friend, what do you think?"

Mirabella bowed her head. "I suppose not," she admitted. "But I'd like you to know that we are friends before we are avowed to any creed. You can trust me, Father." She met his eyes, her heart pounding. "I promise I would never betray you."

Father Alec reached out, covering her hand with his. Mirabella trembled at his touch. "I appreciate your friendship, mistress. But I would never want to compromise you by sharing views that would burden your heart and leave you torn."

"My beliefs are my own," she said. "What I see now is that not everyone will ever agree on a matter as complex as religious doctrine. But maybe there is some way we could coexist and compromise?"

"Then you have grown," Father Alec observed. "To bend but not to break is a great strength, and if this is truly so, then I respect you all the more."

"Then?" she prodded, hating the fact that she was baiting him, that she was lying. She knew in her heart it was either the True Faith or the New Learning. There was no compromise, no coexisting. The battle would be long; many casualties would be sacrificed on both sides before it was won.

"Then what?" Father Alec chuckled, withdrawing his hand to urge the horse in a pleasant canter.

"Then what of the celibacy of priests?" Mirabella asked.

"They won't be encouraged to rove the countryside for ladies of the night, if that is what you're implying," he said in light tones. "But the sacrament of marriage would be made open to them, yes."

"And you, Father?" Mirabella persisted. She chastised herself for her forwardness yet couldn't contain herself. All self-discipline seemed to be lost with her veil. "Would you marry, had you the choice?"

Father Alec sighed. "It is not good for man to be alone," he said at length. "And if the flesh burns, it must be contained in the marriage bed." He paused. "Would I marry? A wise man once told me that permitting priests to marry would allow them a better understanding of the struggles of their fellow man. I cannot say I disagree." He turned to her, his tone thoughtful. "I suppose it wouldn't be abhorrent to have a helpmate, to know that someone will come after me when I pass on." His tone became light. "However, it is all rather moot now, isn't it? Until then, if then ever comes, I am constrained to my vow of chastity. So chaste I shall remain."

Mirabella ignored the last statements, latching on to what she considered most valid. He would marry. Her heart quickened. He would marry. . . .

When Father Alec and Mirabella returned to Castle Sumerton, James Reaves was there to collect the horses.

"Mistress Mirabella, may we have speech?" he asked as he took her hand, helping her dismount.

When she was satisfied Father Alec was out of earshot, she faced him. He kept a firm hold on her hand.

"You have never given me an answer," he noted. "For months now I have been waiting, hoping you would recall that I asked you to marry me. And yet, still I wait, as though my proposal meant nothing to you."

Mirabella bowed her head, her face flushing. How could she give him an answer when everything had changed today, when Father Alec admitted there was a chance *he* would marry? How could she give herself to anyone else? Yet Father Alec never said he would marry *her*. And who could anticipate when or if that reform would ever be pushed through? But if it did go through . . . It made sense that Father Alec would marry her; they challenged each other, they enjoyed each other's company, she loved him. The last thought startled her, but she could no longer deny it. She loved him. She would have him, no one else.

"I'm sorry, James," she said in short tones. "I cannot marry you." She withdrew her hands, turning away from him.

"Then all these years, all the time we have spent together—"

Mirabella whirled toward him. "Have I ever behaved as anything less than a lady? Have I ever indicated any feelings toward you other than friendship? For love of God, James, if you feel you've wasted time on me, then perhaps you have!"

"For love of God," James repeated in quiet tones. "Yes, I rather thought it was the love of God that drew us together. I see now that I am wrong. The love of God does drive you, that is certain, but not toward me." He shook his head, pity lighting his eyes. "It's the priest you want, isn't it?"

It was instinct. She brought her hand across his cheek in a stinging slap that echoed in the stables. From its stall a horse whinnied its disapproval.

James shook his head, unaffected. "You'll not get what you want from that man. He's an honorable one, if he's anything at all. And you'd have to be a blind fool to see that if he were free to love 'twouldn't be you." He drew in a quavering breath. "It would be the Lady Cecily."

Hot tears stung Mirabella's eyes. She shook her head. "You're wrong, James. Cecily is devoted to my father—"

"That is not in question, is it?" James returned coolly. "I only said who he would choose if both were free to. But they aren't, are they? Yet you'll throw your life away on a chance, a slight chance, when before you stands a man ready to give you a life filled with love, children, a home, whatever is in my power to give. But that's too easy, isn't it? That's too safe. You like the risk, the danger. That's why you stayed on at Sumerton Abbey, that's why you went to London, and that's why you throw yourself shamelessly before a man you can't have. My apologies for being simple. My apologies for not being forbidden."

With that, he turned on his heel and quit the stables, his steps brusque with purpose.

Mirabella stood alone, burying her face in her hands and sobbing for herself, for James, and for the fact that he was right.

Father Alec returned to find Hal gone to Lincoln and the children abed. Lady Alice Camden had come calling and was keeping company with Cecily, embroidering in the bower. Father Alec paused outside the door, taking in the scene, his breath caught in his throat. The sun filtering through the bay window created an ethereal glow about Cecily; her hair shone as though it were lit from within. Her skin, bathed in the soft light, radiated with a warm luster. In a peculiar way, Father Alec found himself likening her to the Virgin Mary.

"There is the woman in the woods, you know," he heard Alice tell her.

Cecily inclined her head. "The witch?"

Father Alec knew it was impolite to eavesdrop; he should withdraw. But he found himself rooted in place, curious at the nature of this conversation.

"I would not call her a witch," Alice corrected. "A wisewoman to be sure, perhaps like a pagan druid priestess of old . . ."

"The law would not discern one from the other if she were caught," Cecily warned. "Both witches and druid priestesses burn the same."

The dark statement caused a chill to course up Father Alec's spine. He edged closer to the door.

Alice expelled a sigh tinged with frustration. "Regardless, Cecily, I'm telling you she may be the answer to your prayers. I have not borne a child since seeing her, thanks be to God. She could do the same for you."

Cecily's hands ceased their sewing. She bit her lip. Father Alec noted the beads of perspiration gathering at the base of her throat. "How?"

"Pennyroyal. It's an herb, administered in very small doses." Alice's voice was hushed with the excitement of a conspiracy.

Father Alec had heard of pennyroyal and the damage it could cause. It was an abortifacient. In the worst cases, it could prove lethal to the partaker. His heart raced. No matter the grief of her loss, Cecily could not justify this. A child was a gift from God; she must see that. Basic contraception was one thing, and another difference between Father Alec and the Church of Rome was that he could truly see no harm in regulating the size of one's family. But this . . . this was different. This was dangerous.

He could not bear to see Cecily put herself in any kind of jeopardy.

"All right," Cecily said, the gaze falling upon Alice pointed. "Procure me some, if you will. But I do not want to see her. Not just now."

Alice nodded. The two commenced their sewing in silence.

Father Alec slipped away, his heart heavy, his mind restless.

*   *   *

"You mean to say that Master James asked for your hand and you said no?" Cecily asked, gazing at Mirabella's tear-streaked cheeks, incredulous. "Why?"

They were in Mirabella's apartments. Cecily had all but chased her down when she saw Mirabella flee to them, head buried in her hands.

Mirabella's green eyes were emerald fires of indignation. "You would not understand," she said. "You cannot understand how it feels to know one's first calling is to God. Can you expect me to abandon my inclination just because I am no longer formally tied to monastic life?"

"I appreciate how difficult that would be for you, Mirabella," Cecily told her, her tone sincere. "But it has been seven years. You have had time to adjust. And James has been so good to you. He is a kind, honorable man who shares your convictions."

Mirabella offered a frenzied shake of the head. "I cannot!"

"Mirabella, I understand you have fears," Cecily went on. "But Master James can give you your own home, your own children, your own *life*. Don't you want those things? I often feel for you, watching how wonderful you are with your sister and brother. You deserve to be a mother yourself. Don't you want your own space?"

Mirabella turned away. "I am happy here," she said.

"Are you?" Cecily challenged. "Or is it just that it is safe here? Here you can live through others without ever really experiencing anything yourself—"

"Do you want me gone?" Mirabella demanded. "Is that it? I can leave. I can go to my mother's family in York. I can go to court, to Sumerton Place. If that is it, just say the word."

"You know that is not it," Cecily told her, appalled and frustrated that she remained so obstinate, so impossible to reach. "But I worry that you are not really living here, that you are treading water, passing time. I want you to be happy, Mirabella. I know that if you gave Master James the chance, he could provide a great deal of what you are missing now."

"He is not the one!" Mirabella screamed.

Cecily was silent a long moment. She would not entertain her suspicions. Surely Mirabella was more honorable than that.

Cecily shook her head. "Then who is?" she asked, her voice just above a whisper.

Mirabella said nothing.

Cecily quit the apartments.

Father Alec knew there was no other course but honesty. He sought Cecily out in the stillroom two days later, where she had been gathering lavender to put in the linens.

"Lady Cecily, I must confess that I heard your conversation with Lady Alice," he told her.

Cecily arched a brow, pursing her lips. "You had no right to conceal your presence," she said. Her tone was so cold, so formal. Her distance saddened him.

"Then neither of us are right, me for concealing my presence and you for concealing your child." He drew in a breath.

Cecily's face contorted as tears lit her teal eyes; they shone brilliant as a moonlit sea. "You do not understand, you cannot understand, what it is to lose a child, what it does to you. . . . I will not risk it again. And Hal . . . he doesn't deserve any more loss after all he has endured. He cares not if we have other children; Harry is healthy and secured as his heir and Kristina is our hearts' delight." She shrugged, returning her gaze to the lavender she arranged and rearranged in its basket. "And I do not want any more children."

"There are other ways to prevent that," Father Alec assured her, embarrassed that he should be the one to shed light on such a sensitive subject. "But if you are already with child, you are putting yourself and the child in an incredible amount of danger.

Does Lord Hal deserve that tragedy? Do any of us?" he added before he could help it.

Cecily squeezed her eyes shut a long moment, shaking her head. "I am barely gone with child; it is hardly there, hardly there at all! It hasn't quickened!" She raised her head, her eyes lit with indignation.

Father Alec seized her hands from the lavender, clenching them tight in his. "My lady, I beg you, consider this with care . . . it may be 'hardly there' as you say, but when does God place the soul within the body? At conception? When it kicks? At birth? No one can know these mysteries; ergo, no one can be qualified to speculate, to take that risk. Can you honestly say you would want that on your head?"

Cecily's knees buckled as she dissolved into tears. Father Alec caught her in his arms, pulling her near, stroking the back of her hair. It was like silk against his skin. He trembled as he withdrew, gripping her at the shoulders.

"It is *my* body, is it not?" she cried.

Alec shook his head, his heart laden with profound sadness. "That may be, my lady, but the body within you belongs to God, just as you do. Is it not for God to decide its fate, not you?"

Cecily lowered her eyes. "God will deal with me as He sees fit. I will answer to Him for my sins and Him alone." With this she pulled away, running from the room as though her conscience had taken form and was hunting her down.

Father Alec stood alone, staring at the abandoned basket of lavender, dread pooling in his gut, immobilizing him. Now he knew why he loved his time in London; there he was immersed in doctrine, something intangible, without heart, without life. Though the tragedies of the Crown affected him, they were on the periphery. At Sumerton everything was intertwined; the complexities of happiness and pain seemed to be inexorably tied to one person. Cecily.

Alice delivered the pennyroyal to Cecily in her apartments with her usual nonchalance, infusing it in some mulled wine. Cecily lay abed in her nightclothes, claiming illness. She was unsure as to the effects of the herb and would be grateful for the time alone to recover.

Cecily held the cup in a trembling hand, staring at its contents a long while. Father Alec's words swirled in her head, persistent as a migraine. She closed her eyes, sighing. She could not say she was unlike Mirabella, that she did take care to fear for her immortal soul. Guilt coursed through her veins. The thought that she was perhaps snuffing out the spark of life before it had a chance to truly ignite frightened her. What kind of person had she become? What would Hal make of her now? Would he see her as a betrayer, a murderess? The thought of her being the cause of any pain lighting his loving blue eyes would break her heart.

"Cecily, you don't have to do it," Alice told her in soothing tones as she sat beside her, rubbing her upper arm.

Cecily raised her eyes to her longtime friend. "I know I am selfish, Alice." Tears strangled her. She choked them back. "But I truly do not know how I can bear another child now." She chewed her lip. "Perhaps someday . . . but not now. I feel so tired. Losing little Charles has taken so much from me; it has been difficult to recover my spirit. The thought of going through all of it again—"

"You do not have to explain to me, Cecily," Alice assured. "We are not afforded many choices in this life. We do what we have to do. There may be no justifying it to the world, but if it preserves our sanity one more day, that is all the conviction I need to carry these things through."

Cecily cast her eyes upon the vessel once more. It looked so benign. Just a cup of death . . .

She drew in a breath, expelling it slowly. "Forgive me, Lord, I beg you."

With this she put the cup to her lips, drinking deep, feeling as though she were taking part in some unholy communion. Upon taking in the last of it, she handed the cup back to Alice. Other than the slight mint aftertaste, she felt nothing. What she was expecting to feel she knew not.

"It isn't instantaneous, Cecily," Alice said with a smile. "You must drink of it for five days before anything happens. The pain is no worse than the cramping of your regular courses."

Cecily sighed. She did not want to elongate her sin. She wanted it over.

There was nothing else to be done. Nothing but to wait.

❧ 17 ❧

Cecily was in the garden with Kristina when seized by the pains. She doubled over on the bench, clutching her belly. She had felt fine for a week; indeed, she felt fortunate to not have experienced any symptoms. But now was her time to make reparation. Now she would pay for her sin.

"My lady!" Kristina cried, rushing toward her. She sat beside her, stroking her hair. "What is it? What's wrong? What can I do?"

Cecily met her child's distressed brown eyes and tried to reassure her with a smile that translated into a grimace as she tried to right herself.

"I am all right, darling," she told her. "No worries. You must not tell anyone of this; I do not want to raise any alarm."

Kristina narrowed her eyes. She was too astute for her age. "Why lie about it?"

"It's not lying, child," Cecily said in sharper tones than intended. "It's . . . it's just leaving things out—omission."

Kristina shrugged. "Seems the same to me, my lady," she observed. She took her hand. "But I won't say anything, I promise." She offered a wink. The gesture so belonged to her father that Cecily laughed through her pain.

She had made the right decision. She did not need another child to divert her attention from those already here.

She would tell herself that until she believed it.

Cecily waited for some sign of miscarriage. None came. No spotting, no bleeding. The cramps ceased. Her heart raced. Had it not worked then? Now what?

She sat in the small chapel at Castle Sumerton alone, defeated, and hardly aware of the soft footfalls echoing against the stone floor.

"You got your wish, Father," she said in tones laced with irony.

"Not Father." Hal's voice was soft as he slid into the pew beside her. In his hands he clutched the sandglass he had presented to her years before, the keeper of their hours, of each blessing and each tragedy. He sighed. "I brought this for you to reflect upon," he told her. "See here?" He ran his fingers along the carvings. "Our wedding date. Harry and Kristina's birthdays. Mirabella's return. Charles's birth and death dates. Father Alec's return . . ." He drew in a quavering breath.

"And this?" Cecily asked, noting a date with no known sentimental attachment.

Hal met her eyes with blue orbs softened by tears. "This was the day I felt you slipping away from me."

A lump swelled in Cecily's throat. She swallowed. She took Hal's hand in hers, lacing her fingers through his, squeezing, trying to find the reassurance and security she once derived from his touch. She would not insult his intelligence and insight by denying it.

"It was my hope that Father Alec could lend you some guidance, some comfort," Hal told her. He shook his head. "But I see now that things are never as we . . . expect."

She did not know his implication. This she would not speculate upon. She would not let herself.

Hal reached out, tilting her face toward his, his fingertips soft and subtle as a warm breeze on her skin. In his eyes shone a plea.

"Cecily, you do not confide in me anymore," he said. "I do not think you confide in anyone, not truly." He shrugged. "Perhaps Alice." He sighed again, his shoulders slumping. "I do not know how to reach you."

Cecily's lips quivered. "Oh, Hal, I'm so afraid." Cool tears slid down her cheeks unchecked. She leaned her cheek into the palm of his hand, feeling vulnerable as a child. "Since losing Charles I know I have distanced myself, as though numbing myself from any pain. In my fear, in trying to prevent us from future pain, I have fallen into sin."

Hal furrowed his brows, as though trying to wrap his mind around a weighty issue that was just beyond his comprehension. His voice was soft, non-accusatory. "What sin, my love?"

Cecily bowed her head, her shoulders quaking in silent sobs. "I am with child." She shook her head violently, then leaned her forehead into her hand. "I am with child and by God, Hal, I don't want it . . . not because it's yours, not because I do not love our children, but because . . . because . . . I . . . can't . . . bear . . . to . . . lose . . . it!" Her sobs became audible, gulping gasps of despair. "And because of that I took in pennyroyal to induce a miscar-riage . . . but it didn't work and now—now . . ." She trailed off, burying her head in her hands, weeping with abandon.

Hal was silent a long while. At last he wrapped his arm about Cecily's shoulders, drawing her to his side. She nuzzled in the crook of his shoulder, taking in his familiar, musky scent of leather and horses and strength.

"Then it is God's will that we have another child," Hal said. "Because He knows you are strong enough to bear it. He allowed it to remain because He knows your conscience would not be able to bear the weight of that sin. He spared you. He spared me," he added in quiet tones.

Cecily pulled away. "You aren't angry with me, Hal?"

Hal lowered his eyes. "I am hurt that you would grow so des-perate as to think you would not have help and support, that you would take such a heady decision upon yourself. I am hurt that you give yourself so little credit after all we have endured in this life." He bowed his head, gazing once more at the sandglass. "You are strong enough to bear God's will, for good or for bad. You have proved it before; you will prove it again. And all the while, I will be at your side." He raised his head, facing her once more, determination replacing the momentary pain lighting his eyes. "Only come back to me. Come out of yourself. Join me as my wife once more."

Cecily cupped his face between her hands. "I haven't left you, Hal," she whispered. "I'll never leave you." She leaned in, pressing her lips to his in a gentle kiss. "Mark this day on the sandglass. Mark it as the day I decided to rejoin the living."

"Done, my lady," Hal assured, a smile in his tone. "Done."

Cecily's pregnancy advanced as normal as her others had been. She experienced very little discomfort. The baby quickened, filling Cecily's heart with relief at each kick. When she announced her condition to the rest of the family, Father Alec's face emanated a mingling of relief and a flash of something else. Pain? Cecily cared not to analyze. She focused on the children's reactions. Harry seemed indifferent. He was looking forward to joining the Earl of Surrey's household, where he would receive his formal education alongside the Howard children, and his mind was occupied with the prospect of a new adventure. Kristina's eyes lit with excitement at the news. Cecily knew this would give her a chance to play the little mother. She had doted on baby Charles during the brief span of his life and this baby would serve to fill the void he had left in Kristina's heart.

As happy as Kristina was, her joy seemed muted in comparison to that of Mirabella, who was more demonstrative than she had ever been in her life, fussing over Cecily to no end. Cecily could not help but wonder at the girl's motivation. She had seemed to distance herself as much from Cecily as Cecily had from everyone else these past months.

"After your loss, I am just glad to see you pressing on," Mirabella told her as they sat in the gardens, taking in the crisp air. Summer was ending. Autumn advanced in a subtle flirtation with nature, dusting the foliage with a rich golden hue. "And very glad to see you and Father doing well."

Cecily smiled. "And you, Mirabella? What of James? We have not seen much of him of late. I had hoped you would reconcile."

Mirabella was silent. The moment was thick with awkwardness. "I told you. It was not meant to be," she said at length.

Cecily bit her lip, unsure as to how to proceed. "You seemed so close and so alike."

"Not alike enough," Mirabella said, but she averted her eyes. Cecily wondered whom Mirabella was lying to more, Cecily or herself. "I do not wish to speak of it again, Cecily. Now is a time to focus on your happiness, not my disappointments. Please."

Cecily sighed. "I just do not want you to have any regrets," she said.

"My regrets are my own." Mirabella's tone was hard, inaccessible once more. Perhaps always.

As unattainable as Cecily could be at times, Mirabella was that much more so.

Cecily wondered if anyone would ever be allowed a glimpse into her soul.

Mirabella could not say that Cecily's condition did not fill her with immense relief. This meant that relations were good between Cecily and her husband. This meant that Mirabella had misinterpreted the strained glances exchanged between Cecily and Father Alec. All was well. All would stay well. The Pierce family was strong, loyal. Impenetrable from the forces of lust and sin.

Leaving Mirabella safe to nurture her own dreams.

She still spent much of her time in Father Alec's company. She sat in on many of his tutoring sessions with the children, trying to instill in Harry, the more malleable of the two, a strong foundation in the True Faith. She attended calls with Father Alec to sick tenants, offering whatever assistance she could, feeling that, in a way, she was still fulfilling part of her holy calling.

And she relished his friendship. Their spirited debates, their companionable silences, the work they did together, filled her with purpose, with meaning. She tried to reconcile herself to her decision regarding James. She tried to put him out of her head. Nonetheless, he crept in unbidden, his innocent face laced with disappointment and betrayal and knowing, always knowing, that her intentions with Father Alec were less than holy.

She cursed him for it.

More than that, she cursed herself.

Cecily went into labor during a blizzard one February morning in 1546. The pains seemed close together and intense, despite the fact that her water had not yet broken. She retched violently, clutching her belly and whimpering feebly.

Mirabella attended her, her cheeks flushed with anxiety. This was her first birthing; she hoped it would be her last. She had no stomach for it. She swabbed Cecily's forehead with a cool cloth and tried to soothe her with nonsensical banter, then fell into a restless silence, not knowing how to comfort the girl.

What was worst was that the midwife could not be fetched. The weather prevented it; the snow was thigh deep and mounting. Fortunately, some of the older female servants had some knowledge of childbearing, so Mirabella did not feel completely inadequate and alone.

The hours stretched on. Twilight, then night, at last yielding to an indigo dawn. Mirabella's heart pounded. At last Hal entered the sanctuary.

"This birth echoes too much of Harry's for me to keep away," he told Mirabella in soft tones. "Something is wrong. It is taking too long; she is struggling too much. . . ." He ran a trembling hand through his hair. "Something must be done to ease her pain, to help this along."

"The woman . . ." Cecily murmured in a raspy whisper.

"What?" Mirabella asked, making for the bedside once more. She took Cecily's hand in her own. "What, dearest?"

Cecily tried to open her eyes, revealing slivers of teal against her ivory skin. "The woman of Sumerton Forest . . . the wise-woman . . . Alice's druid . . ."

Mirabella's heart lurched with peculiar dread. "Druid? A witch? Cecily, you can't mean—"

"Find her, Mirabella," Hal ordered. "If Lady Alice trusts her, she's good enough for me. She may be our only hope."

"But Father—"

"Find her!"

Mirabella started at the harshness, so rare in Hal's tone. She nodded her acquiescence and quit Cecily's chamber to seek out a woman she knew nothing of, praying all the while she would not be the harbinger of evil at Sumerton.

Mirabella wrapped herself in furs and found the only conveyance she could think of to make traversing the snow easier, a pair of snowshoes Harry had fashioned for play. With them she trudged through the forest, not knowing where she was going or what she was really looking for. As she walked, bitter wind biting her cheeks, she was reminded of the day she took Cecily through the forest to the convent for the first time, so many years ago. How naïve they were then, how delightfully ignorant to what fate had in store.

Now everything had changed, every plan, every person. Her dearest brother Brey was gone along with her convent, her true mother, her innocence. . . . How she longed for that day in the forest, to reclaim the feeling of hope and a heart filled with dreams. Instead she was engulfed in a shroud of uncertainty.

Through a veil of snow a dark form came into view. Mirabella squinted, sniffling, shielding her eyes against the bright whiteness of the storm. A rough-hewn dwelling with a thatch roof stood before her. Mirabella had no idea who resided there; there was no guarantee this was the wisewoman Alice Camden consulted. Mirabella twisted her lips in frustration as she trudged forward, knocking on the door. It fell open. She bit her lip, peeking in.

A woman stood before a cook pot that hung over a fire, her back turned to her.

Mirabella cleared her throat. "I am looking for a friend of the Lady Alice Camden."

The woman turned.

Mirabella's heart stopped. Her chest constricted. Light danced before her eyes. She willed strength into her quivering legs. It couldn't be . . . it couldn't be. . . .

"My God, what have you done?" she breathed to the apparition before her.

The woman squared her shoulders and tucked a white tendril

that had escaped her kerchief behind her ear. She met Mirabella's gaze with hard blue eyes.

Mirabella shook her head. She did not know whether to leap forward and strangle the woman or turn and run, putting as much distance between her and Lady Grace Pierce as possible.

"I know you cannot understand, Mirabella," Grace started slowly. "But I could not stay. That life would have killed me. I could no longer pretend to be something I am not. In order to preserve my own self, sacrifices had to be made."

"So, instead of leaving, of divorcing Father, you *fabricated your own death?*" Mirabella returned in cold tones. "You are a monster," she spat. "You were always selfish, wallowing in spirits and self-pity. But I never would have fathomed you to be capable of this. And all this time . . . all this time you have been barely a stone's throw from Father and Cecily, who are married, incidentally! Of course, it is invalidated now, thanks to you, their children—their two children—bastards." Mirabella could barely focus through her anger. She could not stop shaking her head.

"I had already shamed your father enough; I could not divorce him. I knew that he would make a good match and in Cecily he did," Grace said. "I have followed your lives; I know everything." Her gaze was pointed. "Everything."

Mirabella clicked her tongue, expelling an exasperated sigh. "I will not even explore that; I couldn't care less about what you think you know. Clearly your vast expanse of knowledge excludes the most basic concepts—taking others into consideration, being selfless for sake of the greater good. . . . You are out for yourself, just as you have always been. You have not changed at all."

"Perhaps not," Grace agreed. "Which is another reason I choose a life of simple anonymity."

Mirabella furrowed her brow. "I have neither the time nor the inclination to pursue this conversation. I only want to know if you are the 'wisewoman'—Lord knows there is no use disputing that blatant misnomer—that Lady Camden associates with."

Grace pursed her lips, nodding. ". . . Why? Need to rid yourself of an unwanted little burden?"

Mirabella's smile was scathing. "This life suits you, indeed.

Who more appropriate than you to dabble in the dark arts?" she spat. "No, it's not my burden. It is Cecily—the *true* Lady Sumerton. She has labored too long and we cannot fetch the midwife in this storm, so you are—and I say this with the utmost sincerity—our last resort."

"I cannot very well go there," Grace said. "Though I do not doubt that out of spite you will reveal my presence—"

"And ruin the lives of those I love *most?*" Mirabella returned. "Despite whatever ill will between us, I am not half so callous as that."

Grace bowed her head, blinking several times. Mirabella did not care if she was struggling with her emotions. Whatever weighed on her conscience was the least she deserved.

"Has her water broken?"

"No," Mirabella said.

"Check her; see if the cervix is dilated," Grace said, her tone soft as she gathered several different jars and vials from a shelf. She took what appeared to be a knitting needle, thrusting it into the flames. "Then use this to break her water," she said. "It will not yield easily; it takes some force. I do not doubt your capabilities in that," she added in ironic tones. "Then rub some of this ointment on her belly and woman parts to ease things along. Shake the bed a bit, too; it may loosen things up. Or have her inhale pepper." She shrugged. "I've never been a believer in such things, but at this point it couldn't hurt." She handed Mirabella the needle and the ointment. "And pray to Saint Margaret; she is the patron saint of women in childbirth, as well you know. Perhaps she will be merciful."

Mirabella tucked the objects in the pockets of her gown. At the door she paused. "You know, it was far easier believing you dead," she said, her tone wistful. "I could make sense of your weaknesses then; I could forgive them, almost excuse them. We idealize the dead, you know. How I wish you would have stayed in that realm of memory, in that ideal. You cannot know how far you have fallen."

Grace said nothing.

With one last shake of the head, Mirabella turned on her heel and left.

There was no time to analyze or reflect upon the newest revelation. Mirabella returned to find that Cecily's water had still not broken and set to work. The girl was unconscious now, her head lolling from side to side, her breathing jagged and short. Mirabella's heart pounded as she set to following Grace's instructions. Upon her crude examination, she found Cecily to be dilated enough to insert the needle, using the necessary force to break through the amniotic sac, allowing the warm liquid to flow forth in a rush. After which, Mirabella applied the ointment, cringing a bit as she applied it to Cecily's intimate parts.

Cecily's breathing seemed to regulate. At once it was as though her body began to push for her and she bore down, clenching the bedclothes in white-knuckled fists, her eyes flashing open, a small moan escaping her parched lips.

"That's it, Cecily!" Mirabella cried, wiping beads of perspiration from her own brow. "I can see the head! Push! Push *hard!*"

Cecily clenched her eyes shut and grimaced, propping herself up on her elbows into almost a sitting position.

"Come on, Cec!" Mirabella urged.

Cecily tossed her head back and held her breath. Mirabella ushered the child forth, cupping the head, slick with birthing fluids, in her hands. Her face tingled in anticipation as a weak mew pealed forth. One shoulder came, then the other as the rest slid into her arms. Cecily collapsed back onto the bed, breathless.

Mirabella's own breath caught in her throat.

"Oh, no . . ." she whispered as she beheld the baby girl. The child's left leg was a great deal shorter than the other, twisted grossly beneath the knee, the foot clubbed almost beyond recognition.

"What is it? Is it healthy?" Cecily asked, her legs trembling as a servant cleaned her. "Mirabella! Tell me!"

Mirabella cleaned the child, holding her close. Despite the deformity, she did not think it possible to love another creature more than the broken little thing she held to her heart. She brought the child to her mother, her vision obscured by tears.

"It is a girl," she told her. "But there is a problem. Her leg . . . is misshapen."

Cecily took the girl in her arms, examining her. Her shoulders began to quake with sobs. "Oh, God, no . . . it is my fault! I have condemned her to this . . . oh, God. . . ." She thrust her back into Mirabella's arms and averted her head.

"But she's still beautiful," Mirabella said as she wrapped her in a warm blanket. "She's still a gift from God. If she is so challenged, it is only to serve as an example of grace under hardship, of long-suffering, that she might teach others."

"No," Cecily said. "This is my punishment, my retribution for sins you know nothing of. You can't know. . . ." She choked on the words. "Now she will struggle the rest of her life because of me."

"Stop it," Mirabella admonished in sharp tones. "Now you sound like Lady Grace . . . did. It isn't about you. It is about this little one; it is her cross to bear, not yours. It is the will of God, not your sin, that brought this forth, whatever you have or have not done. I will hear not another word of such foolishness. You have a beautiful daughter; you must name her."

Cecily gazed at the baby, her eyes misty with tears. "I will call her Emily," she said. "Emily Mirabella Pierce," she added. "For without you, she would not be here."

Mirabella beamed with pride at both the honor of the namesake and the fact that it was true; Emily would not be here had she not delivered her. She clutched the child to her breast, nuzzling against the downy brown hair. "Emily," she whispered. "My sweet Emmy."

She could not be more proud if she had borne her herself.

❧ 18 ❧

Hal did not want to resent Cecily for Emmy's deformity, yet somewhere in his soul he knew that he did. He was convinced that had she not ingested the pennyroyal, the child would have been born perfect. He did not want to be angry with his wife, the woman who had given him four children; the love and the years that they had shared meant too much to him. Yet he could not look at her the same.

On the sandglass he marked Emmy's birth, knowing that to himself he was making note of his own unwanted bitterness. He did not show it. He was solicitous to Cecily and the baby, making pains to tell Cecily that it was not her fault, that, like Mirabella said, it was a part of God's unfathomable plan. But it was forced. He knew it; she knew it. And something was lost between them.

They attended the mundane tasks of daily life. Harry was sent off to the Earl of Surrey's household, where he would learn the ways of a knight and courtier, leaving Mirabella and Kristina to dote on their baby sister. It seemed as though Mirabella had developed a special bond with the child she had helped bring into this world and displayed as much devotion as any mother. Mirabella, despite her protests that she did not want a family of her own, had proved to be a nurturer; she had been close to Harry, and the birth of Emmy saw her skills as a caregiver put to use once more. Hal was proud of her.

"At times I think she is a better mother to the girl than Cecily, God forgive me for saying it," Hal told Father Alec one day as the two rode through the vast fields where the sheep of Sumerton grazed. It was summer. Despite all odds, Emmy was thriving, progressing much like any normal babe, filling Hal with relief. He could not imagine what other effects the pennyroyal might have on the child.

"Your feelings are not misplaced," Father Alec assured him. He sighed as they slowed their horses.

"You know of Cecily's sin." It was not a question.

"I do," Father Alec admitted after a long moment's hesitation. "And no doubt she was wrong. But God's will prevailed and the child has lived. Lady Cecily pays for it with her own guilt far more than anyone could ever punish her."

"Oh, Father." Hal's voice was thick with mourning. "I don't desire to punish her . . . yet I cannot reconcile myself to my own resentment, either."

"You must," Father Alec urged. "It will take time. But you must. Otherwise you may become separated from Lady Cecily by a chasm nothing can bridge."

Hal swallowed the growing lump in his throat, frightened at the prospect. "I do love her, Father, the Lord knows I do. Perhaps I suffer from disillusionment. I never expected to be disappointed by her."

"It was a long fall from the heights you placed her upon," Father Alec observed.

Hal nodded. "I suppose part of the fault is mine, for that and more. I should have taken more precautions if she did not want a child. But she never told me!"

Father Alec shook his head. "You are where you are now," he said at length. "Just remember, my lord. It is far more important to forgive than attain forgiveness from others. It will free you."

Hal nodded. Forgiveness. That which he sought for so long. It would be a long road, but he must traverse it.

Somehow he must forgive, or lose Cecily altogether.

* * *

Cecily sensed Hal's distance. He occupied himself with sport—hawking, hunting, and leaving the estate to indulge in pastimes of old, cards and dice. Though he never treated her with anything but respect, his solicitations adopted a new formality that bordered on coldness. Cecily wondered if they would ever heal from this or if she had condemned their marriage to a slow death.

She internalized her guilt, discussing it with no one. Mirabella tried to comfort her to no avail; Cecily knew confiding her shame would bring her judgment upon her and she could not bear it. She withdrew.

Mirabella was a marvel with little Emmy and included Kristina in all the daily tasks of her upkeep. It was just as well. Cecily could not face any of them and threw herself into the running of the household with the dedication of a merchant for his store. Everything was in order; everything ran smoothly. The rents were collected, the tenants looked after, the household food stores maintained and well stocked. At times she felt she was a better steward than anything else.

She was going over the ledgers one late afternoon when she heard a shouting in the great hall. Abandoning the book, she quit her study and made for the noise, finding, much to her surprise, Master James Reaves with Father Alec and some servants.

James's face was flushed, his breathing shallow. He was covered in dust.

"Master James." Cecily took his hand. "What is it?"

"Fire at Camden Manor," he told her.

"Fire?" Cecily cried, her heart racing. "Alice and the children—are they safe?"

"They are trapped within," James said, as they began proceeding out of doors. "Oh, my lady, it has been a sort of hell there, if you'll forgive the term. Sir Edward and his sons are pigs, unfit to be called men. Many a time I have come between them and Lady Alice or, worse, the girls, that I might prevent grievous sin from occurring." He offered a helpless shake of the head. "But I cannot be all places at all times. . . ."

Cecily closed her eyes. "Oh, Lord preserve them. . . ."

"I heard them fighting. Lady Alice was screaming, telling Sir Edward she and her girls would never again be used for the pleasure of him and his 'demon brood.' She said she was leaving, that she could not bear this world a moment more. Then she took to the nursery with her daughters. Sir Edward dismissed it, saying it was another one of her dramatic scenes." He trembled. "But it was not long before we smelled smoke. Soon it could be seen curling down the hall. It got out of control so fast . . ."

Cecily covered her mouth with her hand, casting her eyes to Father Alec. He wrapped an arm about her shoulder, drawing her close. She was too distressed to pull away.

"We are doing all we can," James went on. "But you are in possession of the only water syringe within fifty miles. We beg use of it now."

"Hal is gone; he took Mirabella and Kristina to visit the Howards. He will not be back for days," she told James. "But we will remove there directly with the water syringe and offer what assistance we can."

They arrived at Camden Manor, Cecily riding on the back of Father Alec's horse as they followed the carriage with the water syringe, which held ten barrels of water. The manor was shrouded in flames. What remained of the staff congregated outside, speaking in hushed tones, while others passed one bucket after another to pour on the conflagration in vain. It seemed to have taken on a life of its own, as if it were the breath of a dragon sent to rain its punishment upon them all.

Cecily and Father Alec did not hesitate. They helped the servants align the nozzle of the great syringe to the base of the fire, while one of the burlier men cranked a large handle at the back of the cylinder, forcing the piston in, which ushered forth a great stream of water. With effort, the piston was cranked back and the great vessel filled with water once more.

"Quick! We need more water!" Father Alec cried to the throng of onlookers who were just as content to remain useless. The assemblage scrambled, gathering as many buckets of water as were at their disposal to refill the syringe.

Sir Edward threw his bucket to the ground. "This is pointless!" he cried. "Do you really think this puny mechanism will stop *that?*" He shook his head at Father Alec, his soot-covered face contorted with scorn. He turned to his sons. "Come, boys, we shall go rescue them ourselves!"

"It is a death sentence," Cecily said to Father Alec.

"He knows," Father Alec told her.

No one tried to stop them. They ran into the firestorm, obscured in flame and black smoke. At once could be heard the sound of timbers cracking. Over the heads of Sir Edward and his sons half of the manor collapsed in upon itself, a testimony of destruction. Tears streamed down Cecily's cheeks despite the fact that she could not imagine a more fitting end for him and what Alice aptly deemed his "demon brood."

Father Alec continued working the syringe with the other men. Cecily retrieved more buckets of water to keep the firefighting device as well stocked as possible. Somewhere in the back of her crowded mind she heard Alice's voice, laced with bitterness. . . . *It is a hard enough world to get along in.* . . . *It is no place for my daughters and me.* . . . Could any statement have foretold these events any clearer? When did she say it? Why didn't Cecily address it with the seriousness it required?

Cecily sobbed with abandon as she poured bucket after bucket into the great mouth of the syringe, feeling as though her tears alone could douse the flames.

Well into the night they worked, yet still it did not wane. The fire lit the night sky, a bright beacon from Hell. All knew that the residents of Camden were gone to a man; there was no saving them. The least they could do was keep it contained to minimize the further loss of life and property.

At last could be heard God's reprieve—a crack of thunder. At first Cecily thought it was more timbers collapsing, but as the first drops of rain could be felt soothing her aching body her bucket fell to her side. She held out her hands.

"Thank God!" she cried. "Oh, thank God!"

It was as though the sky had opened up, sending a great deluge to cleanse the ravaged land. It poured in a torrent. The men ceased their operation, tilting their heads up to the sky. Many crossed themselves in thanksgiving. Thick smoke curled up into the night as rain conquered flame. Despite this, it still took hours for the fire to be vanquished.

When it was deemed safe, a party of men was sent into the rubble to seek out any remains. After what seemed like an eternity, made more intense by the lack of urgency, the party emerged, carrying with them the charred bodies of the Camden family and some servants. Sir Edward was crushed by a beam and could not be salvaged, but Alice and her three daughters were laid side by side, burned almost beyond recognition.

Father Alec stood above them, blessing them with tears streaming down his cheeks. No one rested. Coffins were fashioned on the spot; all knew in the warm weather the risk of scavengers, both human and animal. Father Alec officiated an informal burial as what remained of the staff and tenants who had come to assist stood by, sobbing for the disaster, the fiery veil for an even greater tragedy.

Cecily was overcome by weakness. She trudged away from the graves toward the stables, wishing she would faint, wishing there was some escape from this madness. When at last she came to Father Alec's horse, she leaned her head against its neck and sobbed anew.

"My lady."

Cecily started at the warm hand on her shoulder. She turned to find Father Alec, covered in dust and soot.

"Oh, Father, the sorrow we have known!" she cried.

Without a word he gathered her in his arms, holding her tight as he swayed from side to side in a gentle rhythm. His nearness comforted and tortured her at once; the feel of his body against hers amplified the intensity of their shared experience. She pulled away.

"Oh, please take me home," she begged, her voice raspy with tears.

He nodded, lifting her onto the horse and seating himself behind her. She leaned against his chest and he wrapped his arm about her waist.

Together they rode from one hell toward another, subtler kind of anguish.

They arrived home, where Cecily ordered baths for the both of them. She immersed herself in the hot water, scrubbing away the grime and pain of the day with vigor, as though with it she could scour away the emotions that raged within her. When at last she was cleansed, she found herself plagued with restlessness. There was nothing to distract her, no one with whom she could share her grief. Emmy was asleep, Mirabella and Kristina gone with Hal.

She was left with no choice. She would go where she had always gone in times of trouble, to the only one who understood. She gathered fresh clothes for Father Alec and, almost against her will, made for his apartments. When he did not answer her knock, she let herself in, recalling her childhood when she sneaked into his rooms to leave him little gifts. How far away those days did seem. . . .

Cecily's heart pounded as she beheld Father Alec, still in the large copper washtub.

"I'm sorry—I—" She bowed her head, cheeks burning. For some reason, her feet remained rooted in place. "I only meant to bring you some clothes."

Father Alec lowered his eyes. "I thank you."

Cecily approached, meaning to set the clothing on his dressing table, but as she tried to pass him he seized her wrist. His hand was warm and wet on her skin. She trembled; the clothes slipped from fingers gone limp onto the floor. Without hesitation she leaned in, pressing her mouth to his. He cupped her cheek in his other hand, devouring her mouth in his own urgent kiss. He pulled Cecily atop him into the water, both working frantically to free her of her gown. They discarded the sopping wet garment to the floor beside the abandoned change of clothes.

Cecily did not think. She suspended reality and consequence, yielding to the moment. She roved his body with her hands, stroking every inch of him as he explored her. Unlike the tender couplings with Hal, this union was infused with passion and a yearning so long denied. She staved off her guilt. She had the rest of her life for penance; had not every day become an atonement of sorts? She could not wonder if she would be damned. She could only gaze into Alec's loving hazel eyes, immerse herself in his kisses, savor the feel of him, the taste of him, the scent of him. Alec . . . how long had she loved him like this? How long had she needed him? There was no need for examination. There was but to lose herself in him, if only for this one sacred night.

When at last they were sated, gasping for breath, their sweat and tears mingling with the water, the two settled back into the bath. Father Alec's arms wound tight about her as she laid her head on his chest.

"God forgive me," he said. "I should leave."

"And take my sanity with you?" Cecily asked, leaning her chin on his chest to look up at him. "No. We acted of our own free will. We chose this. Now we must carry our sin with us, as I carry all of my sins with me. . . . Still," she added in soft tones, "I do not regret it."

"God help me, nor do I," Father Alec said. "Years ago I learned that Cranmer had a secret wife," he went on after a while.

"The archbishop?"

He nodded as with one idle hand he stroked her hair. "Do not tell a soul or you will condemn him to death at the stake," he warned.

Cecily offered a wry smile. He knew she would guard his secret.

"And I challenged him about it," he said. "But Cranmer made me understand that to be in true service to God, one must be a true man." He sighed. "Not that it gives license to sin . . . but ever since that insight I could not help but hope for the day when our reforms would both allow me to serve my God and grant me a helpmate of my own." His voice broke. "Cecily, you must know that you are the first woman for whom I have broken my vows."

"Oh, Father . . ." Cecily trailed off. She could no longer call him that. "Alec . . ." she whispered. "I am honored." She reached up to stroke his cheek. He covered her hand with his.

Father Alec swallowed. "We must not sin again," he told her. "I pray your forgiveness and God's that I took you in such an emotional state. But by God, Cecily, I have loved you since the day I helped you out of your mother's wardrobe as a little girl." Tears coursed slick trails down his cheeks. "Not as it is now, but in innocence. I do not think I knew the depth of it till you married my lord. That is why I left that first time. And then I returned to find you so . . ." He shook his head. "So much a lady . . . so beautiful. The love that was but a seedling when I left grew. I fought it; believe me I fought it. But I can fight no longer. What is worst is I no longer want to."

Cecily leaned up to kiss his cheek. "We have both lost this battle," she said. "And betrayed a man we love well. We can neither of us abandon Hal. He has been nothing but good and forgiving of me and a true friend to you." She sighed. "We will not sin again." She drew in a quavering breath. "But we have tonight."

She tilted her face to his to receive his kiss once more.

Tomorrow it would end.

Though they carried themselves with honor, each look, each touch, each word was fraught with a new meaning. Cecily relived the night again and again, using it as a distraction from her grief and guilt. She would not think of Alice and her daughters, charred in their graves. She would not think of her own little Emmy, who had taken to crawling quite adeptly despite her deformity.

She met Hal's eyes, trying to put forth the effort they had abandoned after Emmy's birth. He was kind and helped ease the pain of the loss of her dear friend Alice, whom he grieved for as well. Together they achieved a semblance of what they had known in the beginning, but the façade lacked a key element they could not seem to recapture: their friendship. Cecily told herself it would change. In time. For now there was but to pretend and hope they would someday believe their own charade.

Moments alone with Father Alec were rare. Yet every now and again he and Cecily would allow their gaze to linger, a testimony to what was and what could never be.

One day in late autumn Cecily came upon Father Alec in the stables. He was about to go riding and had shed his cassock for breeches and boots. When he saw Cecily he smiled.

"How are you, my lady?" he asked, his tone soft.

"I am well," she answered. "Better." Her voice broke on the last word. She bowed her head.

Father Alec approached her, taking her hands. "I am thinking of returning to London. After the king spared Queen Catherine this summer from heresy charges, my hope is renewed."

"I thought you told me that it was too dangerous, that you must wait for Cranmer to send for you," she said. "He—he hasn't, then?"

Father Alec shook his head. "Not yet. But I can live conspicuously. I can wait there." He drew her to his chest. "It is better for us, Cecily. I cannot bear to remain here, to see you and not . . . I cannot live in such agony and temptation. Despite my sin, I respect Lord Hal. And I respect you too much to compromise you further."

Cecily's shoulders slumped as she nuzzled in his chest. "I know," she answered, her tone rich with anguish. "I trust you to do what is best." She pulled back in his embrace, raising her head to meet his face. His hazel eyes were luminous with unshed tears. She reached up to trace the line of his jaw. "Stay safe, my dear friend. Promise me."

"I promise," he whispered, reaching up to cup her face between his hands. He pulled her close, pressing a soft kiss against her lips, which yielded to his, hoping to trap one last moment before it was gone forever.

The clomp of hooves against the earth startled them. They turned to find Mirabella in the doorway, returned from a ride. Her face was contorted as though she had borne witness to a great horror, her eyes fiery with accusation. She shook her head as she jerked the reins, whirling the horse about and riding from the stable as though it had burst into flames.

Cecily chased after her, crying her name in vain.

Everything, all good purposes, had all been in vain.

* * *

Mirabella rode through the forest at breakneck speed, listening to the pounding of the hooves against the fallen leaves. Her blood raced. It was confirmed, that which she had tried so hard to deny, all brought to light at last. Father Alec was a man as any other, a lustful, sinful man, and Cecily, the woman she loved so dear, no better than a common whore. It was just like Sister Julia and her father, sin upon sin. Betrayal upon betrayal. The cycle never ended. Oh, God. . . .

Mirabella rode until she reached the dwelling, yet another place of shame, another place of betrayal.

An eye for an eye. . . .

She dismounted and stormed in, finding Grace in the midst of reading cards. She looked up as though she had been expecting Mirabella.

"And so it has all come to pass," she said in wry tones. "And you will make them pay, won't you? 'Vengeance is mine, sayeth the Lord.' " She shook her head. "I imagine you provide quite a relief being His right arm."

"They must answer for their sin!" Mirabella cried as she seized Grace by the wrist, pulling her from the table and out of doors. The frail woman put up little fight as Mirabella nearly threw her over the saddle of her palfrey and mounted. "You will answer for yours as well!" she seethed.

"And you, Mirabella?" Grace returned, her tone calm and cool. "When will you?"

Mirabella said nothing as they cut through the forest, back to Sumerton, back to where it all began.

Mirabella did not bother to stable her horse. She rode into the courtyard, dismounted, and let the beast wander as she dragged Grace behind her into the castle, into the great hall, past wide-eyed servants who paused from their work to cross themselves.

"Where is my father?" she demanded of a fearful Kristina.

"H—he is in his apartments with my lady and Father Alec," she told her.

"Stay here," Mirabella commanded of the child, who looked as though demons themselves could not convince her to move.

"Mirabella, I beg you—" Grace began.

"Speak not!" Mirabella cried. "I am through protecting you!"

She pulled Grace down the hall to Hal's doors, abandoning courtesy and bursting forth.

She held Grace's hand aloft, thrusting her toward Hal, who had been seated before his fire, a tearful Cecily and Father Alec before him.

"Mirabella, what is the meaning of this?" he asked, rising. His face was streaked with tears.

"Don't you recognize her, Father?" Mirabella's tone was low. "Has it been so long that you have forgotten the features of your own true wife?"

Grace stood, mouth parted, tears streaming down her own cheeks as she beheld the broken family before her. "Oh, God . . . Oh, Hal. . . ." But there were no words for this. There would never be any words.

And then something went terribly wrong. In all of Mirabella's plans for revenge, she could not have foreseen it. Cecily and Father Alec rose, their faces wrought with sorrow. But her father, her dear father. . . .

Hal shook his head a moment as he advanced toward them. At once his face was overcome with an expression of pain too powerful to be attributed to emotion. He seized his temples in his large hands, crying out, before collapsing to the floor.

Cecily was at his side, taking his head onto her lap. "Quick! Fetch Dr. Hurst!"

Father Alec rushed past an immobile Mirabella.

"My God, Mirabella," Cecily said, her tone soft as she fixed her eyes upon Mirabella. "Do you hate me so much?"

Mirabella could not speak; she was rendered mute as her father.

"Apoplexy," Dr. Hurst said. Cecily heard the word as if it were an echo from another time. Indeed, Cecily wondered if she had been sucked through some kind of portal, back to the first time, when her love had willed Hal back.

Would her love be enough now, or would Hal succumb to the betrayal she and Father Alec had only just confessed to him, hoping to confront his wrath before Mirabella revealed it? How his eyes shone with the light of disillusionment when he gazed upon them, his dearest friend and his wife, his most unlikely betrayers. The silence that impregnated the room was suffocating as Hal, still casting his eyes in disbelief from one to the other, tried to find words suitable for such an unprecedented occasion. But the words never came.

Mirabella came, her wrath, her hate; she came at them merciless and exacting, her attack as unlikely and unprecedented as their own betrayal. Never had Cecily imagined this would be the form of revenge Mirabella's bitterness would incite. It was all too much to take in.

"I'm sorry, Lady Sumerton," the physician went on, addressing Cecily. "It was severe and he is older now. He will not survive."

Hal lay abed. The muscles had gone slack on the left side of his face; everything was crooked, as though she were looking at him through a mirror as shattered as her dreams. She sat beside him and allowed no one near.

She would keep vigil over him alone, as any good wife would do.

A moan cut through Cecily's haze and she opened her eyes, unaware that they had closed, to find the noise had come from Hal. Drool coursed down his chin. She retrieved a cloth, swabbing it clean.

"Cec . . ." he murmured, opening his right eye as much as would be allowed. It was an eerie blue slit across a face that had gone gray.

"I'm here, my love," she whispered, squeezing his hand in hers. Tears choked her.

"Far," he said. "Faralec," he said again, then with more urgency, "Faralec!"

"Alec?" she asked on a sob. "Father Alec?" She reached out, cupping his face in her hand. "Do you want him, darling?"

"Him . . . you, yes," he answered.

Cecily rose, bidding her longtime servant Matilda to fetch the priest. When he came, he sat beside Hal on the side of the bed opposite Cecily.

Hal's breathing grew labored.

"Oh, my darling, calm yourself," Cecily cooed. "We will solve all of this when you are well," she told him with sincerity. "And I will obey whatever you command, whatever you wish. I do love you, Hal. I've always loved you."

"Forgiven," he whispered at length. With the utmost effort he raised his hand and with it took Cecily's, resting it on his chest. His heartbeat was sluggish and erratic. Cecily trembled. He closed his eye for what seemed like an eternity before summoning the strength to seize Father Alec's hand and place it atop Cecily's. "Blessed," he said, covering the two hands with his own. His hand rested atop theirs, then slid off with a new heaviness. His head lolled to one side as he expelled one long, last jagged breath.

Cecily and Father Alec met each other's eyes, each alight with tears.

Forgiven. Blessed.

Gone.

❧ 19 ❧

Mirabella knelt before her prie-dieu but could not pray. She wanted to ask for forgiveness; she longed for absolution. But the only priest who could grant it was unfit to wear the collar. She shook her head in agony, sobbing. It had all gone awry. She had not meant for this, surely they must know she never meant for this. . . . Had she killed her father, just as she had her mother years before when she tried to stop the heinous act against her person? Her mother had begged her to let go, to forgive. But all her life she clung to the past, to sins that were not hers, sins she assimilated into hers through her own actions, thus mocking her mother's last request. Now her father perished to an apoplexy, the very thing she had once lied to him about when asked how Sister Julia passed. Divine retribution. No one could ever tell her there was not such a thing. Her life was proof.

What had she become?

She rose in a flurry of black damask and headed for the stables. She would go to James Reaves, sweet James who once wanted her. James would comfort her; he would understand. He would know what to do.

She rode alone to Camden Manor, now in the process of being rebuilt and in the hands of Sir Edward's younger brother William, the Sheriff of Sumerton. He had retained what was left of the staff with James as steward.

James received her in the great hall, which still smelled of new lumber and fresh rushes.

"Oh, James . . ." she began, breathless. "Please . . . accept my apologies. I was harsh."

"There is no need," he said, his tone formal but gentle.

"My father died," she said, her voice breaking as she threw herself into his arms. "And I have been so disillusioned by life!"

James's arms went about her in a limp embrace. He patted her back a moment before disengaging.

"You have my sincere condolences," he told her. "Lord Hal was a good man, truly kind and without guile. He will be missed." He arched a brow. "How fare the Lady Cecily and the children?"

Mirabella swallowed burning bile. "The children are handling the situation with as much grace as they can, dear things. And Cecily . . . she is Cecily." Her voice was laced with an anger she tried to suppress.

James did not comment. "I wish the family well. This will be a hard time. You are all in my prayers."

Mirabella blinked back tears, taking his hand. "Oh, James . . . James, we must have speech. I was wrong. You see, I know I was wrong now, to refuse your hand. Forgive the impudence of my timing, James, but . . . may we . . . may we try again?"

James withdrew his hand, backing up. "Now is hardly the time to discuss such things," he said.

"Then when?" she persisted. "After the interment? You may call whenever you like."

James shook his head. "I'm sorry, mistress. You do not understand. . . . I am married."

"Married?" Mirabella breathed, backing away. "So soon?"

"With all due respect, did you expect me to wait for you to come to your senses, mistress?" he returned. "And how long a period would have been acceptable to you? I am sorry that I chose to move on. I am not getting any younger; I put off my dreams long enough, and when you dashed them all I saw no reason to wait.

You are not the only one to have suffered disillusionment, mistress."

Mirabella shook her head. "No . . . James, no. You are angry with me. You are hurt. You cannot be speaking true—"

"Her name is Cynthia," he went on. "And she is a good girl. We are like minded, but she is gentle; she is not always fighting battles she can never win. I am sorry, my dear, but it is true."

Mirabella's face contorted in pain. James married. Her James, her last dream, her last hope for redemption, for something real and lasting. Now he was someone else's dream, someone else's to hold, to love. Someone else would pray with him, would converse with him, would take care of him, have his children, and Mirabella would be alone, abandoned as she had always been. Oh, God, how would she bear it?

There was no hope for her now. There was no saving her. Any chance for salvation was stolen from her the day Alec laid eyes upon Cecily once again, slipping away with brutal finality when Mirabella rejected James's proposal, leaving her nothing but hatred and regret, those miserable, ever-constant companions.

She turned her back on James as the world had on her and ran.

Hal's body was cleansed and prepared for interment. Harry was sent for while Emmy was tended by faithful nursing staff. Kristina clung to Cecily's side, her eyes bewildered.

"But why did he die, my lady?" she asked, her voice strangled by tears.

They were in the solar. Though Kristina was not a demonstrative child, she now sat on the settle as close to her mother as possible. Cecily wrapped her arm about her shoulders and held her to her heart, stroking the silky locks of blond hair as much for the girl's comfort as her own.

She drew in a breath. "Your father was a strong man, Kristina," she told her. "And he lived through an apoplexy when first we . . . married." She swallowed at the word, wondering what Grace's presence now meant for her marriage and the legitimacy of her children. She sighed. She would deal with that as it came. She went on. "He regained his speech and the use of his limbs. But this second apoplexy . . . it was too much for him to bear at his age."

"It was Mirabella, wasn't it?" Kristina's voice was low.

Cecily started, recalling the scene, Mirabella's frenzied eyes and Grace's shamed countenance. Was it? Could she blame Mirabella or was this apoplexy a long time coming?

"Why do you say that, child?" Cecily prodded in gentle tones.

"I am not a fool," she told her. "I see how Mirabella is—so . . . angry. She thinks no one notices. She's a high-minded wench half the time, always wanting us to see things as she sees them. If we disagree, we are wrong. Isn't that so?" She did not wait for an answer. "And I saw Mirabella heading for his apartments that day; she looked taken by the devil himself. I know she had something to do with it; you will not tell me different!"

"I will not try," Cecily said, giving her daughter a reassuring squeeze. "I do not know what forces work for and against us, Kristina. I can tell you it is God's will and expect you to be satisfied with that . . . but I would be a hypocrite." She swallowed a sob. "It is hard for me to accept how life has turned out, hard for me to credit God for all of it when we have made our own mistakes and now must live with the consequence, not only to ourselves but to the innocent as well." A vision of Emmy swirled before her mind's eye. She bit her lip and shook her head. "At times, Kristina, I have acted out of my own self-interest and have made others suffer for it. Mirabella has done the same. Both of us will live with our sins the rest of our lives. The one thing I know for certain is that God will hold us accountable in His time."

"Oh, my lady, I cannot see you ever doing anything wrong," Kristina assured her as she nuzzled against Cecily's shoulder. "Not out of meanness like Mirabella. You may be selfish at times, but everyone is. And you are sorry. That is all God asks."

Cecily smiled. "If it were that simple . . ." She wiped a tear that had strayed onto her cheek. "But I see that Father Alec has instructed you well."

"He is a good man, my lady," Kristina said. She sighed. "I suppose he will marry you now and take care of us since we've no one."

Cecily's heart pounded in her chest. "My darling, whatever would make you say such a thing? He is a priest."

Kristina shrugged. "He loves you," she said simply. "And he needs you more than he needs to be a priest."

"It is not possible," Cecily said, flustered. "And we must not speak of it. We are in mourning for your father. We will be taken care of, no matter what happens."

As she said the words she knew what her next course of action must be.

It was time to confront Lady Grace.

Cecily found Grace housed in a suite of apartments reserved for guests. She had not made an appearance since Hal's death two days before; no one save Cecily, Mirabella, and Father Alec was aware of her existence.

Now she sat before a small fire, clad in homespun, her hair, more white than blond now, arranged in a braid over her shoulder, looking every bit the opposite of a countess.

When she saw Cecily she rose and dipped into a curtsy.

Cecily waved for her to sit, taking a chair opposite her.

"I do not know where to begin," Cecily confessed as she gazed upon her. "I want to know everything."

Grace averted her head a long moment, taking in a quavering breath before starting. "Every dream I had was with Brey. Hal and I, we had no marriage. There was too much hurt; we could not be salvaged. Brey's death drove home that fact. We would have made each other miserable and the cycle of pain would never have ended. I saw how far gone I was. I wanted to end my life. I tried to . . . only to wash up down the Thames." She offered a wry smile. "I could not even kill myself right."

Cecily shook her head, her gut churning in disgust.

"I saw that it was my chance to begin anew," Grace went on. "I began to make my way back to Sumerton; I wanted to be in a land familiar to me and near all of you, that I might monitor everyone's progress. In the forest resided an old woman versed in herbs and white magic. She took me in and taught me her ways. I gave up the spirits. I took care of myself. The life of simplicity suited me far more, I realized, than the one of luxury that I once believed I craved more than anything. Not only did I have a new life, but I felt I was a new person, a better person."

"I am glad that you underwent such a transformation," said Cecily. "But you must know what this means. You are still Hal's wife; you are entitled to all this."

"I know that. Do you not think if I desired it I would have made my presence known long ago, before you ever married him and began a life together?" Grace shook her head. "You have no need to fear me, Cecily. I will not deprive you or your children of your rightful inheritance. Harry will remain Hal's legitimate heir." She bowed her head, sighing. "Mirabella underestimated the course of events that her hatred set into motion. She will be haunted by her choices, mark my words."

"And you?" Cecily asked. "What will you do?"

"I will return to the forest. I only ask that now that you know of me, you will see me now and again. That you will be my friend."

Cecily hesitated, choosing her words with care. "I cannot say I condone any of your actions," she confessed. "But we neither of us are innocent women and have to answer for our own sins. I am relieved to see you well; I appreciate the hardship you have known before making this choice and the hardship you have known since; it could not have been easy watching our lives progress and not taking part. But I am glad that you found yourself," she added. "And I will be your friend. More than that, I will see that you are granted an annuity as such that will see you through the rest of your days."

"It is not necessary," Grace told her.

Cecily leaned forward, taking the older woman's hand. "But it is right."

Grace dissolved into tears, clutching Cecily's hands in hers. "You are a good woman, Cecily. I am proud of you."

Cecily's lips quivered as she took her in her arms.

Despite the conflicting emotions and the tragedy, it was a good reunion.

Father Alec tried to quell his rising sense of dread. After all, what more could happen at Sumerton? How much worse could it get? He would leave. After he saw that Cecily's affairs—the irony of the term was not lost on him—were put in order, he would return to London, Cranmer's summons or not.

He had ruined Cecily's life and incurred Mirabella's vengeance. Despite Hal's touching display of forgiveness, he could not stay on. It was no longer proper. More than that, it was not right. He would go; what Cecily gave him was enough to sustain him the rest of his days. It had to be.

The day Hal was to be interred in the family mausoleum, Father Alec went to his apartments that he might don the proper attire for the service. What he found made him gasp.

The apartments had been ransacked. His possessions were thrown about everywhere; furniture was turned over, papers were strewn about. Father Alec shook his head. Whoever had been here was looking for something. He immediately went to his trunk with the false bottom where he kept his secret writings. Heart pounding, he lifted the bottom.

Gone.

Father Alec sat back on his haunches, his breathing shallow. Beads of perspiration gathered at his temples; his face tingled. Everything he had recorded, all of his thoughts and meditations that could be his death sentence, was gone.

He rose. There was no time to investigate. He would do what he could after the interment.

There was nothing to be done but to head to the mausoleum.

When he arrived Cecily reached him, her eyes wide with panic as she clutched his upper arm. "Mirabella is gone," she whispered. "We cannot find her anywhere. The house has been searched, the stables—everywhere. Oh, how could she miss her own father's interment?"

"I am afraid it is more than that," Father Alec returned. "My apartments have been turned upside down, my personal papers stolen."

"Oh, God, no. . . ." Cecily's hand flew to her mouth. "Not even she would—"

"Now is not the time," he told her. "We will commence with the ceremony."

Cecily nodded and returned to the children as he began the service. After celebrating the requiem mass, Father Alec spoke.

"Today we commend Harold Pierce, Lord Sumerton, to our Heavenly Father," he said. "He was a husband, a father, a friend . . . my friend. He gave me charge over two generations of his children, and all the while as I instructed them it was he who was doing the teaching." His voice caught. "Lord Hal taught me what it is to be a family, a family who see each other through tragedy and triumph. His life serves as an example of what a Christian man should be, not because it was void of sin but because of how he handled it—both his sin and those who sinned against him. Unlike so many, Lord Hal lived by the true meaning of the words 'forgive, that thou might be forgiven.' " He shook his head in wonder. "As a priest I celebrate his entrance into Heaven. But as a man, I shall miss his friendship and guidance more than he could know." He paused a long moment, raising his eyes. Against his will they found Cecily. She stood, head bowed, tears glistening against her fair cheeks. The children were at her sides, all but baby Emmy, who remained in the nursery, protected by her innocence. Harry sobbed openly. Kristina kept her pain internal and looked on with a dignity beyond her years.

He collected himself and commenced with the funeral mass and Hal was put to his eternal rest beside Brey.

Good-bye again. How many more good-byes were they expected to endure?

As the procession made their way from the mausoleum to Castle Sumerton, they were met by Sheriff William Camden and two guards. Mirabella was beside them.

Cecily gripped Harry's and Kristina's hands as Sheriff Camden approached Father Alec. She shook her head, a scream trapped in her throat.

"We come to detain you in the name of His Majesty, King Henry VIII, on suspicion of heresy," the sheriff announced in a tone that suggested his perverse sense of pleasure at carrying out his duties.

Father Alec met Mirabella's eyes. Mirabella had the grace to bow her head.

Cecily rushed forward, laying a hand on the armored wrist of Sheriff Camden. "You come here in the middle of my husband's funeral to take away the officiant? How dare you?"

Sheriff Camden withdrew his arm. "You have my deepest condolences, my lady; however, justice cannot wait. It is best you do not fight this, else you implicate yourself as a heretic as well."

"It is all right," Father Alec said, directing his gaze at Cecily. "I will go in peace. Blessings to you all and not to worry. God's will be done."

With this the guards seized his arms, escorting him from the gathering. Mirabella began to follow the sheriff, but Cecily caught up to her, holding her fast by the upper arm.

"Does your hatred know no bounds?" she seethed.

"Unhand me." Mirabella's tone was cool. "I am beholden to you no longer."

"I see that," Cecily said, but did not free her. "I see you are beholden to none but your own thirst for revenge. Does not the verse 'Vengeance is mine, sayeth the Lord' mean anything to you? Or have you so completely abandoned your religious convictions?"

Mirabella struggled against Cecily's talonlike grip in vain.

"Perhaps I have," Mirabella confessed, her tone almost giddy. Her lips curved into a sneer. "I see how much good they have done the rest of the residents of Sumerton."

"It is not about faith at all with you, Mirabella," Cecily told her, pulling her closer. "It is about not getting what you want. It has always been about that. What has seized you is as old as Eden itself: jealousy."

"Jealousy? Over what? Your sin?" Mirabella returned. She shook her head, tears filling her eyes. "Have you no shame, Cecily? He was a man of God and you brought him down like a common whore—"

"It is you who will bring him down!" Cecily hissed. "You will condemn him, possibly to death, and for what? To ensure he will not sin again? Tell me! For what?"

"I loved him!" Mirabella cried, at last freeing herself from Cecily's grasp.

Cecily was taken aback. Her eyes widened in horror. "If this is how you punish those you love, I sorely fear for those you hate."

Mirabella shook her head, turning on her heel to rejoin the entourage.

"Where are we going, my lady?" Harry asked.

Cecily had ordered the carriage and was making ready in her apartments. The funeral guests, a-thrill with gossip over the latest happenings, ate their fill in her great hall.

"You must stay behind," Cecily told her son. "You will guard the castle for me like a shining knight. You are my shining knight, are you not?"

Harry offered a proud nod.

"Care for your sisters in my absence," she went on, though she had instructed Nurse Matilda to care for all the children. "Comfort them in their grief, especially Kristina. She loved her father well."

"Did you, my lady?" Harry returned.

Cecily was struck. "You know that I did. How could you ask that?"

Harry shrugged. "I never doubted it . . . it's just that lately, before he died, you looked at him with sad eyes."

Cecily blinked back tears, images of her husband, so shocked and saddened when last she saw him, swirling before her mind's eye. "Life is complicated, Harry. When you become a man, you will see." She wrapped herself in the warm otter fur–lined cloak. The sky was gray; she did not doubt it would snow soon. "I am removing to London to appeal for Father Alec."

"But if he is a heretic, surely you cannot!" Harry said, his blue eyes wide with fear.

"Harry, he has been your beloved tutor!" Cecily cried. "Do you think your father would ever engage a heretic for a tutor?"

Harry shook his head. "But Mirabella says that heretics hide everywhere and are even sometimes people we love," he explained. "She said it is our duty to preserve the True Faith by exposing them."

"Harry, I do not want to hurt you by disclosing your sister's nature to you," Cecily began. "But you must not listen to her, at least not in this. She has been much disappointed in life and bitterness has poisoned her heart. Keep in mind, also, that her 'True Faith' is also now considered heretical."

Harry bowed his head, expelling a sigh that betrayed his confusion. "Sometimes I do not know what to believe," he confessed.

Cecily took the boy in her arms, holding him close. She swayed from side to side. "When you are a man, you will decide for yourself in a land that will hopefully let you choose. Till then, we can only all of us do as we are bid by His Majesty, else we shall never know a day of peace." She pulled away, stroking his blond curls from his forehead. So like Brey . . . "Be brave, lad. We will endure to see better times. What makes men heretics are all matters of doctrine, technicalities. But if you have faith in God, He will know you are of a sincere heart and will see you through. That is what matters most."

Harry offered a solemn nod. "I will be brave, my lady," he assured her. "And I will care for the girls."

"There's my good lad," Cecily said, ruffling his hair one last time as she pulled away.

"My lady." Harry seized her hand, pressing it to his lips. He raised his eyes to her. "Be brave as well."

Cecily swallowed an onset of tears as she squeezed his hand.

She must be brave. For herself, for her children, and for Father Alec.

❧ 20 ❧

Cecily went straight to Lambeth Palace, not bothering to stop at her home on the Strand to refresh herself. There was no time. She requested a private audience with Archbishop Cranmer and was shown to his presence chamber. She could not sit, nor sip the sweet wine offered her. She could only pace and wring her hands in agony. It was all too much—Hal's death, Mirabella's betrayal, Father Alec's arrest. She could not wrap her mind around any of it. There was no time to digest the shock, no time to grieve.

"What is troubling you, my dear?"

Cecily raised her eyes. She had not even seen the archbishop enter. He stood there, the picture of serenity and gentleness, his languid brown eyes filled with compassion.

The sincerity of his tone brought tears to her eyes and she dipped into her lowest curtsy, taking his hand to kiss his ring.

"Your Grace," she began. "I am Cecily Pierce, Countess of Sumerton."

Cranmer held on to her hand, pulling her to her feet. "Sumerton, you say? I know of it well. Father Alec Cahill spoke so highly of it. How does he fare?"

Cecily bowed her head. "Oh, Your Grace, I fear he has come to harm. He has been betrayed in the cruelest of ways, his private papers confiscated and turned against him." She met his eyes. "He is now imprisoned, suspected of heresy. I come to you to appeal for his life. I—I did not know where to turn."

Cranmer's mouth was set in a grim line. "This is very serious," he said. "Many have perished in the fires at Smithfield for heresy. Oh, my dear friend . . ." His eyes grew distant. "I thought he'd be safe there. . . ." He shook his head. "I will see to it that the matter is adjourned to me personally."

Cecily's eyes lit with hope.

"He will not be freed," Cranmer said, raising his hand as if to sustain her blind optimism. "But I will see that he is detained until I can review the evidence myself, that we might spare his life. There are changes on the wind, my lady. There may be hope for our friend yet."

Cecily slid to her knees before him. "Your Grace, I have prayed and prayed for you to give me hope for him. I thank you. With all I am, I thank you."

"You must not lower yourself, my lady," Cranmer said, helping her to her feet. "I am not worthy of such a show. Rest now, dear, then get you back to Sumerton, that you might be a comfort to him."

Cecily rose. "He told me you were a good man, Your Grace. I see his description could not be more accurate."

"I am only a man," he said, waving off the praise with flushing cheeks. "Subject to the pleas of a lovely lady."

Cecily smiled as she made her exit. At the door, he stopped her.

"Lady Cecily." His voice was soft. "I think Father Alec may have learned that it is not good for man to be alone. . . . I am glad it is you."

Cecily was about to respond, but he smiled to his guard, who closed the door.

Somehow he knew. This should have troubled her, yet it did not. In a strange way, it relieved her.

The dungeons of Camden Manor may have been the only place the summer's fire had not touched. Father Alec had not even been aware of their existence, but he supposed many homes of the gentry had some place to detain those who broke the peace. Now that the Sheriff of Sumerton had assumed the manor for his own, it was renovated as a jail, complete with instruments of torture, which Father Alec hoped to be spared.

Now he sat shackled at the wrists and ankles in a windowless cell on a bed of straw. Now and again a spider or mouse used him as a kind of bridge and he squirmed in discomfort. The straw had not been changed in a while and dampness seeped into his robes. He leaned his head against the stone wall and closed his eyes. He never thought it would end like this.

That his first visitor should be his ultimate betrayer did not surprise him at all. Mirabella stood before the bars of his cell, clutching her cloak about her. Father Alec resisted the urge to spit at her feet. *Compassion*, he urged himself. *No matter what, compassion.*

"What do you want from me?" he asked, his voice low.

"I have not yet turned over the evidence," Mirabella told him.

"Then what have I been detained for?" he returned, struggling to remain calm.

"I revealed some statements that could be interpreted as heretical," she said.

"Then I imagine that will be enough to see me to the stake," he said.

"I can recant," she said.

"For what?" Father Alec challenged. "What else can I give you besides my life, Mistress Mirabella? Have you not seen what your hatred has wrought upon Sumerton? You blamed yourself for your mother's death. I told you it was not so; I still believe that. But your father . . . it seems you have enough to live with that you should add my death to your conscience."

Mirabella met his eyes. "You try to divert the sin upon my shoulders when it is you who are the betrayer! You and Cecily."

"That is our sin," Father Alec told her. "Between us and God. He has not appointed you His judge on earth."

"No, He has not," Mirabella agreed. "But it is my duty to protect His faith and intervene when I see blasphemy and sin corrupting it."

"Your duty?" Father Alec laughed. "You do nothing out of a sense of duty to the Lord. You are a female first, Mirabella Pierce, a jealous female, and that more than anything has been your motivation. Your jealousy will destroy us all. Years ago I knew of your unholy designs on me. I addressed it once, do you remember?"

Mirabella averted her eyes.

"And since you respected my office and remained my friend," he went on. "How I rejoiced for you when I thought you had a man like James Reaves to give you the life that you so needed. But you refused him and clung to a dream, a silly confession of mine made when I thought—for a brief moment—that I could trust you. If only I had known then what my fatal lapse in judgment would cost me."

"Don't you see?" Mirabella cried. "It is that statement which will preserve your life!"

Father Alec shook his head. "What do you mean?" He understood too well what she meant. But he hoped, he prayed, that there was something still human in her, that she would not say it.

"You said you would marry, if the Church allowed," she said. "I do not know if the Church will push those reforms through or not . . . but what I propose is that you renounce your collar and marry me. If the reforms go through, you can return to the priesthood, I promise you."

Father Alec's eyes grew wide in horror. "Satan once tempted our Lord with the whole world and what did he do?"

"We all know you are not our Lord." Mirabella's tone oozed with contempt. "This is your life we are talking about, Father. Your *life!*" Her lips twisted into a sneer. "Are you so willing to become a martyr? With the evidence I have, you will burn, make no mistake of that."

Father Alec shook his head. "Let us not forget who is first so willing to sacrifice this life of mine." He sighed. "As far as martyrdom, it seems I am made one regardless. Either way I am doomed."

"We are alike, Father, you know that," Mirabella went on. "Both religious, both intelligent—there is no end to what we could accomplish for God together."

"My God, you have lost your mind if you believe that I am anything like you." Father Alec's tone was thick with sadness. "I pity you more than any living being, Mistress Mirabella."

Mirabella shook her head. "All I have to do is show your papers and no one—not the Archbishop of Canterbury himself—can save you. You know it in your soul. This is the only way."

"You think because of one sin that I have no integrity, no honor, and that I value my life above all else," Father Alec said. "Believe me when I tell you I would rather die than abandon my calling and marry you."

"And Cecily and the children?" Mirabella retorted. "What of them? What will your death do to them after so much loss? Will you be responsible for breaking her heart and scarring the children for life?"

"How dare you?" he seethed. "How dare you use them against me when it is you who have caused their ultimate suffering? Do you not think that Lady Cecily's heart would be broken anyway? Do you not think that it is broken already?"

"I know Cecily; we are as sisters," Mirabella said. "She is a woman of practicality; she would rather see you live than die a saint, even if it means she cannot have you." Mirabella cast her eyes toward the ceiling. "You have till sunset to decide. Die a nameless saint or live as my husband and have a chance at shaping this faith that means so much to you. I will stand by your decision, *Father*."

With this she turned and in a swirl of skirts was gone.

Tears streamed down Father Alec's cheeks, slick and warm. There was but to turn it over to God. What would He want? Father Alec knew what Archbishop Cranmer wanted; he wanted him to live, that he might be used in the future, when it was safe. But to give up the priesthood, to turn his back on his calling—was he being a coward? Was it God's will that he become a martyr? Yet what God of love would will people to die so senselessly?

And Cecily, what of her? How much more loss could she take? Was it better to live with her resentment than die with her heart-break?

Father Alec drew his knees to his chest, bowing his head and resting it upon them. If he married Mirabella to spare his life, he was cheating them both. He could never love Mirabella. It would never occur to him. The marriage would be a farce . . . and yet, in that was there hope? If it was a marriage in name only, it could be annulled. With little guilt.

Father Alec raised his head. He believed he was put on earth for a higher purpose, higher than human love, higher than marriage— it would have been an unexpected benefit to future reforms that he truly did not anticipate ever becoming an actuality. If Mirabella was right in one thing, it was that Cecily would want him to live. She was not so selfish as to rather see him dead than not belong to her. He would not have been hers anyway, had reality had its way. He would have departed for London, she would have remained at Sumerton. Till reforms were pushed through . . .

He could not allow his plans to revolve around a maybe. There was only here and now and what to do.

He could see his life and his goals go up in ashes or he could marry Mirabella . . . but at what cost to his soul! Was sparing the fire in life only saving him for an eternity of flame? He shook his head with vehemence, as if to shake himself from a nightmare.

But there was no waking, no sleeping.

There was but to choose.

Mirabella returned to Father Alec's cell stony faced. She drew in a breath, daring him to answer. It may seem wrong, yes, but it was the only way! In time, when he worked through the resentment, he would see that they were meant to be, that they had always been meant to be.

She closed her eyes against what Cecily would make of the union. Could she bear to meet those teal orbs, Cecily's betrayer once again? But what of Cecily's betrayal?! Had she not been faithless perhaps this could have been avoided . . . and yet . . . had Mirabella waited for reforms that may never be pushed through how else could she save Father Alec from himself? That, more than anything, had been her ultimate goal—yes, that was it, truly. Cecily's actions only spurred an inevitability.

She was not saving him from the sin of the flesh but from something far worse: the sin of abandoning his True Faith. She could bear him as a defrocked priest but not a man who sold out his calling to the devil in the guise of the New Learning. Even could he marry then it would not have been right. There was to be a priest or a man, never both. Someday he would see it her way, after time had dulled the sting. Someday . . .

If he made the right choice.

She steeled herself against the possibility that he would choose martyrdom. Could she bear it if he did? Could she ever forgive herself? Yet better to die a martyr than make the wrong choice in life, better to be spared that.

She had paid Sheriff Camden and his chaplain well should Father Alec make the right choice. Sheriff Camden had shaken his head at her, offering a wry, knowing smile when she made the proposition that should Father Alec renounce the priesthood and marry her, he would be dismissed from suspicion. She would guide Father Alec toward right and keep him, essentially, out of trouble. On its own the proposition would never have stood. Three hundred pounds and an emerald from her father's coffers the size of her fist sweetened the deal considerably.

She would not allow guilt to creep in. The world would see her as trapping Father Alec; they would not see it as the selfless preservation of his soul. But no matter. God knew her heart. He knew her intentions and would bless them. . . . He had to.

Mirabella laced her fingers around one of the bars of the cell, peering in. Father Alec's face was drawn, new lines etched upon its countenance as if overnight. She swallowed tears. Jesus endured three days of Hell to get to Heaven; Father Alec could stand a few days in a cell.

She could bear his silence no more. "Well?" she prodded, her tone husky.

His eyes were naught but hazel pools of regret.

"You win," he said. She ignored the defeat in his voice. "I only hope you realize what your victory will cost us all."

Relief flooded through Mirabella, sweet as wine. She tipped her head back, thanking God, before calling the guard. "Fetch the sheriff and Father Michael. Hurry!"

The guard did as he was bid and within minutes Sheriff Camden lumbered forth with the scrawny, fidgety chaplain.

Father Alec offered a bitter smirk. "So. You thought of every-thing."

"She did," Camden said with a slight chuckle as he unlocked the cell. "And I reckon you have more reason to fear life as her husband than pain of death at the stake any day."

Father Alec shook his head, refusing the help of the sheriff as he scrambled to his feet. His shackles were unlocked and he took a moment to flex his chafed wrists.

"And now, my dear Father . . . Alec Cahill," the chaplain began. "We shall begin."

No, thought Father Alec, his bitterness palpable as he fixed his eyes on Mirabella. *Now it shall end. . . .*

Cecily was exhausted. Cranmer's assurance had eased her mind somewhat, but she could not bear to sleep at the house on the Strand. The sooner she conveyed the news to Father Alec, the better. She dozed in the carriage on the way back to Sumerton, hir-ing two drivers to switch shifts, that they may drive through the night, and arrived home earlier than expected.

Rest did not find her at Sumerton, however. Upon entering the great hall, she found her children and servants in an uproar.

"Oh, my lady!" Kristina cried, tears streaming down her rosy cheeks as she flung herself into Cecily's arms. Cecily was unsure if the display was prompted by grief over Hal or a yearning for her company and embraced the child.

"I'm home now, darling," she cooed, swaying to and fro. "Now, now, you mustn't cry." She raised her eyes to find Harry standing behind her, his expression solemn. He was pale and, somehow, seemed older.

"Harry . . . something has happened, hasn't it?" Her heart slowed; each beat was a painful throb against her ribs.

Harry bowed his head. "Oh, my lady mother," he said as he ap-proached her.

Kristina wrapped her arms about Cecily's waist, sobbing.

"Not Father Alec," Cecily prompted, her throat constricting with tears. "They haven't—he hasn't—"

Harry shook his head. "It is Father Alec; he's been spared, thanks be to God."

The knots in Cecily's shoulders eased. "Spared! Then this is a cause for rejoicing, not despair!" she said with a smile. "Has the archbishop's messenger reached the sheriff, then?"

"No, Mother, I am afraid not," Harry said. "It appeared the only way to save his life was to renounce his vows—"

"Oh, the poor, dear man!" Cecily cried as she stroked Kristina's hair. "I can only imagine what that must have cost him. But soon the messenger will be here and all will be made right—"

"I am afraid it is worse than that," Harry told her. "He had to renounce his vows and marry Mirabella, Mother. Apparently that was the only way they would believe he was sincere. Somehow she convinced them that it would curb his—heretical bent."

Cecily could not breathe. The arms that had been wrapped about her daughter fell to her sides, limp. He had not said it. He was misinformed. He had not said it. She shook her head. "Harry . . ."

Kristina looked up. "It's true, my lady," she confirmed. "Mirabella brought him here and told us herself—and I know, my lady, I *know* in my heart she has done something evil to him, else he wouldn't have given up his true dream to marry that—that wicked creature!"

"Oh, Kristina, you mustn't—"

"No, we all know it to be so!" Kristina cried. "You didn't see his face; he was broken, my lady, as broken as a body could be. It was as if they had killed him and she was dragging about an empty shell of who he was. It wasn't our Father Alec. It was . . . a ghost." Kristina shook her head. "And all the while, my lady, Mirabella looked as the cat who swallowed the cream! She could nary contain her delight, her—her *triumph!*"

Cecily lowered herself onto the bench by the trestle table. Kristina and Harry sat beside her. Cecily knew her daughter had estimated the scene with accuracy. Only under threat of death would Father Alec be coerced into such action. He may have had pride, but he was too much of a visionary to sacrifice his life for that pride. And he thought martyrdom, in most cases, foolish and wasteful. Could Cecily blame him? The stake would test any man's integrity. As to Mirabella's treacherous hand in the entire affair she could not begin to fathom . . . To let herself venture into that woman's head would be tantamount to sacrificing her own sanity. Oh, had she arrived a bit sooner she may have spared him this terrible tragedy. . . .

"Where have they gone?" she asked.

"She said they had to call on some tenants before you came home," Harry said.

"She wants to humiliate him, my lady!" Kristina told her. "Can you imagine the cruelty of it, and she who claims to love him?"

"Oh, my dearest," Cecily cooed helplessly, almost cursing her daughter's brightness. Would that she could spare her from the realities of life a bit longer. . . . She sighed. "We can trust that he is strong enough to bear . . ." *That evil,* she wanted to say, but refrained. She was certain her daughter could herself finish the sentence with a few other choice words. She almost smiled.

On that thought she rose. "I best tell the servants to prepare rooms for them."

"You mean to have them back here, Mother?" Harry asked, screwing his brows up in incredulity.

Cecily nodded. "Your father acknowledged Mirabella as his daughter in his will, providing an annuity and allowing her use of Sumerton for all of her days," she told them. Though her children were not yet privy to the circumstances of Mirabella's birth, it remained known, albeit unspoken, that Mirabella was not a legitimate Pierce heir. "And after what Father . . ." She swallowed an onset of tears. "After what Master Cahill has endured—" Master Cahill! There was the ultimate humiliation, being reduced to nothing but the master of himself, not the shepherd called to herd the Lord's flock. Cecily's heart lurched. She drew in a breath, squaring her shoulders. "He deserves nothing less than to be surrounded by the comforts of familiarity and those who . . . love him."

With this she bit her lip and commenced the necessary preparations. She would keep busy; she would go through the motions.

Perhaps then somehow the pain, the pain of losing Hal, the pain of losing Mirabella to her bitterness, and the pain of poor Father Alec's position, would stop.

He was Alec now, Alec Cahill, formerly of Wales, formerly a priest and tutor and man with honor. A string of formers to follow a name that meant nothing. He held no position, no calling, and felt far less than a man. As they returned to Castle Sumerton that evening, he knew it was Mirabella's intent to complete his humiliation and punish Cecily for her betrayal once and for all. He had already suffered Kristina's tears and Harry's stoic disappointment, but Cecily . . . God curse him. It was no less than he deserved to see those teal eyes light with pain and shock. He steeled himself against the confrontation to come as they entered the great hall.

Trestle tables were set up and food was being laid out, great platters of cheese and bread, prawns and boar and sugared comfits. Alec looked about him in wonder. The hall had been strung with pine boughs to usher in the holiday season and candelabras painted the room in cheery hues of gold. Dancing as festive as could be in the hearth was a bright fire. Fire . . . Alec squeezed his eyes shut against a vision of the stake. He could almost smell his flesh burning. He shook his head.

And then, somehow, she was there, approaching them. Her black mourning gown only accentuated her ethereal glow and rose-gold hair.

Alec swallowed an onset of tears. He brought himself to meet those eyes but in them found no condemnation. Only a knowing sadness. But her smile was kind, even sincere, as she extended her hands to Mirabella.

"My dear," she said, drawing her near to kiss her cheeks. "Perhaps a feast is out of order considering our state of mourning, but upon learning of your nuptials and the grace of God, Who has preserved our Master Cahill, I thought it was a necessity."

Mirabella trembled visibly as she looked about her. "I . . . I thank you, Cecily."

"My only wish is that you could have been there to see your father interred. Events deterred us from a proper funeral meal, as

I'm certain you recall," Cecily went on, her tone eerily light. "But no matter. He is with us now and knows all we do."

Alec noted even Mirabella had the grace to avert her eyes at the statement.

"Come, won't you sit?" Cecily asked as she led them to the high table, where Harry and Kristina were already seated with other members of the local gentry. "Now that Master Cahill is family we cannot deny him a seat among us."

Cecily proceeded for her seat at the center of the table, Hal's chair vacant beside her. To her left she sat Mirabella and Alec. Before settling herself, she raised her cup of wine to the guests.

"Please share our happiness with us, so hard won in the face of such recent sorrows," she announced. "And welcome into our fold the newly married Alec and Mirabella Cahill. While starting his new life here at Sumerton with his lovely bride, it will please me to have Master Cahill continue to tutor the Pierce children." She raised her glass. "To new beginnings!" she cried, her cheeks flushing. Only Alec was close enough to note the tears lighting her eyes.

"New beginnings," he chorused with the rest of the guests. Mirabella had made to clink her cup against his. He withdrew it, averting his head and wishing the cup were large enough for him to drown in.

The feast was interminably long, as Mirabella expected Cecily intended, and before permitting them to retire she offered the couple a nuptial gift. With great care she presented them with a sack of orange velvet.

Mirabella untied the drawstrings, sliding the bag down to reveal a sandglass. Her hands trembled as she ran a finger along a series of dates carved in the mahogany top, immediately recognizing the birth dates of her sisters and brother, along with the anniversary and death dates of her father.

"I don't understand," she said, raising her eyes to Cecily.

"It is to keep hours," Cecily told her as though explaining something to a very small child. "Your good father gave it to me in the early years of our marriage, that we might keep a record of all the important events in our life. Now I give it to you to do the same. For good or for bad, mark the dates, that you might remember where your every decision has led you."

The guests who had remained throughout the length of the evening murmured their admiration over the sentimental gift. Mirabella hugged the timepiece to her belly.

"I shall," she told Cecily, meeting her gaze. "May it commemorate many a happy anniversary."

"As God wills," Cecily said, her gaze unflinching.

The face was a portrait of kindness that did not reflect in her eyes. In those teal orbs Mirabella expected a number of emotions, none of which she saw.

There was only irony.

21

A t the end of the evening Cecily led them to their newly appointed apartments herself and bid them good night. Mirabella was content to survey the rooms, ones that had been reserved
for guests. In them was her prie-dieu, along with a portrait of Hal
commissioned just before his death. Her father's knowing blue
eyes seemed to stalk her every move, forcing Mirabella to avert
her head.

"You know more about me than anyone," she told Alec in soft
tones. "My good and my bad . . . and what was almost taken from
me." She raised her eyes to him. "But what was preserved, I
choose to give only to you. I will not allow the past to interfere
with your being a true husband to me."

Alec shook his head, a bitter smile twisting his lips. "Do you actually believe this illusion you have created?"

Mirabella furrowed her brow. "It is no less than what you owe
me. I saved your *life!*"

"Saved me?" Alec's voice was low. "After you turned me in and
allowed me to sit in a rat-infested cell, assuring me I awaited my
death were I not to wed you . . . Saved me, Mirabella?"

Mirabella started. For the first time he had dropped his formal
address of "mistress."

"It was inevitable," she said. "I was sparing you in the long run, from heresy charges that would no doubt be your fate, and something even worse. . . . I could not watch you sell your soul to the devil and had you become a true reformer priest—"

"Which, as I recall, you said you would 'let' me return to once more if the reforms ever were pushed through—" His eyes widened in mock surprise. "Wait. That is no longer so?" His laugh was a joyless cackle. "You mean you were *lying* to me, Mirabella?"

Mirabella shook her head frantically. It was wrong, all wrong. She knew he'd never see it her way and this was her punishment, his eternal resentment. . . . Oh, God, what had she done?

"You don't understand! It wasn't like that—you make it sound so sordid, so vile!" she cried.

Alec placed a hand upon his breast. "What? You mean I made your confiscating of my private papers and having me suspected for heresy, only to tempt me from the stake with promises of life"—he raised a hand as if to exclaim *voila!*—"and marrying you, to sound *vile?*" He raised his head. "Forgive the audacity of my assumptions."

"Your soul was in jeopardy!" she cried, seizing his hands in hers. "I *did* save you! Yes, I connived to do it, but it was worth the risk! You're alive and finally, finally free of the reformer influence that would have cost you your soul!"

At once Alec's face softened. He approached her, cupping her face between his warm hands. She trembled. He leaned in, placing a kiss upon her forehead. When he drew back, his eyes were lit with pity. "My poor naïve girl," he said. "I think you believe that."

Mirabella shook her head once more, clenching her hands into fists. "It's the truth! Yes, I was angry at you and Cecily for betraying my father and felt you should suffer for it—I admit it! But this was about so much more than that when I thought about it—"

"When you convinced yourself of it, you mean," Alec corrected, his gentle tone laced with disgust.

Mirabella bowed her head, closing her eyes. "You will understand. Someday you will understand and then you will thank me for it."

"Until I reach this understanding, you must . . . understand, forgive the redundancy, that this is no marriage," Alec told her in no uncertain terms. He made an expansive hand gesture as he cast his eyes about the room. "You are free to sleep where you like. I, however, will return to my former apartments until I make further arrangements."

"You will not!" Mirabella cried. "We are married now, Alec!"

"In name only, my dear," he told her as he made for the door. "Just until I can obtain an annulment . . . or does that seem ungrateful?"

"Wh-what?" The breath had been sucked from her. Her gut twisted in knots. How could she be such a fool as not to anticipate this? She pursued him, grabbing his upper arm and turning him to face her. "You can't do this," she told him in soft tones. "Please don't do this. Give me a chance to be a good wife to you. Your days as a priest are over now. You cannot return to it after you have disgraced yourself in this fashion—"

Alec withdrew his arm with a jerk. "I disgraced myself? By trusting you, by sacrificing my honor and integrity and choosing a marriage to you rather than death at the stake?" Tears lit his eyes. "Yes . . . well. Perhaps I did," he added, his voice just above a whisper.

Mirabella reached up to cup his cheek in her palm. "I know you don't believe it, but my actions were motivated out of love."

"You are right," he said in flat tones. "I don't believe it. Not for a minute. You were motivated out of anger, bigotry, and jealousy, none of which I have ever confused with love. I have grossly overestimated your intelligence by assuming you could discern the difference yourself. The ability to connive and deceive may fool people into believing one is intelligent for a time, but not for long."

"You should know," Mirabella said in low tones. "Are you not practiced in the art of deception yourself?"

"A dabbler, never a master," Alec said without pause. "In that area, I defer to you, my good wife."

"Just you remember, Alec Cahill, who is in possession of your private papers!" Mirabella hissed then. "I only made statements before but did not turn them over . . . yet."

Alec shook his head. "Holding me with more threats?" He

shrugged. "Do what your conscience advises, Mirabella. If it is God's will that I be subjected to the stake after all, then I will not fight it." He expelled a sigh. "And now, it has been a trying day and I would like to bid you good night."

With this he turned on his heel and fled down the hall.

Mirabella stood alone.

It did not escape Cecily that Alec had taken to his old apartments since his nuptials, leaving an ashamed and humiliated Mirabella to her bridal suite alone. Cecily could not deny a perverse sense of satisfaction at the thought. But it was a short-lived victory; the prize was far too bitter.

And for that prize the household was suffering. The children, especially young Kristina, absorbed the tension like sea sponges. The girl grew pensive, nervous, and agitated at the slightest provocation. Cecily could not condemn the poor thing, always too astute for her own good, and knew some action must be taken to spare the children from the heartbreak that was suffocating Sumerton.

There was no one Cecily could think of to consult but Grace, who had returned to her dwelling and was known only as Mrs. Forest, and to very few at that. Cecily chanced riding to her the next day. A light snow blanketed the earth, insulating it as it awaited the birth of new life, new hope. There was no such anticipation for Cecily as she offered a feeble knock.

Grace answered, her blue eyes widening in the subtlest trace of surprise as she beckoned Cecily's entrance with a thin hand. She could not mask her shock whenever she saw the former Lady Sumerton. Assessing Grace sans the anguish wrought when first her presence was revealed was easier now; Cecily could take her time. Never would she have passed her by and recognized her as the woman who, for all intents and purposes, had raised her. Even if she had not isolated herself, Grace's humble appearance alone afforded her an inconspicuous existence. She was thin but somehow more robust than Cecily ever recalled seeing her, with her ruddy cheeks and calloused hands that set one at ease the way most hardworking folk could. Her now white hair she wore in a simple plait down her back; she could never be mistaken for the young woman she had been. And yet, as Cecily examined her, still could be found the same wry expression, the sardonic half smile as Lady Grace scrutinized through her lashes. Despite whatever deception and betrayal that went before, there was a strange sense of coming home, a rare comfort Cecily had not experienced since her friendship with Alice.

"My dear." Grace's tone was warm as she led her to the bedstead. She poured her something steaming. Cecily took the cup from her with ultimate trust, not realizing till after she sipped that it was hot honeyed milk. The drink, hers and Brey's favorite as children, brought an onset of tears she tried to stifle.

"I did not expect to see you so soon," Grace said. "I hope you understand why I did not say good-bye. I could not bear to see Hal interred." Her voice broke as she shrugged, offering an apologetic smile. "I suppose I would rather pretend all is as it was, that he is at Sumerton well and loving you and the children . . . but it will never be as it was, will it?"

Cecily shook her head. "No, never . . . and I—I do not know where to turn. My dear friend Alice is dead, my husband is dead. I have no one now. . . . Fa—Alec and Mirabella are lost to me."

"Alec has taken a blow. And I daresay Mirabella is lost to herself as well," Grace commented. "But worst of all, lost to that God of hers." Her lip curved into the half smile Cecily had just now realized she missed. "I wonder what He makes of it?"

Grace rose from the bed to pour them more honeyed milk. "And now I suppose you come to tell me she betrayed our Father Alec as a heretic, only to 'save' his life with a wedding ring and renunciation of his vows?"

Cecily's mouth fell agape.

"I have my ways; I've had them all along," Grace added with a joyless laugh.

Tears swelled in Cecily's throat. She swallowed. "It isn't good for the children, living like this, seeing all the resentment and anger, and them mourning their father."

"You cannot think that Father Alec desires to be married to Mirabella any more than she desires to be married to him, God help her realize it," Grace explained. "And, no, it is not a happy home for those children right now, I agree. God knows I've contributed enough to unhappy homes. . . ." Her eyes grew distant a moment. She shook her head, as though with that gesture she could shake the regret, replacing the wistfulness with her devil-may-care smile.

"Mirabella and . . . Alec are miserable. They sleep in separate chambers and he, from all reports, can't abide the sight of her. I suppose I avoid them both and the children are left trying to maintain a relationship with all of us while trying to hurt none of us; it is a weighty lot we've put on their small shoulders."

"The children must be protected for a time," Grace conceded. "But only for a time. You must send them away, all but the weak one, little Emmy. The other two are ripe for fostering and with their blue blood as backing you can have your pick of good families. In these times I recommend you find a family that is religiously ambiguous and has never had any dealings, good or bad, with the Crown that might draw any attention to them. Times are changing and reigns will, too. It is best to find a family that can change with the times."

Cecily absorbed these thoughts with a solemn nod. "But where? And who? Everyone I know seems to be firmly entrenched in either the old faith or the new. No one is above suspicion in Henry VIII's England. I cannot imagine—"

"You do not have to," Grace told her. "Fortunately, I have enough imagination for both of us." Grace leaned her chin on her steepled fingers. "Now. Are you aware of the Hapgood family?"

"Hapgood . . ." Cecily tested the name; it rolled unfamiliar on her tongue.

"They are middle gentry, high and low enough to assure your children a place in society and assure you that they will not arouse any sort of controversy from His Majesty's court or otherwise," Grace told her, her voice ringing with the authority of a well-informed chatelaine. "A little reformist in bent but not dangerously so. And they have children old enough to contract alliances with Harry and Kristina, matches that may be a bit beneath you but guaranteed to satisfy any family with a bit of ambition. They wouldn't refuse your children, in other words. They are far from

here, Cecily, very far, which will be hard for you. Hard but necessary."

"But Harry has been brought up in the Earl of Surrey's household till now," Cecily pointed out, the thought of sending her children to an even more distant destination chilling her to the core.
"Hal had hoped to marry him into the Howards."

"A sinking ship to be sure, until such fortunes reverse," Grace
said, once again shaming Cecily with the fact that she remained
more aware of the world's happenings in her forest sanctuary than
the lady of a bustling castle. "The Duke of Norfolk and his unfortunate son are in the Tower as we speak, arrested for treason—Surrey plotted to kidnap the little Prince Edward, I believe, and
quartered his arms with Edward the Confessor. Norfolk has been
implicated as a participant. Only a fool would ward a child to that
lot as it stands now, let alone sanction a marriage."

"My God," Cecily breathed in awe, sending a quick prayer up
for the tragedy-ridden Howard clan, who had already lost two
queens and countless children. It would be heartless to exclude
them, however conniving and plotting they may be, from compassion. As much sympathy as Cecily felt for their plight, however,
she would never be such a fool as to express it. She nodded in
agreement. "No, of course I can never send him to the Howards
now," she said. "But the Hapgoods? How do I go about introducing myself and presenting the idea of wardship and possible alliance?"

"Leave that to me," Grace said, her smile triumphant.

Cecily's heart surged with fresh hope as she regarded the
woman who had stood as, ironically, her truest friend. She thanked
God that Mirabella's hatred had turned on her to reveal such a
blessing and knew without doubt that in coming to Grace she had
come to the right place.

The Hapgoods were impressed with the letter of introduction
and proposal of wardship and possible future alliance, "should the
children prove compatible." Grace had composed the missive in
Cecily's name and negotiated the terms. For their wardship the
Hapgoods would receive a handsome annuity to cover the ex-

penses of the children's upbringing. They would be received after Twelfth Night, an affair Cecily could not imagine infusing any joy in without Hal, the great lover of all holidays and master reveler.

There was but to tell the children, a task Cecily took on with a generous measure of dread. But she recalled Harry's stoic strength in the light of his father's death and Alec's arrest, along with Kristina's understanding. They were strong children, brave, and had endured much. They would survive a separation. Indeed, most children of noble birth did; it was not an unusual practice, to say the least. Had not Cecily herself begun her life at Sumerton as Lord Hal and Lady Grace's ward?

She took supper with the children in the nursery, laying out their favorites. Prawns Kristina could pop in her mouth like sweetmeats, with a plate of mutton so tender it melted in the mouth for Harry. And for little Emmy, whom Cecily held on her lap to comfort herself as much as the child, hot spiced apples.

The nursery, where her own life began with Brey—such an innocent, happy spirit!—and Mirabella, with her misplaced intensity and fruitless crusades. The nursery witnessed their joys and their fears and, always, their good-byes. Now it would be good-bye again with none but little Emmy as its sole occupant.

"What is it, my lady?" Always intuitive, Kristina could not waste a moment on idle chatter.

Cecily smiled, reaching out to take the children's hands. "My darlings, you know there comes a time in the lives of many noble children to receive a higher education and experience a life their home cannot offer—"

Kristina rose, folding her arms across her chest. "You're sending us away." It was a statement. Her little bow mouth puckered. "Why now? Why can't we wait? Father's only just gone; we haven't had a proper mourning! Besides, you need us to help you! And we . . . we need you. . . ."

Cecily could not maintain any composure in the light of Kristina's argument. Tears stung her eyes. "It isn't that I want to send you away . . . but there are things happening here you need not be affected by just now." Cecily swallowed. "So I crave your patience and forgiveness for what I must do." She expelled a quavering sigh. "You must know, no matter what, that all that has come to pass will not ever diminish my love for you both. That is a constant."

"Oh, my lady, there is nothing you could do that could stop us loving you," Harry assured her. "But are you certain this is the right thing?"

Cecily shook her head, touched. "It is for me and our current circumstances as much as to honor your father's wishes. He would not have wanted any of us to stop living and, especially, to stop learning." She looked to her daughter, hoping to abate the confusion lighting the liquid brown eyes. "Kristina, you must learn to become a great lady. With the Hapgoods you can study the social graces. There are other children your age there—why, I believe there are ten! You will have friends of your own station to grow up with." She turned to Harry, her solemn boy, who stayed his quivering lip, his blue eyes alight with an understanding beyond his years. "Harry, you will have a proper gentleman's education—you must learn to be my brave knight and with the Hapgood boys you can learn. What's more, you will be together. I could never bear to separate you."

"What about Emmy?" Kristina asked, kneeling down before Cecily to take the child's hand in hers. Her face softened when looking at her sister.

"Emmy must stay here," Cecily said.

"And I'll miss everything! Her learning to walk—" Kristina lowered her eyes. It remained unspoken that the prospects of Emmy walking as a normal little girl were slim. "And talk, and write!" she went on as if to soften the thought that hung between them all.

"Darling, it isn't as though we will never take holidays and visit one another!" Cecily assured her. "And I will make certain as soon as Emmy learns her letters that she will be a most faithful correspondent." Cecily forced a little laugh. She raised her eyes to Harry, making a silent appeal for him to step in and cast a favorable light on their fostering.

Harry squeezed Kristina's shoulder. "It will be all right," he told her. "We can't none of us carry on like babies. We will go to the

Hapgoods as brave as any knight and make our lady mother proud. And"—he met his mother's eyes, his mouth tilting upward into the most tender of smiles—"we shall honor the memory of our father with what we learn."

Cecily blinked back tears, her heart swelling with pride. "You have the heart of a knight, Harry," she told him. "You will watch over Kristina, make certain she is not mistreated."

"And if we are mistreated, what then?" Kristina wanted to know, though her voice was softer.

"Then you will come home," Cecily stated. Relief washed over Kristina's features; her little shoulders seemed to ease. "Now, this does not permit either of you to concoct stories against your keepers or behave in a manner that invites strict discipline. You are representing the Pierces of Sumerton; I expect you to behave as befitting of your station."

"We will," Kristina promised, with an earnest nod of assent from Harry.

Cecily opened her arms, and the two children rushed forward to hold her and Emmy tight in an embrace of reassurance.

It did not reassure Cecily, however.

It was only the beginning of another good-bye.

"You're sending the children away?" Mirabella demanded of Cecily that evening after Cecily took to the only refuge she could find—her own chambers, a place Mirabella disregarded as she disregarded everything else, entering without preamble or even the courtesy of a knock.

Cecily, who was lying on her chaise attempting to lose herself in mindless embroidery, nodded. "I should think I would not have to consult you as to the decisions I must make for my own children," she said in cool tones.

"But what of Master Cahill? He is their tutor! And a better tutor you will be hard pressed to find!" Mirabella cried.

"While I agree with you, I am certain this is the best decision for all involved," Cecily told her. "Be assured, there will be no shortage of prospects for Master Cahill. I know how concerned you are after his well-being."

"So do you propose to send us away as well?" Mirabella's tone was petulant, grating on Cecily more than her children could at their worst. From children petulance was expected.

"Do what you like," Cecily said. "Sumerton is large enough to ensure that our lives need not affect one another at all."

"But the children—they're—" Mirabella cut herself short. Tears lit her eyes a vivid emerald. Cecily was unmoved.

"They're growing up," Cecily finished for her. "Harry would have been sent back to Lord Surrey's household as it were, but in light of the earl being imprisoned in the Tower at present, I did not feel it wise to recommence his education there. The Hapgoods are a good family, honest, hardworking, and noble. And since I was sending Harry I thought it best to send Kristina with him; they can be a comfort to each other. Take heart," she added, though her tone was less than encouraging. "Emmy is still here and too young to perceive you as anything but her loving sister." Her gaze was pointed. "Until you prove otherwise."

Mirabella could not seem to summon an argument against Cecily's cool reserve so stood a moment; her helplessness translated into the silence, almost stirring Cecily to compassion. It was a fleeting sensation. She only had to recall Mirabella's recent betrayals and conniving, never too far from her mind, to quell the notion.

"Is that all, Mirabella?" Cecily prompted, taking up her embroidery once more.

Mirabella offered a slow nod. "I suppose it is."

She quit the room.

Cecily's embroidery blurred as tears flooded her vision, tears she would never allow Mirabella to see, tears that were for her and for the friendship that was forever lost.

❧ 22 ❧

My dear Alec,
    It is with the heaviest of hearts that I hear of your
plight. There is no sense lecturing you on the decision
you have made, I am certain you are punished enough.
I cannot say myself how I would fare were martyrdom
in question so I will not be such a hypocrite as to judge
your actions. The flock has lost a shepherd few can
rival, but I am certain God is not finished with you, my
friend. Keep the faith that you remain part of His
divine will and plan.
    I am compelled to share my disappointment that my
missive intervening in your case did not arrive until
after the measures you took to resolve this unfortunate
business. It seems poor Lady Sumerton's visit to
Lambeth Palace was in vain. I suppose I have as much
trouble turning things to God's will as the next man.
    Take heart, Alec. I cannot but keep hope that you
will return to your calling sooner than later. You must
know I will do all in my power to help you. Until then
I remain . . .
    Your obedient servant,
    T. Cranmer
    Archbishop of Canterbury

The hand that held the letter shook as Alec Cahill's eyes scanned the second paragraph again and again. Cecily had gone to London. Cecily had made an appeal on his behalf, not by scheming or deceit but by love and conviction. And Cranmer, his beloved friend, would have helped him. Would have saved him, perhaps. But they were both too late.

Anger surged through him, anger at the circumstances that quickly converted to anger at God. How could He allow this to happen? Should he have just burned? Now he was without calling and soon without the comfort of a profession now that Cecily was sending the children away. He was cursed, as cursed as Job ever was without any of the saint's patient acceptance of loss. No matter how he tried to analyze it, he could not come to anything resembling an understanding of why all had come to pass as it did. It all seemed so unnecessary. So futile.

Since his marriage, if indeed the farcical union could be called such, the month before, he had avoided Cecily as much as Mirabella, interacting with the children and few others.

He could not hide any longer.

Letter in hand, he went to Cecily, who lived out much of her days in either her chambers or the nursery. He found her in the latter, rocking little Emmy to sleep. He gazed down at the unfortunate child, almost too big for her cradle now, and reached down to touch her cheek. His heart stirred with a peculiar longing he could not identify.

Cecily raised her eyes to him; they were teal mirrors of sadness. Alec swallowed a lump swelling his throat.

"I have been a bad friend to you, my lady," he told her, his tone huskier than usual as he sat beside her on the window seat. "I have been so caught up in my own shame and regret that I have been in hiding. And that is wrong."

"We have all been in hiding," Cecily said. "Tending our wounds in our own private hells." She sighed, reaching over to cover his hand with her own. There was a strange comfort in the gesture; in it there were no expectations. He laced his fingers through hers.

"I did not know you appealed to Archbishop Cranmer until

today," Alec confessed then. He indicated the letter with an incline of his head. "If only . . ."

"No 'if onlys,' Alec," Cecily insisted, squeezing his hand. "Else you will drown in them." She shook her head. "I saw no point in telling you." She offered a feeble smile. "But I am glad that you know."

Alec turned on the seat, taking both her hands in his. "I have never railed at God's will so much as now. No matter how I try, I cannot wrap my mind about the sequence of events."

"It isn't God's will, all this," Cecily told him. "It was Mirabella's. God allowed it to happen to teach us something, though I am hard pressed to discern the lesson myself." She sighed. "As it is there are too many present concerns to waste a moment dwelling on even the recent past. I have to get the children settled with the Hapgoods."

"Oh, my Lady Cecily, would that you could keep them with us," Alec lamented. "They are my favorite, and at times only, diversion." He sighed. "But I suppose it is not fitting keeping them here with a deranged half sister and her fool of a husband." He almost choked on the last word.

Cecily bit her lip, shaking her head. "No, Alec, it is not fitting," she admitted. "And my Lord Hal would have wanted it this way. He wanted them to see more of this kingdom and learn; it is for his wishes and their health and happiness that I am compelled to carry on with this." She averted her head.

Alec reached out, turning her to face him with a gentle hand on her cheek. "I am so sorry our decisions have brought such unhappiness to Sumerton, to all of us, that such action is now necessary."

She pursed her lips a moment, blinking several times. "It cannot be undone," she said in soft tones. "We can all of us only move onward and hope for better days ahead."

Alec gathered her in his arms, holding her fast. "Oh, my lady, at times it seems God *is* cruel," he said, his voice breaking.

Cecily pulled away, meeting his eyes. "No," she told him, her voice tremulous with conviction. "We are the cruel ones; we mock God with our free will instead of following His and now we cry because we are paying for it."

Alec could only nod in agreement. Once again, Cecily proved correct. Whether tied to the old ways or the New Learning, Cecily remained closer to God than all of them.

It was reassuring and defeating at once.

Hapgood House was situated on the coast of Devon; the children would be almost as far south from Sumerton as was conceivable in Cecily's mind. Though the region was primarily set in the old ways, the Hapgoods remained obedient to their king and seemed altogether unruffled by the religious climate, a fact Cecily found reassuring.

Despite the bleakness of January and a journey that seemed interminably long and uncomfortable, Cecily could see that spring would reveal a beautiful seaside haven for her children. Indeed, it was the perfect backdrop to grow up by. As Christmas through Twelfth Night proved to be every bit as steeped in muted despair and awkwardness as Cecily had imagined, the journey became an anticipated event and prospect of excitement for the children. The change of scene helped alleviate the sting of mourning and even Kristina perked at her first sight of the rolling gray sea.

Cecily remained with the children the first week to help acclimate them and acquaint herself more with their keepers. They seemed fine people, if a little overwhelmed by their own children, six girls and four boys, all ranging from ages four to seventeen. Sir Richard Hapgood, a justice of the peace with considerable landholdings, and his wife, Lady Beatrice, an able chatelaine of the bustling household, were in their midforties. She reminded Cecily of the evolved Lady Grace, with her forward, no-nonsense manner. They were a hospitable family rife with joyous chaos. Cecily knew by the end of the week what she had suspected all along: that her children were in a good place.

The farewells were tearful, the good-byes laced in uncertainty. When would they see one another again? How much would the children have grown? Would they still love her or would they begin to forget her? How long would it be before her children became polite, noble little strangers? Cecily could not bear to think anymore in this vein and comforted herself with the fact that

Harry and Kristina were swarmed with Hapgood children to distract them the moment her carriage pulled away.

But Cecily gazed out the window until the mass of playing children became an indistinguishable dot against the horizon and the coast faded into the sea.

God keep you, my children. . . .

To cope with the new quietude Harry and Kristina's absence left Sumerton in, Cecily busied herself with the mundane—the ledgers, the mending, the candle making, the tenants. She was grateful little Emmy was left behind; she could not have endured a house completely void of children, and her younger daughter proved a comfort to her.

And then as January drew to a close, the bells tolled the most extraordinary news.

"He's dead!" Mirabella cried as she burst into the bower where Cecily had been mending. Her cheeks were flushed, her lips curved into a smile.

Cecily regarded her, puzzled by her happy delivery of news of a death and wondered just how mad Hal's daughter had become.

"King Henry, Cecily! He's dead!" Mirabella told her, raising her eyebrows and nodding.

Cecily looked past her to see Alec in the doorway. Her smile beckoned him forth.

"It's true, my lady," he told her. "Long live King Edward VI!" he added with a small smile of his own.

"Long live King Edward!" Cecily and Mirabella parroted. "Poor little boy," Cecily commented. "To lose your father at nine is difficult enough." She thought of her own Harry. "Let alone to inherit a kingdom in turmoil. What's going to happen now?" This she directed at Alec.

"His uncle Edward Seymour, now created Duke of Somerset no less, serves as lord protector," Alec said. "And the Seymours move quickly. The Howards were put down just before His late Majesty's death; the Earl of Surrey was beheaded on the nineteenth. The Duke of Norfolk lives, however; the king neglected to sign his death warrant. So he sits with a handful of influential papists in the Tower."

Mirabella shot him a glance at this. "I suppose you think this a good thing?" she demanded. "No doubt the Seymours will see to it that any traces of the True Faith are wiped off English soil forever."

The sarcastic twist of Alec's lips that served as a smile was not lost on Cecily. "This is a positive stride for the Church of England, yes," he answered without hesitation.

"What an exciting time this must be for the archbishop," Cecily breathed, knowing how important Cranmer was to Alec and how much this transition in power meant to him and his cause.

Alec's eyes softened with wistfulness. "Indeed an exciting time for us all."

"We should remove to London," Cecily proposed suddenly. "Take Emmy and perhaps even Lady Grace and open Sumerton Place."

"I thought you hated Sumerton Place," Mirabella said.

"You were brave enough to stay there once," Cecily returned. "And you were right; it is just a house and cannot be held responsible for what happened in it. Besides," she added, a tear in her voice. "Brey loved it there. He wouldn't want us to hide from it. It would be like hiding from his memory."

"But to bring Lady Grace?" Mirabella challenged. "You cannot imagine she would want to confront the memories there after how long she ran from them, from everything."

Cecily shrugged. "That is her decision. As for me, I still consider her a member of this family and would enjoy her company. Of course, Mirabella, you are free to do as you please." She cocked a brow. "But you, Master Cahill? What make you of it?"

"To be in the thick of it . . . would be more than I could hope for," Alec said.

"Then we will make ready," Cecily decided. "If we are lucky we will make it in time for the coronation!"

Cecily and Grace opted to take a second coach with baby Emmy and follow behind Mirabella and Alec. A small baggage train and ensemble of guards accompanied the travelers. They were not halfway to London when Cecily's coach broke an axle. Unruffled, Cecily waved Mirabella and Alec onward.

"We'll be along; we have plenty of help!" she shouted when Alec poked his head out his window, his expression a silent offer, perhaps even a plea, to assist, which Cecily responded to with a bright smile, gesticulating once more for them to keep going.

After the carriage rolled out of sight, Cecily sat back in her seat, a smile of satisfaction curving her lips.

"You never intended to go, did you?" Grace asked, the corner of her own mouth tilting into a smirk.

"But, Lady Grace, we broke an axle." Cecily's tone heralded exaggerated innocence. "What could we do, and me falling ill besides?" With this she brought a hand to her forehead, emitting a dramatic sigh. "No, this is where Master Cahill needs to be, and without me as a distraction to him; I'm sure Mirabella will provide distraction enough," she added with a wry laugh. "Meantime, the threat of heresy no longer hangs over his head and he will have the support of his beloved Cranmer and be free to pursue what he loves, at least in part." She drew in a breath, her shoulders squared. "I will send a messenger shortly explaining that circumstances have arisen which will prevent us from making the journey. A messenger has already been sent to Cranmer announcing Master Cahill's impending arrival."

Grace's laugh rippled forth in sheer delight. "Pray tell, what did it say?"

"Simply that I am sending Master Cahill to him and . . ."

> *. . . Please help him. The reforms the new government will be pushing through with your guidance mean more to him than anything. It is my sincere prayer that he can be a part of that which he holds in such high esteem even if it is not in the way he once dreamed.*
> *Humbly yours,*
> *Cecily Pierce*
> *Countess of Sumerton*

" 'Greater love hath no one,' " Thomas Cranmer quipped as he looked from the letter to Alec Cahill, who stood before him in his privy chamber as bewildered as if he had just witnessed the Second Coming.

Alec knew his immediate summons to Lambeth Palace upon their arrival could not be a coincidence. When he and a disgruntled Mirabella received the dispatch stating Cecily could no longer make the trip, he knew he had been the victim of a bizarre, albeit loving, swindle. Once again, Cecily had obeyed the convictions of her heart with nothing but the sincere desire to help him. Try as he might, and contrary to Mirabella's opinion on Cecily's "deception," he could not resent it.

Cranmer stood up from where he had been seated behind his writing table, linking his hands behind his back as he circled it. He leaned on a corner and fixed Alec with a penetrating gaze.

"This marriage . . ."

"Is a deception of the highest degree," Alec finished before he could help himself. "She confiscated my private papers and still has them hidden, used statements against me to fabricate suspicion of heresy, only to pay the sheriff off that he might abet her with the renunciation of my vows and this . . . this . . . unholy union!"

Cranmer smiled, nodding as if indulging a temperamental child. "It is not an easy situation you have found yourself in," he said at length. "Do you plan to seek an annulment? Surely whatever papers she has of yours hold no power considering that the ruling family are the premier Protestants in England at present."

"It matters not," Alec told him, his shoulders slumping in defeat. "Either way I would be a fraud. I broke my vows last summer, Your Grace. So you see, no matter if an annulment is granted or not, I could never return to the priesthood."

Cranmer seemed unaffected by this newest revelation. "Do you maintain your relations with the woman in question? Do you feel you or she is intentionally sabotaging your purpose for her sake?"

"No," Alec said, entertaining Cecily's selfless actions once more. "She has only tried to help my cause and not stand in the

way of it and reconcile me to my purpose, whatever that is now."
He emitted a heavy sigh. "As far as my self-sabotage, I did that
when I chose this marriage over a saint's death."

Cranmer nodded in understanding. "Well, we none of us can
predict how we'd react under those circumstances," he said. "And
while I cannot condone the breaking of your vows, nor can I condemn you for it. You are not the first man of the cloth to falter. You
will not be the last. But you cannot think this would hamper your
being welcomed back into the fold."

"I no longer feel worthy of my calling," Alec confessed brokenly. "Breaking my vows is the least of it . . . my cowardice, my
inability to become a martyr for God." He shook his head, swallowing a painful onset of tears. "How can I in good conscience return?"

Cranmer's smile was gentle as he laid a hand on Alec's shoulder.
"I commend that you do not easily forgive yourself, but you cannot
put yourself above our Father, Who forgives all iniquities. Before
you decide on any course regarding your marriage and your calling,
you must forgive yourself. You will be immobilized otherwise."

"Your Grace, you have treated me with nothing but compassion
and I thank you," Alec said, dipping over the archbishop's hand
and placing upon his ring a reverent kiss. "And if I have disappointed you, I seek your forgiveness first."

"There is naught to forgive, my friend, but only that you seek
your own forgiveness," Cranmer said, disengaging his hand, bowing his head as though embarrassed by the display. "We have
known much suffering these past few years, and many changes.
But now is a time for healing and a time for reflection. For our suf-
ferings are about to be rewarded."

Alec nodded, knowing the archbishop was referring to the great
religious reforms that were no doubt in store under the reign of
young King Edward.

"And while you are coming to terms with your personal struggles, you can still be of use to me," he went on, his voice infused
with hope. "I need a mind like yours for my panel of gentlemen I
am consulting for my latest work, a book that will outline the
tenets of our faith."

Alec's heart constricted at the honor. "I am at your disposal, Your Grace."

Cranmer clapped his hands with a decisive smile. "Right. Then we shall set to this great and noble process. Welcome back, my friend."

Welcome back, indeed, thought Alec with a rueful smile, once again congratulating Cecily's prowess at getting him to London and thus, he hoped, to his ultimate destiny.

There was but one thing Mirabella could think to do while in London and that was to somehow contact Mary Tudor. The newly restored princess was said to be mourning her father and would not be present for her younger brother's coronation, thus Mirabella opted to write her in the hopes that she could seek refuge in her company. She needed time to reflect in a neutral place unaffected by the tragedies that preyed on her life like relentless falcons. Perhaps with the princess she could do just that. And if Her Highness advised her to annul the marriage and let Alec go for the sake of their common cause, she would do so.

The missive, a lengthy mingling of confession and events since their last encounter all those years ago when Jane Seymour presided over the Christmas festivities, coupled with condolences for the king's death (which she wrote with a trembling, unconvinced hand), was dispatched, leaving Mirabella anxious and restless as she anticipated her response.

Meantime, Alec spent much of his time at Lambeth Palace, conspiring with the heretic Cranmer no doubt. No amount of praying seemed to dissuade him from his path and anger surged through her at the thought that all of her loving actions had been in vain. She could not save him if he would not save himself.

The two existed in separate spheres, both awaiting the coronation of the child-king and wondering what the new reign would portend. Alec was filled with such palpable hope and optimism that he was compelled to treat Mirabella with a formal kindness he had not afforded her since before his imprisonment. Relieved at the apparent truce, Mirabella could but be amicable in turn, leaving the two to maintain a quavering peace at best.

The response from Princess Mary was prompt, drawing Mirabella from the unwanted reflections day-to-day living brought. She nearly shouted for joy when she received the messenger of what might be her only ally, and broke the princess's seal without delay.

> *Mrs. Cahill,*
>   *Your actions disgust us in a way we shall not stoop to describe. You have allowed your resentment to compromise your sanity and any decent contribution you could have made to our cause has been undermined by your despicable, shameful behavior. The priest, if a heretic, should have been left to die for his sin, but instead you sullied your own virtue in the misguided attempt to save him. Perhaps you should save yourself. In any event, yours is a life we desire no affiliation with and we caution you to keep your distance from court. As sister to His Majesty our views are held in suspicion, but our brother is merciful thus far. We cannot anticipate how merciful he would be to one of your station. God be with you, Mirabella, for we certainly are not. . . .*

Mirabella read the words again and again, as though with each reading some covert message of friendship could be discerned in between the lines of the callous dismissal, to no avail. The princess had abandoned her. Mirabella was alone.

Balling the letter in her fist, she thrust it into the fire that blazed in her chambers. She stood alone, watching the flames devour the message and convert the hateful words of the Tudor woman to ash. *And unto dust ye shall return. . . .*

"Some wine, missus?"

Mirabella started at the voice of her young servant Nan. Sniffling, she nodded, beckoning the girl forward with a slight wave.

The girl edged near, setting the tray of warm spiced wine on her breakfast table.

"You may stay and drink with me," Mirabella said, knowing it mattered not if one of "her station" crossed the unspoken boundary that separated master from servant.

She had no one else.

Nan shifted. "Are you quite sure, my lady?"

Mirabella smiled with quivering lips. "Would I have said so if I was not? Come!" she ordered, taking her cup fireside and sitting in her chair.

The girl poured herself a small cup and sat on the rug before the fire. "Thank you, my lady."

Mirabella nodded, sipping the wine, letting the warmth surge through her limbs. She looked into the glass, pondering. "Would that wine were a miracle potion," she mused in soft tones.

"Wine is the oldest miracle potion, dependent on what miracle the missus is hoping to rouse," Nan said, her voice sweet.

Mirabella glanced at the girl, her bright blue eyes sparkling with youth, her red curls glossy, infused with a luster from within. Tragedy hadn't dulled her yet. She had yet to be robbed of her joy and beauty.

"How do you mean, child?" Mirabella asked, grateful for any distraction from the words of the princess's letter that stood bold before her mind's eye, quite intact from the flames.

"Well . . ." The girl grew guarded, shifting her eyes fore and aft. "What type of miracle are you supposing to obtain?"

Mirabella laughed at this. Imagine! A servant girl the purveyor of miracles! Her heart sank. Yet a miracle had once been bestowed upon the humble son of a carpenter. . . . Mirabella yielded herself to the intrigue. She could play this game.

"All right . . . supposing I wanted a love potion?" she quipped, her tone rich with false cheer.

"Ah . . ." Nan's smile was conspiratorial. "To inspire Master Cahill to fall in love with you?"

Mirabella scowled. "What do you mean? Master Cahill is my husband and—"

"Pardon me, missus, how often have you seen a married couple truly in love?" Nan challenged her.

Cecily and her father, Mirabella thought with a sigh. Cecily and Alec . . . but then they were not married. But nonetheless, Cecily never had to fear not being able to inspire the love of a man. The heat of anger replaced that of the wine and she trembled.

"Are you well?" the girl asked.

"Quite," Mirabella snapped. She drew in a deep breath, expelling it slowly, willing some modicum of patience to return to her. "Right, then. So. A love potion. Tell me about love potions."

The girl laughed, a sound that rang slightly derisive. Mirabella bowed her head, embarrassed.

"My lady, it is my belief that none exist," Nan told her. "Though there are enough potions for every other ailment. There are potions for warts, for relieving the curse of our sex, for burns, and for wounds. But love can only come from God and potions are from man."

The words shamed Mirabella. That a servant, and a young one at that, could be so in tune to the misguided pursuit of man to be loved when love itself was ordained by God and no other. Love could not be forced—how aware was she of that! It could not be coerced. When the blessing of love was bestowed, it was chosen by the true Cupid—God. From His divine bow Love's Arrow was driven straight to the heart, and there was nothing to be done. It could not be fought against, it could not be ruled over, it could not be contained. But what of the love that was unreturned? Was it some curse then, some punishment she was meant to endure, to love alone, to find that the object of such emotion was unable and unwilling to withdraw the arrow from her breast?

But is it love?

Mirabella flinched. The gentle whisper in her mind belonged to Sister Julia, her mother, her mother who died for love.

If not love, then what? Mirabella wondered back.

Control. Revenge.

Mirabella shook her head. *No!* She brought a hand to her temple, as if to massage away the inner conversation.

"My lady, are you certain you are well?" the servant girl asked, cocking her head to regard her mistress in puzzlement.

Mirabella started. She had forgotten the girl. "I said I was and I am, am I not?"

Nan shrugged. "You would know."

But Mirabella did not know. When was the last time she was truly well? When she was a child with Cecily, running down the snow-covered trail to the cloister, or before her arrival, before she ever set about on this quest for the oneness with God that eluded her at every turn? Indeed, was she ever well?

Mirabella shook off the thoughts with a shudder, exasperated. "I have kept you long enough from your work, Nan. Dismissed."

The girl rose in a flurry of skirts to obey her mistress but stopped short of the door, turning.

"If I may say, my lady, though there is no love potion that can be relied upon, there are ways to spark forth a man's desire, if that is perhaps what you mean by love. . . ."

Mirabella's heart thudded. If she could not have Alec's love, could she settle for his desire, for his caress, his kisses, his embrace?

There was no meditating on the answer.

She regarded Nan, a savior in servant's garb.

"What do I need to do?"

Nan smiled, looking down at her cup of wine, which now swirled with possibilities.

❦ 23 ❦

The morning of 20 February dawned cool and crisp. It was a
historical day, the day of new beginnings for England, the
coronation of boy-king Edward VI. Alec, who had worked alongside Cranmer with tireless devotion to help make this day possible, stood among the throng that awaited the child's arrival at
Westminster Abbey, his heart swollen with pride. Mirabella stood
beside him, her natural intensity traded for a strange benevolence
of late. Alec cast a sidelong glance at the woman who had become
his wife. For the first time he was able to regard her without the
usual churning of resentment in his gut. She was an attractive
woman; this he had known since she was a girl. Yet at thirty-three
her rich dark hair remained untouched by time, her skin was
smooth, her figure, unmarred from childbearing, remained trim.
Alec could admit that, in her rich green velvet gown with slashed
sleeves to reveal fitted undersleeves of pale yellow, his adversary
was indeed quite beautiful. A wave of pity overcame him as her
life played out before his mind's eye—bastard daughter of an earl
and a nun, betrayed all her life long by secrets intended to protect,
and forever steered by a lost cause. On peculiar instinct, Alec
reached out to her, wrapping an arm about her shoulders and drawing her close, as if in that quick embrace he could gather the girl

and not the woman Mirabella to him, the girl he had known when first he came to Sumerton.

Mirabella started at the touch, then tipped her head to him. Her green eyes swam with a mingling of shock and . . . he could not discern the emotions. A plea, perhaps. Tears knotted a painful lump in his throat. God, what they had come to. . . .

Mirabella leaned her head against his shoulder a moment, before he withdrew his arm to point at the entourage that bore the young Edward.

"He comes!" Alec exclaimed. A rush of excitement flushed his tingling cheeks. The tears in his throat vanished as he watched the grand procession.

Under his canopy, the boy was accompanied by the premier gentlemen in the land. The Earl of Shrewsbury and Bishop of Durham walked beside him, followed by the ever-present John Dudley and Edward's beloved uncle, famed rake Thomas Seymour, who carried his train.

Alec watched them file into the abbey, where after his anointing the boy would later climb seven stairs to the dais and sit on the throne, fitted with extra cushions to compensate for his unimposing size.

Cranmer, Alec noted with an inner chuckle, appeared a font of calm after three weeks of being hassled and harried and hoping this day would eclipse every coronation before and after. As he began his address, Alec was tempted to mouth along the words. He had read and reread the nervous archbishop's epistle, reassuring the man that the people and young king would indeed receive his message with the desired effect.

Alec's heart lifted at what he considered by far to be the most compelling part of the speech. Cranmer's voice thundered forth with confidence and authority.

"Your Majesty is God's vicegerent and Christ's vicar within your own dominions, and to see, with your predecessor Josiah, God truly worshipped, and idolatry destroyed, the tyranny of the bishops of Rome banished from your subjects, and images removed. These acts be signs of a second Josiah, who reformed the church of

God in his days. You are to reward virtue, to revenge sin, to justify the innocent, to relieve the poor, to procure peace, to repress violence, and to execute justice throughout your realms. . . ."

No stronger message to the papists could have been sent. Edward, the "Second Josiah," had come to reform the Church, to bring about a new closeness with God sans the shiny distractions of Rome. Under the reign of Edward, a new era would begin, that of a purer faith, one that called its practitioners directly to a personal relationship with God without the intervention of others. A faith infused with straightforward simplicity.

At his side Alec felt Mirabella grow rigid. He regarded her a moment. Her eyes were hard, her jaw set. It was evident that Cranmer's message, a warning to Mirabella no doubt, had been absorbed. Alec shook his head, dismissing unpleasant analysis in favor of watching the coronation proceed.

Crowned with the imperial crown and that of Saint Edward, the young king was at last fitted with his own, one light enough for his head. He was given Saint Edward's staff, the orb and spurs, and the scepter, which could only be held with help from the Earl of Shrewsbury. The child, though maintaining a regal dignity expected of him, betrayed his youth with his wide eyes as he bit his lip under the weight of the various accoutrements. To his good fortune, he was relieved of them soon enough.

The lord protector, Duke of Somerset, knelt before him first, then a reverent Cranmer. Each man kissed on the cheek the boy who carried their every hope and ambition, after which the nobility knelt before him together, where Somerset declared their allegiance.

It was done. It was formal, written in the heavens and the earth.

Edward, the at once neglected and pampered son of mad Henry VIII, was King of all England.

The celebrating commenced in earnest at Westminster Hall, decorated and freshened for the occasion. The walls were draped with cloths of arras, the hall and stairs covered in rich carpets of crimson, filling the place with festive grandeur. The guests competed with both the hall and one another, their attire sparkling with jewels of every imagining, soft furs, rich brocades, and velvets. Color and life emanated from every corner; the revelry was contagious.

As Alec and Mirabella took to their table among the lowest gentry present, they watched the nobility serve the king course after course only so the entire assembly could move to Whitehall for more feasting and drinking.

By the beginning of the masque, which featured a blatant mockery against the Bishop of Rome, Mirabella's Pope, Alec was tipsy from toasts and drowsy from overeating. Beside him Mirabella sat, unable to disguise the pain that contorted her expression as she witnessed her faith ridiculed for the pleasure of the court. For the second time that day, Alec was stirred to pity. He leaned toward her, resting a hand on hers.

"Would you like to return to Sumerton Place?" he asked in soft tones. Though he relished the triumph of the Church of England, he still could not will himself to throw it completely in Mirabella's face, no matter her sins against him.

Mirabella turned toward him, her eyes lit with tears, and nodded. She appeared a child of thirteen again, vulnerable and afraid, compelling Alec to take her hand in his and lead her from the hall.

"You mean you are accompanying me?" she asked him, mystified.

"I am exhausted," Alec confessed. "Besides, there are to be revels all week."

"Yes, then," Mirabella said, squeezing his hand. "Let us remove to Sumerton Place, to home."

Alec in truth was more than ready. He must have taken in too much wine. His limbs were weak and quavering; he stumbled a bit as he walked, and, for some unfathomable reason, he could not stop laughing.

It had been an effort, but one that had paid off in Alec's response to what Mirabella had sprinkled at great discretion in his wine at Whitehall. The concoction she procured from the servant girl Nan, which could prove deadly if administered incorrectly, contained caraway, lovage, and mint, along with its most potent in-

gredient, something called nightshade. The Italians called it bel-
ladonna and used it for increasing the beauty of the eyes, among
other things.

Tonight it would be among other things.

She willed herself not to think of anything beyond what lay in
the moment. She would not allow guilt, that tool of the devil, to
creep in.

She led a dizzy Alec to his chambers.

"Really I am rather embarrassed," he confessed as Mirabella
turned down the bedclothes. He flopped unceremoniously against
his pillows. "I did not think I took in so much."

"It was a long day," Mirabella said, sitting beside him. "There
was more wine than we imagined and taken over a long period."

Alec smirked. "I suppose . . . and you, did you enjoy yourself
watching this King of the Reformation be crowned?"

Mirabella winced. "It was a good day," she said at length. "I am
glad we went together."

Alec laughed. "Me too." He rolled to his side, fetching the
chamber pot beneath the bed. "I fear I may vomit."

Mirabella rubbed his back, her heart sinking. "You will be fine,"
she said in soothing tones. "I will stay with you until you are
asleep."

"It isn't necessary," Alec told her. "This is not my best hour."

At this Mirabella was compelled to laugh. "Then consider us
even, for you have never seen me at my best hour."

"That I will agree with," Alec muttered as he leaned over the
chamber pot.

Mirabella bowed her head. She supposed she had invited that
remark.

After a few moments of feeble dry heaving, Alec lay back on the
bed, his lids fluttering before closing. Mirabella swallowed. She
could go to her rooms now; she could leave him to rest and recover.
She did not have to do this.

Where was her resolve? Determination surged through her. She
would see this through. She would seize what had been so hard
won. Undressing to her shift, she lay beside him, resting a hand on
his chest, stroking idly.

"I do love you, Alec," she whispered.

"I love you, Cecily," Alec murmured, covering her hand with his.

Mirabella bit her lip. Her heart pounded. Cecily. The name caused bile to rise in her own throat, bitter, repulsive. Cecily . . . Fine. Let him think it was Cecily. . . .

Poising above him, Mirabella began to cover his face and neck in soft kisses, feeling his hands reach up to cup her face.

"You've come to me at last," he slurred.

But his eyes were closed, and as he took the virtue Mirabella had saved for this night at great cost one name remained on his lips: Cecily.

Mirabella lay beside Alec, sore and trembling. She found no pleasure in the coupling. It was an act, nothing more, and if this was what she had saved herself for, she might have remained intact her life long without missing the obsession of poets and bards alike. Perhaps if it had not been under false pretenses, perhaps if he said her name and not Cecily's . . . It mattered not. It was done. Their marriage was consummated and she was a wife truly made.

She drew the covers to her neck and wrapped her arm about Alec's middle, snuggling closer beside him. The light filtered through the window, casting eerie shadows about the room.

For what you stole, you will be made to repay. . . .

Mirabella sat bolt upright. The whisper was familiar. Her mother again? No . . . She began to tremble as her eyes found the source. At the end of the bed he stood, transparent and surrounded by a soft white glow no light source could provide. Was he floating or did he stand atop solid ground?

"Brey . . ." she breathed, reaching out.

Brey, his head crowned in golden curls, his blue eyes containing the wisdom years of life would have afforded him, stood before her. His eyes, the only testament of his age, were those of a man in the body of a child-ghost. He shook his head as though the weight of every disappointment in the world rested atop his slim shoulders. He began to fade.

"Brey!" Mirabella cried. "Don't leave me! I need you. . . . I need help!"

The apparition retreated, fading into just another shadow in the room.

Beside her Alec stirred, his eyes flickering open. They rested on her a moment as confusion washed over his features.

"What are you doing here?" His voice was low. The warning in his tone was not lost on Mirabella.

She drew the covers around her. She could not stop shaking. She scrambled for an explanation. Anger replaced the fear of the apparition's cryptic statement. "You do not remember? I came at your drunken invitation last night," she snapped.

Alec leaned on an elbow, then cupped his forehead in his hand with a grimace. "And . . . ?"

Mirabella leaned forward, her face inches from his. "Our marriage is made true before God," she hissed. "One sacrament your reformation will never change. I am your wife now, in deed as well as name."

Alec did not meet her eyes. "How did you accomplish this? I have taken in many a cup of wine in my day with no such effects." He sat up, his head still in his hand. "What did you give me, Mirabella?"

Mirabella shook her head, wrapping herself in the coverlet and rising. "You cannot believe you wanted me of your own free will? That is too much for your mind to take in, that you would lust after your own wife, the woman who saved you."

Alec met her eyes for the first time, shaking his head. "No, I cannot believe it," he told her. "But getting the truth from you is a useless enterprise, so there is naught to be done but congratulate you once again on your cleverness. Though I must add that it is a pity you had to resort to such means. It should be noted that our marriage could only be made . . . how did you say it? True? Yes, made 'true' with my mind and humors altered. You call it consummation. There is another word for it, my dear. *Rape.* What your mother saved you from with her life, you throw back at her with this act, therefore invalidating an honorable woman's heroism."

He allowed the words to hit her, daggers thrown to the soul, every one of them, and her eyes burned with tears. Rape. It had not been rape. Men could not be raped, could they? He had never screamed or protested or behaved unwillingly. He had never said no . . . yet could her deception be considered such? Had she fallen so far? No. Women were not capable of such things. . . . *She* was not capable of such things . . . was she?

"But!" Alec's voice, light with false cheer, cut through her reflections. "If I had a cap I would surely doff it to you, dear lady." His laugh was wry, his eyes filled with a mingling of sadness and mockery. "You win, Mirabella. You have successfully 'saved' me from every dream and value I held dear. I hope it was everything you wanted."

Mirabella averted her eyes. She could not bear his expression another moment. He did not even look at her in anger anymore. He regarded her as if she were some helpless inmate at an asylum in need of a mercy killing. That look shamed her like she had never been shamed before.

"It wasn't anything I wanted," Mirabella confessed at once, her voice strangled by tears. "Oh, if I could take it all back . . . if I could take everything back . . ." She shook her head, covering her mouth with her hand.

She could not remain. She would not meet his eyes and find in them pity once again.

Sobbing, she climbed out of bed and fled, Brey's words echoing in her mind, relentless and ruthless as she had ever been.

Mirabella would leave. She would give Alec everything he wanted, an annulment, whatever he wished. Anything to be free of the guilt and shame that stalked her, a falcon preying on her conscience, every waking moment. She would return to Sumerton, if Cecily could abide the sight of her, and from there decide her fate. Perhaps she would remove to France, still a favored daughter of the Pope. There she could take her vows once more. Yes, that was what she would do! Hope began to replace shame as she supervised the packing of her things.

There was no need for good-bye. Alec had gone to the jousts in honor of His Majesty as it were. No words were spoken. There was nothing to say now. By the time he returned, she would be gone, his fondest wish granted.

Mirabella ordered her coach.

You cannot run from this.

Her mother. Oh, God, why? Why must she be pursued by these voices from beyond? She was leaving now. She was setting things right. She did not need moral intervention from the living or the dead.

On Alec's writing table she left a quick note:

You are free.

With this, she bid farewell to London.

She was going home, that place that had never denied her no matter her sins.

Sumerton.

Cecily had little time to invest in pondering what was or was not occurring in London. Between running her household, keeping correspondence with her children, who seemed to be flourishing under the care and tutelage of the Hapgoods, and caring for baby Emmy, there was more than enough to occupy her mind. When not consumed with the tasks of the day to day, she kept company with the former Lady Grace. In her she found the friendship she had longed for since the tragic passing of Lady Alice and the sisterhood she had never quite grasped onto with Mirabella.

When Grace was not attending her own flock that included sick tenants and women in search of her various remedies, the two found solace in conversation. No subject remained untouched.

"I think it is harder mourning the living than it is the dead," Cecily noted one afternoon as the two sat before a crackling fire in her apartments watching baby Emmy attempt to crawl. Despite her misshapen leg, the child's ability to compensate displayed a strength of character and determination that swelled Cecily's heart with pride.

"How do you mean?" Grace queried.

"The dead do not choose to leave you, at least most of the

time," she explained. "But the living, when they hurt or abandon—they choose it." She sighed. "I have found more resolve and peace when I think on our dead then I can ever find with the living."

Grace reached out, resting a calloused hand over Cecily's. "Treat the choices of the living as you would a death, done and out of our control. I have never been a woman of faith, my lady. You know that. However, in my later years I have learned that we have no control over our children, our mates, or our family and friends. All we have control over is ourselves. And God? He is the master of all. Give Him that power and trust and you will be more at peace than ever you could have imagined. When you give yourself over, you find that your heart becomes a font of grace, forgiveness, and sincere goodwill." Grace's smile was serene. "I call it divine surrender. Surrender yourself to it, my dear girl, and you will find you have more power than any king."

Cecily offered a smile of gratitude, squeezing Grace's hand in hers. "I am so glad you have been returned to us, Lady Grace. Despite Mirabella's many transgressions, I still thank her for that."

Grace bit her lip, blinking back tears. "Come now, enough of that," she muttered, waving off the thought with a modest laugh.

A light knock on the door of Cecily's apartments brought the women to compose themselves with sheepish grins and the subtle daubing away of sentimental tears with their handkerchiefs.

"Enter," Cecily ordered in husky tones.

The door opened, revealing Mirabella, pale and drawn, her eyes glassy. She had left young and returned an old woman. Cecily's heart thudded against her ribs in a painful rhythm. *What now*, was her first thought. She cursed herself. She must maintain a generous heart. Mirabella would always be Hal's daughter. Any kindness Cecily was bound to show her would be for him, if she could not in sincerity do it for her.

Cecily rose from her settle. She did not know what to say, how to feel. "Master Cahill remained in London. He is much occupied with the king's coronation and doing the bidding of the archbishop," Mirabella began, her voice soft.

Cecily could not yet detect a threat in her manner.

"If I may, my lady, I have come to stay awhile and . . . reflect. . . ."
The knot in Cecily's stomach eased a bit. She willed herself to be calm. She would not reveal her dread or disappointment. She was the lady of this house and so she would remain, with dignity and charity.

Cecily reached out, taking Mirabella's hand in hers. It was cold, clammy. "This will always be your home, Mirabella," she told her.

Mirabella bit her lip, her green eyes luminous with unshed tears. Cecily was mystified. Never had she seen Mirabella more vulnerable or, as it appeared, more broken. Not when Brey passed, or when she revealed the loss of her mother, nor when her baby nephew died. Not even, and perhaps especially, when her father died. She had always been closed off, as if something in her was missing. Was it too much to hope that the key to unlocking her humanity had been restored?

There was no time to ponder it, for at once Mirabella's expression converted to bewilderment as she crumpled to the floor, unconscious.

"She appears undernourished and simply exhausted," Grace said when they had Mirabella carried to her rooms. "I haven't supervised tending this one since she was a little girl," she said, her voice soft, wistful. She sat beside Mirabella, stroking her face.

At rest Mirabella appeared a child, as if she were incapable of procuring a malicious thought. *How deceitful is the face of sleep*, Cecily thought, wishing once again to stave off her bitterness.

"She was never a sickly one," Grace went on to say. "Always too driven to waste time on feeling ill," she added with a slight, albeit joyless, chuckle.

"So she is home now," Cecily commented. "To gather her strength for what? To create more chaos and heartbreak?" Her lip quivered as she wiped away tears of frustration, at herself for thinking the worst, and for this woman who had caused very little in her life but pain.

Grace rubbed Cecily's upper arm. "Now, now, we shall see. Let her rest. Likely she is more than aware of her various wrongdoings, and as you noted just today, some good has come from her actions even if she did not intend such. Remember what I told you about trusting God. If this one had truly been the holy woman she always strove to be, imagine the good she could have done if she had grasped, *truly grasped,* that one lesson."

Cecily conceded her point with a sigh.

"That said, I think I may just stay at Sumerton awhile as well," Grace said then, her smile sardonic. "Call it assurance."

Relief flooded Cecily's heart. She could do this, and in doing so she would surrender. At least she would try.

Together the women tended Mirabella, who lay abed for three straight days. When she awoke she was given bread and fish broth, for Lent was now upon them. She smiled when baby Emmy was brought to her; it seemed the little one was her sole source of delight. She did not speak much and whatever she did say was light and nonsensical. Cecily and Grace exchanged many a glance at this but said little in return. If ever Mirabella wished to steer the conversation to more significant fare, it would be with no prompting from them.

Meantime, Mirabella remained weak. She slept often and ate little. What remained the most shocking of all to both Cecily and Grace was that Mirabella did not pray. Not ever. She had not once utilized the prie-dieu for private worship that Cecily made certain had not been taken from her rooms, nor her other Romish accoutrements Mirabella had used for private worship. Cecily would not disrespect Mirabella's faith. She would strive as ever to be gracious and merciful in the hopes she would receive such in turn.

Winter began to ebb with the last vestiges of February. And as March gave way to the crisp days of April, Sumerton finally received news from London in the form of a dispatch for Mirabella from Alec.

"So?" Grace prodded at last. She could not be as patient as Cecily and would not try. What made them such a wonderful pair was their differences; Cecily was a willow to her oak—despite this, both could bend with the breeze.

Mirabella, abed as she was much of the time, scanned the letter. "He's shut the home on the Strand and has been appointed apartments at Lambeth Palace," she reported. She read further, biting her lip, then discarded the letter to her side. She tipped her head toward the black velvet canopy above, drawing in a sharp breath. "Our marriage has been dissolved by sanction of His Majesty and His Grace Thomas Cranmer, the Archbishop of Canterbury." The words were spoken with no feeling whatever, as if she were reading some text that was too dry to infuse any inflection in. Grace searched her face for any signs of emotion, finding none.

"And," Mirabella added as she expelled a heavy sigh, "Master Cahill is to be knighted for his devoted service to the Church of England 'despite all obstacles that would otherwise obstruct a lesser man.' " She shook her head. " 'Obstacles' meaning me, I am certain."

There was nothing to be said to that. Grace regarded Cecily a moment, whose eyes revealed a melding of pity and hope. She returned her gaze to Mirabella.

"Well, then," Grace said at last. "All is as it should be, Mirabella. Isn't it?" Her tone was not unkind.

Mirabella blinked several times, averting her head. She took in a few gasping breaths before giving herself to sobbing. Grace took her hand in hers, making soft cooing sounds. It would be a cold human being indeed, she thought, who could not be stirred to some form of compassion for this misguided creature.

"Yes," Mirabella said through her tears. "All is as it should be." She raised her head to meet Cecily's eyes. "I am now unmarried and with child."

For a moment all were stunned into silence. Grace looked from one woman to the other. Mirabella's face was contorted in pain, as if making an appeal she could not put into words. Emotions washed over Cecily's countenance so fast Grace was unable to discern them. Shock, anger, hurt, disbelief, to shock again. Cecily shook her head, rising from the bedside. She parted her mouth as if to speak, then clamped it shut once more with another frantic shake of her head before whirling on her heel and fleeing the room.

Mirabella covered her eyes with her hand, her shoulders heaving as she sobbed.

Grace sighed. "And to think I never likened you to the Blessed Virgin before," was all she could think of to say.

Mirabella's eyes darkened with anger. "You are enjoying this," she seethed.

Grace pursed her lips, resting her chin on her folded hands. "No, my dear, I am not. Though I do find irony to be amusingly tyrannical," she added with a slight laugh. "Forgive my impetuousness, Mirabella, but I must ask—is it true?"

Tears streamed down Mirabella's cheeks unchecked. "I would give anything to say it was a lie. You must believe that I came to set things right. But I am too late, like all my life, too late." She dissolved into sobs once more.

Grace drew in a breath. She did not know whether to comfort or chastise the woman who had caused nothing but turmoil the majority of her life.

"Mirabella," she said in soft tones, reaching out to rub her knee. "For many years I raised you as my own," she began, her heart pounding. She had never anticipated such a conversation but knew she could evade the words no longer. "I wanted to love you as a mother would. I blame myself for maintaining the charade when I knew I was unable to look upon you without resentment for what passed before between your father and Sister Julia. You were always a challenge for me, but many of those challenges I imposed on us. I fear my neglect and inability to love you as I should have at the time caused this relentless drive in you to pursue your cause with impure motives. The quest for God should be a joyous one, but for you it was always one of desperation."

Mirabella averted her head, sobbing harder.

"If you had been loved and petted as you deserved to be, perhaps that quest would have been undertaken in the right spirit," Grace went on. "Or perhaps not at all. Who's to say what choices would have or should have been made when we find ourselves at the crossroads of What If . . ." She trailed off, reflecting on her own choices and where they led her. She swallowed a painful onset of tears. "Mirabella, wrongs can never be made right, but that doesn't mean we cannot do right *now*. For my part, I am here now and I will be here for you as long as you need me."

"Oh . . . oh, *Mother!*" Mirabella cried, throwing herself forward into Grace's arms.

Grace held her tight, swaying from side to side. "My dear girl," she whispered. "I am so sorry."

"That is all that is left to us," Mirabella whimpered into her shoulder. "Regrets and remorse."

Grace pulled away, cupping Mirabella's face between her hands. "And forgiveness. This is where it starts, Mirabella, in the midst of sorrow. This is where we begin to let go."

Mirabella regarded her a long moment, then nodded slowly.

"*Forgive . . . let go,*" she whispered. "I . . . have heard those words before."

She nuzzled against Grace's shoulder once more. As Grace stroked her hair she wondered if those things could ever be attained at Sumerton.

Cecily stood in the mausoleum alone. She gazed upon the stone effigies of Brey, so young and innocent even in his stone rendering, and of baby Charles, too young for his features to even be captured with accuracy, left to be remembered as any baby, a generality, more of an idea than a life. An effigy of Grace was there, too. Hal had commissioned it when he awaited the recovery of a body that would never be found, not in the way anyone could have ever anticipated. . . .

And Hal, her husband, her first love. In stone his countenance was captured, its kindness, its consistent ability to forgive, to love. Cecily rushed toward the effigy, throwing herself atop its cool stone chest and sobbing as she stroked its face.

"I am lost, Hal," she confessed. Her voice echoed a lonely remembrance in the darkened room. "I have sinned against you, God knows. You know. But I have endeavored to live right, to honor your memory in my decisions with the children and myself, and even Mirabella and Alec. But now . . . now . . . please do not ask this of me. Please let her be lying. If it is true then it stands to mock everything we ever held dear and constant. Everything will change, even my memories!"

She raised her head to regard the face as if it would somehow answer her. It remained unchanged.

"The dead are our only constants," she observed, her voice laden with sadness. "In a world that just keeps moving." She sighed. "Until I join that realm of constancy, I have but to move with it. Lend me your strength, Hal. Lend me your ability to keep loving and forgiving, no matter the sin. Please." She squeezed her eyes shut a long moment, willing the prayer to him with all her strength.

Then she rose. And kept moving.

Cecily returned to find Grace waiting for her in the bower. She opened her arms and Cecily fled to them, her tears renewed. When she recovered herself, she pulled away.

"It is true, then," she said, steeling herself for the answer that was in Grace's nod.

"It is," Grace said. "And conceived out of another deception, as with anything else in Mirabella's imagining. She infused his wine with some country concoction to dull his senses, thinking consummating the marriage would hold him. Her punishment is the realization that nothing could hold him. Nothing but God . . . and you, of course."

Cecily bowed her head. The story revealed no surprises to her. Indeed, she found a strange sense of relief in the fact that Alec had not gone to Mirabella of his own free will, for what little comfort that could provide. She wondered what this portended, for nothing could bond a man and woman like a child, even if the bond was not a loving one. It was nonetheless two people tied, made one. Alec and Mirabella . . . She bit her lip, shaking her head against the thoughts that played before her mind's eye against her will. She must resist. She must not think of them . . . that way. She never imagined she would have to.

"What are we going to do?" she asked in a whisper, taking Grace's hand in hers as if the woman held the answer to every mystery of life.

"We are going to end the deceptions once and for all," Grace told her, her voice firm with resolve. "We are going to summon Alec Cahill home to Sumerton. And Mirabella is going to tell him the truth."

A novel concept, Cecily thought, her gut churning in a compound of jealousy and bitterness she longed to ignore. She drew in a shaky breath. "You have sent the summons already, haven't you?"

"I have," Grace admitted, wrapping her arm about Cecily's shoulders and drawing her near. "Because it's going to end now, all the lies and all the pain. It's going to end because that is the only way life can begin again."

Cecily squeezed her eyes shut against the burn of more tears. What had she ever done but begin again? Was not her life the constant transition between beginnings and endings? Her lips twisted into a wry smile. Perhaps that in itself was the constancy she had thought belonged only to the dead.

There was nothing to do but wait, yet another reliability that had accompanied Cecily throughout her life. Now it was to wait for the little one who held everyone's hopes and fears as one, and, always, always, for Alec.

The response from London was without delay.

"No?" Cecily asked the messenger, her eyes widening with bewilderment.

The messenger offered an apologetic shake of his head. "That was all he said, my lady. Just 'no.' "

"He did not even send a handwritten message with you?" Cecily asked, assessing the young man from head to foot as if she could detect a hidden note on his person.

Again, he shook his head, shrugging. "No, my lady. I am sorry."

Cecily sighed. Her shoulders ached. Her feet ached. She mopped her brow with her handkerchief and sighed. "Go to the kitchens, son," she told him. "At least be fed for your efforts."

The messenger's eyes sparkled at the notion. "My thanks to you, my lady!" he exclaimed as he retreated.

At least someone still finds happiness in simple things, Cecily reflected, her heart constricting as she made for Mirabella's chambers; Mirabella rarely left them. If the legitimacy of her pregnancy had been in question, it was no longer. Despite that it was too soon for the quickening, Mirabella retched daily and took to her bed, exhausted more often than not. To Cecily's good fortune, Grace stayed with Mirabella much of the time. Cecily as yet was unable to remain in Mirabella's company for any period of length and kept the running of her household and tending of her tenants in the foreground, distracting herself from before sunrise till after dark, when she at last took to her bed. Her solace was found in her work and her sleep; she invested her whole self in both.

Longing for her bed now, she forced herself to enter Mirabella's suite, finding Grace as always sitting sentinel at her side as the two sewed.

Cecily closed her eyes a moment. Baby garments. They were sewing baby garments. She shook her head. How could she resent this? Had not she passed time in the same manner as she anticipated the births of her own children? Why should waiting for the birth of Mirabella's child be spent differently? The child would need clothing, after all. Cecily sighed, exasperated with herself.

"Master Cahill sent word through his messenger," Cecily announced. "And said no. He is not coming back."

Mirabella's expression yielded a fusion of relief and despair.

Grace pursed her lips. "Well," she began in soft tones. "I do not think it appropriate to convey this news in a dispatch. We must find another way to bring him home."

Mirabella shook her head. "We have time. Perhaps we should just wait it out."

"Perhaps we should," Cecily agreed, shocked to share any form of consensus with Mirabella. Both seemed of the same will when it came to avoiding Alec's reaction to this newest happenstance.

Grace emitted a sigh. "No. He deserves the same amount of time as Mirabella to prepare himself. This is going to be fair, as fair as can be for something very unfair. No surprises, no lies, no deceit," she reiterated once again. "Consider this our chance for redemption."

Mirabella lowered her eyes. She drew in a breath as she cast her eyes to the bedside table on which the sandglass from Cecily stood.

"We may have no choice but to convey it somehow," Mirabella said as she reached a hand out to trace the etchings of the various dates in the mahogany.

Cecily regarded her a long moment, reading her intent. It was not the worst idea, she conceded to herself a bit grudgingly.

"There is something else," Mirabella said then. "Something else I want him to have." She raised her eyes to Cecily. "Behind a loose stone in the garden wall by the yellow rosebush, the place where I used to sit with Master Reaves . . ." She blinked several times, averting her head. "Master Cahill's papers are there. Please fetch them. Perhaps then he will know that . . . that I mean no harm."

Cecily nodded to Grace, who quit the room to do Mirabella's bidding.

Redemption indeed.

❧ 24 ❧

At Lambeth Palace, Alec had at last begun to heal. Though the archbishop was much occupied under the new reign of young King Edward, he always made time for counsel and friendship. Under his gentle guidance, Alec flourished. He devoted many hours to prayer and introspection in the hopes he might find forgiveness and atonement. When he was not imbued in quiet contemplation, however, he was working alongside the archbishop and his panel of learned men from all over the realm on the *Book of Common Prayer,* that which was to serve as the cornerstone of the faith of the Church of England. It was a joyous, frustrating challenge inspiring many a stimulating debate on doctrine and many a devoted hour to study, translating, and writing.

In another word: paradise.

Though Alec was knighted at Easter for his devotion and suffering for the sake of his faith, he could not yet bring himself to take his vows once more and return to the priesthood. Despite Cranmer's lectures on self-forgiveness and his urgings to join the fold, he could not. Until he found himself truly worthy and at peace with all that came to pass, he would remain Sir Alec Cahill, a secretary and scribe to the Archbishop of Canterbury. It was an identity he could still at last take pride in.

After Mirabella set him "free," he endeavored to pray for her without bitterness. She was a lesson, Cranmer had told him. A lesson to be applied to his journey toward God. Ah, but how high the price of such learning! Nonetheless, Alec prayed for her and for all those at Sumerton, all but one. Cecily he could not think of, even so much as in prayer. Not after the night of the young king's coronation. It seemed that to think of her now after such a sin degraded her. She was sacred, and until he was worthy of things sacred she remained as unattainable as his collar.

And then the summons, expecting his immediate return to Sumerton. He could not bring himself to make a lengthy reply. "No" was enough; indeed, it encompassed everything. He was not a priest, he was no longer the children's tutor, and he certainly was not Mirabella's husband (a fact he could not help but thank God for daily). There was no reason to go back. If they were in need of spiritual guidance, he could recommend many a man of the cloth who would happily take on the complexities of Sumerton. He no longer had to.

It was early summer when he received the package from a messenger of Sumerton. Exasperated, he opened the plain wooden box to reveal the sandglass Cecily had bestowed upon him and Mirabella at their farcical "wedding" feast. He sighed as he scanned the dates, wondering why the women of the place he once considered his fondest home had the need to send him something so cryptic.

A fresh etching caught his eye. *20th February*. King Edward's coronation day. He swallowed. Of course it would not mark that event but the moment he fell deeper into sin with Mirabella. He resisted the urge to smash the sandglass against the opposite wall of his small quarters. Drawing in a breath, he set the sandglass on his writing table and reached back into the box, where, to his shock, he found papers. Not a random missive these, but his own private papers that Mirabella had confiscated and threatened to sentence him to death with. All of them, every word, bound, protected, and intact.

He looked, mystified, from the papers to the sandglass, then retrieved the heavy timekeeper to gaze upon it once more.

She had set him free and returned his papers. Why? Were her motives pure at last or was this simply a subtler torture device?

He squinted as his fingertips found a much fainter etching in the mahogany.

It read simply: *November*. No specific date.

Alec's heart began to pound as he looked from *20th February* to the lightly carved *November* beside it. Almost against his will, he counted the months. He began to shake his head, his breathing coming in rapid spurts. No . . . No . . .

Mirabella could not have devised a better instrument of agony had she commissioned it from the Spanish Grand Inquisitor himself. Yet . . . was it? Momentary hope surged through him. It could be another lie, another machination to bind him to her. He could pray. The truth would be revealed one way or another.

There could be no avoiding it. He would return to Sumerton.

In November.

The baby had quickened. Life stirred within Mirabella's womb, kicking, stretching, and making its presence known, dispelling completely any remaining doubts as to her condition. Sumerton passed a hot summer that set Mirabella into fits of sweats that caused her to throw her blankets aside in a fit of irritation and bathe her face with cool water to evade the effects of the heat. Relief was found when September yielded itself to a crisp October. As her belly grew, the baby grew more active. Grace insisted it must be a girl, for Mirabella carried high. Cecily, though she remained uninvolved in the day to day of Mirabella's progress, conceded the point, admitting that she had carried both Kristina and Emmy so high that she suffered great discomfort when she was kicked in the ribs. It mattered not to Mirabella the child's sex as long as she could give birth, and soon. She hated every minute of her pregnancy and found little consolation in the vibrancy of the life within. The sooner she was delivered, the sooner she could begin her life anew.

As it stood, Mirabella's life was immobilized. She could not bring herself to rise from her bed. She lay, rubbing her swelling belly and thinking, always, of the past. The missed opportunities and the opportunities stolen from others. Now she was an unwanted resident of Sumerton, kept out of obligation, nothing more. Despite whatever Grace believed about redemption, there was no rectifying what she had done. There was no asking forgiveness. Yet were rectification and forgiveness truly necessary? As yet she was unsure if she was sorry. Did she regret her moment with Alec, the moment that inspired life to renew itself within her? Did she regret saving his life, no matter that he wasted it on the New Learning? Indeed, his life would have been put in jeopardy. She may have rushed that process, but in doing so she removed him from suspicion. She supposed it had worked in his favor, considering the exalted position he held in his beloved archbishop's household.

If she had only been let alone years before, it all could have been avoided. If she had been allowed to remain at the convent to practice her faith as she chose, to devote her life to study and oneness with the God of the True Faith. If she had been allowed that, life would not have come to pass as it did. It was the fault of the king, the mad King Henry. Him and that devil Cromwell, may the demons devour his soul! Archbishop Cranmer could not be excluded from blame, nor even could Father Alec himself. Nor could her own family, whose betrayals and deception spurred her toward the calling that was forever denied her.

She was blameless.

For the hurt she caused in response to the hurt inflicted she *had* made reparation. She freed Alec. She respected Cecily and made peace with Grace. She wrote lighthearted letters to Harry and Kristina and devoted hours each day to baby Emmy. She had set things right.

As to this baby, she had not intended it. The act that conceived the child had been her last feeble attempt at making their marriage real. It had been in vain, all of it. She couldn't hold him with her love; she did not expect the baby to make any difference. If he had hated her before, this would serve to further drive the spikes of his resentment through her palms. There was naught to be done now but tell him the truth, as Grace instructed. His reaction she neither anticipated nor despaired over. Regardless, she planned to remove to France as soon as she was well enough to travel upon its delivery. There she would seek refuge with some of her other ex- iled sisters. The child would be her gift to the Church, the true and only Church, and would be groomed for Holy Orders no mat- ter the sex. It was the greatest offering she could think of to demonstrate her love for the Lord and her sincere desire to attain forgiveness for her sins real and imagined.

Hope surged through her. She would get through this. She would endure and, in the end, be happier than any at Sumerton.

She may have lost her cause with England, but what of that? England was only a small part of God's great world, as irrelevant to His will as a candle's extinguished flame. Its light would be doused from her life forever, replaced with the flaming torch of the higher purpose she had been meant for all along. . . .

"My lady . . ."

The whisper cut through the fitful slumber Cecily had slipped into at her writing table. She found herself roused by a gentle hand on her shoulder and realized she had fallen asleep before her ledgers, her head resting on her folded arms. Embarrassed, she re- covered herself and met the owner of the voice.

"Lady Grace," Cecily began with a smile. "I did not know I slept."

Grace offered an apologetic smile. "I am sorry to have woken you," she said. She drew in a breath. "I have come to tell you that Master Cahill . . . Alec . . . he is here."

Cecily's face tingled. "He waited long enough," she said in hard tones. Her breathing quickened with her heartbeat. She brought a hand to her cheek and swallowed, bowing her head. "Strange how Mirabella's was the summons he obeyed, even if it was a bit de- layed." She bit her lip, averting her head. "I do not know why it is strange. They were married. They are having a child. I . . . don't . . . know . . . why . . . it's . . . strange—" she began to gasp as she dis- solved into sobs.

Grace rounded the writing table to take Cecily in her arms. "My darling, you know the marriage and the child were all under the harshest of circumstances," she told her as she rubbed her back. "Now, now. Be strong. You have been strong all of your life. You grieved when it was time to grieve and put grief aside when it was time to work for the interests of yourself and those in your life." She drew back, tipping Cecily's chin up with a fingertip. She nodded with a smile. "Keep being strong, dear heart. Everything you need is inside of you."

Cecily's lips quivered as she found a foothold in composure. She drew in a quavering breath and nodded her assent, knowing that she was putting her trust utterly in Grace's confidence in her strength, for she was desperately short of it for herself.

Cecily reached out, squeezing Grace's hand. "I cannot see him just now," Cecily told her. "Please. Let me gather this strength you so believe me capable of for a time before . . . before I face him."

Grace cupped her cheek in one hand, brushing aside the rose-gold hair that had strayed from beneath Cecily's hood. "Do what you must, my dear," she said, leaning in to place a kiss on her forehead.

As Grace quit the room Cecily wondered what it was she could do to recover herself and to face all that must be faced, praying all the while she could avoid the inevitable for any amount of time God was generous enough to allot.

God, in your divine mercy, Cecily begged, *remember us. Be kind.*

Grace found Alec lingering in the great hall near one of the trestle tables, his hand tracing idle patterns on the wood surface, his expression wistful. Upon seeing her, his hazel eyes swam with tears. Grace blinked rapidly. He was a handsome man, though the year's events had aged him considerably, streaking his fine chestnut hair silver, creasing his gentle face with a subtle patchwork of lines. Grace approached him, taking his hand.

"I am Mrs. Forest," she told him in hushed tones, offering her sardonic smile. "I am a lady-in-waiting to the Countess of Sumerton."

Alec nodded in understanding. His lips trembled. Grace took his hand.

"Come, my old friend," she beckoned, and together they made for the place she sensed he dreaded most: Mirabella's apartments.

"We have witnessed much at Sumerton," she observed as they navigated the maze of hallways that led to their destination. She looped her arm through his, squeezing his hand. "And if it has taught us anything, that which we have found to be the hardest is that fate is crueler than God." She stopped walking; they stood before the door, the ominous door that seemed to hold the fate of Sumerton behind it. "God is forgiveness, light, and love. Fate is immune to the railings of man; his cries for mercy, vengeance, and justice fall upon ears that are far worse than deaf. They are"—she fixed him with a hard gaze—"uninterested." She rested her hands on Alec's shoulders. "To ensure yourself the benevolence of one you must have the favor of the other. Pray God might command a gentler fate to those who love Him."

Alec drew in a breath, squeezing his eyes shut a long moment.

Then opened the door.

Alec found Mirabella abed. She lay there, her dark locks flowing around her shoulders in thick waves, pale and drawn beneath her olive complexion. Bluish circles surrounded green eyes that had lost their once luminous luster. Upon seeing him they filled with tears she blinked away.

Alec edged forward. "So," he began, his heart pounding. He did not know how to proceed, what to say. What was there to say? What was there to do? He sat in the chair that had been positioned near the head of the bed. "Are you well?"

Mirabella bowed her head. "I am tired. I am in pain often," she admitted in soft tones before raising her eyes to him once more. "But I will survive as so many others before me have." She sighed. "I am glad you came, Alec." She reached out, taking his hand in hers. He could not will himself to respond to the touch. His hand lay limp in hers.

"The papers . . ." he started, swallowing an unexpected onset of tears. "I thank you for their safe return to me. I . . . appreciate the gesture no matter the motivation behind it. It seems whatever you have done in your life for your own will has somehow been met at every turn by the will of God to do good in the lives you wished to destroy," he could not help but add, shocked at the bitterness of the statement, let alone that he had voiced it.

Mirabella remained unruffled. Her lips curved into a wry smile as she withdrew her hand.

"What do you want from me now, Mirabella?" Alec asked, then. Better to hear it now, that he might prepare himself.

"Nothing," Mirabella stated.

Alec paused. "Do you expect me to believe that?" he asked as he rose. "That after all the hell you have wrought upon me, upon everyone, that now, now that you have taken me from all I love, you expect *nothing?*"

"Yes," Mirabella responded without hesitation. "I expect nothing. Our marriage was dissolved and rightly. I meant what I said when I told you of your freedom. I want nothing but to impart the truth. You need not offer any compensation for the support of this child. My father's will ensures that I want for nothing." She cast her eyes toward her belly. "Neither of us will." She sighed. "You know the truth now, Alec, and can do with it what you like. Return to London, return to all that you hold dear and real. If you desire to know the child, know the child. If not, I will not bear a grudge."

Alec shook his head. "I cannot abandon my child. I will do right by it. I will know it." He sat once more, resting his hands on his knees. "And I will once again congratulate your ability to keep me from everything I dreamed of as surely as if I had been martyred." He locked eyes with her. "I can never return to the priesthood now, not ever."

Mirabella scowled. "Come now, no histrionics, Alec." Her voice remained cold, annoyed. "We both know your blessed reforms will be pushed through and priests will be allowed not only to marry but father children. That yours is a bastard will not be uncommon—it is not now."

Alec averted his head. "I will hold you to all you promised me, Mirabella." He fixed her with hard eyes. "If you betray me again, you will pay." His voice was low as he struggled to keep his resentment in check. All the prayers for the ability to forgive her faded away like morning mist and he cursed himself for it. "You will allow me into this child's life, you will expect nothing from me in the capacity of a husband or lover or even, for that matter, a friend. I am this child's father, nothing more, and God help you if you go back on your word."

Mirabella nodded her assent.

He rose. "There is nothing more to be said. I will remain to see this child safely delivered and then I will return to London."

"I am indifferent to where you go," Mirabella said. "I will be removing to France."

Alec paused. He endeavored to remain calm.

"The child and me," she added.

Alec tipped his head back, regarding the ceiling a long moment, begging God for the patience and the resilience to endure. At last he met her gaze.

"I am indifferent to where you go as well," he said at last. "Wherever you are, I will still make time and opportunity to know my child."

He turned to quit the room, swallowing a strange urge to cry.

"Alec." Mirabella's voice was a breath above a whisper.

He stood a moment, back turned. He no longer wished to look at her.

"Alec . . ." Mirabella's tone was stronger yet bore no malice. "Please."

Expelling a sigh, Alec turned toward her.

"Can you ever forgive me, Alec?" she asked, her eyes lit with unshed tears.

Alec paused. Could he? Was she sorry? Did it matter? God did not command forgiveness based on the sincere remorse of those who needed it. Indeed, the unremorseful were a higher priority than the repentant. They needed it the most. But Alec . . . did he forgive her?

He beheld the woman on the bed, the woman who had wrought so much pain in every life she touched. Now she lay, swollen with child, and despite being tolerated at Sumerton, she was not wanted, not truly. The pity that had seized him the day of King

Edward's coronation, the day this child was unwittingly conceived, washed over him.

He offered a slow nod. "I can never forget what you have done, Mirabella, do not expect that of me. But I do forgive you."

It had not been as hard to say as he imagined. More surprising, it was not hard to mean.

Mirabella's sigh was shaky. "Thank you," she whispered.

With that, Alec quit the room.

The pains started on 26 November. The baby had ceased its activity two days prior and Mirabella had grown anxious. Her belly was taut, her ankles had swelled to twice their size along with her fingers to the extent she had to remove her rings, and her back ached. Her heart raced and her throat was always scratchy. When her labor started, cutting through her abdomen sharp as a warm dagger, she cried out as much in relief as pain.

Grace attended her along with the midwife Dorothy Mopps, who had delivered three of Cecily's children. Cecily was also present.

"You attended me with Emmy," she told her in soft tones as she took to one side of her while Grace took the other.

Mirabella's breathing was shallow. "Where is Alec?" she whispered, hating the panic that mounted within her.

"He has been informed and waits in the solar," Grace told her. "He is praying."

Mirabella nodded. Appropriate, she thought, for she no longer had the strength to pray or think of anything beyond the pain. Why must renewing life cost such pain and suffering to the mother?

"I still neglect to see why Eve should bear such punishment when Adam chose to partake of the fruit as well!" she exclaimed when her labor had progressed well into the night with no sign of abating.

Cecily emitted a laugh at this. "You know, I said something similar when first I started my courses," she told her. "You will endure, Mirabella," she assured her.

Mirabella raised her eyes to Cecily. For the first time her voice echoed the woman she knew before she learned of her betrayal with Alec, the honorary sister of her youth. Her face bore no malice, no hatred or anger.

Mirabella sighed, relieved as at once the room swirled before her. The pains seared through her, each as merciless as the one preceding. Something warm was rushing from between her legs. She began to sob.

"She has hemorrhaged," she heard the steady voice of Dorothy Mopps explain to the women beside her.

"I feared as much," Grace said. Mirabella felt a warm cloth daubing at her woman's parts and legs.

"What of a Caesarian?" Cecily's voice, panicked. "You performed it successfully on me—"

Dorothy's tone adopted another note, one that Mirabella could not discern. Sadness? Fear? "I am sorry, my lady. She is worse off than you were at that point. We best allow her to labor through. The blood loss from a Caesarian would kill her."

Mirabella's lips parted as she struggled against emitting a scream. She must be strong. She must not expend strength on a scream when she could save it for this birth. She felt Cecily mopping her forehead with a damp cloth.

"Fetch Alec," Grace ordered. "Hurry!" Odd, thought Mirabella. Men were not present at birthings and that Grace should want him unnerved her.

Cecily retreated to do as she was bid.

Cecily found Alec seated in the solar before the fire, his eyes closed, his head bowed to his folded hands. Her heart clenched. They had not spoken beyond cursory greetings since his arrival at Sumerton. She could not bear to look at him. Unbidden the thoughts entered her mind, images of him and Mirabella creating the child who was set to enter a life its parents ensured would be a difficult one. She could not think of either of them without resentment churning her gut and bitter bile rising in her throat.

Now she gazed at Alec, as if for the first time since his return.

She no longer felt resentment. She could not say it was pity either. What she did know was that neither he nor even Mirabella had asked for what came to pass, despite the irresponsibility of the actions that ushered forth this day.

What's more, she knew that she would always love him. Nothing could change that. She wanted nothing to change that.

Alec opened his eyes to regard her. They were hazel orbs of sadness and fear.

Cecily rushed forward, on impulse taking him in her arms and sobbing. "She is bleeding, Alec. It is bad, very bad," she whispered as she held him close, relishing for one moment his scent, the feel of his doublet against her cheek, the heat of his breath on her face. Alec held her in turn in an embrace without awkwardness, without trepidation. It was an embrace between the truest of friends.

Cecily pulled away, taking him by the hand as he rose. "Lord Hal had insisted on being present for my complicated birth; you deserve the same right," she told him.

"Mrs. Mopps and Grace are capable," Alec said as they proceeded toward Mirabella's rooms. "She could not be in better hands."

They had reached the door. As Cecily was about to push it open, Alec stopped her, placing a hand on her arm. "Cecily . . ."

Cecily turned her face toward his. He was obscured by a veil of tears.

"I have loved none but you," he said then.

Cecily offered a feeble smile. "I know."

They entered the room.

How many minutes had passed before Cecily returned with Alec, or was it hours? Pain obscured time. Mirabella supposed she no longer cared; what was time but another of man's vain attempts at controlling their world? There was no time; there was no controlling anything. Somehow, it no longer mattered. Alec and Cecily were here now and now was all she had.

When at last she was able to draw Alec into focus, she searched his face. His brows were furrowed in concern as he made toward her. He raised his eyes, meeting Cecily's. His lips parted as if to speak, before he shook his head.

"Don't say anything," Mirabella told him as she struggled to keep him in focus. She removed her gaze to Cecily, finding her a willing prisoner to Alec's eyes.

What use were words with a look like that? Alec's eyes conveyed nothing but the love Mirabella had tried to extract in vain, love that was given devoid of any expectation or solicitation, love that Cecily's own gaze suggested was returned wholly and without any anticipation in return.

Mirabella looked toward Alec once more. He had broken the gaze from Cecily, returning his eyes to her. His face bore no trace of the usual bitterness he saved for their encounters. While he did not look upon her with affection, it was not, at least, with hatred. She turned her head toward Cecily once more, Cecily, sister of her youth, Cecily . . . *oh, Cecily.* . . .

"Are you my friend, Cecily?" she asked, her voice a husky whisper, almost unintelligible between her gasps of pain.

Cecily shook her head, lowering her eyes with a forced laugh. "Would I have allowed you to remain here were I not?"

"You will write to me in France?" Mirabella pressed. She had not meant to reveal it now, not just yet . . . but it did not matter . . . Cecily would understand. She would let her go. What was life but learning to let go? Her mother's voice swirled around her once again. The halo of blood that had surrounded her head in death was replaced with the light, the pure and unadulterated light, of eternity.

Forgive. . . . Let go. . . . Sister Julia's lips did not move. How was it that she was there yet not there? Mirabella reached out, finding not Sister Julia's outstretched hand but Cecily's.

Cecily had screwed up her face in puzzlement. "France? I do not understand. . . ."

France. Oh, yes, France . . . they were talking about France. "I am leaving Sumerton," Mirabella said as she clutched her belly. How could the pain be sharp yet dull? "I am . . . taking the baby to a land that will still have me and my faith."

"Oh, Mirabella!" Cecily shook her head, her tone thick with exasperation. "Faith or doctrine?" she cried as she retrieved the cloth to swab her brow once more. "I swear you and Alec are more alike than I ever conceived of. Both of you devoted to one doctrine or another and never truly to God! Will God care who believes the— the technicalities of his body and blood transforming to bread and wine, or whether or not it brings comfort to those unlearned, those peasants who can*not* devote their time to dissecting doctrine, to look upon statues and lovely things devoted to God, so long as He and His son are worshipped and not those—*things?* Doctrine separates man from God far more than any Romish icon! The rest just makes for a good debate! If all could but agree that faith is about trust in God and *love*, there would be no need of reforms!" Her speech was rapid, her tears streaming down her face in an unchecked torrent. When she finished speaking she was breathless, her eyes wide in bewilderment, as though she had been shocked to embark on such a tangent at this of all times.

Mirabella gazed at Cecily as if seeing her for the first time. Perhaps it was. Perhaps she had been asleep all her life; perhaps she had always been fumbling in darkness, blinded to all those around her. Now she was awake, the scales removed from her eyes. Before her stood the girl her father had taken on as ward all those years ago and she was meeting her for the first time. The girl would live with her as a sister now. And they would be friends. Mirabella smiled.

"I think it was you who have been called closest to God," Mirabella said then. Her voice she pulled from some inner source of strength that still allowed her to speak. Was it her strength or Cecily's? Or the God Cecily described? Strange it should be the same God she had searched for all her life. "All along it was you," she went on. "You carried out God's will without question, without hesitation, with the pure-hearted trust that God commands and so admires in children. Oh, Cecily . . . It was you, never Alec, never me. It was you." Tears. Oh, how they flowed, warm as the blood that she gave, warm as the sacred blood shed to save them all. . . .

Your payment . . . Brey's voice.

"Ah, yes," Mirabella answered him. "It is only right that it should be so," she whispered. And it was. A life for a life. It was the right thing, finally, truly, the right thing.

"Mirabella." Alec's voice. Why did it sound sad? The baby was coming. He should not be sad. "I—I have something for you," he said. In his hands he held a velvet sack. From within it, he produced the sandglass. The sandglass . . . "We must put a date by 'November,' " he said. "You must have this baby now. The rest . . . the rest can wait. Bring us our child, Mirabella."

Mirabella reached out a trembling hand to trace the mahogany of the timepiece. A feeling of warmth obscured the pain, but it was not the warmth of blood. It was her father's warmth. She could almost see him carving the dates. She could hear his laugh. Was he laughing now?

"Yes, the sandglass," she breathed. "The sandglass that marks our every choice . . ."

"Hold on, Mirabella!" Grace cried from the foot of the bed. "The head is coming! Such dark hair! The baby is nearly here. Save your strength and push, darling!"

Mirabella bore down, clutching the hands of Cecily and Alec beside her.

"Push!" Dorothy and Grace cried at once.

Something slid from her. She could not see. She could not focus.

"A boy, Mirabella! You have a son, and a bluff, bonny boy is he!" Grace exclaimed as the child announced his presence with a lusty cry. She brought the child to Mirabella, laying him upon her chest without cleansing the birthing fluids and blood away just yet.

"We must name him, Mirabella," Alec told her, his voice thick with awe. She felt his gaze upon her and the child she lacked the strength to hold.

He was born in truth, soaring above the deceit and betrayal that stalked Sumerton like a relentless . . . "Peregrine," Mirabella said. "Peregrine Richard. Our little bird . . . our Falcon of Truth . . ."

"It is a good name," Alec conceded as he took the baby to be cleansed.

"Yes," Mirabella agreed.

I am waiting. . . .

Brey again. His eyes were no longer laden with disappointment. They were beckoning, appealing. Brey . . .

Forgive. . . . Let go. . . .

Her mother again.

Mirabella returned her gaze to Cecily and Alec, who stood on either side of her bed, the baby nestled close to Alec's heart. Where he belonged, Mirabella reflected. Alec's face was washed over with love as he beheld the little one. Somewhere she was aware of Dorothy and Grace discussing her condition. She felt again the cloth wiping clean her body.

With all her strength she reached out her quavering arms, taking Alec's and Cecily's warm hands in hers. His felt so strong, and Cecily's . . . it was the hand of a great lady. She squeezed; joy surged through her as she felt them return it. Her eyes threatened to close. *Not yet! Please . . .* She brought their hands closer, closer together, till at last she joined them. Alec and Cecily gazed at each other, their faces a blend of exhaustion and surprise. Mirabella allowed her hands to slip from theirs as she fell back against the pillows. They did not disengage.

The words did not come from her. They were given to her, a gift from God or was it her own father?

"Forgive me," she whispered as her gaze found Hal. He stood beside Brey and Sister Julia, reaching out his own hand toward her. Tears strangled Mirabella. "For *all* the wrongs, forgive me. Care for Falcon. Raise him in love, truth, and light. Teach him . . . teach him right and love him without condition, as I should have loved all of you," she begged with all the strength she could summon. "Please, oh please, can you forgive me? Can you care for Falcon?"

"Yes," Cecily answered without hesitation, reaching out to stroke her forehead. "I forgive you, my darling. And I will raise Falcon. I shall tell him all the good things that you are."

Mirabella's eyes searched Alec's face; in it there was no hatred, no resentment. Nothing but compassion shone from his gentle hazel gaze.

"I forgive you, Mirabella," he told her. "And I, too, will care for Falcon; I will love him well; he will be a son to bring you pride."

Mirabella could not speak. It was done, all done. She could go; it was good and right to go. It was her last gift to her family, to Alec, that she leave them.

Mirabella smiled one last smile as a single tear trailed down her cheek.

And then . . . she let go.

Further Reading

Elton, G. R. *England Under the Tudors*. London and New York: Cambridge University Press, 1955.

Elton, G. R. *The Tudor Constitution*. Cambridge: Cambridge University Press, 1960.

Gies, Joseph and Frances. *Life in a Medieval Castle*. New York: Harper Colophon, 1979.

MacCulloch, Diarmaid. *The Reformation: A History*. New York: Penguin Books, 2005.

MacCulloch, Diarmaid. *Thomas Cranmer*. New Haven and London: Yale University Press, 1996.

Power, Eileen. *Medieval English Nunneries*. Cambridge: Biblo & Tannen, 1922.

THE SUMERTON WOMEN

D. L. Bogdan

ABOUT THIS GUIDE

The suggested questions are included to enhance your group's reading of D. L. Bogdan's *The Sumerton Women*.

DISCUSSION QUESTIONS

1. Did Lord Hal and Lady Grace love each other? Could their marriage have been saved?

2. What was the source of Hal's guilt? Was it an automatic response based on his upbringing, or was it sincere?

3. By medieval standards, did Hal make the right choice in marrying Cecily?

4. Did Hal and Cecily love each other?

5. Why was Cecily drawn to Father Alec?

6. Was Mirabella truly driven to her calling as a woman of God, or was this an escape for her? If so, what was she escaping from?

7. What drew Mirabella to Father Alec?

8. Describe Mirabella's relationship with Sister Julia. Did Sister Julia do right by her daughter?

9. Should Mirabella have chosen James? Would they have been happy?

10. What was the turning point for Mirabella that drove her beyond the edge of reason? Was there any point in the novel where she could have been "saved"? Was she a victim or a villain?

11. Did Father Alec make the right decisions throughout the novel? What decisions impacted him the most?

12. Lady Grace made some extreme choices throughout the novel. Were any of them justifiable?

13. Cecily and Mirabella's relationship was complex. Was it founded in genuine closeness or obligation?

14. What was the Reformation about to Mirabella? What did it mean to Alec? To Cecily?

15. Who in this novel would you describe as being closest to God?